OCTOBER'S GHOST

Also by Ryne Douglas Pearson

Cloudburst

OCTOBER'S GHOST

A Thriller

Ryne Douglas Pearson

William Morrow and Company, Inc.
New York

It is the policy of William Morrow and Company, Inc., and its imprints and affiliates, recognizing the importance of preserving what has been written, to print the books we publish on acid-free paper, and we exert our best efforts to that end.

Library of Congress Cataloging-in-Publication Data

Pearson, Ryne Douglas.
    October's ghost / Ryne Douglas Pearson.
      p. cm.
    ISBN 0-688-12984-6
    1. United States—Military relations—Cuba—Fiction. 2. Cuba—Military relations—United States—Fiction. I. Title.
PS3566.E2343025   1994
813'.54—dc20   93-47456
                                                            CIP

Printed in the United States of America

First Edition

1 2 3 4 5 6 7 8 9 10

For Irene,
the fairest and sweetest of souls

Acknowledgments

Twisting history, and writing about such, is more a team effort than one might think. Thanks must be given.

To Clyde Taylor, my agent, the bulk of the gratitude goes, for listening to a far-out story idea and nurturing it through the inevitable incarnations. It is better because of you.

To Tom Colgan, my editor, for entertaining the same story idea during an October lunch at Mickey Mantle's, and for the continuing support.

To my family and friends, for sticking with me when things get crazy.

To R.H., S.H., and M.G. once again, and for always, for showing me the value of words.

To Mickey and the staff at Vroman's Bookstore in Pasadena, California, for being a class act.

And, definitely not least, to the countless Cuban-Americans who long for the land of their birth to be free again ... it shall be.

"The Soviet government has reached certain accords with the American government. But this does not mean that we have renounced the right to have the weapons we deem convenient and to take steps in international policy we deem convenient as a sovereign country."

FIDEL CASTRO
January 2, 1963

"Those who make peaceful revolution impossible will make violent revolution inevitable."

JOHN F. KENNEDY

OCTOBER'S GHOST

PROLOGUE

Brinkmanship

The Cuban sharpshooter, aiming from a rise above the clearing, trained the crosshairs first on the green shoulder boards that adorned his target. These he could not identify by color in the low moonlight, but to see them at all was sufficient. It was less a confirmation than a final, purposeful act of disrespect for the entity that the unit insignia represented. A smile formed as he brought his aimpoint up, centering on the back of the head. He said a silent curse and increased pressure on the trigger. Quite fittingly, the KGB would be the first to die.

Ten Mosin-Nagant rifles, accurized for use as sniper weapons, fired within a split second of each other from the jungle on the east side of the bulldozed oval of earth. There were only seven "primary" targets, and all were hit at least once. One KGB guard, a junior officer, survived the first volley, as his intended killer's shot was low, striking him in the shoulder blade, but a quick follow-up shot felled him before he could lift the Kalashnikov and fire.

The guardians of the prize were now gone. Just its keepers remained.

Twenty-two heads turned in unison as the fire erupted from the jungle behind. They had formed up just a moment earlier in an inspection line as a courtesy for the final visit of the Cuban colonel, whose unit had provided perimeter security for them during their stay. He, to repay the show of respect, drew the American-made .45-caliber pistol from his side and shot their commander, a young captain of *raket* artillery, in the side of the head as he looked to the east.

Turning back at the sound, the missile crewmen, none of whom had felt any need to take their weapons from the equipment truck, saw their commander fall into a heap. Half of them froze, while the other half bolted away from the scene, running for the only safety in sight. Safety, however, was nowhere to be found.

From the vegetation at the clearing's north and south sides, short, controlled bursts from the Cuban Kalashnikovs caught each fleeing crewman as he neared. Some slowed as the flashes ahead lit the collapsing bodies of their comrades, but that only hastened the inevitable. Other shooters concentrated on these easier targets.

In the clearing the Cuban colonel pointed his pistol at those who had chosen to offer some kind of surrender, which, of course, would not prevent that which had already been fated. The even dozen crewmen backed toward the weapon they had stewarded as their country came to the aid of the tiny island nation in its fight against the imperialists to the north. They slunk lower as the colonel, now joined by two better-armed soldiers from his unit, advanced closer. Finally they were on their knees, their heads just below the trailer that held the weapon, the prize, that they still had not gathered was the cause of their demise.

"Someday Premier Khrushchev will join you in hell," Colonel Juan Asunción said in forceful, if imperfect, Russian. "When he does, tell him the Motherland is a whore!"

The Russians' eyes went wide at the blasphemous comment, but whatever rage it might have motivated was left no time to manifest itself. Asunción squeezed his shots off carefully and was joined by the soldiers at his side. Single shots, several for each crewman, finished the job that the colonel was honored, and more than happy, to carry out. And with that the killing was done. Almost.

"Inform the *presidente*," Asunción ordered, which sent one of the soldiers scurrying off to the unit's radio. From the jungle he saw the remainder of his men emerge. They went to each body and ensured that the job was finished. It was. No coup de grâce shots were necessary. Not yet, at least, the colonel knew. It was a cost of success he had come to accept.

Asunción waited for the bodies to be dragged away from the weapon and placed in a neat row on the damp earth before approaching it. A dark green tarpaulin covered the entire missile, which rested horizontally on its Transporter/Erector/Launcher. He ran his hand along the slippery covering that hung from the weapon as he walked slowly from the tail to the nose. There he stopped. The moment was mystical, almost as he imagined it would be. Magical even. Just beyond his reach, but now within the grasp of the nation—and the man—he served, was the power that had been promised them by their "brother Socialist" ally, which was now bowing to pressure from the *yanqui* imperialists in the name of peace. Ha! Asunción nearly strangled on the taste the thought of such cowardice brought to his mouth. Looking to the ground, he saw the bloodied cap of a fallen crewman, the proud hammer and sickle surrounded by golden boughs of wheat forming the emblem on its front. With force the colonel spit on the emblem before driving the cap into the soft earth with the heel of his boot.

Asunción turned as the sound of engines racing drew closer. Headlights, their beams dimmed by slit covers, appeared from the access road and pulled into the clearing, more than twenty soldiers of the presidential guard jumping out and securing the area before the *presidente* arrived.

That he did a moment later, riding in the passenger seat of an open-topped Jeep of American manufacture, hundreds of which were still in service after their capture from the Batista regime overthrown just a few years before. The vehicle pulled into the clearing through the gauntlet of soldiers and came to a crisp stop next to a rigid Asunción, his right hand at his forehead in an arrow-straight salute.

"Presidente Castro!" The hand came down and swept toward the weapon in a gesture of offering. "I present to you this gift."

Fidel Castro Ruz, founder of the Revolution, a man who had climbed the muddy Sierra Maestras and led a tiny band of guerrillas in a fight to bring prosperity and honor to the people of Cuba, could now also give them true power. The power to deter aggression without the worthless promise of protection from a weak and boastful ally. The power to never fear the threats of the Western World. Before him was that power, and its deliverer.

"Colonel Asunción!" Fidel shouted gleefully, his hands coming together as he bent over in a joyous, almost childlike expression. "You have done it!"

Asunción knew of no higher praise than to be entrusted with such a great responsibility by this man, for whom he would go to the ends of the earth. "For you, *Presidente.*"

Fidel looked over the covered weapon, then to the row of bodies in the distance. "And no damage?"

"None," the colonel responded with pride. "The men performed excellently." *It is such a shame. . . .*

Fidel needed only to see the colonel's eyes to know what emotions had not been expressed by words. It would be a loss, but a necessary one. "Yes. Excellently."

Asunción followed his leader as he walked along the TEL. Fidel avoided the urge to peer under the tarp, realizing, correctly, that the physical appearance of the weapon was quite secondary to the importance of it being under his control. Looks meant very little in the game he had begun to play.

Asunción waited until they were to a spot out of earshot of the others. "The premier is being notified?"

"Raul is doing so as we speak," Fidel said, referring to his brother, General Raul Castro, leader of the nation's military. "It will be just a short message." A wry smile spread across his face. "Just to tease and make him twist. I will finish the humiliation in the morning."

Asunción nodded. Anything to make the bastard squirm. "You believe he will remain silent."

"He will. He has no choice." Fidel noted the smiles on the faces of the soldiers. "He will do as we will to maintain the secret. For him exposure will mean death. For us . . ." His shoulders came up. "We will not have to worry about that. You have chosen those to trust?"

"Two men," Asunción confirmed. "Single, no family, and fiercely loyal. They and I will 'debrief' my men and your guard troops individually before the sun is up."

Fidel nodded soberly. More must die. He looked beyond the row of those who had already been sent to their supposed maker. The four tank trucks attached to the unit were being driven into position near the corpses. "A mighty explosion it will be."

Asunción heard the comment but did not connect it to the *presidente*'s meaning. For the briefest second he thought that . . . "Yes," he agreed with relief. "Nothing will remain. Just pieces."

"The perfect excuse," Fidel observed. It wasn't, he knew, but it would suffice.

The colonel noted that all was ready for the next phase. "*Presidente,* we must go now. The missile must be moved."

"Yes. A moment." Fidel took some steps back and let his eyes fall upon the weapon. What was at its top interested him most. The power of a million ordinary aircraft bombs in a device that weighed no more than three of them. A beautiful piece of engineering, made possible by the application of years of brilliance toward a common goal to harness the power of the inner universe. Yet that was applicable only to the so-called superpowers, technological behemoths who had acquired their strength through much testing and sweat. Fidel Castro Ruz had engineered his nation's entry into the realm of true power with the sacrifice of blood.

That in itself was cause for celebration, though it would be only of a personal nature. For the power to be of the use he intended, it must remain in the deepest, darkest shadows of existence, removed for use only to protect the Revolution. Would that ever be necessary? Would the secret be revealed? Fidel hoped not, thought not, content himself to know that the island nation of Cuba, in the early-morning hours of a fateful autumn day that would end with the world breathing a collective sigh of relief, had become the fifth member of the nuclear club, not by way of technical mastery, but by a calculated act of thievery.

Chapter One

Events

"There he is."

Jorge leaned forward against the van's dash, looking to the left past Tomás. The man was walking with the crowd in the pedestrian crossing, hands pushed deep in his pockets and his balding head moving from side to side. "Right on time."

"He looks nervous," Tomás commented.

"He has reason to," Jorge said, sitting back.

Tomás scooted forward in the driver's seat, his slight paunch pressed against the steering wheel, and removed the revolver from his back waistband. He kept it below the window line and slid it between his legs, the barrel pointed bravely backward. He would not do the same with the semiautomatic pistol under his coat. It was cocked and locked, ready to fire, with the safety on, but he trusted safeties as much as he did weathermen. The nice thing about revolvers was that they went off only when one wanted them to, without the risk of jamming, features that still made them popular with many American policemen, and equally popular with men in his line of work.

"Going inside," Jorge reported. He, too, was armed, carrying the identical mix of weaponry, though he left his concealed for the moment. There was no rush. The time would come soon enough.

*   *   *

"One for lunch?" the hostess inquired.

The man's eyes searched the room. *¿Dónde está?* He wasn't there.

"Sir?"

"Yes. No. I . . . I am meeting someone."

The hostess smiled politely, her blue eyes twinkling benignly below the perky blond coiffure. *Fucking immigrants.* She had to work her *ass* off just to survive while attending UCLA, and these people came over the border and somehow ended up with all the money they needed. His accent wasn't Mexican, though. Probably a fucking chiropractor or something trained in Guatemala. Her smile widened as she led him toward a table at the back corner of the restaurant. *If I have to work two jobs just to make it through pre-med, you can live with some kitchen noise.*

"Will this be all right?"

"Yes," the man answered. "Very fine."

He watched the hostess walk away. She was young and might have received closer attention at another time, but his gaze soon shifted outside, through the window on his left. He felt somewhat more comfortable where he sat. The entire dining room was visible, as was the entrance.

"Water, *señor?*"

"*Sí. Gracias.*" He looked up at the busboy and slipped him a dollar. It was truly the underlings who deserved the tips.

"*Gracias,*" the young Salvadoran said, his eyes beaming. "*Gracias!*"

The man lifted the glass to his lips but jumped at the sound of dishes falling behind. A splash of water leaped from the glass and spilled on his trousers, drenching the left side. He quickly grabbed the napkin from the table and set it on his lap.

But it wasn't the clothing he was concerned with.

"Are you ready?" Jorge asked.

Tomás nodded, straightening himself as much as possible in the seat and tucking the revolver in the front of his waistband. He buttoned the coat next.

"Let's go."

He was killing himself. There was no doubt about it. Frankie watched him put the end of it in his mouth. It was only a matter of time.

"Mmmmm." Art Jefferson bit into the bacon-chili cheese dog with a satisfaction he had avoided for almost six months.

Frankie Aguirre shook her head and sipped her flavored seltzer. "You gonna make me watch you do this? Huh? Is this so I can testify at the probate hearing? 'Yes, Your Honor, I saw him do it.' "

Art heard his partner's protest but continued anyway, chewing the first bite until swallowing was a necessity. "Ooooh. That is goooood!"

"Yeah, right." Frankie drained the bottle and set it down on Pink's streetfront counter, her fingers picking at her chips.

Special Agent Thom Danbrook nursed his root beer and took in the good-natured exchange as an eager observer. "Does he always eat this stuff?"

"Hey, twice a year," Art said, explaining before his partner could do his culinary reputation harm. "That's what I give myself. Kinda like a vacation from boring food."

"From healthy food," she corrected him.

He did plenty of that, Art could say, eating healthy and all. Lots of salads and fruits, chicken, pasta, veggies till his mouth tasted like broccoli all day. Bush had it right on *that* green hunk of nutrients, he believed. It had been just over a year since the heart attack, and he was doing fine. Even his cardiologist said an occasional divergence into cholesterol land was acceptable. The whole idea was moderation, something his partner exhibited little of in the area of overprotectiveness.

But that's what partners were for, inasmuch as the Bureau had "partners" (the correct term was "team"), and Special Agent Francine—"Don't call me that"—Aguirre was top-notch. She and Art had been paired since he left desk duty and returned to real work, as he called it. A true Bureau street agent, just the way he began his career in the days of old J. Edgar. It was also the way he wanted it to end. Three more years to a full thirty, and he was damned glad he'd gotten out of the bureaucracy end of things. *That* would have killed him. The heart attack had been a very clear warning that the stress of command and his screwed-up personal life was too much, and Art had heard it loud and clear.

"I could just shoot you, if you want," Frankie offered.

Art brought his right elbow down against his side in a reflexive action, the hard grip of the Smith & Wesson right where it should be. "I'll take the slow way out, if you don't mind. Okay, pardner?"

"Art, trust me, you'll never get used to 'Mother' here," Danbrook informed him. He had been teamed with Aguirre for two of his first three years fresh out of the Academy before transferring to the San Francisco field office, giving her up to Art.

"I hear you," Art said between chews. "So, you think old Barrish will go down this time?"

"That's why I'm here." Danbrook was back in his old Bureau stomping grounds in order to testify in the case of United States of America versus some white-supremacist asshole. He hated to dignify the man by using his name; *the suspect* would do just fine. "This place have any burgers?"

Art nearly choked on his dog at the remark that bordered on heresy. "At Pink's? Didn't Aguirre ever bring you here?" He got a smiling head shake in response. "Frankie!"

"I don't believe in killing my own partners," she answered, deadpan. "If they want to do it themselves, well . . ."

Danbrook laughed fully at that. Frankie was a wiseass if ever there was one, and the number-one wiseass to have on your side when the heat was on. He had learned well from her. "Is there someplace around here I can get something to eat that doesn't have pig snouts as a main ingredient?"

This time Frankie was the one to laugh, while Art gave Thom a purely devilish look.

"Out the back, across the alley," Frankie directed. "Clampett's has what you want."

"Thanks. Back in a minute." Danbrook walked through Pink's and out the back door.

Frankie saw another third of the artery torpedo disappear into Art's mouth and a look of pure ecstasy come to his face. "Live it up, Arthur."

"Sure will, Francine."

He was a reporter, and that meant he had to do things like wear bad blazers, drive a never-new, American-made car of some sort, and, of course, buy lunch for people who had a story to tell. It was all part of the persona, and George Sullivan fit into it with no effort at all.

The three-year veteran of the *Los Angeles Times* turned his eight-year-old Chrysler left onto Melrose, sneaking a sip from the flask in his coat pocket, a necessity, he believed, to survive the streets of L.A. He was a transplant from New York, a former Gray Lady staffer who had gotten tired of the cold and the crowds and traded them for the smog and the crowds, and he still hadn't figured just *who* had taught Californians to drive. Not that they were nuts, but they all drove like old women. They even used turn signals! Hell, he had learned to drive in the city—Manhattan— where you changed lanes if you wanted, and if someone was already there, they would hit the horn, or maybe scream something. It worked, and it was a lot more interesting.

This fine autumn day, when the parts per million of some airborne carcinogen or something equally as horrid had reached the magical level where the weathermen colored the Los Angeles basin orange on their air-quality maps, George was off to meet what was supposed to be a story: some Cuban exile who had a juicy bit of nostalgia to share, it had been alluded to by his boss when he assigned it to him a week earlier. At least Bill had checked the guy out and verified that he *might* be someone who knew something. But, then, who wasn't someone? Everybody had something to tell. Or something to sell, he added cynically.

His own conversations with the guy, all over the phone, had been pretty noneventful, a bad signal for a reporter. News, generally, meant something of interest, and to this point there had been no indication of such. But today was supposed to be the day when the guy gave up his secret, the terrible secret he kept referring to in their conversations. The guy had actually been testing him, making sure that he wasn't a cop or some foreign agent out to steal the wondrous knowledge he possessed. Give me a break, George thought. Just give me the straight poop, and I'll decide if it's earth-shattering.

There it was. Clampett's. Another trendy L.A. eatery that had degenerated into something—surprise!—quite ordinary. They served *food* there, George thought, not fucking Picassos. Angelenos had a tendency to think themselves somewhat superior in just about anything they attempted, even the mundane. It was amusing, at least, and made for good stories every now and then.

That must be him, George thought, as he waited behind a row of cars to turn left into the alley alongside the restaurant. He could see him sitting in the corner, fiddling with something on the table, his features darkened by the tinting on the restaurant's large front windows. The description the guy had given of himself was pretty good. Sixtyish, balding, a bit of a gut, though the guy hadn't put it that way. Sullivan could see his bulk widen at the waist.

The light ahead was red, creating a backup of cars trying to turn left onto La Brea. Sullivan was stuck in it, not yet close enough to the alley to turn. He kept looking back and forth between the light and the man. Then their eyes met. Only about forty feet separated them. George smiled, but the man did not return it. He checked the light again. Green. Good, he thought, and looked back to the . . . Who are those . . . *Oh, shit!*

"Yeah, can I get a burger, plain, to go?" Thom asked the hostess. She smiled almost seductively at the request. He was a good-looking guy, attractive to women, something he had been told on numerous occasions, and almost monthly by his mother. Oh, well. At least she accepted it now.

"One burger plain to go." The hostess walked back toward the kitchen, her day starting to brighten up. *Hey.* Who were those guys? They didn't wait to be seat—

"Portero," Jorge said in a normal voice, waiting for the man to react and turn. His hand unbuttoned his coat and reached behind his back. To his left Tomás was making much the same move.

Francisco Portero turned his head toward the voice, knowing as soon as the word was spoken that something was wrong. His eyes confirmed that fear a second later.

Both Jorge and Tomás pulled their revolvers at the same time and leveled them at their target from a distance of five feet. The caliber meant little at this range. Both men squeezed the triggers twice in even, steady pulls, Jorge using one and Tomás two hands. The four rounds impacted above Portero's waist, half in his head. Tomás's doing. He preferred the head shot.

The body, unlike the result of movie murders, fell easily against the chair back and slumped left, the head coming to rest with a thump against the glass.

The first shot surprised Thom more than alarmed him, and he looked up from the menu at Clampett's front counter to see what was happening. That was when the warning was flashed from his visual sensors to the brain, starting a trained response that was automatic, developed from patterned repetition. His left hand slid his jacket back as he twisted slightly right, the Bureau automatic he had been issued a few years before coming out of its hip holster and to his front.

"Federal agent!" he yelled, both hands now on the Smith & Wesson, the right hand wrapped around and on top of the left, his gun hand. It was the grip ingrained in his mind from the endless hours of firearm instruction at Quantico, where he had been trained using the Bureau's former standard-issue weapon (the Colt .357 revolver), and it was a mistake. A grave mistake.

Tomás began spinning when the first word of the shout from behind reached his ears. He also dropped low, bringing his gun around to find the ... there! Jorge had also turned and was aiming at the same target.

Thom knew they were turning to fire, but there were people scrambling all over the place, running in front of him toward the door and toward a window someone had smashed out. He shifted his aim a little to the left, drawing a bead on the one who was closest to firing, and squeezed the trigger. The power of the 10mm kicked his hands back, causing a fiery pain on his right hand that had never happened before. But that was inconsequential. He was in a fight for his life, in a test of speed. His mind directed his finger to squeeze the trigger again. . . .

But nothing happened. It was strange. He could *feel* his eyes widen at the surprise. He looked at his weapon, still held at eye level. The slide was forward, no obvious jam, but what was that on his thumb? *Blood?* What was—

The first shot entered Thom Danbrook's torso just below the sternum and continued through his lean body, exiting out the back with a vital portion of his spine. The muscles below his chest immediately registered the cessation of controlling signals from the brain and began to relax. But before that effect could be manifested, seven more shots were fired, three of them connecting. One shattered his right elbow. A second hit low, doing massive damage to his left hip. The third was a gut shot that punctured intestines and fragmented into several pieces, peppering the liver four times.

Thom fell backward, his weapon still in his gun hand, and crumpled like a rag doll against the counter, his mouth open in surprise and his eyes staring at the floor.

"Get it," Jorge ordered as he pulled the Browning and

stuffed the empty Ruger in his waistband. He centered the pistol on the fallen cop—*What did the guy yell? "Something" agent?*—to make sure that Tomás could get what they had come for.

Tomás turned back to Portero and spread his coat, checking the inside pockets. Nothing. It had to be . . . the shirt pocket. There was a rectangular bulge, which he reached in and retrieved. "Got it."

"Come on."

Sullivan's eyes were locked on the scene, his hands holding the Chrysler's wheel with a death grip. *Oh, shit! Oh, shit! I was supposed to be there!*

The two men were moving outside, a crowd of terrified lunchtime eaters preceding them. Were they coming for him? He was not about to wait and find out. Traffic ahead was not moving, so he cranked the wheel all the way to the left and floored it, heading across traffic for the alley.

The last of Art's bacon-chili cheese dog was on its way to his stomach when the distinctive sound of gunfire echoed through from the back of Pink's. "What the hell?"

Frankie drew her weapon first, followed quickly by Art. "Call nine-eleven," she said calmly to the cook, her eyes looking through the back windows. *Where's Thom?*

"Let's check it out," Art said. He led off through the inside of the hot dog stand's small interior dining room, which opened to a parking lot on the alley at the rear. He stopped at the building's corner and listened. Screams told him where to go. "Clampett's." *Oh, my God.*

They moved quickly through the lot toward the back of the restaurant across the alley, Art in the lead as he and Frankie—

"Jesus!" Art swore, the right-side tires of a beat-up car almost taking his toes off. "You get the plate?"

"Partial," Frankie said, her eyes watching the gold sedan speed away from them. It could be whoever did the shooting, or just someone trying to get out of the line of fire.

Art walked quickly along the windowless wall at the building's east side, his gun to the front. Frankie was behind him, her attention focused to the rear. A good number of people were running east on Melrose, passing the alley entrance in front of Art.

That was a sure sign that trouble was to the west. "Where the hell is Danbrook?"

He reached the corner just in time to see two men jogging across Melrose toward a van on the opposite side. One went around the back, out of Art's view, and the other went for the driver's door, his free hand holding a . . .

"FREEZE!" It was an automatic response cops have when a weapon is sighted. Art brought his 10mm up to eye level in a two-handed grip, his knees bending slightly, centering it on the— *Damn!* Another wave of frenzied pedestrians rushed past, just feet from the barrel of his Smith. He instinctively cleared them, lifting the barrel skyward, waiting for them to—

"COVER!" he screamed at the sight of the gun pointing directly at him from across the street. His body started down as the first shot rang out, sending things into a weird kind of slow motion that blocks out all things not directly related to one's survival. Art heard another shot, and he rolled to the right, trying to get closer to the stuccoed wall of the restaurant. And another shot, which he heard impact just above his head.

Then the sound of tires grabbing at asphalt broke the trancelike state, and his head came up. He saw the van, a white windowless model, cross to his front, going east on Melrose. His weapon was pointed at it, but he knew he couldn't fire at it as it sped away. There were just too many people around, and the thought of sending a two-ton vehicle crashing into a crowd was not his idea of a successful felony stop.

"Goddammit!" Art swore, jumping up from prone using his free hand for a push-off of the alley's rough surface.

"You okay?" Frankie asked from behind.

"Yeah. You?"

"Close one," she commented, her breath coming in mild heaves. Getting shot at had the tendency to do that to a person.

"I got a good look at it," Art said as he moved around the corner to Clampett's front. It was all glass. He looked inside carefully and saw, not two feet through the glass, the recipient of the gunfire. His eyes swept left across the dining room toward the entrance, looking for . . . *No. NO!* "Thom's down. Let's go!"

They raced to the entrance, keeping their weapons out as they entered the almost-empty restaurant. The only obviously live person they saw was a young blond woman standing less than ten feet from the man slumped against the window, her eyes locked on the body, both hands covering her mouth.

"Thom!" Frankie holstered her weapon and dropped to her knees, easing her former partner's weapon from his fingers and laying it on the counter above. "Thom. Thom. Can you hear me?" She could see his chest moving, and his eyes didn't have the far-off look of someone on the edge of death. She had seen that before. Thom didn't have that. She was sure of it. He couldn't look that way. She wouldn't let him. Would not let him!

Art swept the room as his partner did what she could for Thom. He walked to the other victim, passing the obviously cata-tonic woman standing among the upended tables and chairs. This guy was dead. No question about it. The brain matter that hadn't been blasted through the back of his head to the wall behind was dropping in tiny, bloody clumps from the exit wound.

The door to the kitchen, on Art's left, opened slightly. He trained his weapon on it, but only a frightened, weeping busboy was behind it.

"I call . . . I call the *policía.*" He buried his head in his hands and stood against the wall.

"Anyone else in the kitchen?"

The young man took several deep, heaving breaths. "No. The men who do this, they run." He pointed to the front door. "They do this. Why?"

Art patted the young guy's shoulder and put his weapon away. The kid had probably left his home to get away from stuff like this. "Dammit!"

Frankie had Thom's head in her arms, his body braced against her legs. He was still alive. "Talk to me, Tommy. Come on." The tears were streaming down her face. "Talk to me."

Art stood over the scene, the memory of what had happened a year before to his previous partner bringing past and present together in a collision of emotions that left him numb.

Frankie looked up, her face asking what to do. Art knew the truthful answer would only add to the anguished feeling of help-lessness. "Ambulance is coming. Keep talking to him."

She did just that, encouraging, almost willing, him to answer, but there was no response. The sirens a minute later announced the arrival of the first Los Angeles Police Department officers. The rescue ambulance of the L.A. City Fire Department rolled up right after them, and, after a quick look at the wounded FBI agent that convinced them there was no time to waste trying to stabilize him on scene, loaded him into the R.A. and, with Frankie in the back, headed straight for Cedars-Sinai Medical Center behind a caravan of police cars clearing the way.

Looking down at the carnage remaining where Thom Danbrook had fallen, Art knew that the heroics surely to be attempted once they reached Cedars would be for naught. It was the most painful admission a cop had to make. One of his own was going to die. Art would never say that, just as he hadn't to Frankie. The living often needed hope more than the dying. He stared down at the blood until the rhythmic wail of the ambulance faded to nothing.

Nothing. It was all that could be done for Special Agent Thom Danbrook. It was all Art had been able to do for his first partner, more of a mentor, right out of the Academy. You couldn't bring back the dead.

But you could bring those responsible to justice. That was something, despite the hollowness that the concept of "justice" held when compared to the fate just dealt his brother agent. And to the other victim. Art looked to the body of that man. It was the starting point in a very familiar, and a very distasteful, process. Art Jefferson knew that the investigation of a murder had just begun.

But he could not imagine where it would lead.

The gleaming white Gulfstream descended from the blue Colorado sky and touched down on runway one-seven at Falcon Air Force Base, a relatively small site that served primarily as a support facility for the North American Aerospace Defense Command located deep inside Cheyenne Mountain. It slowed and swung right onto the last taxiway, heading north toward the group of men who had awaited its arrival—some eagerly, some otherwise.

"The Devil is strapping on those ice skates about now, the way I see it," General Henry Granger, chairman of the Joint Chiefs of Staff, theorized, capturing the realized likelihood of the historic event. He looked to the man just behind. "What do you think, Paul?"

"Hmmm," General Paul Walker, commander in chief, NORAD, grunted, eyeing the approaching jet, which bore the marking of his beloved United States Air Force. He felt no such endearment for the human cargo just delivered to Falcon, and only slightly more for the man who had made this all happen.

"Still not on board, General?" National Security Adviser Bud DiContino asked, looking over his shoulder at CINCNORAD.

"I was never invited."

"Oh, hell, Paul!" Granger protested. He and Walker went all the way back to the class of sixty at Colorado Springs, a lineage also shared by the NSA, who had paraded past the spires of the United States Air Force Academy Chapel that last time two years later. "This is going to make your job easier in the long run."

"I suppose." CINCNORAD really didn't. He was part of this because he had to be.

"You promised to make nice with our Russian friends, remember," Granger pointed out for good measure, though he knew Walker would not let his personal feelings mingle with his duty.

"I'll take them home for dinner to meet the Mrs., if it's necessary," CINCNORAD assured his boss and friend. "Sufficient, Mr. DiContino?"

Bud let the cynicism slide. "Just make sure they don't have any reason not to trust us. The only thing making this possible is trust." *And a whole lot of work.*

The twin-engine jet, identical to those in use by many of America's larger corporations, stopped fifty feet short of where Bud and the two Air Force officers stood, its door folding downward less than a minute later. Its two special passengers emerged behind the Air Force captain who had accompanied them on the entire four-leg journey from Moscow.

"Ugly-ass uniforms," Walker commented, aware that his opinion of the puke-colored Russian dress greens was shared by many in the service. Ivan never could make anything pretty, weapons or battle dress. Function—what there was of that—came before aesthetics in their world. America had learned to make things bad and beautiful. CINCNORAD defied anyone to watch a Strike Eagle unload a stick of thousand-pounders on a target and dispute the claim.

"What's that about beauty being skin-deep?" Granger wondered jokingly as the two Russians left their escort at the jet and began to approach. "My guess is that you can strip old Vasiliy there down to his unmentionables, and you'd *then* see the purpose of those dashing dress greens."

Bud suppressed a laugh. The guests whose visit he had arranged were too close to risk an errant chuckle escaping. "I'll have the President bust you down to a junior bird, General, if you make me lose it. Straight faces."

General Walker pasted on a sweet smile as Marshal Vasiliy Kurchatov and his aide neared. "Two weeks, DiContino?"

"Guaranteed," Bud affirmed from the side of his mouth. "The Japanese will have the new computers up and running at *Voyska PVO* in ten days, tops. That's the promise."

"My last protest," CINCNORAD began. "I do not like giving access to *our* strategic systems just because the Russians couldn't build a BMEWS worth crap. That and pulling our boomers in just pushes it, DiContino."

"Trust, General Walker. We can't very well have our missile boats running around during this. The Russians have to be able to *see* our strategic platforms. We can't leave the ICBMs and bomb- ers out for all to see and expect them to overlook the subs. Quid pro quo, General. Theirs are in as a gesture during this, and ours have to be, too. You'll be glad we were able to work this out once the new warning system is up and running over there," Bud said with certainty. "That last false alarm their computers gave them left them forty *seconds* from a launch order." The NSA swiveled his head a bit toward the general. "That kind of fuckup could ruin *everybody's* day . . . Marshal Kurchatov!"

"Ah, my friend!" The huge Russian, as round as the most reverent artist's depiction of Saint Nick, pulled the NSA into a hug that ended with kisses to both cheeks. The same gesture was given by both Russians to each of their three hosts. "My English is improved, yes?"

"Very good, Marshal Kurchatov." Bud gestured to his two companions. "You have met General Henry Granger before, at the Force Reduction Conference in Geneva."

"Yes. Yes." Kurchatov dipped his head respectfully toward the chairman.

"And this is General Paul Walker, commander in chief—"

"I am very familiar, Mr. DiContino," Kurchatov interrupted tactfully. "The general and I share a passion."

"Oh?" Walker probed passively.

"A fine deer hunter you are, I am told. Your exploits have been chronicled in many sporting journals." The marshal smiled admiringly. "Those have become more available in my country in recent years. A *Boone and Crockett* record, I believe."

Walker's eyes widened with some astonishment at the Russian's knowledge of his third love, after the Air Force and his family. "You are a hunter, Marshal?"

Kurchatov stepped closer. "Sometime soon, when the work of the coming days is finished, I will make arrangements to show you the finest hunting on this earth. The Siberian reindeer is a formidable quarry."

You are gooood, Walker admitted. "I look forward to it."

Kurchatov stepped back by his aide. "This is Colonel Mikhail Belyayev. He is an expert on the things that are to be done. I am here just as baggage!" the marshal proclaimed with a laugh that degenerated into a hacking cough. "The air is so clear, so cold. Much different from the thick air of Moscow."

"Then we should go inside," Walker suggested. "You can rest here before we go to NORAD."

Departing words were exchanged, and then Walker led the Russians into Falcon's old main building. Atop it was the tower that had seen many a busy day during the Cold War, but now it sat almost idle. Days often went by without as much as a T-2 from the 94th Flight Training Squadron out of Colorado Springs dropping in. More important arrivals were even less frequent. Much had changed at Falcon. Much had changed in the world. One needed to look no farther than the trio of men walking through the soundproof steel door to find validation of that truism.

"The Russian Defense Minister and their top missile guy hanging out in Cheyenne for two weeks." Granger shook his head. "You pulled off something I never thought I'd see."

"It wasn't just me," Bud said, getting a "Yeah, right" look from the general. "Well . . ."

Granger heard the door into the building close with a metallic slap. "Old Vasiliy knows how to sweet-talk, doesn't he?"

"If he can mellow General Walker, I'm all for it. In any event, this *should* be done when the Japanese say so."

Granger's head shook again, once more in astonishment. "I'm still surprised this hasn't leaked out on their end. They're gabby little buggers, you know. Love to brag about their coups, especially of this magnitude."

"They also respect the almighty buck, and this contract is worth a couple billion dollars to them," Bud explained. That it was a couple billion *American* dollars made it all the more lucrative to the contractors, Sony and Panasonic among them. The complete replacement of the signal-processing end of the Soviet-era Ballistic Missile Early Warning System—the huge radar antennae facing north and west from the frozen wastes of the country would be retained—was a monumental undertaking that would bring the Russian system on par with its American counterpart. During the changeover, though, the nation would be half-blind, able to detect launches from its array of early-warning satellites but unable to confirm any threats by radar. That was where Bud had come in, suggesting that high-ranking Russian military personnel could be given access to one of the command centers from which the United States would wage nuclear war to ensure that the weapons slated for such use were sitting benignly in their silos, on their tarmacs, and tied alongside their pier. The latter, pulling the entire U.S. fleet of ballistic-missile subs in from their unknown patrol areas, had been the hardest to achieve. After protests from people like General Walker, the other CINCs, and, initially, Granger himself had been overcome, the first steps in the highly secret operation to upgrade the Russian BMEWS had begun. Japanese contractors—any from the United States had to be ruled out, for obvious reasons—under Russian and American supervision, designed the components and software in record time, and were at this minute awaiting the final word to begin dismantling the old to make room for the new, in figurative ways as well as literal.

"Us, the Russians, the Japanese, and the Chinese," Granger said, listing the non-European parties who were knowledgeable of the operation. "What did Beijing have to say about this all?"

"Good luck," Bud answered. "The thought of a nuclear exchange"—"exchange" sounded much more palatable than "war"—"starting by accident thrills them as much as it does anybody. Besides, the system pointing south will be unaffected; it was upgraded in '89. This is good for everybody, General." Bud, old "Colonel DiContino" from his Air Force days, couldn't bring himself to call a former superior by his first name. "The world will be a safer place when our neighbor can see if we throw rocks over his fence as well as we can see him."

Granger saw that the Gulfstream, which would take him and the NSA back to Washington, was being refueled from a tank truck—Falcon's underground pumping system was now out of service and unlikely to be repaired. The Base Closure and Realignment Committee was sure to recommend its demise by the end of the following year. So much that was familiar was disappearing. The general knew it was necessary, but that could not remove the pangs of loss from his gut as he watched the finest fighting force the world had ever known shrink toward a smaller, equally capable—he hoped—force that would continue to protect the nation in perpetuity. The warriors had made the world safe for peace, and they were now fading away.

"Our work here is done," Granger observed. He started to walk toward the jet.

"Back to Disneyland," Bud said, exhibiting a touch of cynicism himself. "And to the same old same old."

"Isn't that the truth," Granger agreed.

It wasn't.

He was a businessman before all else.

"Soothe my nerves, Gonzalo. Give me the total again," José-Ramón Alvarez directed. His eyes, aged but still filled with the fire born in his youth, added a silent admonition for his aide to be certain of the figure.

"Sixty-five million dollars," Gonzalo Parra repeated, sure of his accounting.

Alvarez smiled. "Information is very valuable."

"The correct term is intelligence," Parra corrected. He was the only man to hold enough favor with the executive secretary of the Cuban Freedom Society to chance such a seemingly mild rebuff.

"I think still as a businessman," Alvarez told his trusted aide, a man equal in age to his sixty-one years.

"You must begin to think as the leader of a nation." The suggestion was delivered with an expression that those who had wielded absolute power would recognize clearly, though this was in anticipation of such power. "Think what we will be able to do once we have the resources of an entire country at our disposal. That sixty-five million will be multiplied by ten times ten. With such money, with such power . . ."

"Yes." Power came in many forms, José-Ramón Alvarez knew. In the form of money it could purchase and persuade. In others it could deter and defend. Soon the combination would be in his possession. With it he would see that his people, enslaved by a failed ideology for decades, would prosper, as would he. Strength would be theirs. They, under his guidance, would be seen no longer as the weak. *The weak . . .* "I wish I could speak to Avaro once more before we go."

"It is not wise. Not at this time. He will contact us when the problem is taken care of." Parra heard the sound of approaching feet outside the door to the CFS inner sanctum, which was innocuously located in a converted minimall in Miami's Little Havana. "He has run the network for months now. This is not much different."

Alvarez knew that lack of trust or comfort was not his motive for desiring a final call, but his aide was very right. Great, momentous things lay ahead. Sentiment would have to wait.

The door opened after a quick knock. One of Alvarez's security men stepped in. In the hall stood two men in suits, both Anglos. Their jackets were unbuttoned for quick access to what was undoubtedly on their hips.

"Mr. President," the CFS security man began, looking directly at Alvarez. "It is time."

José-Ramón Alvarez smiled at the somewhat early use of the title that would soon be officially his. It would take very little getting used to.

It was the beginning of a catastrophic failure.

The *USS Pennsylvania,* an Ohio-class ballistic-missile submarine, was arguably the most complex platform in the arsenal of the United States for the employment of strategic nuclear weapons. On board she carried a mix of sophisticated sensors, machinery, and weapons, all of which worked in harmony to make the eighteen-thousand-ton sub a silent and potent deterrent to aggression against the country she served. Costing more than a billion dollars, the *Pennsylvania* was a reliable boat but one that required regular maintenance to ensure her effectiveness. Everything that could be done to keep her in tip-top shape was.

But there had been a mistake.

"Cap'n, that harmonic is gettin' worse," the chief of the boat reported.

The *Pennsylvania's* captain finished his notation and snapped his personal logbook closed. A gift from the crew of his old boat, the last Lafayette-class boomer to be in service, the waterproof box, slightly larger than a clipboard and an inch thick, had the name of his present command stenciled boldly across its front. He sneered at the reminder. The *Pennsylvania,* despite being the

most advanced inhabitant of the aquatic world, had been nothing
but a pain in the ass this cruise.

"Still the shaft gears?"

"Aye, sir."

The *Pennsylvania*, like all submarines in the U.S. inventory,
was powered by a nuclear reactor, a General Electric S8G natural-
circulation model in this case. But unlike other submarines, the
propeller shaft of the Ohio class had no direct mechanical contact with the steam turbines. These were turned by steam produced when water in the "cold" loop passed through heat
exchangers, which transferred thermal energy from the superhot
reactor by way of the circulation of coolant through the "hot"
loop. This two-loop system isolated the "hot" radioactive coolant.
The turbines, instead of transferring their circular motion directly to the shaft by way of lifter rods or gears, turned an electric
generator, which powered a quiet electric drive system that drove
the propeller shaft. The process, known as turboelectric drive, was
highly efficient and exceedingly quiet, a must for survival in the
life of a boomer, whose mission was to go to sea and cease to exist.

But it was that search for silence that had begun a series of
events the result of which would soon manifest itself.

During the *Pennsylvania*'s last refit, completed two months
earlier, the gear assembly that transferred power from the electric
motor to the shaft had been replaced with newly designed ones
that had proved less prone to harmonic transmission—the prop-
agation of even the slight machinery sounds from the electric
motor through the shaft and into the water. The new gears used
a unique sound-dampening system of assembly to cut the sub's
acoustic signature a further 10 percent. The twin cylinders of
high-stress alloy into which grooved channels had been machined
were basically reengineered into twelve "slices" of gears that fit
together over a main connecting core made of a layered combination of titanium, ceramic laminates, and more titanium. Each
slice was fit over the core in sequence, and in between each was
a doughnut-shaped gasket made from a carbon-fiber laminate,
which was the true trick of the new assembly. Quite literally, they
cut the transfer and reflection of sound from gear to gear, and
thus helped remove a source of harmonics that had plagued all
subs for decades.

Key to the successful use of the new system was its proper
installation and maintenance, and the crew of the *Pennsylvania*

had done well following every safety and operations check the assembly required. But there was one thing they could not check, as it was an installation item, designed to be configured during refit and left alone until the sub's next stay in port.

Holding the twin gear assemblies—one lay on each side of the similarly geared propeller shaft—tightly together as one unit was a single twelve-inch nut at the aft end of each cylinder. This nut was set and torqued during refit according to a very tight tolerance, as even the barest variance could negate the positive effects of the system and actually add to the problem of harmonic transmission. But the nut on the starboard assembly had not been torqued properly—it was recessed inside the aftmost gear by almost six inches. The technician responsible for its installation had added four-and-a-half foot-pounds too much torque when mechanically tightening the fifty-six-pound nut. That alone was enough to cause an excess of harmonics because it compressed the composite gaskets too tightly and degraded their sound-dampening qualities. But in combination with another phenomenon, one the crew of the *Pennsylvania* had no control over, the error was about to prove deadly.

Traveling on a course of three-four-five, skirting the Bahamian Island chain to port on her way to the relatively feature-free Blake Plateau, the *Pennsylvania*, running at six hundred feet, was in the midst of the Gulf Stream, which flowed northwest along her route to King's Bay, Georgia. Sixty miles off the island of Eleuthera, in a water depth that exceeded fifteen thousand feet, the warm current was moving at more than five knots, a direct result of the exceedingly hot winter months the Southern Hemisphere was experiencing. This warm water rushed northward, and was, at the moment, giving the *Pennsylvania* a much appreciated "tailwind" that turned her self-produced twelve knots into a nature-aided seventeen. It was also doing something else.

The huge bronze propeller at the rear of the sub was absorbing tremendous punishment—which it had been designed to accept—from the unstable water it was churning. The five-knot current was acting upon the water propelled aft and away from the sub, creating a doughnut-shaped area of lower than normal water pressure nearer the ends of the propeller's seven blades. As they turned, they were alternately "sucked out," away from the sub into the pressure void, then pushed back as they found "clean" water. This fluctuation was not an entirely abnormal phenomenon, but it was very powerful. The motion was transmitted inside the submarine through the shaft to the gear assembly, which rested upon a sound-absorbing sheet of high-density voided polymers. The assembly actually moved the few millimeters with the shaft. Back and forth. Back and forth. The motion was barely perceptible to the human eye and raised no alarm with the sensitive instruments that monitored all facets of the sub's propulsion system.

But it did register on the nut that had been torqued beyond spec. The repetitive motion, driven by tons of force, was transmitted to the nut that had lost much of its ability to absorb such fluctuations. As the geared cylinders spun with the energy of more than thirty thousand shaft horsepower, additional stresses were placed upon the nut that held the twelve slices together. At full speed the effect would have been similar to that of a jackhammer with the shaft snapping in and out in fractions of an inch while the gears absorbed the punishment. This took longer. After an hour in the current the nut developed a tiny hairline fracture on its inner face. Ten minutes later the fissure had spread through the nut. A minute after that it separated in two with a loud snap that caused heads farther forward in the engine room to turn. The pieces came free of the core that ran the length of the gear assembly and spit aft, impacting the bare metal bulkhead. Less than a second after that the aftmost gear slice, following its natural rotation and now free to move, slid off the core, spinning with a force unimaginable.

And with that there was nothing that could be done.

The starboard gear assembly was on the downside of the rotation, meaning the propeller shaft was spinning over its top to starboard. As the gear slice came free, its teeth still enmeshed with those on the shaft, it was pulled under the shaft. But there was not enough room for the foot-diameter slab of metal to make it. With only a four-inch clearance between the shaft and the polymer-coated deck, the gear was pulled into the inadequate space like a wedge, the power of thirty thousand horses ensuring an uneven match between force and matter. The sound of the event, louder than the fractured nut ricocheting through the engine room, was transmitted throughout the sub, causing brains to register the fact that something was very wrong. Before any heads could turn, though, another, more horrifying sound radiated from the back of the boat.

The propeller shaft, continuing to turn, had nowhere else to go but upward as the gear was driven between it and the deck. A four-inch clearance expanded instantly to more than twelve as the ten-ton shaft broke free of the bearing rings that held it in place. Its forwardmost end, where the gear assemblies were attached, sprang up like the vaulted end of a fulcrum, lifting the eight-ton electric-drive motor upward with it. At the top of the motor were stabilizer bars, looking much like extended shock absorbers, that helped dampen any motion of the machinery and held the unit in place. These bars had three inches of play, which was not enough to absorb the extra eight inches the unit was being forced to move. Their top ends transferred the force of the event, now exceeding a million-and-a-quarter foot-pounds of energy, to the number-eight structural ring, to which they were connected. Seventy-eight of these rings, over which an inch-and-a-half-thick skin of HY-80 steel was welded, formed the structure of the pressure hull. The number-eight ring, like all the others, was designed to withstand tremendous pressures squeezing it from all sides, but not a point impact of the magnitude being delivered. It was as if a mighty scissor jack had thrust upward against the ring. The result was a complete failure of the structural member, which cracked outward, separating the steel skin as it pressed toward the sea. The directional force continued for a millisecond more, expanding the rupture in the pressure hull, tearing the inner and outer skin of the *Pennsylvania* for a hundred feet along the starboard side of its topdeck as if a can opener had sliced through it.

No emergency drills could have saved the sub or its crew. The seawater, under tremendous pressure at six hundred feet, sprayed through the ruptured hull, flooding all compartments from the missile room aft. The huge electric-drive motor, lifted more than a foot off its base, came back down with a violence the deck and supports had never been intended to sustain. They failed completely, sending the unit crashing through to the bulkhead supports below. In the process the propeller shaft, free of any moorings, smashed around the engine room, impacting the steam turbine a few feet to port, knocking it off its supports and separating the steam pipes from their welded flanges that mated them to the reactor room. High-pressure steam at 1,000 degrees Fahrenheit shot into the flooding compartment. Those who had survived the initial venting of the hull were burned to death without as much as a spark of flame.

One compartment forward, in the reactor room, automatic controls registered the event and began to SCRAM—or rapidly shut down—the nuclear pile, but radiation was not what was to doom the *Pennsylvania*. The emptied steam pipes that fed the turbines one compartment back quickly overheated. Though they did not enter the reactor vessel, they passed side by side through the heat exchanger with the pipes that transferred the high-temperature coolant from the reactor. When the empty turbine pipes were doused with the ice-cold seawater flooding the reactor room, a vast quantity of steam was instantly generated, more than the confined space could handle. What engineers called an explosive overpressure event occurred. This ripped through the aft part of the sub, buckling the hull more than it already was and punching bulkheads fore and aft. The resultant overpressure blew watertight doors all the way forward through the control room just as the captain ordered the emergency buoy released.

The command was never carried out. A tremendous *pop* shook everyone in the forward section of the sub, then a strange white wall of fluid poured through the doors facing aft and slammed into every living thing. Men were thrown forward as the water raced toward the nose of the sub.

The entire process, from catastrophic failure to destruction, had taken under ten seconds. The *Pennsylvania* continued on course another two hundred yards before the weight of the water filling her hull overcame her momentum and stopped the big sub. As most of her weight was closer to the stern, she slid backward and down at an angle that grew ever steeper. She impacted the sea floor at a depth of 15,030 feet, her stern pointed almost straight down. Traveling at forty knots, the mass of the *Pennsylvania* drove the crumpled hull into the soft ocean bottom and collapsed the sub, bow upon stern, like an accordion.

With that, the *USS Pennsylvania* had disappeared into the watery depths of the Atlantic for the last time, and the United States of America, which had counted itself lucky for more than three decades, had lost its first fleet ballistic-missile submarine in an accident at sea.

CHAPTER TWO

Libertad

There were ten of them, all dressed in the dirty blue coveralls that they wore each and every day in the execution of their duties at the Cuban Revolutionary Air Force Base near Santa Clara in the central part of the island nation. On evenings such as this they would routinely spend the six hours of their first duty shift cleaning and preparing the base's twelve operative MiG-23 fighters for use the following morning. The likelihood that any would be taken skyward was rare these days, so the limits of their efforts were largely directed at keeping the aircraft clean and rust free. A pretty picture they would make, but the squadron—which had boasted sixteen functioning MiGs just a month previously—was supposed to be more than a showpiece in its intended role, something these ground crewman were, in a grand switch of motives, going to prevent from ever coming to fruition.

In pairs they went to each aircraft, working as normal, cleaning debris from the landing gear and strut assemblies. The officer overseeing their work sat idly a hundred meters away in a straight-backed wooden chair that he leaned against a hangar's outer wall. His attention was focused on one of the "unauthorized" publications so readily available in Santa Clara, particularly upon a pretty young woman whom the caption said was a frequent visitor to the sands of Playa la Panchita. From the absence of tan lines he was certain it was an accurate statement.

But while the risqué pictures held his attention, the crews under his watch were able to spend just a short amount of time longer than normal at the front wheelwell of each MiG. In less than four hours their work was done, freeing the crews, half of whom were unofficial "replacements" for those who were not inclined to cooperate in the somewhat historic venture soon to begin, to spend some much needed additional time on the four Hind helicopter gunships based at Santa Clara. There they focused on the tail rotor assemblies, lubricating the exposed fasteners and checking for the required torquing on the bolts. When the desired tightness was achieved, they moved on to the repair shop to clean and secure their tools, most of which were specialized and irreplaceable, as was much of the machinery in the building.

With a full shift of work behind them, the group, with the approval of their uninterested duty officer, proceeded to their barracks and, as every good soldier in the Cuban Revolutionary Armed Forces was expected to do, cleaned and prepared their personal weapons for use in any eventuality.

This final task they completed with particular care and haste, knowing that a certain "eventuality" was soon to occur.

They called him Papa Tony. It was a term representative of respect more than lineage, though the blood that filled Antonio Paredes, Jr.'s veins was of the same land as his hosts. Yet his years were insufficient to allow for parentage of any of the men he was now with. They were all senior officers in the Cuban Revolutionary Armed Forces who had served their country with pride and distinction for decades, from a time before young Antonio had learned to walk. Some may even have taken up arms against his father in the disastrous Bay of Pigs Invasion. It was possible that one was even responsible for the elder Paredes's death. But the past was simply history, Antonio believed, and it was time to write a new chapter for the books. Things changed, societies matured, and people who were once cattle in a pen had come to see the benevolent rancher as little more than a guide to the slaughterhouse. Yes, the past was very different from the present, except in one way that few would ever know. A very ironic and appropriate way. For the same reasons as his father Antonio had returned to the land of his birth, the land his family had fled more than three-and-a-half decades before, to help bring freedom once again to a simple, beautiful people. And, as Antonio felt was a tribute to the father he never knew, he had come at the behest of the same, secretive American employer as *his* Papa Tony.

"Papa, do you wish to watch?"

Paredes turned toward the voice. It was Colonel Hector Ojeda, executive officer of the Second Mechanized Division, a unit located some twelve miles to the east at Falcon. It was a position he would occupy for fifteen more minutes. At that point he would become Colonel Ojeda, rebel officer and leader of the battle for his nation's freedom.

Ojeda held a pair of French-made night-vision binoculars out for the CIA officer, who took them and followed his host to the edge of the vegetation on the hill just four miles north of the Santa Clara airfield. They settled in among a sparse grove of palms that opened into a moonlit clearing where the rise sloped downward. There was no fear of detection. The unthinkable would never happen. All threats were outside the borders, across oceans. Akin to the American maxim of personal freedom and safety, the door was unlocked on this warm autumn evening.

That was the essence of the plan to free Cuba.

"Ten minutes," Ojeda reported. He was a tall man, thin from head to toe, which would make him appear weak if not for the eyes. Bulging, brown on white, they were set in a gaunt face that showed a tired determination known only by those who had traveled a long road to an uncertain future. His frame, never beyond wiry in his fifty-nine years, had obviously suffered from the strain of the previous three months. So much planning, so many things to accomplish in the shadows. And at any time his actions could have been discovered, with only one result imaginable. It was that knowledge that had pushed the already driven Ojeda to secure an opportunity for the future with a ruthless abandon that had silenced many of those who would not join in the fight for freedom. The affair had changed him, and he knew it.

Paredes had been changed, also. In his one month living among those who were about to inexorably alter their future, he had found an attachment to a place he had no memory of. It contradicted what he had been taught during his education in the United States about nature versus nurture. Where environment had shaped his being, it was this place, this land, that had formed it. And though the part he was to play, an officially deniable role as liaison between the rebel military commanders and Langley, was important, if small, he had come to realize that with success there would be a freedom of sorts for him personally as well as for his hosts. In essence he was a thirty-eight-year-old man who had come home.

"Watch the line of aircraft," Ojeda directed.

Antonio braced himself against the coarse surface of a palm and brought the glasses to eye level, using his arms to form a sturdy triangle and steady the view. His left thumb activated the enhancement function of the binoculars, and a soft green luminescence escaped the viewport to paint the upper portion of his face with a glow that matched closely the color of the surrounding flora as seen in daylight.

"How long now?" Paredes inquired as he slowly swept the twin rows of Soviet-built fighters.

"Just a few minutes."

All was still on the tarmac. Nearly an hour past midnight nothing else would be expected. But shortly a display of ingenuity, determination, and deadly ability would be offered, not only for the eyes of Papa Tony, but for the eyes of his masters, for whom a final act of convincing was necessary before committing support to the rebellion.

Antonio both heard and felt the breath of Ojeda on his neck. It surprised him some that the colonel chose not to watch the scene more closely, but then the man had lived it for so long. In each safe house—a generous term in a country where the accommodations depicted on *Gilligan's Island* were ostentatious by comparison—he had been moved to, twelve in all, Ojeda had kept him intimately informed of the preparations and the participants who were signed onto the plan. So strange it was, Paredes had come to realize, that a man whom Ojeda and his comrades had respected for decades could destroy that trust and loyalty with such a minor act. They would have killed for Fidel Castro, but now they would kill to unseat him from power, from his throne of arrogance. The bullet that had killed General Eduardo Echevarría Ontiveros, hero of the Revolution and *true* leader of men, might just as well have been fired by volley at the *presidente* himself.

But acts seen as insignificant by the mighty often propelled lesser men to counter the injustice they perceived with a fury never imagined. And fury was the proper word, for it was some-

thing Antonio knew was key to Ojeda's being, and it was something to be revealed momentarily before his very eyes.

The flashes were rapid in succession, like a string of noiseless
firecrackers exploding to one's front. The brightness flared the
night-vision glasses and were compensated for automatically, the
optics fully recovering by the time the sharp cracks reached Paredes and Ojeda four miles distant. A joyous yell erupted from
beyond the grove of palms as the sound passed over the rebel
command staff.

Like a coach looking for evidence of mistakes or missteps on
the part of his team, Paredes watched for several minutes as may-
hem erupted on the base below. Pilots, alerted by the blasts and
the subsequent alarm, ran from their quarters to the flight line
where they stood, bewildered, as they stared at their suddenly
grounded aircraft. To the west of the planes a flash erupted from
the base's maintenance hangar, followed quickly by a bright orange fireball that did not subside. Fingers of orange licked out of
the half-open door and the shattered windows as equipment vital
to the operation of the aircraft was consumed by the inferno. A
few minutes later, as the Hind pilots and crew scrambled to their
ships and took to the sky, the final blow of the opening was struck.

Antonio lowered the glasses as obvious muzzle flashes
erupted around and in the control tower. He turned to Colonel
Ojeda, who stood in the same position as before, his eyes cast not
upon the successful operation unfolding, but toward the sky almost straight up. "Sufficient for your government, Papa Tony?"

Paredes smiled, wishing in vain that the cameras a hundred
miles up could see the look in the colonel's eyes, for no further
confirmation of the viability of this rebellion would be necessary.
"Ample, Colonel. It is a fair fight now."

Ojeda's gaze came down upon the American's satisfied face.
At several other airfields across the country similar actions would
be happening, effectively taking the Revolutionary Air Forces out
of the fray. The skies would belong to no one. Still, it was a fact
only of tactical convenience to the colonel. "Papa, I would fight
this war with a stick, a stone, and the hate in my heart." The
expression on his face changed slightly, to something that seemed
to perplex and slightly frighten the American. "It was fair when
they had an air force. Now the battle is mine."

Grandiose, some would label the claim, but they were not
standing in the shadow of the man who, as lit from above by the

bright, full moon, resembled the earthly embodiment of the grim reaper. Antonio Paredes was, and he pitied the enemy, for any foe of this man was at a disadvantage simply by nature of his allegiance.

Ojeda reached out and touched the American on the shoulder, leaving his hand there for a moment, conveying the gratitude that words would fumble over. Then he turned and went to his men, leaving Paredes to stand among the palms that towered like sheltering sentinels over him. Activity on the base was picking up, with more flashes, more sounds, and the beautiful scenes of confusion as soldiers loyal to the government struggled to comprehend what had happened and where the enemy had come from. Ten men, Antonio thought. And Ojeda has thirty thousand. He could only smile at the thought of what was still to come.

The liberation of Cuba had begun.

Deputy Director, Intelligence, Greg Drummond hated the hour. The sun was barely up when his CIA driver arrived at his suburban Virginia home, the crisp beauty of an autumn morning not yet fully realized. And it wouldn't be for the man who headed the Agency's Intelligence directorate. He had missed a slew of sunrises and sunsets in his eighteen years at Langley, half of those in the past six months, and he had begun to wonder if life was anything more than work marked at both ends by meals from the Agency's mess.

The drive in took thirty minutes, a little more than usual because some knucklehead had tried a right-side pass on a big rig and ended up transforming his forty-thousand-dollar Beamer into a thirty-thousand-dollar Beamer with a ten-grand repair bill attached. Drummond was deposited in the VIP area of the CIA's underground parking garage and took the VIP elevator directly to the seventh floor, the home of the VIPs. Being a VIP had its pluses.

"Greg, hurry up," one of the minuses said as he saw the DDI step off the elevator.

"One minute, Anthony." Drummond walked past Director of Central Intelligence Anthony Merriweather's office, which, unfortunately, was but one from his, and checked the night dispatches on his desk. There was no reason to rush, despite the DCI's urging. The DDI slid out of his overcoat and laid his soft leather case on the desk, which, to his chagrin, hadn't magically swallowed the ponderous "to do" list, courtesy of his micromanager boss, that would pop up on his computer screen when he coded in for the day.

He let out a breath and tried to convince himself that this day would pass quickly and productively, then picked up the Significant Events summary prepared by the night desk and felt his hopes of a second earlier fade away.

"Damn," he said softly, folding the single sheet in half and pulling the corresponding detail report that explained in depth the event of concern. He has to listen to this, Drummond thought, knowing that "has to" was a term that rarely applied to Merriweather. He was in the DCI's office a minute later.

"We have SNAPSHOT stuff coming in," Merriweather reported.

"Oh? This soon?" the DDI asked, only half-interested.

"Healy's guy gave me an eyeball description of what he saw. Very impressive," the DCI commented, tearing the sheet of his notes on the conversation from the legal pad and sliding it into the shredder atop his wastebasket.

"Christ, Anthony!" Drummond's jaw would have dropped if he didn't know the added emphasis would be wasted. "*You* should not be in direct contact with field officers when they are engaged in a mission. Especially this mission."

Merriweather made his disagreement clear with a look. There was a fine line between security and paranoia. "It is a secure communication link, Greg."

"Secure is a fantasy we all hope is true," the DDI said. "We do not take risks with it when they are not necessary. Mike could have gotten the information." Mike Healy, Drummond's counterpart in Operations, ran the spooks in the field.

"Hmm." The DCI wasn't sure he wanted Healy being the point of contact on something as big as SNAPSHOT. Like Drummond, the DDO had a tendency to filter too much, Merriweather believed. "Well, it's done now. We'll have another KH-12 pass in an hour. After that we go to the President. He'll want to see that everything is going as planned." *And won't DiContino be surprised that his Russia operation isn't quite the most important thing going on,* he added to himself, knowing that the man sitting across from him would neither appreciate nor understand his opinion of the NSA. It was clear enough without words, he figured.

"Now that Cuba is free," Drummond began, the sarcasm mild but undeniable, "we have to talk about CANDLE."

"What about it?" Merriweather was impatient with his deputy's seemingly endless search for a leak that he believed existed somewhere in the Intelligence Directorate. The days of James Jesus Angleton were long past, he reasoned, making the present search for a supposed leak reminiscent of the famed hunt for "K" by the former agency official. CANDLE was Drummond's internal operation to locate the supposed exfiltration of information and plug it.

Drummond handed over the night summary and the detail report supporting the first item on it. Merriweather scanned it quickly, jotting down his own observations and giving it about as much attention as he had to his deputy's suspicions from day one. It was *his* directorate, after all, and if there was a leak, which Merriweather doubted anyway, then it was *his* responsibility. He almost wished it were true so he could convince those diehards on the Hill that he needed new people for new times, not holdovers who were there just because of longevity in the position.

"So? The president of the Panamanian legislature changed his schedule for the day after tomorrow." The DCI looked up. "Do we have a problem with that?"

Drummond told himself that all nightmares came to an end, and that he would soon wake from this one. "We had a damn complex surveillance set up on him, Anthony! He was supposed to meet with reps from the Peruvian drug cartels at location *X.* Now he suddenly changes to location *Y,* and we have no idea where that is." The DDI let it hang there, wondering why his boss couldn't see the seriousness of the implications.

"And?"

"Anthony, this is the third time we've had a meeting scheduled weeks in advance between Coseros and unsavories that was suddenly changed at the last minute. Not a week or two ahead, but *days* before the meet. That doesn't give us enough time to find the new site and shift our assets. Someone is tipping him off."

"I thought you checked your Latin-American section," the DCI said.

"I have, but apparently not close enough," Drummond admitted. "But beyond the fact that we have a leak—"

"Possibly," Merriweather interjected, allowing it just for the sake of argument.

"All right, possibly have a leak. The important thing is to recognize who is benefiting from what is getting out."

"Come on, Greg. Don't beat that old horse anymore."

Christ, is he blind? "Coseros is a government official in Panama, and his ass has been saved from indictment because of these leaks, and he has been funneling money to your CFS guys down in Miami. Their bank account is busting, Anthony!"

"Funneling? That is not what the Bureau found in its *three* separate investigations before this one." The Agency, as it sometimes did, was assisting the FBI in an investigation that required some of its special abilities. "I believe the term they settled on was 'contributions.' As for your narco-corruption theory, you know damn well that money Coseros has given them doesn't even begin to amount to what is in their accounts. The CFS has other supporters, Greg. Big ones." Merriweather seemed suddenly disinterested in any further correction of his deputy's off-the-mark position. "Besides all that, the Justice Department has found no compelling evidence to support an indictment of Coseros," he pointed out correctly, ignoring the other connection his deputy was implying.

"Because every time we get close, someone tips him!" Drummond sat back, letting the frustration subside a bit. "And he is supporting the people you want to put into power in Cuba."

"*I* do?" The DCI chuckled. "So you consider yourself not a part of this?"

Bad choice of words, Greg. He'd learned that his boss was a master at catching misspeaks and using them to the fullest advantage. "Look, I want Castro out as bad as anyone. He's one of the last of a dead breed. But we can't overlook the connection between the Peruvian cartels and Coseros, and between Coseros and the Cuban Freedom Society."

The DCI's face went instantly red at the direct link the DDI was suggesting. "You are not to repeat that assertion outside of this room. Never! I will not tolerate even the hint of such linkage without irrefutable evidence to warrant it. Is that clear?"

"Have I yet?" Drummond responded with a challenge.

Merriweather ignored the question. "I will not jeopardize SNAPSHOT simply because you have doubts about the integrity of your directorate, and because you place fiction above fact in forming your opinions."

"Anthony, I—"

"You will keep your unsubstantiated ideas to yourself until the time that you have something concrete to back them up. Is that very clear? A yes or no, please."

What the hell was concrete? Drummond wondered. His job was supposed to involve speculation, and now his boss was telling him to reign in his brain? "Very clear."

Merriweather was still flushed. He was not a man to calm from provocation or questioning easily. "Good." He checked the time on the small desk clock left by his predecessor. "We have to be at the White House in a few hours. Be ready."

And with that it was over. The DDI walked into the hallway, closing the door himself. It was still too early for the majority of Langley's workers to have arrived, so he felt comfortable just standing in the hall. A better man had occupied the office he'd just left, until a microscopic, indiscriminate bug had taken its toll. Herb Landau just wouldn't have run things this way, Drummond knew. He was sure of it, as sure as he was that the director's *cause célèbre* was inherently flawed. Yet he could do nothing. The President had given it the nod, without even letting his closest advisers in on SNAPSHOT. That was an entirely different problem, but one the DDI saw as potentially more dangerous than having an autocrat at the helm of the Agency. His eyes searched the ceiling for a solution that was not there. He was certain where the problem was, however, and equally confident in his belief that things were going to get worse before they got better.

He would have been surprised, however, at just how much of an understatement his last thought had been.

The dacha of Gennadiy Konovalenko, president of the Russian Federation, was a hundred miles from the Russian capital, nestled along a river among a stand of firs that kept the expansive deck at the rear in a perpetual shade. The sunlight that did penetrate the canopy from the yellow globe low in the southern sky lit the rippling water below with sparkles and flashes, and cast a harsh, pale coloring upon the birds that flitted through the beams. The scene was in stark contrast to the dirty, dull pallor that was pervasive in the great cities of Mother Russia. All the brightly colored spires and fine statuary could not reverse a course of decay initiated almost eighty years earlier. It would take much longer to right the wrongs done the Russian people. Much longer to make the nation a reflection of its inherent beauty.

"We should have such a place in Red Square, eh?" the president suggested from his reclining wooden chair on the deck. It was reminiscent of the Adirondack style favored by the leisure-loving Americans and had actually been built with those in mind after the president's return from a particularly enjoyable trip to the United States.

"Then what reason would we have to journey here?" Foreign Minister Igor Yakovlev responded with his own musing. He walked along the deck, sliding a gloved hand on the rough railing as he moved. The chill of the autumn afternoon caused a cloud of whitish mist to spurt from his mouth with each word and each breath. "And where would we hold court?"

The president laughed, his paunch shaking beneath the fur coat that took the bite out of the air but left his reddening nose unprotected. A man of only middle age, he was perhaps the most crucial leader his country—in whatever incarnation or by whatever name—had ever had. And "holding court," as his trusted adviser called it, was but one tool he had developed to placate his critics. Bring them out here, to the dacha his father, a onetime member of the old Soviet Politburo, had built using prison labor imported from the east. Get them away from that dreadful place called Moscow, where power was the goal of all the players. Even he fell into that trap when the days in the Kremlin stretched to weeks, and weeks to months. But always there was his dacha, as modest as it was by Western standards. His escape. His domain.

A servant stepped onto the deck from the main building and announced the arrival of those who had come to do battle with the president. Court was in session.

"Igor Yureivich," Interior Minister Georgiy Bogdanov said, greeting the man who should have been his equal in government, but the president's favor had placed the foreign minister in an elevated state of importance. He turned to the leader of his nation, who was rising from his seat. "Gennadiy Timofeyivich, your dacha looks lovely as always."

The president welcomed Bogdanov with the accepted firm kiss on each cheek. "Georgiy Ivanovich, you are welcome here always." A polite smile masked the hollowness of the offer. "And you bring the good general with you."

General Aleksandr Shergin, commander of *Voyska PVO,* the Russian air-defense forces that had changed little from the days of allegiance to the Soviet Union, nodded crisply to the man he grudgingly accepted as his commander in chief. "President Konovalenko."

The president expected no more informal a greeting than that from a military man, and would offer none in return to General Aleksandr Dmitreivich Shergin. "Come, sit."

Yakovlev took the seat beside the president, across the small drinks table from the men who were their adversaries. A platter of *omul,* a smoked fish imported from the eastern expanses of the country, appeared from the hands of a servant, as did a bottle of vodka and four glasses. The small talk that followed lasted several minutes, until its purpose as a prelude to more serious discussions had been exhausted.

"And now to the less enjoyable matters at hand," the president said. "Your choice of a traveling companion leaves little for me to guess at, Georgiy Ivanovich."

The interior minister smiled obligingly at the friendliness of the comment. "General Shergin is an expert in these matters."

"As is his superior—Marshal Kurchatov," Yakovlev offered. "And Colonel Belyayev."

"Yes. Yes." The interior minister laid a strip of the pinkish fish on his tongue and chewed it quickly to a swallow. "But they do not represent the opinion of all in the military."

The president bristled at the veiled meaning. "You do not suggest that the military would try to hinder our efforts, do you, Comrade Bogdanov?"

It was "Comrade Bogdanov" now. Soon it would deteriorate to "Comrade Interior Minister." Beyond that, just invectives. Bogdanov hoped to avoid that, but, with the president's well-known temper and his fervency on this point, doing so would be difficult. He had to try, however. His duty to the Motherland demanded such.

"Hinder?" Bogdanov answered the question adequately with a nonresponse. "It is simply a matter of advisement. To place so much trust in the Americans is, well, presumptuous, would you not say?"

"No, I would not say that." The president pulled his collar up against the breeze that was picking up. "They have given Marshal Kurchatov unprecedented access to their strategic systems. Their *raket* submarines are being recalled for the duration of the operation. In a few hours he will observe the process by which a launch of their strategic missiles is ordered, something that is such a closely held secret the KGB was never able to determine the exact process." His head shook emphatically. "No, Comrade Bogdanov, I would not say that our trust of the Americans is presumptuous."

"I would," the interior minister countered, drawing the philosophical line between himself and the president. "And so do many others . . . in all areas of our government."

The president saw the general straighten at the minister's words. What was being implied was clear enough. He had already survived one coup and had squashed two others before they ever got past the planning stages, mostly because they lacked any sort of catalyst to spark and inspire the plotters. The dismantling of his nation's missile-warning system about to begin with American assistance could be just such a catalyst. Warnings of such a situation had been given since the plan's inception. There was deep, vitriolic disagreement within the government over the plan. To trust the Americans or not. There were only two answers, with no gray area in between, and these men had been dispatched to be convinced that the president's decision was correct. Anything less could lead to something the country neither wanted nor needed.

"Igor Yureivich," the president said, signaling his foreign minister to do that which he had hoped would not be necessary. As a smart political maverick, though, he had prepared for the eventuality that it would.

"We have proof that the Americans are sincere in this effort," Yakovlev began. "From inside the Central Intelligence Agency."

The revelation caught both Bogdanov and Shergin off guard, and each looked to the other for some bearing as to what should be done now. The interior minister went on with the obvious. "We have an agent *in* the CIA?"

"Not exactly," Yakovlev said with a smile, explaining the full story for the visitors after a sip of vodka. "As you can see, it is an unusual arrangement. But we have validated the information. The spy that State Security caught earlier this year—the damned Lithuanian in the shipyard—was foretold by the information we received from our source. And several other pieces of information have proven very helpful, and very truthful."

Bogdanov thought over what he'd just been told. It was quite out of the ordinary but very elegant indeed. State Security, the leftovers of the former KGB, still held domain over the gathering of intelligence, but not in this, it was apparent. "And the reason for having the Foreign Ministry handle this . . . source, instead of State Security?"

The president laughed. "Even you, Georgiy Ivanovich, cannot believe that our vaunted intelligence agency is free of all the powers that corrupted it in the past. This arrangement is more secure, if somewhat more cumbersome. The chain consists of two persons in America. One of them is an American who has given us advance word of media reports for more than a decade now—their press is often more adept at information gathering than the KGB was—and can be trusted completely. Now his use is mostly as a courier. The other is a liaison at the embassy. Reports are delivered to the American by means that are not important, then to our man at the embassy. They are then brought directly to Moscow and hand-delivered to Igor Yureivich. He then brings them to me for review. And now the both of you are blessed with the knowledge." He said the latter with a warning glare. "Where this information comes from is beyond compare, especially because it is given . . . how would you say? . . . unwittingly. Without embellishment or filtering. To let on that we have access to this information would surely end its availability. Hence the extreme precautions. I alone make the decision as to how the information is to be used."

"This could be trickery," Bogdanov suggested.

"Not with what has been allowed to slip out," Yakovlev responded. "We have learned such secrets that you would not believe."

"And those may be useful in the future," the president said, knowing the value of inside knowledge during negotiations in the international arena. "I tell you all this only to stave off any foolish moves by 'other parties.' You must convince them that such would be a grave mistake, and you must do so without revealing what you have been told."

Shergin caught the president's attention with his stare. "I trust that you are right to believe this information. Inoperable radars will do little to protect the Motherland."

"As will malfunctioning ones," the president shot back. "A safer tomorrow will come only from trust today."

Interior Minister Bogdanov, in a position of allegiance that was odd considering his seemingly benign place in the government machinery, had to decide whether to report in the positive or the negative to his fellow dissenters back in Moscow. The 106th Airborne Division, a unit that had saved the president once by refusing to participate in a failed effort to unseat him, was poised to move into the capital with just a word from General Shergin, its allegiance this time opposite of the past by way of a new, conversely loyal unit commander. Would Bogdanov set such a thing in motion? Could he?

"The next two weeks will be somewhat tense," the interior minister theorized, his decision sure to disappoint many of his political bent. "I hope events bear out your trust in the Americans."

"I have no doubts," the president said confidently. "All will go well."

"I hope so," Bogdanov said. "For the sake of the Motherland." *And for yours.*

"Tomás, look. Quick," Jorge said, the CNN anchor's words sounding much too awake for such an early hour, then reminded himself that he was on the *West* Coast. He had been out here too long, he knew. "Turn it up, Tomás. Turn it up."

Tomás set down the plastic cassette case and jeweler's screwdriver and rolled off the motel bed. He twisted the volume knob until the sound came up. No fucking remote, he thought, realizing that fifty-six bucks a night didn't necessarily guarantee the latest in amenities.

"Early reports from Havana indicate that the apparent coup has caused widespread disruption of communications systems." The anchor fiddled with papers that were being fed to him, obviously trying to sort out that which was before him and the flow of words through his earpiece. Fast-breaking news was never as pretty as the produced stuff. *"And, uh, we are now getting some confirmation on an earlier report that this may be a very large and a very well organized uprising. Sources at Guantánamo Naval Base near the eastern end of the island are reporting that there is heavy fighting in the nearby city of Guantánamo. Flashes . . . I am reading this as I receive it, so bear with the roughness of it. Flashes are visible from the north and . . . If these reports are correct, and we believe they are, then this fighting is hundreds of miles from the initial reports from the area near the country's capital of Havana. And . . ."*

Jorge switched the set off. "I don't believe it."

"Shit. No wonder they want this thing out of circulation." Tomás tightened the last of the small metal screws that held the cassette together. "Does this do anything to us?"

Jorge's head shook. "Fee up front, Tomás. We have our money, we do the job." He looked at the work his partner was finishing up. "How long?"

"Just ... a ... there!" Tomás held up the tape. "You should go for the head like me next time."

"Like I should have known," Jorge protested. One of his shots had not only found its mark in the man's chest, it had also clipped the cassette he was carrying in his shirt pocket, destroying the transfer rollers but sparing the tape itself. That had necessitated a hurried search for the required materials and tools. A cassette of the same type had been purchased, along with the tiny screwdrivers, and was simply dismantled and the undamaged spools of tape inserted. It had taken some time, as Tomás was careful to remove all fragments of the shattered plastic. Thankfully, the tape had been pulled from Portero's pocket quickly enough, saving it from a drenching in the man's blood. Liquids, especially thick ones like human blood, were devastating to the thin magnetic tape that depended on stability in its environment for longevity. Anyone who had ever left one exposed on the dash of an automobile on a hot day would understand the fragility completely.

A thump from outside the door made Jorge turn his head. It had to be the complimentary *USA Today,* one of the reasons he had chosen this motel. The one extra he wanted, actually needed. It would save him a trip to the liquor store across the street. "Let's hear it."

Tomás reached for the portable cassette player and inserted the tape, pressing Play next. A few seconds went by before there was speaking to be heard. Thank God it ...

"What is this?" Jorge asked. It was not what they had been told to expect.

"Who is that?" Tomás added another question. "This isn't the fucking tape! What the fuck is going on!"

"Shut up!" Jorge said, looking at the walls and hoping they were thick enough to contain his partner's outburst. He listened for a few minutes to the conversation's end. "Damn."

"Jorge, that is *not* what we were supposed to find." Tomás stood from the bed and began to pace.

"That had to be Portero speaking," Jorge said. "But the other one?"

Tomás stopped his stalking, looking directly to his partner. "Jorge, we fucking killed an FBI agent today to get that tape, and it *ISN'T EVEN IT!*" The news on both radio and TV had spread the word quickly, along with vague descriptions of the pair that, thankfully, weren't very accurate.

"But it is something."

Tomás, the younger of the two, snorted. "Yeah. A lot of good that'll do us. Fuck!"

His partner was right, Jorge knew. They were supposed to get the tape and verify that it was *the* tape. What they had been briefed to be on the lookout for was definitely not what they had just heard. "You still have that reporter's name, the one he was supposed to meet with?"

"Sure do. You think he might have given it to him ahead of time?"

"It's possible," Jorge figured, even though he didn't see how it could have happened. "But we're going to make damn sure about it. But first we've got to report this."

"But we're not supposed to ..." His partner's look convinced him that arguing was not a good idea at the moment. "They're going to love this." Tomás watched Jorge go to the door and open it gingerly, peering through the crack into the early-morning darkness before retrieving the paper from just outside.

"Dial it," Jorge instructed his partner while he pulled the slip of paper out of his wallet. On it was the number of a phone booth he had selected a few days before. He had selected others and would use each only once. Next he opened the paper to the sports section. It was baseball season, so he found the first story nearest the upper left of the page concerning America's favorite pastime. ANGELS STILL ALIVE, the heading read. Hard to believe, he thought. But his interest was in the body of the story. *Just when the team from the land of Disney* ... He had his key. *D.*

"Ringing," Tomás said.

A minute later, almost three thousand miles away, ten digits appeared on the readout of a pager clipped to the inside of a man's pocket. With just a single look, he knew what to do. His *USA Today* had been finished hours before with his breakfast.

Art Jefferson walked off the elevator on the fourth floor just after sunrise, at a time when the L.A. office would normally be quiet for another two hours. This day, though, there were more than a hundred agents already on duty, more than half there on their day off. That was just the way it was. You didn't kill an agent without striking a chord in the collective body of the FBI. Art pitied the perps who had robbed Thom Danbrook of his life.

"Art." It was Cameron Lowe, the supervising special agent of the L.A. office's Homicide Section—Art's boss.

"Morning, Cam." Art walked to his desk in the bullpen area of the floor, which was divided into dozens of "rooms" by attractively upholstered shoulder-high dividers. He and Frankie shared one on the north side of the floor, near the row of glass-enclosed offices that housed the supervising agents of the office's sections. Art had rated one once as head of the OC (Organized Crime) Section. That time was now just a fond, detested memory.

"How's Aguirre?" Lowe asked, leaning his short frame against the pseudo wall that surrounded Art's and Frankie's desks.

"I made sure Shelley got her home last night." He slid out of his jacket, hanging it on the single metal hook clipped to the divider's top edge. "It ain't easy, Cam. She's hurting."

"Are you going to need someone else to back you up on this? I mean, if she needs some time . . ."

Art's head shook. Frankie had made it clear that she wanted in on this, and Art expected no different. He'd never known an agent to back away from the chance to catch the killers of a fellow agent. The offer had to be made, but . . . "No. She'll be in. Is everything squared away with LAPD?"

"All set." The LAPD, which had jurisdiction over the area where the murders were committed, had technical authority to be the lead agency on the case. But the fact that a federal officer had been killed in addition to the other victim had prompted the local police to cede the lead to the FBI. Now they had two murders to solve, and that of the other victim presented the best chance at finding the killers. Thom Danbrook had just been in the wrong place at the wrong time. "TS figured out what happened with his gun."

"What?" It was a subject of interest to the Bureau as a whole, as *every* agent carried the same Smith & Wesson Model 1076 that had somehow failed at the critical moment. The office's Technical Services Section had immediately gone to work to determine the cause of the failure.

"Shooter error," Lowe explained, pulling his own 1076 out. He removed the magazine and cleared the round in the chamber before proceeding. "Look." He gripped the weapon in the proper manner, with the off hand supporting the front and underside of the gun hand. "Danbrook had a nasty gash on the skin webbing between the thumb and forefinger of his off hand."

Art's head dropped. "You're kidding."

"Nope. He held it like a revolver, off hand wrapped over the side with the thumb on top. When he fired his first shot, the slide hit his hand and didn't travel far enough back to pick up the next round. He reverted to Academy training when the stress kicked in. Unfortunately we were still with revolvers when he went through." Lowe reloaded and reholstered his weapon. "That's why the weapon failed, but I don't know if he could have done anything to change the outcome."

It was a cop's nightmare: walking in on something and having the initiative in the bad guys' favor.

"Anything on the getaway vehicle?" Art inquired, sitting down and turning on the ten-cup coffeemaker strategically placed on his side of their area. Frankie had her own on the small credenza, the result of the caf-decaf wars soon after their pairing.

Lowe had been there all night, giving Art a chance to come down from the adrenaline high and get some sleep. "LASO found it in back of the Pacific Design Center, on fire." The Los Angeles Sheriff's Office patrolled the recently incorporated city of West Hollywood, just blocks from the site of the murders. "Listed as a stolen out of Culver City."

"These guys get around," Art commented.

"Listen, I appreciate you taking this on," Lowe said.

Art waved off the gratitude. "Cam, it's no trouble. You knew his folks. You should be there." Lowe and his boss, Assistant Special Agent in Charge Jerry Donovan, were leaving on a midday flight to St. Louis to deliver condolences to Danbrook's parents. It was common for ranking members of the office where a fallen agent was assigned to visit the family, and at the request of the San Francisco office, Lowe and Donovan were going to do the duty. It was fitting, as the young agent had spent the majority of his short career in L.A. "How'd Bill take it?"

"Like a sock in the gut," Lowe answered. Special Agent in Charge William Killeen was at the Bureau's Quantico, Virginia, academy for a meeting of all fifty-eight SACs to advise the deputy director on budget and manpower needs for the next fiscal year. "He wanted to come back, but I convinced him to stay there. He can't do anything more than we already are."

The machine was only up to cup number two, but Art couldn't wait. He switched it off and poured himself a cup, then turned it back on. "You want any?"

"Leaded?"

"Un," Art answered, getting a polite shake of the head in response. "Where are we at?"

"Jacobs is going to bring down an evidence list in a while and anything that might help." They could use anything at this point.

"What about the other victim?" Anyone other than the dead agent was an "other."

Lowe motioned with his head to the file folder on Art's desk. "Not much more than last night."

Art read through it quickly. "Francisco Portero. Sixty-five. Florida driver's license." He looked up. "Miami have anything yet?"

"Luke Kessler promised it by seven," Lowe replied.

"Hmm." It was the slimmest of the slim. Art was in charge of an investigation without a well-defined starting point. "Witnesses sure aren't plentiful."

"That blond waitress is still in shock. The only thing she gave us was that Portero said he was meeting someone. No descriptions from her, though. Looking at the statements, I'd say your busboy is the best so far. His description matches the one you gave of the van's driver more closely than any of the others."

A sudden hush fell over the room, the silence soon filled by condolences and comforting words as Frankie Aguirre waded through the sea of her fellow agents. She set her purse on the desk and went to the open arms of Cameron Lowe.

"How're you doing, little lady?" The senior agent, a father figure in the L.A. office, was entitled to call her that, probably the only guy in the place she'd let get away with it.

"I'm okay." Her eyes were a little swollen, but there were no tears. She had cried them all out the previous night.

"Much sleep, partner?"

"A few hours," she answered, stepping back from the security of Lowe's strong arms. "Enough for now."

Lowe reached out and placed his hands on her shoulders, bending his head to look her in the eyes. "You go easy."

"This is where I need to be, Cam. I need to help find the guys." *I want them.*

"We will," Lowe said, bringing his hands away. "I've got to run home and get cleaned up before Jerry and I leave. Lou is senior here until Jerry gets back." Lou Hidalgo was deputy assistant special agent in charge. "He'll be in about nine, but he's wrapped up in that investigation group that's running with ATF."

"Right. Pass along my . . . you know." Art hated these moments. Death had never been something he'd handled well. When his grandmother, the woman who'd raised him, had passed, he had withdrawn for almost a year, secluding himself in the dorm at the University of Alabama. His grades went up, but A's and B's had seemed almost meaningless at the time. Now he knew better. It was what she had wanted, what she had pushed him to do. This death, though, was an aberration. His grandmother's time had come. Thom Danbrook's had been chosen by another with no authority to do so. There was only one power in the universe with that authority. The ultimate power. The ultimate protector. The ultimate judge. Thom's killers would come to know the latter intimately, Art vowed.

"You want some coffee?" Art asked once Lowe had left.

"Yeah, I'll settle for your stuff today." Frankie slid her empty mug across their adjoining desks, which faced each other. "I don't need anything wiring me today." She took the steaming cup and sipped it gingerly for a moment. "A lot of bodies here this morning."

"You've never seen this before, have you?" She shook her head. Art knew she hadn't. "It's terrible when it happens, but it really shows you what people are made of."

"I saw a few folks on the way in who rode Thom pretty hard when he was here," Frankie said, remembering that Thom, the perfect gentleman, had kept his private life just that. But rumors were rumors, and they always found a way of starting. The truth had started the ones circulating about Thom, first quietly questioning his sexual orientation and later openly attacking it. Still, he hadn't run away from his life. The request for a transfer to the

Bay area had been made when he first arrived in L.A. years before. Frisco was where he had been accepted to law school on a
part-time basis. Thom Danbrook, attorney. Frankie wanted to cry
at the thought of it never happening.

"Mortality is a powerful teacher," Art said. He hoped it would
be enough to end the stupid, silent discrimination against those
who just wanted to do their job. Thom had drawn his gun and
faced down two shooters, for Christ's sake! Wasn't that enough?
"We've got 'em all at our disposal."

"What's the plan?" Frankie looked at the roster that Art
handed her.

"Omar Espinosa is coordinating the field teams. He's got
three of them over at the other victim's place."

It occurred to Frankie that she had no idea who the man was.
"Who was he?"

Art related the particulars. "He had a little apartment up off
of Highland. Manager's card was in his wallet, which was a break.
We wouldn't have had an address this fast otherwise, 'cause the
DL is out of Florida.

"The other teams are going to start hitting the areas where
the van was stolen from and where it turned up."

Either the killers had someone waiting for them, or they had
other wheels already procured. That was the way pros would have
done it, and these guys were looking like pros, which didn't bode
well for a quick resolution. Still, the agents had learned that all
criminals, by way of their choice of profession, had some innate
stupidity that, somewhere along the line, would cause a slipup.
Catching the mistake was the trick.

"I'd say we have to find out why these guys wanted to kill
Portero," Frankie suggested.

"The busboy said one of them . . ." Art flipped back through
his notes. "Medium height, curly black hair, mustache. That one
called Portero's name before they fired. He also saw the other
one, the balding guy who shot at me, bend down and take something from Portero's shirt pocket."

"If this leads to anything, I think we owe that busboy a
lunch."

"I told him we'd put in a good word for him with the INS,"
Art said. "He's been trying to naturalize for a couple years now.
Anyway, so we have two shooters who knew their intended victim

and who wanted something from same." His eyes asked for Aguirre's read of the situation.

"Contract hit," she observed flatly. "But still, why Portero?"

There were several possibilities that Art could think of, and probably a dozen more he knew would crop up along the way. "Okay, all the primary participants are Hispanic. One is from Florida."

"Could have some OC involvement," Frankie surmised, the activity of investigation easing the pain of grief. "There are several Cuban crime families that are trying to expand their influence, and they're pretty ruthless from what I remember of the briefings."

"Salvadoran and Panamanian, too," Art added.

Frankie drained her first cup and slid it back for a refill. "That gives us a few thousand suspects, not counting the million or so we haven't thought of yet."

"Slow and steady. That's how we win this race." Art had come across that lesson after much grief. His natural tendency was to push, push, push. Getting past that sometimes destructive trait had been one of the biggest hurdles in his life. "We've got ten teams slated to run down things once we get a little more from Miami."

Art's phone rang. "Jefferson." He smiled at Frankie. "Speak of the Devil. How're you doing, Luke? . . . Yeah, it's appreciated. He was a good kid. You have anything?" It took a minute for the Miami agent to relate the information. "Well, that *is* interesting. Sure appreciate your help. Hey, get some sleep. Bye."

"Well?" Frankie inquired, wanting desperately for there to be something they could start with.

"Francisco Portero fled from Cuba earlier this year," Art explained. "He came over on that commuter flight that just hopped across the Keys. There were a couple other flights that did the same thing back in '92 or '93. Can't remember which. Maybe both. But that isn't even the frosting." His partner's eyes scolded him for the pause in his release of the information. "Portero, up until he left, was translator for the Cuban ambassador to the UN."

"So this was a defection," Frankie observed, a question immediately coming to mind. "What language?"

"Lang—" Art smiled with embarrassment. It was the little

things, the nuances, that he missed. He was a global thinker, while Frankie saw the trees in the forest. "I forgot to ask. I'm sure it'll be in the hard copy he's faxing."

"Kind of a new spin on things," Frankie commented. "A former Cuban diplomatic type defects and ends up dead before year's end. Hit from home?"

It couldn't be ruled out, Art thought, but the evidence didn't point that way. "I don't know about that. The busboy said the guy who called to Portero didn't trill his *R*'s. He said it was pure gringo talk. If it is the case, though, then it points toward a silencing. Like Portero knew something that someone at home didn't want him to tell."

"Or he had something they wanted," Frankie countered, remembering what the busboy had seen. "Or both."

"Two places to check," Art said. "INS and State. Portero would have automatically been granted asylum because of where he came from, so he would have had an interview with the immigration boys. They might know if he made any declarations when he came in, or if he asked to meet with any of the exile groups. That's pretty common. They all offer some sort of assistance to newcomers. There might be something in there to help us."

"And State?"

"I want to know what Portero did over the years, what sort of information he might have had access to. What other positions did he hold? Who he knew? Anything that could point to what he had that they wanted."

Art jotted the requests for information down and had them taken to the office's communication room for immediate transmittal to the respective government agencies.

"Good morning, folks." It wasn't, Special Agent Dan Jacobs knew. As supervising special agent of Technical Services in L.A., he had been there for the duration of this one. He had seen where Thom Danbrook had fallen and had made the tragic discovery of why the young agent's gun had malfunctioned at the moment of truth. Bad news all around. But now he brought what could be some positives to the morning. "You want some leads?"

"What do you got?"

Jacobs pulled the first item from a manila envelope. "First is this."

Art took the item, a business card advertising a place called

Tony's Tacos on Pico. He flipped it over, finding the real clue. "No area code," he commented, handing the card with the scribbled phone number on the back across to his partner.

"The exchange is right for this area code," Frankie observed. Her fingers squeezed the flimsy card. It was moist. "What's with the dampness?"

"That brings me to number two." Jacobs removed a clear plastic cassette tape from the envelope.

"Is that condensation?" Art inquired, noticing the fogging inside the unmarked protective plastic housing.

"You've got it. We found it balled up in a napkin on the table, like the dead guy had been trying to dry it off. The card was in his left-front pants pocket, and there was a good deal of wetness there. From what I could tell, he might have spilled some water on himself. There was a glass a little less than half-full still on the table. My guess is that the tape was in his pocket with the card, some water got on it, and he took it out to dry it off."

"Any chance of getting to hear what's on it?"

Jacobs nodded confidently to Art. "Luckily it was just water. We should be able to clean it up and at least get something off of it.

"Finally we have this." He handed over a see-through evidence bag with tiny shards of clear plastic captured at the bottom. Several were stained dark by what appeared to Art to be blood. "We pulled these out of his shirt pocket."

Bingo. "Shirt pocket. You're sure?"

"Yeah," Jacobs assured him. "They're fragments of the same kind of cassette you have there. Identical, actually. Same manufacturer. There were also the same type of fragments in the wound right behind the pocket."

Art looked to Frankie. "I think we'll add that lunch to the 'thank yous' we give that busboy." He turned back to Jacobs. "So we can assume that there was a similar tape in his shirt pocket that was hit by a bullet?"

"I think so," Jacobs affirmed. "Oh, we also got the caliber of the guns. Three fifty-sevens." Revolvers, unfortunately, did not give up their spent shell casings, requiring analysis of the bullets recovered from the victims. "I should have some model information later today, maybe tomorrow."

"Great." Art handed back the tape and the bag with the fragments. "Can I hang on to the card?"

"No prob." Jacobs laid a hand on Frankie's shoulder. "Hang in there."

Frankie smiled and reached up, touching Jacobs's hand with hers. "Thanks."

Art called over two teams of agents after Jacobs had departed and tasked them with checking out the establishment on the card. Someone at Tony's Tacos might recognize the photo taken from Portero's driver's license. An employee or patron might know him. Or it could be a cold trail.

But there might be a hot one to pick up on. "So our shooters took a tape."

"And left one," Frankie pointed out. "Why do you suppose that was?"

"Well, let's assume they came for *a* tape, and to shut Portero up. Both of those are more 'probable' than 'possible' now. If they came to do what they did, I'd sure bet they'd have a complete wish list."

"Then one of the tapes might have been, what? A decoy? Maybe just another tape? A duplicate? Which one?"

Art thought back to what Jacobs had given them a minute before. "It would have to be a decoy, something he could give up easily if challenged. You ever read some of the travel guides for New York? They suggest keeping a second wallet with a twenty-dollar 'mugger's fee' in an outside pocket."

"Like a shirt pocket," Frankie said. "And keep the real thing in your pants pocket. The front one."

"Right where the one we have came from." Art smiled with satisfaction for the first time in eighteen hours. The others had been motivated by nervousness. "Our shooters may have gotten the wrong tape."

"Which means they may be back for the real one." Frankie knew that a question was inevitable. "But back where?"

Art held the business card up, flipping it over and over before stopping the motion with the number facing his partner. "Our freaked-out blond hostess said Portero was there to meet someone, and I doubt it was the two who showed up."

"The card was in the same pocket as the tape," Frankie carried the thought on. "You want to do a reverse search on it."

"Why bother the phone company?" Art mused, scooting his

chair forward and lifting the handset to his ear. "Fingers crossed it's a two-one-three number." He punched the seven numbers and waited.

"City desk," the female voice answered on the other end.

Art's face puzzled over the words. "City desk?" *Oh, boy.* "Uh, what paper is this?"

There was a quiet laugh. "The *Los Angeles Times,* sir."

He hung up without carrying the conversation further. Just another wrong number. "It looks like Portero might have been about to give something to the *Times.*" The silencing theory was gaining credence exponentially.

"Let's hope we have whatever it was," Frankie said. "And now?"

Art stood and put his jacket back on, ready to go do some real work. "We visit an old friend."

"Of whose?" Frankie gathered up her purse and followed her partner out of their cubicle, getting the answer only after they were in the elevator.

The car pulled up around the corner from the yellow bungalow in one of Los Angeles's disappearing nice, quiet neighborhoods, its two occupants exiting and checking their surroundings before walking off.

They were dressed nicely, the elderly woman noticed, and very neat in appearance. But it *was* very early for anyone in the neighborhood to have visitors. Maybe they were police, she thought, as she muted the television, leaving Joan Lunden without a voice. As chairperson of the neighborhood watch, she was ever-vigilant. The gangs had stayed away from the middle-class area she had lived in for fifty years, but of late there had been gunshots at night in the distance. What was the world coming to?

So, from her early-morning perch behind the huge bay window her late husband had installed as a birthday present some twenty years before, she watched as the two strangers disappeared around the corner. They were walking normally, not hurried, not overly cautious, but it was her duty to watch over the block. There was no reason to call the police. They were busy enough with emergencies, she knew. But she did do a simple thing that the very pleasant lieutenant from the local police station had suggested when unknown visitors appeared in the neighborhood.

CHAPTER THREE

Skirmish Lines

The West Wing of the White House was built as a much-needed addition to the executive mansion at 1600 Pennsylvania Avenue in 1902, forty years before the smaller East Wing was completed during the Second World War, and had developed into the second tier of power in the executive branch. The various working spaces of the President's executive staff are there, spread over two levels, none more than a quick jaunt from the Oval Office in the southeast corner. Traditionally the ground floor housed the offices of the closest and most visible advisers, with the upper level saved for policy and council positions designated by the President. Located in the northwest corner of the roughly square wing, the office of the President's national security adviser was farther in steps from the Oval Office than any of the close crowd on the ground floor. Only a few policy assistants one level up had to travel as far, though they were unlikely to ever have the access to the President that Bud DiContino had. That was something that transcended being simply "near" the Man. Bud had his ear, and his trust.

Sitting behind his dark wood desk in the office that he had spent more hours in than his own bed during the previous year, the NSA noted the time. The morning meeting called the night before by DCI Anthony Merriweather was not completely unexpected considering the fireworks that had erupted in Cuba within

69

the last twelve hours. Bud's head had barely hit the pillow in the wee hours when the call came notifying him that "something is going on in Cuba." He was a bit surprised that the call had come not from Langley, but from the National Security Agency out at Fort Meade, the government monolith that did amazing things with communications and cryptographics. Signal intercepts of chaotic communications between Cuban military units had been the first indication of a "Significant Event," to use intelligence parlance.

Why the word hadn't come from the Agency, however, could be summed up in one word—Merriweather. The DCI had not taken anything close to a liking to Bud, who often found himself arguing the opposite side of positions held by the former senator from Massachusetts, who had also chaired the Joint Congressional Committee on Intelligence Oversight. That had been his path to the position he now held; that and some strategic arm-twisting by friends of the President on the Hill. Others should have been considered before Merriweather, Bud believed. Greg Drummond, for one, though his "junior" standing in the Agency had worked against such a move. The same for Pete Miner, the CIA's number-two man. This had been a political appointment, it was clear. A return of favors not yet performed. Those would be delivered in two years—campaign time.

This was D.C., after all.

The NSA took his briefing folder and jacket and walked into his deputy's adjoining office. "Nick, I'm heading over."

Deputy NSA Nicholas Beney looked up from the computer display. "Good luck."

"Thanks. Don't fry your eyes on that thing," Bud said.

His boss was computer paranoid, which was funny considering the high-tech work he had done in the Air Force. Or maybe because of it. Beney found it quite amusing. "I can order one up for your office."

"That's all I need," Bud said, turning away and beginning the same walk—right turn, left, then right again—he had made twice that morning already. One was for the President's daily intelligence briefing—nothing much on the platter, other than the scant information on the fighting down South—and the other for a brief update on the modernization of the Russian BMEWS about to begin in earnest. He had handled both well, as usual.

Bud was last to enter the Oval Office. The President, DCI

Merriweather, and DDI Greg Drummond were already there. There was a good-sized security case resting upon the single coffee table to the left of the President's desk, its contents obvious to the NSA. *Imagery.* The Agency must have turned the cameras on Cuba *real* fast to get pictures this quickly. It wasn't really a surprise. Ninety miles south of Florida there was, according to preliminary reports from the intelligence services and the four major networks, intense fighting. That was close, and worth keeping an eye on.

"Bud, good morning again," the President said, standing as his NSA came in. The others stood also. "Have a seat."

A couch was aligned along one side of the low table and two chairs along the other. The President sat at the head of the table, nearest the room's center, in a chair the woodworking of which dated to the late 1700s. The DCI and his deputy were on the couch, leaving a simple choice for Bud, who took the chair closest to the President.

Drummond gave Bud a subtle nod and a smile. The DDI was a straight shooter and knew the NSA well. They had worked closely during the first six months of Bud's tenure but not much since Merriweather's arrival. The new DCI had pulled his people in, in an effort to define their roles more clearly as he saw them. In reality it was a semismart move, as Congress was trimming the intelligence agency's budget with a sharp, unselective budget ax. To make the Agency lean and productive was essential, as some on the Hill were trumpeting for the dissolution of the Agency, arguing that it should be consolidated into some pseudo-diplomatic/information-gathering arm of the State Department. The idea was a crock, but at least Merriweather was playing smart to stave off any serious effort to do away with the CIA. Despite the director's aloof manner with him, Bud had to credit the man with having some foresight.

"James, you're looking good," Merriweather commented, looking up while laying the case flat and zipping it open. His eyes were a foggy brown, with small black centers that were further miniaturized behind the thick glasses he wore. The old-fashioned thick black frames looked awkward on his small head, which was covered by a full crop of short hair that matched closely the color of his gray tweed jacket. By appearances he could have been a college professor or a car salesman.

"I'm getting back into my morning jog." *And the name is Bud.*

The DCI took his educational and social lineage, which stretched from Exeter to Yale, quite seriously. Nicknames were not among his repertoire of verbiage, and only recently had he taken to calling those Agency personnel closest to him by the more casual forms of their given names, much to the delight of "Gregory" Drummond.

The DDI looked up from his own set of materials. "We'll have to do that crack-o'-dawn run thing again."

"None of that sprinting crap at the end like you did to me last time," Bud insisted with a chuckle. "I've got almost a decade on you, remember."

The DDI smiled. "Old men need motivation."

The President watched the exchange with amusement. His advisers were normal people, just like him, though his California background had not lately manifested itself in the kind of relaxed, playful banter he was witness to. Just a week shy of his thirty-ninth birthday, he was the youngest President ever to serve, and, if all went well, in two years he would be the youngest elected. Age, though, had been warped during his short tenure. To look at him was to see the aging process accelerated, just as it had for each man to hold the highest elective office in the land. Responsibility brought with it work, and worry, and planning, and so many other elements of the job that he was certain his main recollection of his term in office would be the constant state of tiredness.

But it was times like these that gave value to all the exhaustive efforts, particularly when a President was able to be witness to something historic that he might not have started but that he had offered assistance to. There were actually two such things happening; that which his NSA had taken from concept to reality, and that which the same man had no idea of. It was time to change that.

"Bud, I'm afraid we've left you out of something."

Left me out . . . Bud saw there was some regret in the President's eyes, but more satisfaction. Merriweather had only the latter expressed on his face. Greg Drummond was without either, just a flatness to his expression. "What is that, sir?"

"Operation SNAPSHOT," the DCI answered for his boss. "The liberation of Cuba."

"Excuse me?"

"I know this may be a little hard to fathom, but hear Anthony out, Bud. This was too good to pass up." The President leaned to one arm of the chair, a single finger coming to his chin as he turned his attention to the DCI.

Too good? Something in Bud clicked at that characterization. A quick look at the wooden DDI confirmed his intuitive addition of "to be true" to the phrase.

"Some months back we received word from one of the Cuban-American exile groups that they had been contacted by a representative of the Cuban Revolutionary Armed Forces." Merriweather stopped momentarily, as if there was nothing more to explain. "They wished our assistance in removing President Castro from power."

"What members?"

"The leader of the rebellion is Colonel Hector Ojeda," Merriweather answered. "Do you know who he is?"

Bud nodded. Ojeda was probably the most highly decorated and best-trained officer the Cubans had. A veteran of Angola, the not-so-secret secret detachment sent to Afghanistan, and every special training program their former "brother Soviets" had to offer. He was the cream of a very sparse crop.

"And to him you can add thirty-two thousand. Sufficient, wouldn't you say?" the DCI inquired unnecessarily.

"More than, actually." Bud looked back to the President. "Sir, why was this kept from me?"

"It is a CIA operation," the DCI answered out of turn.

Bud acknowledged the DCI with the briefest glance. It wasn't from him that the NSA wanted an answer. "Sir?"

"Bud, like Anthony said, this began as an Agency operation. The two ranking members of the Joint Select Committee have given the Congress's stamp to it. My belief was that you had a full plate working with the Russians, and this really does not fall under your area of National Security." The President saw his adviser's jaw drop at that. "This is low risk, Bud."

"Sir, a war raging ninety miles from us is *precisely* what I see as in my domain. That *is* a national-security issue, with all due respect," Bud said firmly. He had never backed down when he believed himself to be right in any disagreement with the Man. He owed the nation's leader no less.

"Your point is noted," the President responded with no mal-

ice. He had expected his NSA to react just this way, which had
partly influenced his decision to keep him from the initial stages.
"It was my call, Bud."

"Understood." Bud's eyes swept over the DCI. A slight expression—never a smile—edged up from the wrinkled folds at his
mouth's corner. *And your prompting.* "But 'low risk' is not always as
low as we'd like to believe."

"Our exposure here is one man. Anthony, if you would . . ."

"Of course, Mr. President." Merriweather faced the man
he'd seen as his nemesis in the West Wing since day one, guessing
correctly that James DiContino now was party to that analysis as
well. "What the rebellious faction wanted from us was intelligence. The location and movement of loyalist forces once the
fighting began, and similar reports. That was all they asked for,
but with that they would be at a distinct advantage. To accomplish
that, we attached a field officer to the rebel command staff some
months ago. His job was first to validate the viability of the pro-
posal—it would do us little good if this was all a crazy show to be
put on by some disgruntled officers. His job now is to receive the
reports from here—all the information is to be gathered by satellite reconnaissance, of course—and give them to the rebel command staff."

"And what prompted Ojeda to do this?"

"The economy, the miserable living standards, among other
things. But the execution of General Eduardo Echeverria Ontiveros appears to be the real spark that lit this fire." The DCI
could see recognition on the NSA's face. "Castro was none too
happy with his support of that Russian after the hijacking, you
remember."

How could he ever forget? His baptism by fire. And the forced
demise of the general, one of the more pragmatic and capable
commanding officers the Cubans had, was easily reason enough
to foment a revolt. Good soldiers were loyal to good, competent
leaders, and equally disdainful of deskbound commanders who
passed judgment upon them and their actions. Ontiveros might
not have been a friend in the eyes of Cuba's neighbor to the
north, but he certainly was to the men who had served under him.

"And what do we get from this? I mean other than a new
leadership in Cuba if the coup succeeds."

"It will succeed," Merriweather said with an arrogant confidence, as though a suggestion that any other outcome was possi-

ble was somehow blasphemous. "And we were able to choose the new leadership."

"Choose?" Visions of Panama after Noriega flashed in the NSA's mind. "How so?"

"Bud, it's not like that," the President interjected. "It's not some insertion of a puppet regime. The rebels agreed to accept civilian leadership drawn from the exile community here."

"And how were they selected?" Bud asked.

"It was logical to choose members of the group contacted by the Cubans to serve in an interim government," the DCI explained. "I brokered the arrangements personally with Jim Coventry."

He's "Jim" and I'm still "James." I see . . . "You told the secretary of state, but not me?" Bud sat back and blew out an exasperated breath. "Who else is in the loop?"

"That's it, until you brief Secretary Meyerson," Merriweather said, passing a task rightly his own to the NSA. "We are going to need certain assistance from the military very shortly."

The "low" in low risk was rapidly losing its accuracy in describing what the NSA was being told. "Assistance."

Merriweather nodded. "Greg will fill you in after the presentation."

Drummond gave a courteous nod when his boss looked his way but said nothing. His place in this had been made perfectly clear without explanation.

"And the purpose of this presentation?" Bud inquired, motioning to the case before the DCI.

The President shifted forward in his chair. "Validation. I insisted that we have some proof that the coup could succeed beyond just the planning stages."

Someone was thinking half-smart, Bud thought. The Man was no slouch in the brains department. Maybe he'd looked at this all carefully enough to ensure that nothing stupid was being done. Maybe, he thought, looking as the DCI reached into the case. Hopefully.

"Mr. President, are you ready?" Merriweather saw the chief executive nod, an anticipatory smile on his face, and laid out a series of four twelve-by-twelve-inch photographs.

Bud leaned forward, as did the President after putting on the reading glasses he had come to hate.

"Sir, these are images from a KH-12 pass two days ago," the

DCI began. "All four are of the military airfield near Santa Clara in the central part of Cuba. The first two are shots from about forty-nine degrees above the horizon. Distance is one hundred and seventy miles." Merriweather directed the President's attention to a line of aircraft obvious in the picture. "These are MiG Twenty-threes, all operational. This angle shows clearly their lineup, all on three good sets of landing gear."

Bud studied the images with his head and body cocked to the right. The shots were clear, with only a hint of clouds that had been digitally removed, he suspected. "These are a combination IR and visible?"

"Correct," the DCI answered. He noticed the President shoot a quizzical look his way. "Sir, this is somewhat of a hybrid photograph. The satellite, as it came over the horizon, focused both its visible light sensors, the cameras, and the heat-sensitive receptors, what is called imaging infrared, on the airfield. Pictures, if you will, were taken by both systems in synch, then, once the images were downlinked, NPIC—that's the National Photographic Interpretation Center—processed them together to enhance the portions of the visible light photos that were degraded by cloud cover and other atmospherics."

"I see," the President said. "Go on."

The DCI jumped right back in. "The second pair of images are from a ninety-degree aspect—straight overhead. It's a wider view of the airfield, so the same aircraft are visible in relation to the other facilities."

"What are these and these?" the President asked, pointing with his pen to two groups of what he surmised were aircraft.

"These objects nearest the maintenance hangar, here, are cannibalized MiGs. They've had to strip perfectly good aircraft to keep the others up and flying."

"What's their rate of removal from service been?" Bud asked.

Merriweather turned to Drummond. "Wasn't it fifty percent over the previous two years?"

"That's right," the DDI confirmed. "At that rate they'd—"

"That point is moot," the DCI interrupted.

Another look was exchanged between Drummond and Bud, this one not hinting at anything friendly or pleasant.

"And the others, sir, are something we'll touch on in a few minutes." Merriweather motioned to the Oval Office's television and VCR, which he already moved to a position where the group, other than Bud, could watch it unobstructed. The NSA would have to look over his shoulder to see what was going on. "Before that, though, are these."

The President noted that the four photos the DCI had just laid before him corresponded in views to the ones just covered up. Bud noticed this, too, and something else. *Damn.*

"Sir, these were taken from the same KH-12 just over an hour ago. Look carefully at the front of the aircraft in the low-angle views."

What Merriweather wanted the President to see was obvious. All twelve of the MiGs, while appearing intact, were nose-down on the tarmac. Some had odd-looking bulges in the area aft of the cockpit.

"What was done here?" the President asked. "It looks like the front landing gear is gone, but I don't see any other damage." He looked alternately at Bud and the DCI.

"Bud, you have extensive BDA experience from your Nam days, right?"

"Right." The word was spoken flat and quickly. He would have preferred no part in the validation of this, but that wish was now out the window. "Mr. President, what you see before you is artwork." Bud swallowed imperceptibly.

"Explain."

Both Merriweather's and Drummond's eyes were on him, though each subtly expressed very different emotions. The DDI's showed empathy; the DCI's, satisfaction.

"What has happened is the same thing the Viet Cong sappers did when they snuck onto Tahn Son Nhut airbase back in '69. The aircraft's nosewheels have been severed, actually the entire strut. Apparently the rebels were able to get their own people close enough to place a small amount of explosives on the upper portion of each strut. It can be placed up in the wheel well with a simple timer so that no one would notice it unless they took a real close look. That probably gave them time to get away or do other damage."

"So what does this mean? Are these planes out of commission?"

Bud was hoping the DCI would answer the President, but the silence dictated that he finish his line of thought. "Down for the count, Mr. President. It's a smart way to disable an aircraft. When the strut blows, the weight of the aircraft comes straight down.

The strut then impales the fuselage and does major damage to the airframe and the innards. That's the bulging you see at the back of the canopy there. The strut is pushing equipment up and to the sides and deforming the fuselage."

"But why not blow the planes up completely?" the President wondered. "Wouldn't you get a bigger bang by tossing a bunch of explosives in the air intake? I admit I saw that in some shoot-'em-up movie somewhere, but it seems logical. Couldn't these be repaired?"

"Not really, sir," Bud responded. "If you're trying to just take out a target, you want to use the minimum force necessary. As for repair—not with the reduced capability the Cubans are exhibiting. There's not much left to cannibalize." The NSA let it sink in, for himself as well as the President. "And the most intelligent aspect of this is the fact that the aircraft *will* be able to be repaired in the future, when they might want them. It appears the rebels have thought this out. They're being very, very smart."

The President was obviously pleased, very much so. He allowed a slight smile, then looked to the DCI, whom he had had doubts about before being convinced to nominate him to fill the position. The critics, however, were being proved wrong.

"You saw this in Vietnam. Bud?" the President inquired.

The NSA nodded. "A very effective technique."

"Proven by the winners, you might say," Merriweather commented.

It was an effective jab, notching up Bud's internal "Nam meter" to a place it hadn't been in years. Veterans of the Indochina experience had dealt with crap of the sort the DCI had just dished out frequently in the years following the fall of the South, but not so much recently. Bud was fully aware that Merriweather, a fervent Yalie who had ironically held the History chair at Harvard in the late sixties, was no fan of the war. It was becoming more apparent now that, despite any effort to counter it, the DCI was never going to be a fan of Bud's.

"Well, not everybody who wins deserves to," the President observed. "Anthony, what about these other aircraft? They look like helicopters."

"Mi-24 Hinds. Russian-built gunships. They're wonderful against insurgents, like they proved in Afghanistan."

Jesus Christ! Bud was having trouble believing his ears. Merriweather was using positive examples of the Viet Cong and the Cold War era Russians to flavor his little performance.

"They lost in Afghanistan, Anthony." Bud's retort was sprinkled with the barest amount of sarcasm.

"Tell that to the mujahideen who are still fighting to get the crony government out of Kabul." The DCI sniffed a quiet chuckle, with no smile attached to it. "Then again, we pulled out of South Vietnam also. But it didn't take the North Vietnamese Army that long to take what they wanted after that."

He couldn't stand it anymore. "Anthony," Bud began, his head shaking slowly from side to side as a smile that could only be one of disgust came to his lips, "some of us were there, you know, unlike—"

"Hold on. Hold on." The President leaned farther forward, looking alternately at both of his advisers. Drummond had shifted back to an upright position on the couch. "We are here to discuss Cuba. Not Vietnam. Christ, I was barely out of high school when all that came to an end. But I am here now, and we may be able to do something to put one of those checks back in the 'democracy' column. All right?"

To be castigated by the President was not entirely unheard of, but it had not happened to Bud. Worse yet, he deserved it, and he had allowed Merriweather to advance his apparent agenda that much further by behaving as a reactionary. Bud looked to the DDI but did not engage in any eyeplay to test the situation. There was no need to draw Drummond into this if he was able to maintain a working relationship with his boss. *God dammit, Bud. Play smarter.*

"Go on, Anthony."

"Yes, sir. If you'll watch the monitor." The DCI lifted the remote from the coffee table and clicked on the video player, pausing it as soon as a picture appeared. The scene was in black and white, very high contrast, and was filmed from a very high angle. "This is a video record from the KH-12 on a pass over the same airfield as the stills, except this was timed to concur with the beginning of the attack. It was taken using the same type of IR imaging as the stills. Remember, this is in darkness, with low moonlight, so what you will see are the heat signatures of objects."

The President nodded while keeping his eyes on the screen.

"Watch the left top corner of the screen." The DCI started the video. From where he had indicated, several objects came into view, their forms growing in a white intensity as the camera slowly crossed the area. "Those are the Hinds. They've just fired up their engines—that's the heat you're seeing there as it bleeds off of the exhaust and radiates from the engine through the body of the helicopter. And there." Merriweather noted several small white blobs crossing into the frame. "Those are people, probably soldiers, running to where the aircraft were blown."

Bud was watching with interest. As a spectator in a game where he should have been on the field, it was all he could do.

"See how the heat signature is growing in intensity? They're readying to take off." Merriweather paused for just a moment, a look of anticipatory satisfaction obvious on his face. "Watch carefully."

Two of the Hinds moved slightly, a perceptible jump upward, then each turned to the right and began moving low above the ground. Suddenly, from the tail of each helicopter, within a second of each other, a bright flash and shower of white erupted, and instantly each Hind changed attitude and spun violently to the right. The motion ceased abruptly a few seconds later, an obvious crash.

"It's amazing to watch this without sound," the President commented. "Can you imagine what that sounded like on the ground?"

"Impressive," Bud had to admit. "How did they do it?"

Drummond sensed that it was his turn to join in his boss's presentation. "It looks like some sort of tail-rotor failure. Not an explosive of any kind; otherwise, that bloom you saw when it failed would have been a hell of a lot brighter. Somehow they tampered with the rotor housing or something, because when it came up to speed, the thing just came apart. If you look real closely, you can actually see blades flying off as it disintegrates."

"And the other two Hinds suffered the same fate a few minutes later," the DCI added. "The Cubans must have thought the first two were shot down. You can imagine the confusion there. Unfortunately the satellite was not able to keep its sensors on that area of observation."

Bud perked up at that comment. "Why not?"

"There's a problem with the stabilization system for the real-time sensors," the DCI explained. The "real-time sensors" were the video camera systems, which were often used to transmit images as they happened, hence the name.

Fantastic! The only platform to observe and provide the intelligence the rebels wanted wasn't fully functioning. There were three KH-12s in orbit, two of which were tasked with monitoring the removal of the former Soviet ICBMs from the Ukraine. The more capable KH-12 ENCAP (Enhanced Capability) was almost out of fuel. It was presently, as it had been for the previous year, running a straight orbital path at five hundred miles altitude. Budget cuts and the lack of any real threats had resulted in the refueling flight by the Space Shuttle being postponed indefinitely. Bud knew there were other means to maintain the country's "eye in the sky" capability, but this situation damned sure didn't warrant the risk of exposure or the expense.

"Would the information we can get from the satellite still serve the purpose?" the President asked.

"Absolutely," Merriweather answered without hesitation. "The still imagery is what we need in order to provide information to the rebels."

The President sat back in his chair, his eyes fixed on the frozen image at the end of the videotape. "What about other facilities in Cuba?"

"We have stills from seven major airfields taken on the same pass as these," the DCI responded, pointing to the second set of photos on the table. "Sir, the Cuban government effectively has no air force remaining."

It was really happening, the President thought. The second-to-last bastion of communism was finally crumbling, and it was on his watch.

And now it was time to commit. "Anthony, get things moving. Our investment in this may be small, but the return could be tremendous. I don't want to miss this opportunity."

"Gladly, sir." Merriweather looked to the NSA with a look that begged of a challenge, but there was none.

"Then let's do this," the President said. He stood, as did the others in his presence, and wished them well before going to the adjoining study to complete work reviewing several policy papers.

Merriweather headed out, leaving his deputy and the NSA alone in the Oval Office. The younger man avoided the NSA's stare for a moment. "Sorry, Bud."

"Just what does he think he's doing?"

Drummond looked to the door that had closed behind the President. "Not here."

"Come on." They were in Bud's office a minute later, Old Executive partially visible through the windows facing west. "Your boss is now officially on my shit list. What in the hell does he think he's doing advising the President to do this!"

The DDI knew it wasn't a question, despite the wording. It was a release. "Anthony is out to prove history wrong, Bud."

"What does that mean?"

Drummond took a seat on the liberally cushioned couch. "You remember old Professor Merriweather's book, *Victory in Vietnam: Winning the War We Lost*. He crucified Kennedy and Johnson for failing to seize the initiative in the early stages of involvement. For some reason he left Ike out of the equation, which is kinda funny, considering his politics. Attacking two Democrats must have seemed more salient, I guess." Drummond, the conservative Republican, let his personal politics slip into an official conversation. It was a rare enough happening that Bud's expression changed from one of anger to one of wonder. "He thought we should have been more aggressive in trying to destabilize the North by insurrection, rather than let them do the same thing to the South. Remember the final four chapters." A nod signaled him to proceed. "My esteemed director explained in detail how such a plan to defeat the North could have worked. First, commit minimum resources. Second, find disgruntled officers in the military. Third, use the carrot on the stick to get those officers to take out their own government. Kind of like 'We'll give you this, but you have to do this first.'" He looked to the dark carpeting at his feet. "When the Cubans practically walked in ready to fulfill his twenty-year-old prophecy, well . . ."

Bud leaned against his file-strewn desk. "Jesus, Greg. Does he have any idea what . . ." He stopped in midsentence. "Stupid question."

"Anthony knows exactly what this could mean, but he chooses to ignore anything that might get in the way of his theory of 'baited revolution' being proven. He chooses to ignore a lot of things."

"I can't believe this. I really can't." Bud walked around his desk and fell into the highback chair. "Do you know what the Russians would do if they found out about this? Christ, Greg, Cuba may not be their little brother anymore, but that doesn't mean they think there's an implied *carte blanche* to kick Castro out. Dammit!'' He spun the chair to face the window. ''Any hint that we're involved in Cuba would make trust a moot point. The modernization program would be down the tubes.'' Bud turned back to the sullen DDI. ''And Konovalenko, and his reforms, well, he doesn't need any other pressures right now.''

''I argued for a timing change,'' Drummond explained. ''But Anthony wouldn't go for it.''

''You should have gone to the President.''

The DDI raised an unsure eyebrow at the suggestion. ''Right. I bypass my boss and go to the Man. Aside from the fact that I like to be able to feed my family, you know as well as I that he wouldn't have bought it. You saw him. He's as much into this as Anthony. Mainly *because* of Anthony.''

Bud knew his friend was right. It was a suggestion, really a wish, born of frustration. ''Dammit, Greg. Why now? Even if it is going to work, why now?''

''Because he's an idiot,'' Drummond said. The characterization might have been harsh, but he could have said worse at the moment. ''All he sees is success, and he's got the President believing that, too. And they want it now.''

It wasn't hard to see why the President was going along with this so willingly. Merriweather had carefully orchestrated it so that only he would advise the President on SNAPSHOT until it was actually under way. Then it would be too late to do anything about it.

So that was the reason for the show. The realization of what had really happened a few minutes before in the Oval Office came to Bud very suddenly. ''Your boss is no idiot, Greg. He's smart.''

''How do you figure?''

Bud laughed openly. ''He keeps the President isolated from any negative analysis of SNAPSHOT by restricting knowledge only to those who won't or can't challenge the plan. Namely he was worried about me. You know as well as I that he's never been a fan of mine, and he knew I'd have serious reservations about his operation. He also knew that the President would listen to me. So what does he do? When it's time to let me in, he uses *me* to give credibility to the results we saw in there by asking for *my* analysis. I couldn't lie; it looked impressive. The rebels were obviously well prepared for this, and that imagery didn't just give Anthony the validation the President wanted—he used it to solicit my tacit approval for the President. Like you said, all they see is success, and now he's negated the person who would have squawked the loudest."

"I'm used to the abuse part from him," Drummond said. "How does it feel being used?"

"It's not so bad when you don't know it for ninety-nine percent of the time it's going on," Bud joked.

Drummond couldn't see where his friend was finding humor in this. "I wish I could laugh it off like you."

" 'Once the derby starts, the horses don't run backward,' " Bud said, the familiar quote bringing a smile to his face and a slight lump to his throat.

"Herb Landau sticks with you, doesn't he?" the DDI said. He had heard the same words from his former boss in some of the darker times when events seemed to be overtaking those who were supposed to be in control. "So what now?"

"We try and keep any major fuckups from happening," Bud said confidently. "If I know you, you've kept Anthony as much on the straight and narrow as is possible."

"Except for his choice of who's to take the reins down there."

"Some things will have to straighten themselves out once this is done." Maybe like in Panama, Bud thought to himself. That was still to be resolved.

"I hope so," the DDI said. "Now would be a good time to fill you in on what we need from the military."

"Shoot."

It took only a few seconds to explain. "Sort of a bodyguard and escort service."

"I think they have a less flattering term for this kind of mission," Bud commented. The boys in black were again being tasked for a mission that was a waste of their talent. But being special, he reminded himself, didn't always guarantee the glory. "Drew is going to love being kept out of the loop on this." Secretary of Defense Andrew Meyerson, though not always of the same mind as the NSA, was likely to have the same reaction at having been kept in the dark on SNAPSHOT.

"You can share some of your empathy," Drummond suggested playfully. The feeling that he was alone in the world was finally subsiding.

"Time for teamwork," Bud said. "I'll keep the President

from getting only a rosy picture of things, and you keep your boss from tripping over his satisfaction."

"Mike will be glad to know it's not just him and me against the world anymore." The DDI got up and started for the door.

"Your duet just became a trio."

"Wanna try for an orchestra?" the DDI asked with a smile, then left the NSA alone in his office.

Solitude was conducive to thought, and thought to worry, in situations such as this. What had begun could not be stopped. Herb Landau's words might have said the same more poetically, but neither statement could tell Bud what lay ahead. That was his question of the moment and was sure to be the one of the hour, day, and week until there was a resolution to that which he really had no control over. Influence was the best he could hope to offer, and that only in limited quantities.

But he did have his own operation of sorts to see to, one that was itself gaining steam. He looked at the clock. The convincing move in the plan to assuage any final fears in the Kremlin was about to take place. After that things would happen too fast to turn back. That was his hope. It would also become his fear in short order.

"This is our force-monitoring panel, Marshal Kurchatov." CINCNORAD gestured across the five-foot console and directed the two Russians to take the seats on either side of the watch officer, an Air Force major. "NORAD is an alternate command center, as you know. Our normal mission in any strategic conflict would be to monitor, track, and advise the National Command Authority. If necessary, though, we can run the show."

"How do you say . . . redundancy?"

CINCNORAD nodded. "If the command center above is knocked out, the one below takes over immediately. And so on. The same as your forces, Marshal."

"Yes, the same," Kurchatov agreed, lying as best he could behind the smile. The Americans would be horrified to know how little redundancy their Russian counterparts had built into their strategic systems.

"For our purposes today, though, we will not actually have control. We will be monitoring orders given by Strategic Command. These displays will show you the status of every strategic system we have. Even the missile subs," Walker added with some coolness. "This is the first time even I've known where they all are. They usually go where they want within a very large patrol area."

"It is true, then," Kurchatov said with some surprise. "Your *raket* submarines elude even you?"

General Walker nodded. "That's their job: to disappear. Except for right now." The general's plasterlike smile masked the difficulty he was having with this as he noted the positional notations of the United States' ballistic-missile subs, which were out of their element, not hiding in the protective waters of the oceans but tied up at dock. Up and down both coasts the subs were spread, many at bases that usually handled only attack subs. This was done to keep observant eyes from noting unusually large numbers of the metal leviathans at their usual ports of Bangor, Washington, and Kings Bay, Georgia.

Colonel Belyayev took the one eared headset lying on the console's flat deck and slid it on. There was none for the defense minister, but then, he was an observer. His presence was to add credibility and surety to the operation, so that any unforeseen happening would not need to be explained to Moscow by a junior officer. The fact that there was *none* more senior than Kurchatov made his presence all the more desirable.

Belyayev touched the trackball to his right, which operated a digitized pointing device on the large display before him, though not as large as the screens in a separate room—actually more of a theater—of the Cheyenne Mountain Complex where the activities of "enemy" missiles inbound on the United States would be watched. He deftly moved the arrow-shaped pointer to each of the notations that corresponded to the subs, his lips moving as he counted. Russian satellites had done passes over the ports on both coasts that serviced the American missile subs, verifying that the electronic images Belyayev was seeing were not just ghostly manipulations. One leg of the American strategic triad—land-based ICBMs and long-range bombers were the other two—was being temporarily taken out of service. Except . . .

"Pennsylvania," Belyayev said, the pointer circling the sub base at Kings Bay, Georgia. "He is not here."

General Walker knew this was coming. The last Russian satellite pass, whose information had been quickly transmitted to his two guests from Moscow, had shown the *USS Pennsylvania,* an

Ohio-class ballistic-missile sub, still not in port. When the orders went out two weeks before instructing individual subs—none knew that *all* of their kind were coming in—to return to port and tie up by a specified time, *Pennsylvania* had acknowledged the transmission as expected. But now she was overdue, though not technically in Navy terms. Missile subs generally had a twenty-four-hour window in which to arrive when returning to base. This was no ordinary return, however, and *Pennsylvania*'s twelve-hour delay was beginning to sound alarms.

"She may have some mechanical problems," CINCNORAD posited. It was both a guess and a sincere hope.

"She." Belyayev remembered that the Americans referred to their ships and submarines the opposite of the Russians. "*She* was due in Kings Bay, yes?"

CINCNORAD nodded. "She and four others." Norfolk and Groton would split the remainder of the missile boats in the Atlantic.

"You do not know where she is?" Marshal Kurchatov inquired seriously. The joviality had left his manner.

"Like I said, their job is to disappear. Strategic Command doesn't even know." The Strategic Command, a joint-service command headed by a Navy admiral, had replaced the Strategic Air Command, and was keeper of the nation's entire nuclear arsenal.

"Have you tried communicating with hi— her?" Belyayev asked.

General Walker paused for just a second. "Yes, we have, and there has been no reply."

"It is possible, then, that *Pennsylvania* is lost?" Marshal Kurchatov wondered, looking briefly to Colonel Belyayev.

"We hope not. In a few hours we will have to assume the possibility, though, and begin a search." The United States had never lost a boomer, and now was by far the worst time for that first to occur.

The marshal, resplendent in his dress greens and breast of medals and ribbons, looked briefly to his subordinate. A decision had to be made. If the Americans were lying, concealing one of their missile submarines out in the waters of the Atlantic, then the Motherland would be vulnerable to a surprise attack once her radar-warning system was shut down. He glanced at the highly technical displays to his front. Could some electronic wizardry perpetrated by the Americans mask a secret launch by the *Pennsylvania*? Was he being duped?

Or were they telling the truth?

A brief moment of reflection convinced the marshal of the latter. "Let us hope it is simply a mechanical difficulty."

"Yes," General Walker agreed. "Shall we begin?"

"Yes."

CINCNORAD gave the go-ahead to the duty officer. The major pressed a single button on his communication console. "Red Bird, Red Bird. This is NORAD Alternate Command Console."

"This is Red Bird," the major's counterpart at Strategic Command acknowledged.

"Red Bird, CINCNORAD requests execution of RANDOM LANCE."

There was a brief silence. "RANDOM LANCE approved."

All eyes shifted to the largest display. Colonel Belyayev already had a zoom box squared around the area in southern Wyoming that they were watching. A click brought the magnification up to reveal an electronic representation of the missile fields surrounding Francis E. Warren Air Force Base. The Minuteman missiles of the 90th Strategic Missile Wing, spread over 12,600 square miles, had dwindled in number after the Strategic Arms Reduction Talks (START) from two hundred to just eighty. The MIRVed LGM-30G Minuteman IIIs remaining had given up two of their three 335-kiloton Multiple Independently Targeted Reentry Vehicles to comply with START, and one of those missiles, number six in Hotel Flight, had recently had its single warhead replaced with a benign-range instrumentation package, a common payload for test launches.

"Notify PMTC," CINCNORAD ordered. The tracking radars supporting the Pacific Missile Test Center, headquartered at Point Mugu in California, normally watched launches from Vandenberg Air Force Base, just miles from Mugu, or from White Sands in New Mexico. It took a few minutes for the radars to be slewed in the proper direction to cover the launch from the Northeast.

"PMTC is ready," the major reported. "Red Bird, Alternate is ready."

"Hotel One reports launch ready." Strategic Command was

relaying word from the launch control center of Hotel Flight's ten missiles that number six was ready to fly. All that remained was for the two officers buried deep underground in the LCC to concurrently turn their keys jointly to the "enable" position.

"Colonel, on your word," the major said.

Colonel Belyayev focused his attention on the informational readout printed next to the number-six silo on the display. "Launch."

The order went through the open channel to the LCC. Miles from the underground control center, the heavy concrete blast lid was propelled away from Hotel Six, exposing the silo. Immediately the Minuteman III missile bolted upward from the silo using the cold-launch technique, which allowed the undamaged silo to be reloaded (in theory). Its first-stage solid-rocket engine ignited fifty feet above the prairie and rapidly accelerated the former weapon, now little more than a big radar target, toward the Pacific Missile Range in the Southwest.

"I verify launch," Belyayev stated. The notations on his display changed as the missile left its silo. He looked away for the phone he was supposed to use.

"This one," the major prompted. "Just pick it up. It's predialed."

The colonel lifted the black handset to his ear and was immediately connected with the headquarters of *Voyska PVO,* the Russian Air Defense Forces. "This is Colonel Belyayev," he said in Russian. "Have you detected a launch?"

"Yes," the male voice answered in its native tongue. "Warren Air Force Base. Missile number six, Hotel Flight. We show a thermal launch signature." Several minutes of silence followed as they waited for the still-operating Russian BMEWS to pick up the missile as it rose above the radar horizon. "We show a missile track, southwest course, high to low aspect. Confirm launch and flight, predicted target is in Pacific Ocean."

Marshal Kurchatov turned back to General Walker. "Very fine. Very fine."

"You now have as much access to the monitoring systems for our strategic forces as I do." *And more than I would have given you . . .* "If a missile is launched, it will be registered right here. If a bomber as much as taxis, you'll know it. And the subs, well, you've seen it."

"Except for the *Pennsylvania,*" Colonel Belyayev said, his eyes locked with CINCNORAD's.

"That will not be a problem," Kurchatov said. "Colonel?"

"Not a problem."

"Good," General Walker said. "Major, the duty officer is from this point forward to report any occurrences directly to Marshal Kurchatov and Colonel Belyayev. They will be in the VIP quarters." CINCNORAD looked back to the Russians. "Right through those doors. You'll be twenty feet away, and you are welcome to monitor the console with the duty officer at any time."

"Very fine. Yes." Kurchatov thanked the major and stood. "The colonel will remain here, General Walker. I must now inform my government to proceed."

Maybe this was good, Walker thought. If the Russians were willing to trust them with one boomer still out there, then they might not just be blowing smoke. He sure as hell wouldn't have trusted them had the situation been reversed. Things really were changing. He'd waited more than thirty years to believe it, and the feeling wasn't all that bad.

"I'll show you to the com center, Marshal," General Walker offered. "Then maybe we can talk about those Siberian reindeer you're so boastful about."

He sat ramrod-straight in the chair, his hands loose at his side. Bad guys were on both sides and behind in the darkened room. A window was to his left, behind the reflective surface of which were the witnesses to his fate.

The beeper on his watch sounded, and he closed his eyes behind the polycarbonate glasses.

Boom!

The door was directly to the front of Major Sean Graber, ten feet away. It folded downward under the force of the entry charge. From both sides forms in black entered, four in all, their faces hidden by ungainly-looking devices that covered their eyes and protruded in a single Cyclopslike lens. Two went high, two low. Three fired in rapid succession, quick double taps on their pistols, long, oversized weapons that emitted little sound.

Sean kept his eyes closed until the shooting ended. Twelve shots, four for each bad guy. "Exercise over!"

The lights came up in the hostage room, and in the observation room behind the thick bulletproof glass. Sean stood and turned to the left. The five visitors were exchanging amazed looks and words of wonder at the display they had just seen. The major motioned to Captain Chris Buxton, squad leader of the unit that had just "rescued" the number-two man in command of Delta from three cardboard cutouts.

"Unbelievable!" the chairman of the House Armed Services Committee commented as he entered from the observation room. The smell of gunpowder was heavy in the room but was purged by exhaust fans a few seconds after the entourage, all members of the congressman's staff, entered.

"Glad you enjoyed it," Sean responded. He wasn't really, but selling the capabilities of Delta to what his superior, Colonel William Cadler, called "the briefcase brigades" had become part of his duties. That meant occasional shows for whomever the secretary of defense deemed in need of convincing. *Budgets!* Now they were quibbling over how many rounds of ammunition Delta should be burning in their training!

"AN/PVS-7?" the lone female member of the group wondered aloud, looking at the monocular goggles flipped up on the four troopers' heads. She was the congressman's resident expert on the technology side of things.

"Antonelli."

The big Italian lieutenant stepped forward at the behest of the man he had rescued a minute before. "No, ma'am. Our own modification. Well, our idea, but the EO lab at Belvoir put it together. You see, ma'am, the standard 'seven' is best for image intensification—taking what light is there and amplifying it. The IR capability—that's infrared—was limited in a zero light environment. Not quite up to snuff to use with our new toys."

"That toy," the staffer said, pointing to the ungainly weapon at the lieutenant's side.

Antonelli held up his unloaded weapon. "This is the OHWS: Offensive Handgun Weapon System. Basically it's a specially designed HK pistol chambered to fire forty-five-caliber rounds." The weapon was quite ordinary-looking from the grip to just before the trigger housing. There forward it jumped into the twenty-first century in appearance. "This thing under the barrel is an IR Laser Aiming Module, or LAM. It paints the area you're aiming at with IR light that lets us see through our new goggles damn good in the dark. That was why we needed the new ones, 'cause they are primarily tuned to the IR spectrum. We gave up some I2—that's image intensification—capability for it. Trading some 'low' light for better 'no' light capability, you might say. So we can see what the LAM paints, and it also puts a focused aimpoint where our shots are going to hit. We have the same capability on our other weapons now, also."

"Well, that explains some of the precision," another member of the group commented.

"Some of it," Captain Buxton observed. There was more to it than gadgets.

"And this long box coming off the barrel?" the lady asked, pointing to the device that lengthened the weapon considerably.

"Sound and flash suppressor, ma'am. We not only like to be accurate, but invisible and quiet also." He smiled as his presentation ended.

"Look at this," one of the aides said to the congressman, pointing to the four holes punched in the cardboard cutout. They were all within an imaginary two-inch circle above the nose.

"That's called turning off the switch," Captain Buxton explained. "Bad guys don't pull triggers with four bullets in their brains."

"My son's a cop, Major Graber," the Honorable Richard Vorhees began, turning to Sean. "They train them to go for center-mass hits. The bigger target, you know. Upper torso."

"That's correct, sir. But we can't do that. We have to make sure the bad guys don't get to pull the trigger. Our job is to make them dead fast, before they make some innocents dead."

The congressman shook his head in some disbelief at the skill exhibited. He was not unfamiliar with things military, as evidenced by his slight limp. A Cuban mine had taken his leg off at the knee in the Grenada invasion, ending a planned military career with just a pair of oak-leaf clusters on his collar. But that had led to a career in Congress, which he was now enjoying after a meteoric rise to one of the governing body's most powerful positions. "That's a pretty tall order, Major. The chance for a miss has got to be much greater."

Sean smiled agreement at the analysis. "That is right, sir, which is why we have to be that much better. Our business functions on a zero-defect basis."

"What's that?"

"No mistakes. We hit everything we want to every time we try. Period."

Vorhees's eyebrows went up at that. "Come now, Major. Isn't that a bit overstated?" He ended the question with a chuckle.

Sean's expression went dead serious, something the visitors immediately picked up on. "Do you think I would sit inches from these targets and let *my* men shoot at them if I doubted their ability one bit?"

That hit home to the congressman. The men he was among were not just soldiers, as he had once been—they were technicians. The term "professional" did not do them justice. Their job, and their skill, were unique. And must remain so, he had just been convinced.

"Major, I think I can assure that you will get your full budget request. And I doubt Congress will quibble over it." Vorhees offered his hand, which Sean gladly took.

"Then I can assure you, we'll be ready if we're needed."

The entourage followed Captain Buxton and the four men from his squad outside to answer any questions about the tactics and equipment they had just seen employed.

Sean went into the observation room and sat down, removing the glasses that had protected his eyes from powder discharges during the exercise. Chalk another one up for being shot at, and for being able to display it. The new facility that housed Delta at Fort Bragg was known as Wally World, an homage to the mythical amusement park in one of the National Lampoon movies, and the moniker was appropriate. All kinds of wonderful "rides and attractions" were theirs to practice on. The hostage room with its viewing area was one of them. No such capability had existed at the Stockade, Delta's former home at Bragg. Without it Sean wondered if he would have been able to demonstrate the unit's need for the millions of rounds of ammunition it used each year. *Miss with a thousand to hit with one when it counts.*

The phone in the observation room rang. "Graber here."

"Major Graber." It was Colonel Cadler, Ground Forces Commander of the Joint Special Operations Command (JSOC). "How did our little pre-sentation go?"

Sean marveled at how his boss, a Texas native, could make any word sound like someone in Waco had invented it. "We'll get our ammunition."

"Hot damn," the colonel exclaimed. "Good work. Now that you're done giving tours, we've got some real work to do. I want you to get a squad ready for deployment ASAP. Clear, Major?"

"Yes sir," Sean replied. "What kind of job, Colonel?"

"Baby-sitting."

CHAPTER FOUR

Discovery

The offices of the *Los Angeles Times* are located in an externally beautiful facility in what is known as Times Mirror Square. It is a visual oasis of sorts in an area of downtown Los Angeles that is reminiscent more of the urban centers of the former East Germany than of the perceived ideal associated with great American cities. The usual gathering of denizens and the down-and-out abounded in the area, mixing with the workday crowd of suits and blueshirts to create a patchwork representation of social standing that existed on a nine-to-five schedule, five days a week.

"Depressing," Art commented as he pulled the Bureau Chevy into a space marked with a familiar No Parking placard.

Frankie stepped out of the car onto the sidewalk. "Things sure have changed."

The senior agent nodded at the observation as he came around the rounded nose of the shiny blue Caprice. As much as he loved the feel of Los Angeles and its architectural mix of old and new, the city was becoming something he'd never dreamed it could. "Let the social theorists come hang out down here for a week."

Francine Aguirre, product of the Pico Aliso housing projects in what had become one of the city's worst areas, knew firsthand just how much things had changed. She had seen her community begin a slow downward spiral over the years. People she had

grown up with were now more likely residents of Sybil Brand
Institute for Women or the men's central jail than the old stomping grounds they had shared. Times were simpler then. Funerals
came when cancer, old age, or a car accident took one of the
neighbors whom everybody knew. Now they happened weekly,
and the young were passing at a pace that had surpassed the
mortality rate of the community's elders. The place of her youth
was dying, and the disease that caused it had spread to envelop
areas once thought untouchable. And people, she thought.

"Quite a bed we made," she said, walking past a man covered
in the tattered remnants of what had once been a coat. His hand
was out, reaching up from where he sat against the building, his
eyes locking Frankie's in a plea for spare change. She remembered the "we" in her last statement and continued into the
building without acknowledging his presence, much less his existence.

The agents showed their shields to the guard in the lobby,
who called up to the city desk to announce their presence and
were directed to an elevator. They stepped off on the sixth floor
a minute later and were immediately set upon by a giant of a man.

"Art, you old rascal," Managing Editor Bill Sturgess bellowed, his hands coming *down* on the six-foot-two agent's shoulders.

"Bill, damn good to see you again." Art gestured to his partner. "Frankie Aguirre."

Sturgess offered his hand in a much gentler greeting. "Hell
of a lot prettier than Toronassi. How is he doing, by the way?"

"Working his way up at the Academy," Art explained. "He's
supervising the OC Section there now."

"That old mob stuff of yours rubbed off on him, huh? Come
on, my office doesn't smell as bad as this place."

A chorus of mock protests erupted from the newsroom near
the elevator. Bill Sturgess, all six foot nine of him, was an editor
from the old school of journalism, where facts superseded con-
jecture and glitz. It was a code he lived by, and one he insisted his
people adhere to, though his reach extended only as far as the
borders of the city. The national and international correspon-
dents were run by another group of men and women, people
whose education had stressed business and sales above ethics and
accuracy, resulting in a slant that not all observers and critics
agreed with. Sturgess was an internal critic with a loud voice, one

booming enough to keep his people from stumbling over their own desire for *the* story. Find it, check it, confirm it, write it, confirm it, edit it, confirm it, print it. Those were his instructions, and God help the reporter who was foolish enough not to follow them.

"Sorry about your loss yesterday."

"Thanks," Art said. "Good kid. Anyway, I'm sure you guessed why we're here."

"What can I do for you?" Sturgess asked, closing the door to his glass-walled office and taking a half-sitting position against his desk.

"The hit on Melrose yesterday," Art began, knowing that his friend of more than ten years hated preliminaries when there was a main event to be seen. "The victim had a card on him with the city desk's number penciled on the back. Did you have anybody set to meet with someone in that area?"

The managing editor's eyes looked briefly at the floor before meeting Art's again. "You have an I.D. on him?"

Art knew there was no reason to hide that fact. "Portero, Francisco. But you can't print that just yet."

"No problem. Yeah, I had a guy who was supposed to meet with him. Good reporter, lots of potential, but he has a problem with his mouth."

"His mouth?" Frankie asked.

"Yeah. It tends to open too frequently when there's a bottle around. Too bad. It looks like he might have had a story out of this one." Sturgess shook his head with true regret at the loss, and at his reporter's bleak future. "Wasted talent."

"Is he here?" Art inquired.

"Haven't seen him since yesterday before it all went down. Told me he had an eleven-forty-five lunch set up with this Portero."

"I'm a little surprised he gave you his name," Art admitted.

"I told him we'd have to confirm his background before I committed someone to listen to him. He claimed to be a translator at the UN and said he was an assistant to Castro's Russian-language translator in the early sixties. I verified the first claim, but the stuff in the sixties was pretty much a wash."

Well, CNN had proved that the media was sometimes the preferred method of gathering and presenting intelligence quickly. Art figured print shouldn't be much different on the gathering end of it. "We knew about the UN stuff, but I'll admit that the other is news to us. Interesting."

"I presume he didn't give up this story or whatever he had to you," Frankie surmised.

"If he had, I couldn't tell you, but, off the record, he didn't give us anything but enough bait to keep me interested. Sullivan was supposed to get the whole spiel from him yesterday."

Frankie took out her notebook. "Sullivan . . . two *L*'s."

"Right. First name George."

"You say eleven forty-five?" Art probed, the timing jogging his memory.

"Yep."

"What kind of car does Sullivan drive?"

"Damn, let me think. It's some old bronze or tan-colored thing. Dodge, think. Why?"

Art started his own notes. "He may have almost taken my foot off bugging out of there. You say he hasn't come in or called?"

Sturgess checked the time. "Well, it's early still, but I get the distinct impression that he's not going to show. Gut hunch based on past performance." Again his expression was one of regret. "I had to put someone else on the story." The big man paused for second. "I don't know if I can keep him on much longer. He had the same problem in New York, but he wouldn't own up to it there either. Just said he preferred warmer weather and came out here with the same baggage. Guess I'm a soft heart."

"We need to know where he lives," Frankie said. "He could be in danger." And he might know something, she silently hoped.

"He's always been in danger, young lady." Sturgess walked around his desk and flipped through his Rolodex, pulling the card out and handing it to Frankie. "If you see him, tell him to give me a call."

"Sure will, Bill." Art stood, shaking his old friend's hand before heading back to the elevator with his partner.

"Nice guy," Frankie commented in the solitude of the elevator. "How'd you two meet?"

"I had my gun in his ear one night," Art said calmly. "Had to talk him out of blowing the head off the guy who raped and murdered his wife."

"Jesus, I didn't know."

Art turned to his partner. "Neither does anyone else. How do you blame a man for wanting to do that?"

You don't, Frankie answered silently, her world having suddenly changed to allow an intimate empathy for the desire.

"You should have seen it. Bill with this big old cannon of a handgun pressed up into this guy's mouth, and me with my old Colt shoved in Bill's ear. Took me half an hour, but I got him to let it go. The perp screamed and moaned as soon as I got him out of there, telling everyone what Bill had done. Kidnapping, assault with intent. All kinds of good stuff."

"Sturgess didn't do any time?"

Art's head shook as the *3* lit up above them. "Never happened, Frankie."

Her lips parted slightly with shock. "You mean you . . ."

"Lied? Yes, I did that. I lied to keep a man who was damn near destroyed from going over the falls because some lowlife took his world away from him. Have I ever done it again or before? No. Would I?" Art paused momentarily, the door opening to their front, and the answer to the self-inquiry hanging somewhere inside his conscience.

"I'll drive," Frankie said. She'd never have expected it of her partner. He was the finest and most human cop she had ever known, and *he* would do that! The motivation was easy to understand, on both sides of what had happened. Art didn't want to destroy a man, and that man wanted desperately to avenge a loss. One, though, was much stronger for her.

Art's hand retrieved the Chevy's keys and something else from his pocket. He handed the keys to Frankie as they stepped into the sun and placed a dollar in the hand of the old beggar.

"Let's go find Sullivan."

"Sure thing," Frankie said, seeing something new in her partner that she hadn't expected to and feeling something new in herself that, despite its source, was strangely satisfying.

It was best to die in one's own land, Antonio Paredes believed. His father had fallen during the invasion of the *Bahia de Cochinos,* just thirty miles from the home in Juragua he had fled when the Communists came to power. The men strewn across the field south of Santa Clara had seen themselves as patriots also, but they were defenders on the wrong side of two rights in this instance. They had died at the hands of their comrades who were fighting to free them. What an incredible juxtaposition of purposes, Antonio thought.

"Papa Tony." It was Captain Emilio Manchon, assistant to Colonel Ojeda. "The colonel wishes to see you."

They walked toward the gathered command vehicles belonging to Ojeda's old unit, the Second Mechanized Division, which he had appropriated en masse from the Cuban Army. Across the nation, Ojeda's collaborators were waging the war with their own units, some of which they seized control of by subterfuge and threats, and some, like Ojeda, by elimination of a hated commander. And, surprising to some of the participants, they were winning. Ojeda was not among the doubters.

"Papa Tony." The colonel was seated in the passenger seat of the familiar American Jeep of World War II vintage, hundreds of which were in use by the Cuban Revolutionary Armed Forces, and now by the rebels. He offered the American a drink from his metal canteen, also a vintage piece of equipment, though this from the former East Germany. "We have secured this area. Santa Clara is ours, and from here we can slice the island in half."

Antonio noticed that the words were not said with glee but with precision, like a surgeon describing a procedure. A surgeon had certainly visited this field, though not of the healing kind. "Who were these men?"

A shot rang out nearby. Antonio jerked his head to see one of Ojeda's men finishing off a loyalist who had not been killed outright. He felt a wave of coldness envelop his body.

"They died like they fought," Ojeda said. "With a lack of proficiency. As for who they were . . . Captain?"

"The Thirteenth Infantry Brigade, Papa," Manchon answered. "Nine hundred men."

"Dispatched with in half a day," Ojeda added. "We move tonight toward Cienfuegos. Major Sifuentes is closing on Mariel from Los Palacios. In the east Colonel Torrejón will have Camagüey in our hands by tomorrow evening."

"And the people?" Antonio asked. "What are they doing? How are they reacting?"

Ojeda looked puzzled at the question. "The people? Papa, tell me, if you lived in the house of a slave master for thirty-five years, and suddenly the master was gone, what would you do? Eh?"

"I'm not sure."

"Exactly. Did you think these people, who have known only one way of life, had only one man who told them what to do, what to eat, how to behave, did you think they would run into the streets and celebrate?" Ojeda brought up a long finger that waved back and forth. "No, Papa Tony. They cannot. They are afraid. Their world is changing. It will take time for them to understand what is happening. Much time."

"I see your point, Colonel." The man was wise, Antonio decided. Fierce and wise. He might have made a good leader for the nation under different circumstances.

"Papa," Manchon began, "when will we have the locations of the loyalist units?"

"Tonight," Antonio replied. "Each night we will get the report."

"We will go over the information together." Ojeda pronounced the directive like a dictator, then signaled his driver to take him away from the place where only dead enemies abounded. He wanted to find where there were more loyalists to remove from the rolls of the living.

"It was an appropriate place for the men to die," Captain Manchon commented, pointing to an overgrown patch of rough earth off to the east a hundred yards or so. "The old cemetery at St. Augustine's."

Antonio walked toward the site, leaving Manchon behind. It was a diversion of sorts, something to relieve his mind from the constant thoughts of the newly dead by visiting those who had met their maker long before. From the looks of the graveyard it had been decades since any had been planted in the ground beneath the lush canopy. What church might have been near was reduced to rubble, a result of some battle in the Revolution before he was born. The headstones were mostly toppled, some broken, a tangled tapestry of weeds and vines covering the dark gray slabs.

"Witnesses to history," Antonio said aloud. He bent down and moved the foliage aside with his hands, exposing several of the markers. "Mariana Lopez. Died 1962. Age twelve." The grim reaper took whom he took, regardless of age, Antonio thought. His gaze moved across the other names, all people who had . . .

Wait. Antonio went back to one of the names, then to the next one, and to the one beyond that. There were several of them, all names foreign to the island. Well, not entirely correct, as they had probably come as invited guests. *Huh!* Only to die for some reason. It must have been an accident or something. Maybe a transport went down. That would make sense.

While not of any real consequence to his mission, it was of an interesting nature and worthy of a mention in his situation report for the night. Langley could take it from there. Something for the history books, Antonio figured.

He pulled out his notebook and began taking down the names from the headstones, careful to get the correct spelling for each, thanking the stars that whoever had buried these fellows had opted for the English spelling of the names, rather than the traditional Russian.

The night's sleep had done him wonders, as had the bottle of bourbon. The company hadn't hurt either, though she had cost five times as much as the liquor. George Sullivan knew he could have had cheaper, but Loretta was a favorite, and, hell, just *thinking* about her expertise in certain matters made him realize that she was worth every penny.

But today. *Damn.* How was he going to explain to Bill that the guy he was suppose to meet the day before got the shit blown out of him? Just like those two gangland hits he'd covered in New York. The whole damn world was turning into a slaughterhouse.

"Guess the guy might have really had something," Sullivan said to himself as he pulled into the driveway of his house. *And guess I have a real story, now.* If only he hadn't run from the scene like a scared schoolkid afraid of the bully. Now he'd have to start digging almost twenty-four hours after the fact.

He closed the car door with a kick, hearing the familiar groan of old metal. Maybe it was time for a new car. His eyes scanned the front of the house as he trotted onto the porch, deciding it was *definitely* time for a new paint job for the house. Yellow peels were not attractive.

He took yesterday's mail from the box and went through the front door, tossing his keys to the right as he checked what wonderful bills had come for—

The sound of his keys *not* landing on the bookcase just inside the entry caused him to freeze. Then his eyes came up from the mail, the sight immediately erasing the semblance of normalcy he had attained from the night just ended. *Oh, my God.*

Everywhere there was chaos. The furniture was turned over, the tables upended. Pictures were off the walls. Sullivan let the mail slip from his hands as he stood and listened for any sign that the intruder might still be there. He was just feet inside the door and could have bolted out with no problem, but there was quiet. Utter, disconcerting quiet.

He began to take steps forward, his eyes looking left to the kitchen. It was empty, though no less disheveled than the living room. Then the hallway. Stripped of the pictures and other decorative items that had adorned the wall. Still silent as he gingerly stepped over the debris littering the carpeted hall, past the bathroom, to the bedroom.

The same there. The mattress was off the heavy oak-and-steel frame, lying against one wall, its fabric covering sliced open exposing the springs. Drawers pulled out and left lying on the floor, along with all their contents. The fucking robber had . . .

But nothing is missing. The VCR was there, in the corner on a pile of clothes, its cover *torn off?* The same with the television. *What the . . . No way!*

Someone was looking for something. They weren't here to rob him, they were here to . . . *What if it's the same ones who . . . ?*

Sullivan backed out of the bedroom and went to the kitchen, his feet sliding through the glass littering the linoleum floor. There was something there he had to get, something he needed. No fucking work today, that was for sure. So who would give a— There! He found the bottle, still intact, thankfully, and twisted off the cap. The sweet, smoky flavor rolled down his throat a second later.

The drink hit him where he needed it. He had to get his head on straight and figure this out. He thought of calling the police, but what would he say? *"Hi, I witnessed a murder yesterday and just ran away. Oh, and by the way, the guys who did it were just over at my place."* No way on that one. He took another swig, still thinking, the ideas racing through his mind. He had to relax. Had to calm down. Another drink. But what if they came back?

That question hit him like an unwelcome brick of sobriety, which he washed away with a long, steady draw on the Jim Beam. *What if they do?* He knew what to do about that, or at least what he could do, or maybe what he might be able to do. *Shit!* He went back to the bedroom and fished through the piles that had been his life until sometime between yesterday and today. The box was

under a mound of his various sweats and T-shirts, its lid open and
. . . the contents right under it.

George picked it up, holding it tightly in his right hand while
his friend stayed true in the other. He was really safe, now, he
believed, but had no idea what came next. None whatsoever. With
such a stunning plan he sank to the floor, his back against the
wall, and waited. For what, he hadn't a clue.

He was in the basement of the Defense Ministry in Havana,
the Plaza de Revolución fifty feet above. Buried by the Revolution,
Fidel Castro thought. A proper way to go.

What the president had heard from his brother so far led
him to wonder if his destiny did lie in failure. Yet it was early.
Though the threat was serious, the gravest he or the country had
ever faced, they were still in power. Still the chosen leaders. The
people would come to the defense of their land as they had been
trained to do. All would be well. All would be fine.

"We have almost no aircraft remaining to fight with," Raul
Castro said in exasperation, hoping to break through the disbe-
lieving trance his older brother had fallen into. As defense minister, he knew the gravity of the situation, and it fell on him as his
brother's closest confidant to explain it. "The last two MiGs we
had capable of flying, both out of the capital, did not return from
their mission. They were more than likely shot down by antiair-
craft fire, or . . ."

"Or what?" Fidel asked, the spell broken by the trepidation
in his brother's words.

"They may have gone north."

The aged leader rose up, his right fist clenched as it came up
even with his face. "The cowards!" His fist crashed down upon
the makeshift map table before him, causing the group of senior
military officers present to jump where they stood. "If *ANY* man
so much as *THINKS* about surrender or defection to the enemy,
I want him shot dead *ON THE SPOT!* Is that clear?! *IS IT?!*"

"It is, Fidel," Raul said. "Every man here knows that. They
are all loyal to you, to the Revolution."

Fidel turned sharply to one side and paced two steps, then
back to where he had stood. "We will defeat this *coup d'état*. The
perpetrators will be captured and hanged in the plaza!"

"*Sí*, they will." Raul acquiesced more than agreed. He had to
get the seriousness across to his brother somehow. "But we have

to ensure your safety. If the rebels are fortunate, they may—"

"Fortunate! To hell with their fortune! Wars are fought not on the basis of luck, but by men with vision! By men with a fire in their belly!" The president looked down at the map table, noting the location of units in the center and west of the country. In the east there was less fighting, mostly from ragtag partisan bands, he suspected. From there the crushing blow to this coup would be struck. "Raul, listen to me carefully. This is what I want done. From Camagüey I want Colonel Torrejón to move west and strike at the flank of the units moving southward toward Cienfuegos. This will force them to halt their advance. I know Torrejón. He will take the fight to them and destroy them!"

Raul looked away from his brother and cleared his throat before looking back. "Fidel, Torrejón is not responding to requests from us. He is apparently among the plotters."

It was as if an invisible fist had struck him in the stomach. Fidel grimaced and slid backward into his chair, the air leaving his lungs in a loud, wet gasp. He was literally in pain. How could Torrejón have done this? How? He had been with Fidel and Raul aboard the *Granma* when the cabin cruiser brought them from Mexico to Cuba in 1956 to begin the Revolution. He had marched with them through the Sierra Maestras. He was a patriot! How could this have happened? Who was responsible?

"Fidel. Fidel." Raul leaned over the table, watching helplessly as his brother's head shook in disbelief.

Who is responsible? Fidel repeated it over and over, searching for a guilty party to strike out at. Looking for those culpable. There had to be . . .

Yes. His eyes came open and met Raul's. There was a responsible party. One that bore the blame for more than this episode in his country's history. A true enemy of the Revolution. The would-be destroyer of his nation.

But not before a price was exacted for the actions that allowed this to happen. A lesson in the cost of war would be taught to the responsible one. A lesson to never be forgotten.

Fidel sat forward in his chair and lifted the phone from its cradle. It was answered immediately in the army's communication center. "Get me General Asunción at once."

"Dios mío," Raul said aloud, invoking the name of a being whose existence he doubted but whose wrath he suddenly feared.

CHAPTER FIVE

Soundings

"What do you think?" Drummond waited patiently for the reply.

"I think Anthony has a lot to learn," Deputy Director, Operations, Mike Healy answered. "I didn't even know he was talking to Paredes." He shook his head ruefully.

"This is his thing, Mike, and I mean *his.*" Drummond took a long drink from the red-and-white can held tightly in his fist. "You and I are window dressing on this one. Talking to Paredes isn't the half of it. He's micromanaging SNAPSHOT all the way. All my people in Miami have been reporting directly to him, and *only* to him, since this op came to life." "All" meant the two Agency screeners attached to the INS for the purpose of identifying those of lesser character who might come through the favorite port of entry for those fleeing Cuba and other Caribbean nations. That Langley had people operating there at all was a closely held secret, even though the practice did not technically violate the restriction on the CIA operating within the United States. They were "consultants," though certain civil-liberties zealots would obviously see it otherwise. "He's afraid the other Cuban-American groups might get wind of us being sweet on the CFS and wants to *personally* know if that's happening, or if any scuttlebutt is coming over with any refugees."

"Why the CFS, Greg?"

The DDI gestured futility at trying to decipher any of his boss's decisions.

"Hmm," Healy grunted. His enthusiasm level with the men supposed to fill the void once Castro was gone had barely reached the low threshold maintained by his Intelligence counterpart. "I can't figure him out, Greg. Those guys he's championing are bad news, and the company they keep doesn't do anything for their social standing. Anthony can't dispute that their benefactor is hooked up with the druggies, can he?"

"He sure can, plus he refuses to believe that the CFS is mixed up in it." Drummond gave a "Go figure" shrug. "The tooth fairy is putting bags of hundreds under their pillows."

"Still no luck on figuring out who's signing the checks?"

"Zip. S and T is still trying with DIOMEDES," the DDI answered, referring to the Science and Technology Directorate's section that was linked to Federal Reserve computers and those of foreign banks with holdings in the United States. It was all very quiet, and borderline illegal. "He hates it, but as long as Coseros is in the equation, I can look wherever I want to find my leak. If something turns up on the CFS in looking, too bad. Anthony can't stop me on that, despite what he believes."

"His head's in a hole," Healy commented with disdain.

"Evidence, Mike. He wants evidence. Short of an indictment, I don't know what will convince him. He doesn't trust the Bureau, he doesn't trust you or me. I don't know who he trusts."

"Himself." Healy's chest heaved with a suppressed chuckle. "The worst possible person."

"I know." The DDI's secure line buzzed before he could depress himself anymore. "Drummond."

"Greg, it's Seth." Seth Feirstein was roughly the DDI's equal in the National Security Agency, the supersecret government monolith based at Fort Meade that did wonderful things with communications and cryptographics. "Listen, remember the watch we put up for you on the satellite lines out of Panama?"

"Yeah," Drummond confirmed, his mind silently praying for good news. "Please tell me you've got something."

"We've got something."

The DDI gave a thumbs-up to Healy and mouthed the name "Coseros." He got a beaming smile in return. "Go on."

"Three groups of lines were finally pegged as his primary

nonsecure international links. Once we nailed those down, we ran back on the U.S. long-distance calls to them."

"I don't want to know how," the DDI said. He already did know how. The National Security Agency had the best electronic witch doctors on their staff, men and women who knew how to skirt the bounds of legality with the deftness of a ballerina and how to cross it with the stealth of an apparition.

"I've got two numbers for you. Both have called at least five times in the past month, and one over twenty."

"Where's the higher one located?"

"Area code three-zero-five."

"Miami," Drummond said. "Give them both to me."

The DDI noted both but circled the Miami one. Immediately after hanging up with Feirstein, he hit the speed-dial button for the Federal Bureau of Investigation.

"Think you may have something?" Healy asked before the DDI's call was picked up.

"I damn sure hope so." The DDI tapped his pencil nervously. "Gordy?"

"Yeah. Greg, is that you? You sound kind of pumped up," the FBI director commented.

"I am. Hey, you feel like helping me with some plumbing?"

"Is this about that little drip you think you had?"

"Exactly, except I have a possible stateside contact now. Just a phone number. Think you can manage?"

"I'll need a wiretap warrant, but we can do that quietly." The Justice Department, of which the Bureau was part, had a regularly assigned liaison judge from one of the federal courts whose responsibility, in addition to adjudicating cases, was to provide swift warrant processing in matters with potential national-security concerns. The present situation fit that profile to a T. "Two-way street on this. If anything incriminating toward or by Coseros is said . . ."

"It's yours." Drummond nodded with satisfaction. Coseros was a prize to be had, but the DDI had a greater desire. "I want the ass of whoever is wasting water."

"I hear you. Oh, and isn't Cuba interesting this time of year?"

The DDI smiled. It was a secure line, and Gordon Jones was not known to be a dummy. "Weather's looking up a bit here, too."

*   *   *

Frankie slowed the Chevy along the street, checking house numbers. "There."

Art undid his belt as Frankie swung into the driveway. "Bingo."

The car was twenty feet ahead, nosed toward the closed garage door.

"That's the partial I got," Frankie said. "Guess he's home."

"Let's go have a talk."

The two agents walked quietly toward the front of the house, their eyes instinctively searching for that which was out of the ordinary.

"Nice morning," Frankie observed. "Would *you* have all your shades drawn?"

"Hmm." Art stepped up onto the porch, his partner staying in the driveway with her eyes alternating between the front and side of the house.

Art stood listening for a moment, hearing nothing, looking to Frankie for ideas. She shrugged. If Sullivan wasn't home, then why was his car still there? And where was he? They were questions that would not be answered by them just standing there.

Art tapped on the screen-door frame four times, his body reflexively standing to one side of the opening. "Mr. Sullivan. This is the FBI. We need to speak to you."

"FBI, my ass!"

Frankie dropped low first, bringing her gun out during the motion. Art did the same, stepping farther aside from the doorway and clear of the windows.

"I've got a gun, and I'll use it!"

The words were strong but slurred. Art and Frankie noticed another thing in them: real fear.

"Listen, George, this *is* the FBI," Art said loudly without shouting. He didn't want to appear to be giving commands. This wasn't a suspect, after all, just an apparently juiced guy who was afraid for some reason. Seeing someone get wasted could do that, the agents knew.

Art looked to his partner. In barricade situations it was standard to not reveal the locations of all agents on the scene for purposes of security and response potential. In this case, though, doing just the opposite might be the way to go.

"Sullivan, this is Special Agent Aguirre of the FBI. My partner and I just want to talk to you. We know what happened yesterday. We were there. Think . . . you drove right by us in the alley. You almost creamed my partner."

The doorknob clicked soon after Frankie's plea ended. Art cringed, remembering the event that had sent his former partner to the hospital, and nearly to the grave. But this was different, he told himself, repeatedly, as the man behind the door came into view. His hands were empty.

"Frankie," Art said calmly, his Smith now pointed at the floor and held one-handed.

"The gun's on the floor," George Sullivan said, his eyes red and moist. He looked up at Art. "Sorry about yesterday."

Frankie walked past Art and Sullivan, checking the interior to ensure that all was clear. She was back on the porch a minute later. "Quite a mess in there."

"Yeah," Sullivan said, wiping his mouth and eyes with the back of his hand. He leaned to one side, aiming for the doorjamb, but missed. Art caught him, and lowered him to the porch floor.

"Take it easy. You hurt?"

Sullivan looked up at Art, his picture of the dark figure fuzzy. "I knew it couldn't be the guys, 'cause I heard a woman. Where . . . ?"

"Right here," Frankie said, stepping closer.

"Yeah. I mean, I thought they might come back, so I had to, you know . . ." His face went blank, the alcohol and terror combining to turn his stomach into a cauldron of boiling fluids. He rolled to the right and vomited heavily, sitting back up after a few dry heaves. "Sorry."

"I think whatever you filled your belly with is better off on the porch," Art observed. "Did you see who did this?"

"No. No." Sullivan spit the taste from his mouth. "I found it like this. Man, I don't want to end up like that guy at Clampett's."

"How do we know it was them?" Frankie asked her partner.

"We don't, but this fits too neatly. Better roll a forensic team out here and get LAPD to string us a crime scene. I'm going to try and sober him up a little."

Ten minutes later the first of two LAPD units turned the corner. The officer began stringing "banana tape" to cordon off the house, as the other started his own report that would explain why the Bureau was in charge of this scene although in LAPD jurisdiction. The first forensic team would not arrive for another half hour, at which time Art hoped there would be something worthwhile found that they could use to identify and locate the perpetrators. Leads, after all, did not just walk up and bite you. Well, almost never.

"George," the elderly woman called from behind the police line.

Art noticed that Sullivan, after two cups of straight black provided by a neighbor, was still a bit wobbly. "I'll help you." They were at the end of the driveway a few seconds later.

"Mrs. Carroll."

"George, what happened? I saw the police cars. Are you all right?" Her tiny hand reached across the police line and touched his chin. She knew what part of his problem was, just like she could tell when her late husband stopped off at the bar on his way home from work.

"I'm okay. Someone broke in, that's all. I came home and found it."

"Broke in?" Her hand recoiled from its comforting touch and pressed against her lips. "Oh, dear. I should have called, but I wasn't sure. My stars!"

Art's sensibilities told him not to read past what had been said to what he wanted to hear, but . . . "Mrs.—Carroll, is it?"

"Louise Carroll," she affirmed, her eyes falling upon his badge. *FBI?*

"Did you see something?"

"Well, yes, but it didn't seem like an emergency, so I didn't want to bother the police."

Art's head nodded acceptance. "I understand. Can you tell me what you saw?"

"Yes," she began. "There were two men. They got out of a very nice car early this morning, right after *Good Morning America* started. I watch it every morning. They walked around the corner, and then I didn't see them anymore. I guess I didn't see them leave because I started my wash for the day."

"That's very helpful," Art told her, easing into the questioning. "Can you describe either of the men?"

She looked downward momentarily, thinking carefully back the few hours. "They were well dressed. Both wore sport coats, but no ties, I believe. I think they were both Mexican, and one had a very thin hairline and a bit of a waist. He was the driver. The other had short, curly hair—it was black—and a mustache. It was quite a distance away, so I'm sorry I can't tell you more."

Art could have kissed her. He looked to Sullivan, and, by his expression, he knew that the men Mrs. Carroll had described were the men who had popped Portero. "Mrs. Carroll, I can't tell you enough how helpful what you just gave us is. Extremely helpful."

"I'm a neighborhood-watch chairperson, so I try to keep an eye open for strangers," she explained. "I just wish I'd called the police right then, darn it!"

"I'd like to have my partner talk to you to write down what you've told me, if that would be all right?" Art's head dipped slightly as he finished the request.

"Of course, but would you like this also?" Mrs. Carroll asked, holding a small slip of notepaper out to the FBI agent.

"What is this?" Art asked.

"The license number of the car."

This time, the rules and all else be damned, Art Jefferson bent forward and gave the senior citizen a much-deserved peck on the cheek.

They were high-tech dispatchers, directing the movement of billions of dollars of equipment thousands of miles from where they sat. When a customer requested a move, the technicians at the Consolidated Space Operations Center in Colorado Springs carried it out through a series of computer commands that were beamed up to a Milstar communications relay satellite that "bounced" the commands to the intended recipient. Sometimes several bounces were required between the ground and two or three relay satellites before the commands could be acted upon.

The customers, almost exclusively the CIA and the DOD, then were free to use their people to control the activities of the newly positioned satellites and to interpret whatever data was retrieved. CSOC's job was done at that point, until another move from any planned orbital path was required. It was all very routine.

"Goddammit!" the senior watch technician swore, his section's routine broken by the single flashing light on his console. He switched his intercom to the channel for the Air Force duty officer for his watch, a two-star general.

"What's the problem?"

"We've got a reactive rotation on number 5604," the technician reported, referring to the twenty-ton KH-12 just beginning its pass over western Cuba. "As soon as NPIC started shootin' pictures, we got a warning."

The National Photographic Interpretation Center, a complex of windowless cubes on the grounds of the Washington Navy Yard, was the arm of the CIA and other governmental intelligence agencies that collected and analyzed imagery from the array of reconnaissance satellites orbiting the globe. Their actions this morning, though quite ordinary, had initiated something unexpected. More than that, actually, something was terribly wrong with number 5604.

"How bad?" the major general, located a hundred feet away in a separate section of CSOC's modest facility, asked.

The technician checked his status panel for the satellite. "Bad. It's off eighteen degrees on the lateral, and we're getting indications of an end-to-end shift."

"Damn." The KH-12 was now pointed uselessly off to one side, a problem that could have been dealt with had the satellite not also have begun a slow end-over-end spin. Though only minute in relative terms—an expected revolution every three hours, the sensors were showing—it effectively put the bird out of commission. "Any ideas on what happened?"

The technician stared furiously at his status panel, which, other than the attitude and motion-warning indicators, gave him not a clue as to why the malfunction had occurred. "Not a light to tell me shit, sir." A civilian, the technician was a bit more free to color his language around the staff officer. His thirty years of government service didn't hurt, either. "My best guess is the stabilizer for the real-time sensors. NPIC was starting to shoot some video, doing a half-degree lens sweep, when the bird started to tilt. I'll bet the dampers failed, and the lens assembly locked up. When it spun, the bird just spun with it."

"But why no indicator?"

"Ask the boys at Lockheed," the technician suggested, his morning now screwed up beyond repair.

The major general would be doing precisely that, through accepted channels and otherwise. But first came the necessity to report to his "customers" at Langley that one of his birds, one they had depended heavily upon during the previous weeks, was now out of the show.

It was quiet in the West Wing, the majority of the staff attending a pre-lunch cake party for the departing secretary of the Vice President. Bud DiContino had stopped in quickly to say a farewell before returning to his office to square things away on the military end of the Cuba operation and await word from the Navy on its overdue boomer. It was troublesome, but at least the Russians weren't letting it become a wrench in the works. Even General Walker seemed to be more in synch with the plan after the test shot. The charm Kurchatov had laid on couldn't have hurt either, Bud thought.

The NSA had just dropped a stack of files on his desk when the phone buzzed. "DiContino."

"Bud, it's Greg."

"Oh."

"Not happy to hear from me?" the DDI said playfully.

"Hoping to hear from Granger." He explained about the *Pennsylvania.*

"And they're still on board? Wow. I guess there is something to be said for this trust thing. You'll have to teach me it sometime," Drummond joked. "We don't do much of that here."

"It's a correspondence course. What can I do you for?"

"We have a little problem."

The DDI's voice didn't betray anything beyond the "little" label in his sentence. "I'm listening."

"Our satellite tasked to get the intel on Cuba just went down."

"Down as in malfunctioned?" the NSA asked, hopeful that it wasn't more like succumbing to gravity and burning up in the atmosphere. *Bye-bye nine hundred million.*

"Yeah. CSOC says it's a major one." The DDI took a drink of something on the other end of the line. "Guess there'll be a shuttle mission for this."

"Yeah, and who's gonna pay for it?" The budget battle had stretched to all agencies and departments, choking off contingency funds that had once been earmarked for instances like this. "Greg, we've only got two more functioning birds up there, and we can't pull them off their missions. No way."

"I know that, but we do have other options." The DDI let that hang without further exposition. He knew none was necessary.

"You can't be serious, Greg!" Bud fell back into his chair, pushing the reclining mechanism to its limits. "Do you know what you are really suggesting? I mean, besides the security aspect of it, the cost would be enormous."

"Look, we could cut back on the amount of imagery we interpret for delivery," the DDI suggested. "A few passes a day instead of sixteen."

Bud's head shook as he leaned forward, his eyes downcast into the hand supporting his forehead. "Greg, this is like asking for the keys to the new 'vette before I've even driven it."

"Anthony will get them from the President if you don't hand them over," the DDI said. "I thought it would be better coming from you. The teamwork thing, remember."

He was right. Bud's resistance would only strengthen the DCI's hand, and give *him* the opportunity to hear the President say yes to another request. It wasn't on the far side of smart, but it really wouldn't be a major undertaking. Not the intended use, for certain, but also not beyond the system's capabilities. Not much was.

"All right. I'll clear it with the President. But you're paying for gas," Bud informed the DDI, quite seriously despite the euphemism.

A couple million a fill-up. Well, the Agency had wanted the damn gas guzzler in the first place. "Thanks."

"Just don't get it shot down," Bud said. "We've lost 'em there before."

"Long time ago, Bud. And they ain't got nothing that can touch this." It was a partisan boast, but also one quite rooted in fact.

The Japanese technicians had been waiting in the poorly heated housing near the *Voyska PVO's* headquarters for just over a week. An hour after dark the word to get to work had finally come, much to their delight.

Eight trucks deposited the joint technical group, made up of senior engineers from six major Japanese companies, outside the access building atop the underground command center. The elevators were loaded with the requisite tools in just a few minutes, then, in four trips, the three separate cars descended to the twenty-five-thousand-square-foot facility, which was divided into five operating areas that were all connected to the main access shaft. The joint technical group followed their Russian escorts into the area in which most of the facility's work was done, yet there were the fewest people there.

The first reaction at seeing the antiquated computers was a collective snicker, then bemused curiosity as the technicians wandered about the room, examining the equipment—much of the designs obviously pirated from American, French, and Japanese systems—and marveling that any of it was still operating. There was even rust on some of the back panels!

"Time to do it," the leader of the group said.

General Shergin, there because of duty and no more, looked to his aide, hesitated, then nodded. The junior officer walked to a red box on the wall, unlocked it, and swung the large cover downward. Three levers—looking as old as the computers—were attached side by side. The same number of supply cables entered through the top of the box, but only one exited the bottom. Heat radiated off of the center switch from the thousands of volts flowing through it to the equipment.

The first switch disengaged was that of the primary backup power supply, a diesel-powered generator that would kick in automatically in the event of a power failure. The second switch connected a large array of batteries to the system. These were the last resort, for use only after the generator failed. All that remained was the primary switch, which carried electricity from the Moscow central power grid to the computers. The commander's aide lowered it completely.

The whine of cooling fans ceased, as did the electronic hum associated with older processing equipment. Performance-monitoring screens went blank, and the old reel tape machines ended their constant recording for eternity. "Done."

"Okay," the team leader said. "Let's do it."

The men who had been trained in the best technical schools in the world, who could perform complex mathematical operations in their heads, moved toward the six rows of machines with pry bars, cable cutters, and mallets. There was no reason to spare anything. The brand-new equipment was waiting a half a mile away in a climate-controlled warehouse. This room would soon have the same humidity and temperature control installed, as well as the computers and software to bring the SRF into the twenty-first century. What was here was, simply put, scrap.

The first cabinet unit broke free of its corroded moorings and toppled to its side with only two men pushing it. General Shergin watched this with some interest. His position made a man well aware how much easier destruction was than creation.

The convoy of four vehicles pulled through the gate into the complex located on the western shore of the Bay of Cienfuegos. Soldiers exited the two lead cars, their weapons at the ready. Security was quite adequate out to a mile from where they stood but, as General Juan Asunción knew from the events of the past days, the scorpion that struck was often in one's own bed.

From the third car a small Caucasian man in handcuffs emerged under the forceful grasp of two more soldiers. He was marched quickly to the general, who stood outside the doors that they had together passed through a countless number of times during their acquaintance, a period at one time cordially accepted but now enforced upon one by the fear of a painful demise.

"Welcome, *señor*," Asunción said. "More work to be done."

The man looked up. He was in his forties but appeared older about the face. Deep lines and loose folds of pale skin attested to some form of confinement away from a sun that had once tanned the thin body to a leathery brown. That had obviously faded, as apparently had the man's desire for anything beyond that which he was commanded to do.

"I was here last month, General," Anatoly Vishkov observed in a voice that was pathetic in its mild attempt at defiance. "A visit every three months was deemed sufficient when—"

"When we agreed to let you live, you miserable little insect!" Asunción brought a hand back to slap the insolent weakling, but the rumble of a distant explosion ended the action before it began. The general noticed the puzzlement on the Russian's face. "The exercises are close today, it seems."

Vishkov listened as another blast echoed across the water of the bay to his rear and reverberated through the man-made canyon of buildings and equipment in the complex. The valleys north of Cienfuegos did twist and distort sound quite frequently, a trait common to areas with similar geological and weather conditions. The physicist in him rationalized it as possible.

"If you work quickly, you can be finished by nightfall," Asunción posited, opting for a different tack to gain compliance without questioning. It was preferable that the Russian be kept blissfully unaware of the troubles just twenty miles distant, lest he be motivated by some sense of humanity to refuse his assigned task. The general thought that quite unlikely, as the onetime honored guest of his nation had proven himself to be quite susceptible to the mere threat of physical violence. Still, to take a chance at this stage would be foolhardy.

"What more work can I do?"

"Make it ready," Asunción directed.

The Russian hung his head as a tired man did, a smattering of tears already on his cheeks. "It is ready. It is always ready."

"No, *señor.*" Asunción reached out and lifted the Russian's head by his chin. "Ready to use."

The look on Vishkov's face changed from frustration to horror. "To use? You mean to . . ."

"*Presidente* Castro wishes a complete readiness test." It was a lie, one without precedence but one the Russian had little reason to disbelieve.

Another roar rolled in from the water. Vishkov turned his head toward it, then back to his tormentor. *What is happening?*

"*Señor . . .*" The general stood aside and gestured grandly at the entrance as a hotel doorman would for a visitor.

The Russian physicist had no choice. Where once he had been a man respected for his ingenuity, he was now a prisoner of his value . . . and of his weakness. To stand up to his taskmasters would mean certain death, or, that which he feared more, a painful precursor to the release of the hereafter. Death, while not a welcome concept, was preferable to that which he could suffer, yet he was incapable of bringing that on to stave off the other. It was a circle of defeat few had mastered as well as the man who, in his brighter days, had mastered the atom and its destructive power. That mastery now remained as the sole bit of control that Anatoly Vishkov maintained over his existence.

And, in a twist of perception that he was incapable of realizing, it made him supremely powerful over a game he suspected he had just begun to play in the familiar role as pawn.

CHAPTER SIX

Imagery and Icons

It was known as Area 51 to most officially acquainted with its existence. Those more intimately involved with the goings-on at Groom Lake in the barren desert expanse of Nevada gave it more literal and crafted monikers. Dreamland, a name often shared by the nearby Tonopah Test Range, was one. The Black Hole was another. All, though, succeeded only partially in describing the mystical happenings in a place that, despite evidence to the contrary, didn't exist.

The early afternoon light was painting the imposing mountains of the Timpahute Range a washed-out white and tan, and, unfortunately, was robbing Groom of the welcome cloak of darkness in which operations were almost exclusively conducted. Secrecy, normally a concern for intelligence and military agencies, was a well-crafted paranoia on the dry lake-bed facility that was surrounded by a piece of restricted government land the size of Switzerland. But, in homage to one of its nicknames and despite the oppressive and serious nature of the business that took place there, dreams not only existed at Groom, they took flight and soared as none could have imagined.

The aircraft was rolled out behind a tug into the harsh, breezy environment and was positioned at the threshold of Groom's six-*mile*-long runway. Only ninety feet in length, it weighed in at 180,000 pounds, two thirds of which were the exotic supercooled liquid-methane fuel that both fed the delta-winged aircraft's twin propulsion systems and helped to dissipate the heat generated by high-speed flight from its airframe.

After allowing time for the tug and its operator to clear, the tower gave clearance to the pilot of the craft that had come to be known as Aurora, though the official government designation of the Special Access—or "black"—program was *Senior Citizen*. The pilot, more a mission manager, was an Air Force major who had logged more hours now at Mach 5+ than any of her fighter-driver cohorts. Four feet behind her the Reconnaissance Systems Operator sat, two high-resolution displays dominating his console of instruments, which controlled the array of imaging and signals sensors that were the real heart of the billion-dollar bird.

With the entry of a command into the flight-management system, the aircraft accelerated under a highly advanced form of rocket power down the concrete slab, the pilot providing only steering to keep the bird on the centerline. A thunderous, resonating roar, the product of Aurora's unique two-phase propulsion, swept across the desert base, penetrating every structure above and below ground. Fifteen thousand feet after it began its roll, the computer brought the nose up. The climb-out was slow as the aircraft turned to the southeast, but once pointed in the right direction, a battery of microchips decided it was time to accelerate to operating speed and "pulled the trigger," adding thrust that pushed the ninety-ton bird through Mach 2 in less than thirty seconds. With a nose-up attitude of seventy degrees, the Aurora was passing through thirty thousand feet when its forward momentum was sufficient (Mach 2.54) to switch over to the ramjet propulsion. Passing sixty thousand feet and somewhere over the Nevada/Utah border, the aircraft was breaking Mach 4. Directly over Cedar City, Utah, it passed Mach 5 and 120,000 feet. At this point the flight-management system eased the climb, leveling the Aurora out at thirty miles over eastern Texas, and set a constant throttle at Mach 6.2. Aurora was moving faster than any rifle bullet in the world just fifteen minutes into its flight.

Because of the relatively short distance to the target, no in-flight refueling would be needed on the return leg, making this an easy quick-pass mission. The pilot kept constant watch on the flight systems, particularly the surface and airframe temperatures, the former of which was hovering around a quite acceptable one thousand degrees.

Somewhere over the Gulf of Mexico the RSO activated three of his sensors. They had crossed through two time zones in just under thirty minutes, so the day was two hours older over their target. No low-light or IR imaging would be necessary, though. Today they would need just the two visible-light Casegrain telescopic cameras and the Synthetic Aperture Radar.

"Uprange one minute," the pilot warned.

Sixty seconds meant sixty miles, give or take a few. That time evaporated quickly. Their pass over the long axis of the island of Cuba took just twelve minutes, the cameras and SAR dumping gigabytes of image data into the ample computer-storage capacity onboard. After turning back, the RSO began preprocessing the data, selecting the images that most closely matched the mission requirements. As the descent to Groom began over eastern Texas, he transmitted the selected data to a Milstar satellite in geo. NPIC had it a minute later.

The Aurora touched down seventy minutes after taking off, the total distance covered over forty-five-hundred miles. Its crew, after having spent $2 million of Uncle Sam's money on what they considered to be an E-ticket ride, debarked in a hangar at the north end of the runway. Dinner was in a few hours and, thanks to their somewhat special ride, they rarely missed a meal.

They were legally breaking the law.

The white van pulled up adjacent to the third utility pole from the corner, its two occupants exiting and setting up their work area. Orange cones directed any traffic in the curb lane to move to the left, and their blue work overalls were properly soiled enough so that questions would not be asked.

But there were always those to whom curiosity was not a feeling but a driving force.

"Whas za problem?" the old man asked, sauntering up to the nearest workman.

Special Agent Chris Testra looked up from the loop of cable he was unspooling, the smell of alcohol having reached him with the old man's words. "Cable-TV trouble, Pops."

"Sheeeeit! The fize on anight." He swung a disappointed fist at the air.

Testra laughed. "Don't worry, Pops. You won't miss it. Guaranteed."

"Oh, man. Thainz."

Testra and his partner, Special Agent Frederico Sanz, watched the old man stumble away.

"His life is bliss, man. Eh, Freddy?"

"Guess so. Come on."

Their work was rather simple, and only a schooled observer would have recognized that the two workmen were not working on the thick black cable-TV lines but on thinner wires belonging to the phone company. Wiretapping had come a long way since the days of splicing and stringing additional wires to carry the eavesdropped communications. The method chosen for this operation, authorized by Federal Court Order (Sealed) #76-a-1212-5, was known as "shroud interception." It required a relatively simple procedure that was only slightly invasive. A black-colored cylinder, five millimeters thicker than the standard nineteen-millimeter telephone line, was at the heart of the operation. It was actually two sections, split lengthwise, that were placed over the existing line and reconnected, creating an almost invisible "shroud" over the line. Several tiny, sharp probes, made of polished copper, pierced the protective synthetic coating on the wire and made contact with the cable bundles housed inside. The agents then plugged a remote dialer into one end of the shroud, which actually contained more computing power in its body than a second-generation PC. Special Agent Chris Testra then dialed the number they were authorized to tap into, waiting a few seconds before it was picked up.

"Yeah?"

"Is Raji there?" Testra inquired in his best feigned Pakistani.

"Wrong number." *Click.*

Testra cleared the line and dialed another number, which rang in room 145 of the Golden Way Motel four blocks away, their home for the next few days at least. It rang only once before being answered by a machine that emitted four long beeps. Connection made. Any calls to or from the intercepted number would now be automatically relayed to the monitoring station in room 145 for recording and instant analysis.

They completed the operation in just under a half hour and picked up their cones, making a U turn on the street to drive past the house in question once again.

"What do you do in there, Meester Spy?" Sanz asked in his best Speedy Gonzalez as they passed the older-looking house.

"Hope he does whatever it is soon," Testra said. "The boat has a new coat of paint."

"Well, maybe he'll hear your heavy breathing on the line and just invite us over, Chris," Sanz joked. "Surrender and confess right then and there."

"I'll pant my ass off if it gets me off this by Friday."

A ten-power loupe was hung on the wall as a deferential tribute to the practitioners of their art who had come before. Trailblazers, really, men who had perfected the innocuous act of looking at pictures into a form of educated soothsaying that had saved their country from embarrassment, missteps on the international stage, and from being hoodwinked into situations with potentially deadly consequences for the unaware.

Much had changed since the first days of light tables, foggy slides, and long stints hunched over with a loupe stuck to one's eye. Much had evolved at NPIC. Photointerpretation was now more correctly known as imagery analysis. Computers had replaced the three-by-three slabs of backlit Lucite mounted on boxtops as viewing apparatuses. Cataloging, storage, and retrieval of data were now instantaneous. Yes, the men who practiced the craft had a new, sophisticated array of tools with which to perform their wizardry, and, not surprisingly, some of those "men" were no longer of the anticipated gender.

Senior Analyst Jenny MacNamara, while differing in anatomy from her ancestors in the field, had all the skills requisite in a top-notch interpreter, namely a good pair of peepers and an innate sense of curiosity. To look at an image and see trees was one thing, but to look at the trees and wonder what kind they were was another. To take that wonder one step farther and determine the last time a mountain alder in the rolling foothills west of the rockies had received rain based upon the growth rate of its leaves was the type of self-enforced lunacy that made Jenny one of the best. It had also earned her a place of respect in the eyes of her colleagues, and the nickname Spot, which was representative not of her looks, which were above average by any standard, but of her ability to spot the incongruous. To some she saw what was not there. That was, of course, until she politely pointed it out to them.

The data dump of images had come in a few hours before.

Over fifty image "packages" were received, some containing a thousand separate pictures that had been assembled into larger, more telling representations of what was really there. While Jenny knew what sensors obtained the images, she was not supposed to know from where. The same way she wasn't supposed to imagine a red elephant when her logic professor at MIT had suggested that one couldn't help but do so when the mention of one was made. *A big, fast bird.*

She pushed herself away from the workstation to the small refrigerator, retrieving a clear bottle of flavored seltzer that hissed open with a twist. The computer continued its task without its operator's attention. Inside the four tower cases on a riser to the display's right were parallel arrays of microprocessors, four hundred in all. The process was logically called parallel processing and took the simple analogy that two hands were better than one to a new exponent. Enough processing power was built into the system to allow image compilation that had only been possible in machines like the Cray some years before.

Still, the process Jenny had initiated was complex and time-consuming. More than looking at the visible light images, which she had done an hour before and noted that which deserved noting, she was now feeding the data from the Synthetic Aperture Radar through the computer to build a picture. In reality she was building an island.

The capability, which had revolutionized her job, was made possible by the SAR. Actually a grouping of thousands of small radar transceivers and receivers arrayed along a long, flat slab, the SAR took a radar picture of a target as it moved over its area of observation. What resulted were detailed pictures of a target from a variety of angles. These images were then combined to form a stereoscopic contour world consisting of billions of bits of digitized data, portions of which could then be called up for close analysis.

A series of quick beeps signaled the end of the computer's task. Jenny slid back to the workstation's thirty-inch monitor. "Harry, it's up."

Her assistant, Harrold Fastwater, moved to the adjacent identical display. Grandson of one of the famed Navaho codetalkers of World War II, he had come to NPIC after a stint in the Navy, following the same career path as his senior partner. The Navy, as was recognized by those not in the rival armed services, had a superior cadre of image analysts, and surprisingly allowed them to migrate to other government agencies quite easily. Spreading the blood around, the Navy brass quietly joked.

"Jesus!" Fastwater exclaimed at the data count on his screen.

"Ain't nothing, Harry. Remember, you're not playing with that real-time garbage anymore." Jenny herself had graduated to the more complex assembly-and-analysis process eight months before. "You want to watch TV, tune in the soaps. This is big-time data."

Harry shook his head. He had only been on board with Mac-Namara for a week, but he still didn't understand her disdain for real-time imagery. To him it was damn exhilarating watching things from a hundred or more miles up *as* they happened. But his enthusiasm for the former was about to be dampened.

Jenny typed a command on the keyboard before switching her right hand to the mouselike digitizer. Upon the two-and-a-half-foot diagonal screen a jagged finger of green and brown appeared, a field of blue surrounding it. "Welcome to Cuba, Harry."

Harry noted that the detail was on a strategic scale. The topography looked as it would on a visible-light topographic plate, but this was done with radio waves? "Yeah, it's good, but . . ."

"But nothing," Jenny said. "Watch."

She moved the digitizer to the right, a cursor appearing on the screen and mimicking the track of her hand. A click brought one corner of a box to the screen, somewhere in the central part of the island, and a drag expanded the area of its coverage. "Area one."

A touch of the digitizer brought a zoom down to the bordered area, which now filled the screen with increased clarity.

"Wow," Harry commented. He had expected to see a degradation in detail, not enhancement.

"Your first SAR shot, eh?" she asked, smiling at the image, which was taken down two more steps.

"Uh-huh." Fastwater stared wide-eyed at the image. "Incredible."

"You think this is something, wait till next year this time." The image of the area north of Cienfuegos became the focus of Jenny's attention. "Your clearance covers it, so no big deal in telling you, but once we get those stacked-parallel machines in here, we'll be doing flybys just like that Grand Canyon stuff you've seen."

"No shit?"

Jenny looked to her left. "No shit, buddy."

It was time for work. "Okay, let's find out what's there."

Harry, manipulating his own controls, started tagging objects as man-made that didn't fit into the natural terrain. The anomalies were distinct from the usually smooth surrounding terrain because of their boxy shape. Most were buildings, but those showing a computer-enhanced motion distortion were obviously vehicles. Dimensions were extrapolated by their relation to known objects, a job the computer handled with a simple command.

"Lots of trucks going somewhere. Zil models, looks like," Jenny guessed, the computer unable to distinguish between the several models of the Russian-built transports. "Look at this."

"What?" Fastwater, his screen duplicating what the senior analyst's showed, focused his attention on a group of dark rectangles in a line. A convoy.

"See how the outlines are sharper on this—let's see, that's south—on the south side?"

"Yeah."

Jenny swept the area with the bright dot, drawing an imaginary circle around the convoy. "Those are the front ends of the trucks. See, there's more distortion at the other end, which means the SAR got fewer returns from the objects as it passed over. Just like a picture of a runner in motion. From a camera it'd be like the effect from a slow shutter speed."

"Or an IR image," Fastwater added, catching on to Jenny's explanation. "On that you have a ghost trail when there's movement."

"Right. Same thing here. So what does it tell us?"

"Other than the obvious?" Harry asked, aware of the senior analyst's rep as a near photopsychic.

"All of it." Jenny rotated the chair and faced her partner.

"Well, they're moving south. We can peg the road designation and tell where, more or less, they're going."

"And . . ." Jenny knew what she wanted him to see.

Harry looked back at the scene and shrugged his shoulders. "Correlate with the camera shots to peg the units involved."

"Harry, which is more important: going to the grocery store

or coming from it?'' Jenny drilled the question into her partner with her eyes. *Come on.*

Fastwater knew there had to be more to the question than the obvious, but . . . "Coming home.''

"Why?''

"Because I've got . . . Because I've got the goodies!'' Harry's eyes lit up.

"Do they have the goodies? Are they running full or empty?'' Jenny turned back to the display, her point now ready to act on. "If they're running south empty, toward their supply bases around Cienfuegos, then it means they're going back for more.''

"Might make a nice artillery ambush,'' Fastwater mused.

"That's up to the boys with the guns. But what if they're running full?''

"Why would they go back with supplies?'' Harry couldn't fathom that.

"You don't have to return with the same load you left with,'' Jenny observed as she took the view down farther to a point just behind the lead truck in the convoy.

"Troops.'' It was said as both a realization and a hope. "You think they might be retreating?''

"We'll know soon enough.'' Jenny manipulated the enhancement functions of the workstation on the SAR data. Besides being able to construct a photomosaic representation of the surface of a target, the SAR could also penetrate into the soil or water a few feet, depending on conditions. This function had such diverse abilities as determining subterranean structures helpful to oil exploration and also in detecting minute subsurface ocean displacements to aid in the hunt for submarines. But when in the hands of a skilled image analyst, it could do much more.

"What are you doing?'' Harry gave up trying to follow Jenny's actions on his own display and rolled his chair next to hers.

"Well, we're going to do this by the numbers. See, behind the first truck. The tread impressions.''

"Right,'' Fastwater said. "We determine the depth, and we can extrapolate the load!''

Jenny glanced at her partner. "Hey, I'm not a witch. It ain't that easy, anyway. There's been rain, so we won't have a uniform depression depth. Just thank God they're keeping off the paved roads.''

"Guess they're getting hit hard there," Harry surmised correctly.

"Yeah. So, we have to go with this first truck's tracks before any of the ones behind it roll through them. Now, we're going to take a subsurface reading on the depression and measure the lateral spread. Then we go to the soils book. . . ."

"The what?"

"You are new." Jenny chuckled. "The Agency has soil data from just about anyplace you can imagine. Rate of percolation, etcetera. So we take that data and run a simple computer simulation on the load-distribution characteristics of the soil with the amount of rain received factored in. From that we get a PSI requirement. Bingo!"

"Oh, I see. That easy, huh?"

"Well, we'll have to run variables for the different types of trucks those could be. But we'll still find out if they're running home full or empty. Ready to get started?"

Fastwater laughed. "I thought you were done!"

"Funny."

Harry moved back to his own workstation, amazed at the magic he was becoming part of. He knew that he'd like it here, especially working with the woman who was right about everything except possibly one mundane assertion she had made. To Harry Fastwater, his partner might just be a witch.

The six men stood outside the makeshift housing hurriedly set up for them in a secure area of Cape Canaveral Air Force Station. They were waiting in the chill of the early evening, looking to the south as the Air Force security police assigned temporarily to protect them watched from several blue Humvees surrounding the crude accommodations. What the men were looking toward was beyond their vision, but people the world over gave reverence to unseen places of meaning. These six men, none younger than forty-eight, were doing something not dissimilar, imagining the place they knew they would soon be. A place they had once lived in. A country of unlimited opportunity. A nation they had been tasked to rule.

But it was from the opposite direction that something approached and pulled their attention from the south. It was a sporadic, rhythmic thumping at first but grew in intensity and frequency as the seconds ticked by. Within a minute the sound was identifiable, intimately familiar to three of the men who had served their adopted country in the jungles of Southeast Asia.

The craft descending from the darkness, however, was similar to the Bell Aircraft Hueys of Vietnam fame only in function, and that little more than partially. It was long and squat, with thick, stubby wings coming from each side below the main rotor shaft. From each wing there were suspended pontoonlike objects that gave the aircraft a wide, menacing appearance. And from the front there protruded a long tubular device that, if this were a mongrel insect of some kind, would be seen as a potent stinging weapon.

But the weapons with which the MH-60K Pave Hawk was fitted were not of the mechanical, thunderous kind that would strike a foe from afar. Its weapons were of the quiet variety, like nocturnal hunters, whose approach was swift and silent, but whose strike was violent and precise.

Delta had arrived.

"Bux, check out the security, then form the squad up," Major Sean Graber directed, pointing to the Humvee with its rack lights blazing. He followed the eight men of Charlie Squad, his old unit, out of the Pave Hawk, which lifted off immediately and headed for an out-of-the-way hangar in another area of the Cape.

Graber peeled off from the line of Delta troopers and trotted over to the six men, his charges until the appointed hour of their delivery. They were dressed like any suburbanite middle-aged men out for a weekend visit to a distant relative, faces somber and impatience the dominant trait in their demeanor.

"Gentlemen, I'm Major Sean Graber, United States Army." Sean stood there momentarily, waiting for a response to his presence, or a question, or anything, but the disinterest he had detected while approaching continued. "Which one of you is Mr. Alvarez?"

José-Ramon Alvarez shifted his rotund frame slightly. "I am President Alvarez, Major."

Well, that's the game then. "Sir, I have been instructed to have my men escort you to your country at the time the situation permits it. I am *not*, sir, allowed or required to offer any official representation of my government concerning your status. Once you reach your destination and assume the duties that will be bestowed upon you per the agreement, then I will treat you as a head of state. Until then, sir, I and my men will afford you the utmost respect . . . no less, no more."

The future leader of the nation of Cuba eyed the soldier who towered over him. He held his rifle casually one-handed at his side. Equipment pouches hung from his webbing, as did a helmet not of standard issue to infantry soldiers. This man was special.

"What are you?" the executive secretary of the Cuban Freedom Society asked, acquiescing to the fact that he would not be referred to as "president" by this man.

"An American soldier, sir," Sean responded.

From behind, the others of his kind approached. They formed a loose half-circle behind Delta's XO.

"Security's set, Maj," Buxton reported.

"Mr. Alvarez, gentlemen, let me introduce you to the team that will escort you in." Sean stepped to the side. "Captain Chris Buxton is the squad leader. Next is Lieutenant Michael Antonelli." The CFS men looked with some awe at the huge blond Italian officer. "Sergeant Chuck Makowski. Sergeant Jerry Jones. Sergeant Bruce Goldfarb. Sergeant William Lewis. Sergeant Tony Quimpo. Sergeant Alfred Vincent." The major moved back to the center. "These men are all highly qualified to protect you as you return to your country."

Alvarez looked over the men. Two were black, Jones and Vincent. One, Quimpo, was Asian, probably Filipino. The rest were Caucasian. "Tell me, Major, do you think it wise to provide escorts who cannot even speak the language of my people?"

The major looked over his shoulder to Antonelli. "Miguel."

"Estoy a sus ordenes," the lieutenant said. *"Con muchisimo gusto."*

Alvarez scoffed at the display with a snicker. "Very *proper* Spanish, but very simple."

Graber smiled, his head bowing momentarily as he rubbed the bridge of his nose. "We all have adequate language skills, and, with any luck, we won't need to use them. Survival and escape, you know. But this shouldn't be all that difficult, Mr. Alvarez, so I'm certain you will let us know if we misinterpret anything."

The man said nothing in response to the mild jab. "Of course." An electronic ringing interrupted the conversation, then a pocket-sized phone was passed to Alvarez from one of the others. "If you will excuse me, I have business to attend to with my cabinet."

Sean nodded, holding his words as the six men walked away.

"It's always a pleasure to watch over folks like that," Buxton commented.

"Real down-homers," Jones added.

"Well, we won't be getting locked into any long conversations with them," Sean pointed out. "All right, we make the best of this. Chris, set up a schedule. Twelve and twelve."

"Yes, sir."

Major Sean Graber stood alone for a moment after the squad dispersed to be put into guard shifts by their leader. *I get shot at so we can baby-sit these boneheads.* It didn't always make sense, but then it didn't have to. There were orders to follow, and even the distasteful ones had to be carried out as if they were of the highest urgency. It was the mark of the professional.

"Thule, Fylingdales, and Clear all registered the cessation of signals from the Russian radar-warning system," Bud told the President, referring to the three American BMEWS sites in Greenland, Great Britain, and Alaska respectively. They were in the privacy of the Oval Office, enjoying a relaxed late dinner. "Finally it's here."

"Your hard work, Bud," the President said honestly. His expression changed after the compliment. "What about the sub?"

"No word," the NSA said. "The Navy is starting an air search as we speak. The Coast Guard is going to help, also. Two attack boats will be on station in a few hours. The problem is—"

"I know," the President said, letting out a worried, exasperated breath. "They just disappear and go where they want."

"Within a patrol area," Bud added. "A very big area. This one was Mid-Atlantic."

"Don't our subs have some kind of emergency locator?" the President inquired. He poured himself a final cup of coffee—his personal physician would have had a fit at the number he'd had already this day—and finally undid his tie. Bud was still in a jacket.

"Emergency buoys, yes. They're set to release at the captain's command, or if the sub exceeds crush depth. There are a whole bunch of things that could prevent that, but no way to know until we locate her."

"How many men on board?"

"A hundred and sixty," Bud answered. "Men and women, sir."

The President knew his feelings shouldn't distinguish between women and men in a situation like this, but, politically correct or not, he did. "I hope this is just some major communications screwup. God, hope so."

"Everyone does, sir," Bud observed. Going down in a sub had to be the worst way to go, he thought. But that was worst-case. There was still time, he tried to convince himself. By the look on the chief executive's face, he was having as much success at that as his NSA.

The phone buzzed, and the President snatched it up. "Yes. Come on over, Anthony." He hung up. "He's over in Ellis's office."

The chief of staff's office was just down the hallway. It wouldn't be long. So much for a relaxing evening, Bud thought.

The DCI walked into the Oval Office with a gait propelled by whatever sense of enthusiasm the refined Merriweather allowed himself. "Mr. President, we have new images from a pass over the island. The Cubans are in full retreat."

The pleasure was overflowing from the DCI, and the same emotion soon spread to the President, almost wiping away the less pleasing contemplation of a minute before. If the prediction was correct, he would be the first chief executive in almost forty years to set foot in the free nation of Cuba. Bud had to go along with the sentiment also, despite his misgivings. Success was success, and the naysayers who Monday-morning-quarterbacked were taken about as seriously as congressional spending limits. Credit due was credit due.

"Your idea changed the world," the NSA said to the DCI.

Merriweather accepted the token congratulation politely. "Another wall down."

"Wall, my ass," the President said, beaming. "We just busted down our bitchy neighbor's fence!"

Bud just took in the exchange between the President and the DCI for a moment. Surprises still lay ahead, but informing his boss of that reality would be fruitless right now. They would have to be dealt with soon enough. The real surprise, though, had been just how easily the government had fallen. Really, he had expected more. Some sort of parting shot. They had had intelli-

gence for years that Castro had intended to attack such targets as
the Turkey Point Nuclear Plant in Florida if ever he was threat-
ened. But, then again, attack with what? His air force was gone,
knocked out in the first hours. The survivors of that had hightailed it to the southern United States as soon as they could get
airborne. The "Saddam Maneuver," it was being called by the Air
Force pilots sent to intercept and escort the Cuban MiGs to selected airfields along the Gulf Coast. "Fly to your nearest enemy."
At least that had been anticipated.

Still, that Castro went out with a whimper confounded Bud.
It would certainly be researched and written about by the think-
tank literati and doctoral candidates alike for years to come. Bud
figured it proved that no man could be cut out in historical terms
and fit into a neatly selected hole in the puzzle of his life. Existence was not only transitory, it was without a rudder. Currents
pushed one to where the water flowed. Somehow they had
avoided being drawn onto the rocks with the likes of Fidel Castro,
a half reality that the landlubbing NSA had lapsed into, forgetting
about the reefs that were more dangerous, and quite elusive,
lurking just below the calm surface waters.

To free a people. To rule a land. To watch it all slip away.

Fidel Castro was in the unique position of having traveled
from the valley to the mountain peak, only to be sent tumbling
down the slope by treacherous footing. The work of a lifetime was
coming to naught.

Strangely, though, he could accept that it was coming to pass.
The fates were proving to be against him, just as they were during
the assault on the *Moncada* barracks before the final push that
had begun the Revolution. That attack had failed also, and he
had spent time imprisoned at the hands of the corrupt government. Yet he had emerged from that to strike again. It was not a
death knell. From that he had learned that setbacks would happen, as would outright defeats. And from those events the defin-
ing legacy was not that a man or an idea had failed, but rather that
a man and an idea had persevered.

Sitting alone as he was in his library two floors above the
below-ground command center where the dismantling of his nation was being fought by old men, Fidel Castro drifted back to the
days of youth that had formed his character. The deprivation he
suffered even though the son of a well-off landowner. The Jesuit

education that had instilled in him more doubt about God than a belief in one. His sister and brother. A wife. Baseball.

All paled, though, in comparison to the Revolution. It was supreme over all, and it would be until his last breath was expended. To say more of it would be to distort its simplicity, which was the essence of its perfection. What did the Dumas characters say? *One for all, all for one.* Meaning could be found in the strangest places.

And so it would come to some conclusion. A failure it was certain to be, and in that he found a sense of peace. Failure, the feared consequence of a strategy gone wrong, would breed defiance, as it had already in him. To lose was not dishonorable, for it painted clearly those responsible for both victory and defeat. Sometimes the parties were one and the same. Other times, as in this case, the architect of defeat was an entity removed from the immediate fray but no less culpable. And, fortunately, as the weapons of war were expended in forestalling the inevitable, some sense of retribution could be brought against those who had deserved such for a very, very, very long time.

With that knowledge, and with a plan rich in irony, Fidel Castro could sleep peacefully, content that the Revolution would be avenged against those who had been the source of its undoing.

Chapter Seven

Skeletons

The sign on the door said "Interview Room," a departure from the term "interrogation" that had fallen out of favor with law enforcement agencies recently. The reality and the bullshit of political correctness, Art thought, closing the door as he left the room, leaving Sullivan alone with a pot of coffee. He was sober now, which was a blessing and a curse. It made him more lucid, but it also turned the expectedly frightened drunk they had come upon into a mildly arrogant combination of bloodshot eyes and a smart mouth. Art was glad Frankie had been elsewhere checking on the license number and keeping an eye on Mrs. Carroll, who was patiently describing the suspects to a Bureau computer artist. Aguirre would have wanted to slap the guy.

Art went straight to the communications room, which was the size of a large closet. In it were the regular fax machines for communications with nongovernmental agencies, high-speed color facsimile machines connected to secure lines that were routed through the government's new Secure Voice Communications switching centers, and teleprinters that spit out continuous reports from law-enforcement agencies throughout the country and overseas.

"Here you go, Agent Jefferson," the com clerk said, handing over the faxes from State and INS. They had arrived almost simultaneously.

His eyes read down the reports as he walked back toward his desk. Frankie was at hers, just hanging up the phone.

"How's Sullivan?" she asked.

"He makes a better drunk than he does a human being." Art laid the faxes on his desk and leaned back against the divider wall. "Anything on the car?"

Frankie nodded. "These guys are pros, Art. We ran the plate, came up with an address, and checked it out. Nice blue Lumina parked right in the driveway with—guess what?—no plates. LAPD set up a perimeter and called the residents out on the P.A. Not our suspects, if you haven't guessed already. Just some bewildered guy and his girlfriend wondering why the cops had their guns on them. Hell of a way to spend his day off. And he was just as surprised to learn that his plates were gone."

"Did Mrs. Carroll take a look at the car book?"

"Pointed right to the Lumina," Frankie confirmed.

"Smart," Art commented. "They get a car—rented or stolen—then get plates from a lookalike car and ditch the others. How many people would notice their license plates missing?"

"Cops wouldn't be too concerned, either," Frankie added. "The car was new. The guy said he bought it two months ago. No plates is pretty normal under those circumstances."

It was a clean move, Art thought, agreeing with Frankie's belief that the suspects were real pros. And pros didn't like to leave jobs unfinished. "Our jerk in there might still be in danger, you know."

A loud, forceful breath escaped from Frankie's lungs. She was tired, the lack of sleep from the night before catching up with her. It had been a thirteen-hour day already. "Anything useful from him?"

"Nothing Bill didn't already fill us in on. I think Bill cut him loose. I was in the room when he called in. Hey, tough decision, but we both saw . . . the guy is a basket case when he's lubed up."

"Guess so." Frankie gestured to the faxes. "Anything?"

Art handed them over. "INS has diddly. Just the standard stuff when he came over, except he didn't request any help from the exile community. That's kind of strange. Most of them coming over do. He did request a meeting with a representative of the government, though."

"Doesn't say here whether he got one or not," Frankie noted.

"We'll check on that later. I hear a lot of asylum seekers try and offer something for sale, and Portero at least had the background to know something."

"The tape, maybe," Frankie said.

"Yeah. Maybe he was going to the paper with it because he couldn't get anyone in the government to hear him out." That was worth looking into further. "Sullivan said that Portero kept insisting he had something terrible to share, something that could affect millions, he said."

Frankie looked to the State Department fax. "He wasn't lying to Bill, either."

"Nope," Art said, looking down the hallway to ensure that the door to the interview room was still shut. "Portero apparently was an assistant to Castro's interpreter back in the early sixties. Russian language, it says."

"A really busy time back then," Frankie said, no real memories of the crisis in her consciousness. She had been in diapers then.

"My senior year in high school had just started." Art looked away, remembering the time. "My grandma was worried to death. Hell, no one knew if we'd wake up the next day. Scary time, Frankie. Busy doesn't do it justice."

"Anyway," Art went on. "State says they'll try some other avenues tomorrow to get the proper classification of Portero."

"Like what?"

Art smiled knowingly. "Once you've been through these hoops as many times as I have, you'll learn that the term 'share and share alike' means little in government. Every agency and department has their own way of doing things, and their own sources of information. They'll probably ask a liaison officer to 'pull a favor.' Happens all the time."

Frankie's head shook at the stupid bureaucracy, then yawned deeply, her arms stretching out and up. "Man, I am beat."

Art looked at the wall clock. "You want to knock off? I can set Sullivan up with a sitter and get him bedded down." As a material witness, one who saw the shooters pull the trigger, George Sullivan was a valuable witness. He was also a person the suspects obviously had an interest in, most likely because they thought he had something which they wanted. Something they had proved they were willing to kill for. For these reasons he would now be under Bureau protection, tucked away under constant guard.

Not really, but . . . "I think Cassie might want to see her mommy before she turns eight. You mind?" Cassandra was the jewel of Frankie's life, the beautiful product of a marriage that had ended when her ex took to loving the bottle more than her.

Art's phone rang before he could answer. "Jefferson."

"Art, Dan. We have your tape ready, but there's a problem."

"Yeah?"

"It's in Spanish and another language, sounds like Russian or something. We don't have any Russian speakers at all, and my lone Spanish speaker left with the nine-to-fivers. Is Aguirre still here?"

Art pulled the phone away, pressing it into his chest. "Sorry, Frankie. Your genes are needed."

She looked at her partner with a funny expression. *"Jeans?"*

"I'll explain on the way down." He brought the phone back up. "We'll be there in a minute."

The agents gathered their notebooks and headed not for the elevator, but for the interview room.

"You doing okay in here?" Art asked, poking his head in.

Sullivan pulled the hands away from his puffy face. His hair, a mass of thinning brown strands, was tousled and matted by sweat. What green there had been in his eyes was overcome by the fine rivers and tributaries of red that had subsided somewhat from earlier. "Wonderful." *How would you feel if you'd lost your job and had guys out to kill you?*

"Good. Stay here, we have to check something out downstairs." Art gave the man as comforting a smile as his humanity would allow. "We'll get you to a nice, safe place in just a while." He saw Sullivan nod with little interest and pulled the door shut.

"He's feeling pretty low," Art said, turning for the elevators, his partner alongside.

"At least he's alive," Frankie offered. "If he weren't such a lush, he might have been on time for his meeting with Portero."

"You calling it a redeeming quality?" Art asked, looking with some shock to his partner, the same one who had kicked her alcoholic husband out of the house and her life two years before, having had enough of his shit. "That's mighty generous of you."

"Not really," Aguirre responded, the subject bringing an unpleasant past to her mind again. " 'Cause he'd never admit that his problem saved his life. He doesn't have a problem, remember."

Art pushed the glowing "down" arrow at the twin elevators. "They never do, partner. Never do."

Sullivan's eyes were fixed on the off-white wallpaper as his hosts left, trying to pick out the tiniest specks of discoloration. The exercise hurt his already throbbing eyes tremendously, but he had to focus on something. Something to occupy his mind. Just anything that would not allow the thoughts to get in, just to keep them out. Out. Out! Out! *OUT!*

His fist balled up tight and came down on the table hard. The impact sent his Styrofoam cup of coffee tumbling to the floor.

"Dammit," he whimpered softly, asking whatever supreme being there was just why these things had happened to him. *Why me?* It was a question he found himself asking more frequently these days, usually when he was . . .

No, that's not it. That's not it. If *other* people couldn't handle their booze, too bad, but there was nothing wrong with his drinking. It was just something he enjoyed, something he had done for so long that it seemed second nature, something he . . . *needed?*

No! NO! What the hell did Sturgess know anyway? He was just like that Fields asshole in New York. *"You need help, George."* What a line! It was easy to cast stones at others when you had your own problems. That was the real thing behind this, he knew. *They* needed a punching bag, someone to throw their shit at. A convenient target. Why not George? It was that simple and that clear.

Well, he could show them. He could prove that what they thought was a problem had no bearing on his life. It was just a . . . a thing. A thing he did, like lots of people. Right. If they thought he couldn't do his job, then he'd just prove to them he could do it better than anybody.

Sullivan stood quickly from the table, putting his blazer on and eyeing the coffeemaker with disgust. He opened the door and stepped into the hall. There was no one around. He didn't know why until the time on the wall clock caught his attention. *That late?* No wonder there was no one there. He walked slowly to the elevator, aware that he really wasn't supposed to leave, but what could they do—*make* him stay?

He walked out the front of the building into stuffy air of early evening, walking down the block with a crowd before a cab came into view. Hailing a taxi in L.A. was nowhere near as easy as doing so in New York. Sullivan slid into the backseat.

"Where to?"

He thought for a moment. There was a lot to do. So much. He had to get started, but he really needed . . . wanted to relax first. "Freddy's up on Sunset."

"That a bar, fella?"

For some reason Sullivan couldn't bring himself to answer. He simply nodded to the cabbie in the rearview mirror.

"Just hang back," Jorge instructed, instinctively looking over his left shoulder as Tomás pulled into traffic.

"We should have taken him when he came out." Tomás stepped on the accelerator hard, cutting in front of a stretch black limo that looked so out of place, it wasn't even funny.

"In front of the FBI? Good plan, Sherlock."

Fuck you, Tomás thought, as he kept their blue Chevy Lumina a half-block back from the bright yellow cab.

"I was surprised they saved it all," Dan Jacobs admitted. "Usually don't get it all."

He dropped the cassette into a sophisticated triple Record/ Play deck in the TS lab. He, Art, and Frankie were alone in the room, which was packed with millions of dollars' worth of equipment, enough to give a professional sound engineer wet dreams.

"I thought you were into bullets and tire prints, Dan," Art said with intended good humor. "Not this high-tech stuff."

"Yeah, well, I always wanted to be a rock star. Never told you that, huh?" Jacobs plugged a trio of headsets, each with one earphone, into a splitter jack on the unit. "While I was in college and working, I used to play in a band."

"No shit," Art exclaimed, putting on the headset and trying to picture the straight-laced forensics agent as a long-haired musician.

Jacobs laughed, a little embarrassed. "Yeah. Good old CCR and Doors kind of stuff. We mostly played frat parties, and we weren't very good. But"—he let out a wistful breath—"I got into recording gear. This stuff, right here, is my passionate closet hobby. My wife loves me when I crank it up."

Art couldn't believe it. It reinforced his belief that it was damn near impossible to paint someone with a broad brush, because you inevitably missed some of the more porous areas of their character.

"We're set," Jacobs announced. "Frankie, I'm going to have you speak into this microphone. It's hooked up to this second deck. That way we'll have a preliminary translation on tape. We can get a real detailed one tomorrow."

"I'm ready, but remember I was raised with barrio Spanish, so this may be rough."

"Confidence in you, partner." Art took out his notebook and pen. "Hit it, Dan."

There were a few seconds of alternating static and silence before the meat of the tape began. Frankie translated the words as they were spoken.

"The date is October twenty-eighth, 1962. Tape one, reel one, Alejandro Cortez is the . . . the interpreter."

There was an obvious stop in the recording after the verbal date stamp, a common practice in official recordings.

"Portero was Cortez's assistant," Art told Jacobs, recalling the fax from State.

"Good evening, Premier Khrushchev." Frankie's eyes went wide, a second voice converting the words into another language—Russian, she thought. A response in Russian came quickly.

"Good evening, nothing! You are a thief, Castro! A thief!"

There was laughing from the Spanish speaker, the one referred to as . . . Castro? *"You spoke to my brother, I gather. A thief, you call me? Then I shall call you a coward. You let the Americans walk all over you. You come here—"*

"You cannot—"

"No! You will listen to me, Premier Khrushchev! I have heard enough of your boasts, and your promises, and your lies." Frankie could imagine him gesturing grandly. *"You came here to thumb your nose at the Americans, and as soon as that pig Kennedy stands up to you, you crumble. Like a brittle piece of glass. The smallest amount of pressure made you break."*

"You have no right to challenge the Union of Soviet Socialist Republics this way! No right on this earth!"

"I have every right, just as every person in my country has a right to expect protection when it has been promised. Promised by you. By YOU!"

"This will not be tolerated, Castro. You cannot expect to come away from this with what you have taken, or with your life."

"Then take it back. Come take your precious missile back!"

"What!" Art said aloud, his eyes finding those of the other two agents. They were as huge as his.

"I am waiting, Premier Khrushchev. I am waiting. . . . Come take it. Let the world see that not only can the United States of America make you bow, but let them see that a small country—an ally, no less—can make you kneel. Let the world see this."

There was a long pause, time enough for the agents' imaginations to shift into high gear. The scenarios envisioned were all equally frightening.

"President Castro—"

"Do not think that because you suddenly use my title that you can stroke me like a lover. No, no, no."

"What do you want? What will make you return our property?"

"It is no longer your property. It is ours. It will remain ours."

"You cannot keep it. I cannot—"

"You can, and you will have to. It is all very easy to explain to your government, Premier Khrushchev. When my soldiers captured the missile, they killed all the crew, and the security troops, of course. Tragic, yes, but necessary. And there was a devastating explosion of the fueling trucks very soon after. It consumed everything. You see, Premier Khrushchev, there is nothing to send back. It is very convenient for you. I will obviously not reveal anything. The only reason anyone would ever know of our acquisition would be if I must use the weapon to defend the Revolution."

"But . . . But . . . President Castro, it is an atomic weapon. How can I . . ."

"You have no choice. None. If you go to war over this, you will lose. How will your other allies see their benevolent protector if you crush a small country such as my own? You know what they will do. You will have revolt along your borders. Is it worth this, Premier Khrushchev? Is it?"

"I must . . ."

"Your Politburo will not understand. This secret is yours, and it is mine."

"It will remain as such?"

"It will. We can even send you the bodies of your soldiers who died so tragically. They can be transported from La Isabela with their associated units. A fine funeral for the heroes will placate your Politburo."

"No. No. There must be no hint of bodies. I suggest that they were consumed in the fire. Dispose of them as you wish."

"They were soldiers, following orders. They will receive a fine burial."

Again there was silence on the tape, but none of the agents spoke. What was there to say, other than a few choice expletives that could scarcely express the gravity of what they had just heard?

"Yes, I hope that they . . . that they will. I hope that . . ."

"It is done, then, Premier Khrushchev. Done."

"Yes. Yes. It must be."

"It is. Good-bye."

The sound of the connection being broken clicked loudly.

"Lock the tape away, Alejandro. The good premier is not to be trusted. His memory of what transpired here may need to be refreshed someday."

"Yes, Presidente."

A shift from static to total nothingness signaled the end of the recording. Jacobs slid his headset off and stopped both tape decks, hitting the Rewind button next. Frankie and Art pulled theirs off a second later.

"Oh, my God," Frankie said, summing up the collective feelings completely.

"Can this really be true?" Jacobs asked, wondering just who could answer the question.

"I don't know," Art answered, afraid to be more certain. "I've heard early tapes of Castro's speeches. That sounded like him."

Frankie's eyes narrowed, her head swinging slowly from side to side. "But how could that be . . . I mean, if it is true, then there could still be . . ."

"I know." Art shifted his thoughts from the past to the present, not wanting to deal with the future quite yet. "This puts a more sinister spin on the shooters who hit Portero. You may have been right before—they could be working for the Cubans. There certainly is a motive for the silencing aspect of this now."

"Jesus." Frankie had never wanted to get into the counterintelligence stuff the Bureau had to deal with, but now an uglier side of it appeared to be rearing up right in front of her. "If so, then Sullivan could be in more danger than we thought. Much more."

There was no hesitation in Art's response. "Get downstairs and sit with him. Now! Don't let him out of your sight. They've already proved they'll kill for this. Go!"

Frankie needed no more prompting. She was out of the TS lab and hitting the stairs a few seconds later.

"Dan, you say nothing of this. Clear?"

"Hey, who the hell would believe me?" He popped the two cassettes from their respective machines. "Do you want copies?"

"Yeah. Two of each."

"All right. There'll be a little degradation, remember. That recording is at least a second-generation copy made from the original reel tapes."

"Okay. Okay." Art was thinking fast, trying to plot the proper avenues of action in his head before setting anything in motion. It was quite a foreign manner of operation for him in this type of situation. "I've got to get in touch with the director. This has to go to him."

Dan knew that the special agent in charge, William Killeen, was not keen on having street agents go over his head. "What about Bill?"

"Remember the SAC conference." The Bureau's SACs were gathering at the academy in Quantico, Virginia, for a so-called budget summit. Everybody was feeling the heat. "You think this can wait with what's going on down there?"

"Not my call." Jacobs thought for a moment. "What about Lou? He's in town."

Step by step, Art. "You're right."

"He can give you the go over the phone. He'd have to."

Shit! "No, that won't work. This has got to go over a secure line. He doesn't have one." Lou Hidalgo, Art's boss's boss, lived in Mission Viejo, a good hour away. Too far. Too long to wait. "I've got to do this."

"Like I said, your call," Jacobs cautioned.

Frankie burst through the door to the lab. "He's gone!"

"Gone?" Art stood quickly. "To fucking where?"

"Don't know," Frankie answered, her breaths coming fast and hard. "The lobby guard said he saw him leave about ten ago."

Dammit! "I knew I shouldn't have left him." The senior agent let the rush pass, measuring his breathing, just as he was supposed to do. *You idiot, Jefferson!* "Okay, get a bulletin out. I want a protective warrant issued for Sullivan." He paused again, straining to regain his composure, knowing he would need it when talking to the man who had authorized his de facto demotion a year before for pushing limits that he shouldn't have.

Art Jefferson knew this could be construed as similar behavior, but he didn't really give a damn at the moment. He was doing what he had to . . . his job.

*　　*　　*

"There is a problem."

General Asunción studied the Russian's expression. "What problem? It will not work?"

Anatoly Vishkov shook his head. "It will work, but you can not carry out a complete fueling of the booster." He pointed to the series of valves and gauges that were connected to the underground storage tanks for the fuel and oxidizer three hundred meters distant. "There is contamination in the tanks."

"What!" It was not a question, for no answer would truly be acceptable. "How?"

Vishkov wiped his hands on a rag, rubbing it nervously. "Water, I believe. But there is more. I will show you."

Asunción followed the physicist to the mass of gauges and flow meters that would allow the weapon to be fueled.

"The fuel gauge indicates one hundred and eight thousand kilograms of propellant. Here, see?"

"I see. What of it?"

"There are only supposed to be an even one hundred thousand kilos of UDMH," Vishkov reported, referring to the undimensional dimethyl hydrazine. "A similar reading comes from the NTO tank." That contained the oxidizer, nitrogen tetroxide. "I suspect that rains of a week ago infiltrated through a rupture in the upper portion of the tanks."

"So the water makes the fuel useless?" the general asked disgustedly.

"Not the water, so much, as the soil residue that was sure to seep in also." Vishkov tossed the rag onto the tree of silver pipes and valves. "Filters and traps will remove the water and residue, but the soils here are high in nitrates. It is a process of the swamps to the east and natural fertilization. There was certainly a nitrate infiltration, which can upset the balance of the oxidizer to the fuel. We cannot know how much the ratio has been altered, so fueling the booster would contaminate the internal tanks." He paused, thinking on the increasing sounds of explosions. "Any attempt to actually fire it would likely fail."

The general turned away, taking a few steps toward the weapon that had become his life, his friend, and now his nemesis. "What can we do?"

"We need fresh fuel and oxidizer," he said to Asunción's back, cursing the stupid decision he had made to not use the storable liquid propellants as they were intended, leaving them in the booster tanks for long periods. But that still would have required occasional draining and flushing, a process made difficult by the lack of trained personnel. No, this had been the right decision, to store them away from the missile, but now the problems associated with his prudence would require remedying. "We will have to pump directly from any trucks that bring them."

Asunción looked to his right and nodded to his assistant, signaling that the Russian's suggestion should be carried out. To secure the needed materials in this situation would be a tremendous undertaking, but it would have to be done. The refinery at Los Guaos would have to come through. "But the other systems are ready?"

"Awaiting only a target," Vishkov said, letting his suspicions surface for the first time.

The Cuban turned quickly back, signaling with a toss of his thumb to get the Russian back to his maximum-security villa at Castillo de Jagua. He would enjoy his life there for but a few more hours, then that would end. *One death plus a million,* Asunción thought, looking at the tower of destruction standing before him and wondering what deserving population center would be the recipient of it.

Chapter Eight

Whispers

Jorge picked the phone up on the first ring. "Yes."

"Why did you page me?"

Tomás noticed the discomfort on his partner's face. Lights from passing cars were distorted as they filtered through the phone booth's cheap glass, casting unflattering shadows on his already scarred face.

"We have the reporter in sight. He's in a bar in—"

"What the hell are you doing anywhere near him? Why is he still alive? His house, what did you find?"

The questions came rapid-fire, leaving Jorge little time to flower his answers. "There was nothing at his house; we turned it upside down. For some reason he was at the cops—"

"The *WHAT*!!!"

Tomás heard the shout from where he stood, the traffic noise not sufficient to drown out the sound from three thousand miles away. He was glad it was Jorge having to deal with their contact, much preferring the task of watching the bar's front door down the street.

"Look, I don't know what's going on, okay? Our source at the paper told us the cops had him," Jorge explained, careful not to mention the FBI. It would only make their contact more volatile. "So we staked it out and waited. At least he turned up, so we can find out once and for all from him if he has the tape."

"If he had the tape, then the police would have it now, you dumb fuck!"

"Hey!" Jorge turned away from the booth's opening, looking downward. "You want to come out here and clean this up? We aren't idiots, man. Do you think the cops would have let him walk out of there if he gave them the tape? He's a reporter, man. They've got that fucked-up code of ethics and shit. Never reveal a source or anything. They like talking to cops about as much as I do."

"All right. All right. Just find out if the guy has it."

"No problem. When he leaves the bar, we're gonna take him."

"Do it right. Where are you staying? The location?"

"Why do you want that? You're not supposed t—"

"Don't fucking question me! I'm sending someone out to get the tape you *do* have. Understand?"

Asshole. Jorge reached into his coat pocket and pulled out the motel key, reading off the address and room number from the tab. "We switched places this morning. Anything else?"

"Don't page me anymore unless it's important." The line went dead.

Jorge stepped from the booth and sat on the car hood, rolling his neck three full times. "They don't pay us enough, man."

"Your blood boils too easy, Jorge. Relax." Tomás checked the bar's front again. "This guy ain't got nothing. We pop him, then it's done with."

"We make sure he's got nothing," Jorge corrected. It was a job, after all, and he'd never blown one yet.

"Then we pop him," Tomás reiterated, hoping for a clean end to it all.

"Whatever."

Testra pulled one earphone off and set the Italian sub down on its paper wrapper. "Did that sound like a setup to you?"

"Yep," Sanz answered, his reply distorted by the mouthful of meatball sandwich. He paged through the phone-activity record they'd received from the phone company, then swallowed. "A good number of calls to L.A. numbers, especially lately." He looked at the recipient codes, which showed only the type of station called—residence, business, public phone, or cellular. To find out any more, they would need additional warrants. "All phone booths. That's funny—the only ones not to phone booths are the ones to Panama."

Testra was looking at his copy of the records. It was as if their subject was operating some kind of switchboard. "They paged him, huh? Clean. These guys he's dealing with send the phone-booth number to him by pager, then he calls them back. Smooth." He flipped through the activity log to earlier dates. "Lots to L.A. lately. Some Miami. A lot in D.C., too. All phone booths."

Sanz recalled the conversation just heard. "Reporter. A set-up." He shook his head. "We come looking for espionage, and what do we find? The same old shit." Drug hit, he thought. Co-seros was mixed up in enough of that to spill over this way. His and his partners' work on the Coseros case had gotten them onto this one, with the anticipation that the leak and the Panamanian were connected. Slime was everywhere, he figured.

"Smoking gun, but not what we're looking for," Testra said.

The agents, both Bureau veterans, knew they had just heard a murder being planned.

"Well, if this goes nowhere else, at least we can pop him on conspiracy to commit murder."

"Yeah, but until then, what do we do with this?" Their wire-tap warrant was issued under a national-security request, effectively sealing everything they heard and recorded from the moment it arrived in room 145.

Sanz thought on that, taking another bite of his dinner. "The same old shit. No variety to this job at all." They couldn't just let a murder in the planning stages, possibly close to being carried out, sit under a federal seal. "We gotta go to the SAC."

"Can't," Testra said. "He's at that get-together in Quantico. Went up a day early."

Their options were limited. The agents, both of whom held Top Secret security clearance from their work on previous cases with national-security aspects, knew they couldn't just call the cops in L.A. and tell them they had a hit about to go down.

"I say it's important enough to send it through the channel," Testra proposed. "The director is supposed to get our stuff directly. Why not this?"

"Fine with me."

"Good." Testra was relieved. The thing would be off his conscience now, but not out of mind. He was too smart a cop to think that. "Hey. Did that name sound familiar to you?"

"What, 'Portero'?" Sanz asked. "Yeah. There's about ten thousand of them on my block."

"Smartass," Testra commented, the name still sticking in his head but not setting off any alarm bells. He went back to his dinner, cursing the extra paperwork this would require, plus the inevitable court appearances if the L.A. cops got the word and nailed the yahoos who were dense enough to do their business over the phone. What they lacked in honor, Testra thought, criminals made up for in predictable stupidity.

"They blew it," the contact said in Spanish.

"How?" The voice on the other end was demanding.

"Some reporter who was cozying up to Portero got picked up by the police. Our guys were supposed to check his house and get rid of him, but they screwed it up."

"Wonderful. And now?"

"They've got the reporter under surveillance. They will verify if he has it this time."

"Good. And them?"

"I said I would send someone for the tape they *did* get off Portero."

"That is a wise move. Of course, there is no reason for them to remain in our employ after that."

"I've arranged it."

"Very good. We must assume that Portero hid the tape then. Somewhere it would not be easily found. Otherwise we would have known by now."

"Right. We would have known, but it's been quiet up North."

"Silence is golden."

The contact smiled and switched off the phone, his temper having subsided after the talk with his employer. *Employer.* That was a different way to think of it, but very professional, and very necessary. They were walking on a very narrow ledge, and he knew it, but things were now going to slow down. Soon he wouldn't have to worry about the idiots on the coast, and they would soon have nothing to worry about either.

*   *   *

"We have more information, Colonel."

Ojeda was sitting on an empty fuel can, slicing pieces of pork jerky with a large knife and sliding them into his mouth. Paredes handed him the report just received over the satellite manpack that was his, and their, link to Langley. The four-page summary of maps and descriptions of unit movements and locations was not of the quality available from the stationary satellite terminals. That they could receive facsimile transmissions at all had been a surprise to the colonel, who had expected only verbal reports. So much the better, Antonio knew. Trust was a two-way street here, and the fact that Langley was giving this the premier treatment had established a sort of invisible chain of respect in which Paredes was the strongest link.

"Something is wrong," Ojeda said matter-of-factly, his jaw moving slowly as it pulverized the hard, spicy meat.

"What is wrong?" Antonio asked, but Ojeda waved off his concern, motioning instead for Captain Manchon to come over. "Look at this."

Manchon studied the report, particularly the description of unit movements. "This makes no sense."

"Colonel, if there is some problem with the intelligence, I can contact my superiors for clarification," Antonio offered.

"No, Papa Tony, the intelligence as presented is adequate." Ojeda swallowed a mouthful of jerky. "It is what it shows."

"Did we underestimate their strength in this area?" Antonio asked, concerned that the level of quality he had worked hard to ensure was somehow suffering.

"No. No." Manchon pointed to the map diagram. "These units are pulling back toward Cienfuegos. It appears they are leaving only a token force to delay us."

"A retreat to the city," the CIA officer said, wondering if the situation was truly that desperate for the loyalist forces.

"No, not to the city," Ojeda corrected him. "They are moving too many men west, to the opposite side of the Bahia de Cienfuegos. The city itself is on the northeast shore of the bay."

Antonio studied the map, matching it to the one Manchon carried at all times. He wasn't a military tactician, but the move, if it was happening, had no logic to it. The positions they appeared to be heading for at Guilermo Moncada, just fifteen miles north of his family's former home at Juragua, were backed against several natural obstacles. The bay was one. To the south and west the swamps of the delta would block any tactical movement. In essence they were backing into a bottleneck.

"Very peculiar, Colonel," the captain commented, a hand rubbing his stubbled chin.

"These are the bulk of the loyalist forces in the center of the country," Paredes observed, checking the report for any other appreciable opposition in the area. There was none. "We have them, Colonel. It is almost over."

"We have always had them, Papa." Ojeda took the map from Manchon. "Captain, is the road between here and Aguada de Pasajeros open?"

"It is ours, sir," the captain reported happily.

Ojeda thought for a moment, more concern on his face than Antonio thought warranted, considering the evidence that victory would soon be theirs. "Captain, I want one battalion to continue the move south toward Cienfuegos. I want them to press hard. Make it Captain Cresada's battalion. The rest of the force we will move west to Aguada de Pasajeros, then swing east to attack from the position we should not be in."

Manchon pondered it for a moment. "It is bold, and it carries risks. Many risks."

Antonio decided to add his own cautionary tone to the analysis. "The battle is yours, Colonel Ojeda. The war is almost won. To risk delaying the outcome, is that necessary?"

Ojeda took the concerns not as an insult to his leadership or tactical decisions, but as questions from those not versed as he in the rigidity and predictability of the comrade commanders he now faced in battle. "Their moves are not logical, nor are they smart. They are not by the book." He saw Manchon nod slightly. "That worries me. Papa Tony, when is a wounded animal most dangerous?"

"When it is cornered, of course." Antonio still didn't grasp the totality of the colonel's thought.

"Correct." Ojeda slid the knife into its sheath on his belt and stood, pulling his green fatigue cap on. "Unless it is a possum playing dead."

It was now clear to the CIA officer. "I understand."

"Good. Now it is time to kill this beast before it wakes from its false slumber."

*   *   *

He rated a nonassigned space in the employee lot on the north side of Langley's two-hundred-acre complex. That was rarely a problem, as the hour he arrived at work was long past the time when the rest of the Agency's workforce had left for their suburban Maryland and Virginia homes. Those nice, big brick things that he had driven past many times and dreamed. Just dreamed. Fifteen years, and he still could only dream.

And he worked like a dog. But that wasn't good enough. No. They had to move him to the graveyard shift to fill the space that some longtimer had retired from to spend his time with some stupid powerboat he always crooned about. Now he couldn't even spend the night with his wife. Twelve years of marriage, and he had to spend it away from her. That wasn't right. They didn't even *ask* him if he wanted to change shifts. No. Just did it. And still for the same damn money thanks to the damn shift differential being yanked because of the budget mess. Wonderful. They spend their money like idiots, and *who* has to pay?

But that was just the reality of it. Only the big shots got the frosting on the cake. Not the real workers. His head shook with disgust enough for ten men.

So, he had sought his own renumeration for the years he had been underpaid and the recent times when he had gotten the shaft. *He* was now a big shot. What he did mattered to someone, and that someone was willing to pay for it. Just another way to reap the benefits of government service, he thought, pushing his hands deep in his coat pockets as he walked through the chilly night air toward the workers' entrance.

His name was Sam Garrity. He was, in simple terms, a spy. He was also a janitor.

The laughability of it all was enough to make him smile wide as he passed through the first security checkpoint on his way to the seventh floor.

CHAPTER NINE

Parry and Thrust

"You're going over when, Thursday next week?" Bud asked.

"Leaving late Wednesday," Secretary of State James Coventry answered. He lifted his briefcase onto the coffee table in the NSA's office and opened it. Pieces of furniture meant for more congenial purposes had been warped into usage as map tables, surrogate desks during crises, and, most commonly, as feeding troughs for the assorted visiting nondignitaries. Bud's dark cherry model was piled with stacks of briefing and position papers on the proposed retargeting agreements. "Here," Coventry said, unloading another stack for the wide-eyed NSA.

"Thanks," Bud said, running his hand over his head to the back of his neck, where he pressed tightly on the muscles. A quick neck rotation completed the attempt at relief.

"This is everything I have on the British side of this. There's some interesting stuff going back to parliamentary discussions about the initial Polaris deployment." Coventry was well known for his level of preparedness, a process he seemingly accomplished with ease. Bud knew better. The man worked his ass off, rarely relying solely on his staff to research important matters. As such, he expected that everyone else would be as prepared. It was motivating, and, at times, maddening.

"You want me to look it over?" It was an unnecessary question, Bud knew. But at least he could hope.

"If you could. Let me know if there's anything you think should be—"

The NSA's phone buzzed. He stood from the small couch and went around the desk, sitting before picking it up. "DiContino."

"Bud, it's Gordy. I've got a call you better take." FBI Director Gordon Jones sounded out of breath.

"Sure. What is it?"

"One of my agents in Los Angeles has something you had better hear. His name's Art Jefferson."

Jefferson. Yeah. Bud remembered from the debriefing conferences after the Flight 422 hijacking. He was the guy in L.A. who found the person who helped the assassins and . . . Had a heart attack after his partner was shot. Went back to street duty. Supposed to be a pit bull when it came to investigations. "Yeah, I remember him." Bud checked his watch. It was already after ten on the East Coast, nearing the end of another nineteen-hour day. "Urgent?"

"I'm afraid so, Bud." Jones went very quiet. "We may have big trouble in Cuba."

Cuba? Bud looked at the phone. The call had come in on a secure line. "What the hell is going on?"

Coventry perked up and was waved over by Bud. The NSA reached into his desk drawer and retrieved a plug-in headset for the phone. He attached it and handed it to the secretary.

"Jefferson's on another line. I'm going to put him through."

"Okay. I've got Jim Coventry here on the extension."

"What's up?" Coventry asked.

Cuba, Bud mouthed, for which he got an appropriate *Oh, shit* in response.

"Hello?"

"Jefferson? This is Bud DiContino. How is the connection?"

"Fine, sir. I'm in the Los Angeles field off—"

"Director Jones told me where you are. What is going on?"

"You're not going to believe it."

Five minutes later, after a call to the White House Library to soothe his doubts, Bud had no choice but to believe that which he would rather have dreamed.

Art Jefferson sealed the original cassette in a security pouch and handed it to two agents. "LAX fast. A plane is waiting."

The investigation was no longer only the search for the murderers of a federal officer. It was now much more, though only
the three agents who had heard the tape and the Deputy A-SAC
were privy to what was actually happening. All the others knew
was that the Melrose Hit was now something beyond even a
priority-one investigation.

Art turned to the eight teams remaining around his cubicle.
The rest had already been dispatched on various assignments.
"Okay. We don't have much time. We *have* to find the shooters,
and we have to find Sullivan. You all have a picture of him, and
Frankie passed around the computer sketches of our perps. But
the best thing we have on them right now is the car. License is no
good, but they had to get it somewhere. If it's a stolen, there's
probably a report. No one with a new car would not miss it if it was
gone this long."

"Unless they were quieted, too," one of the agents surmised.

"We'll deal with that if we come to it. If it's not a stolen, then
it probably was a rental. We have a good description, so the rental
agencies might give us something on that front. What we need are
names. Names." Art's stare was motivating and somewhat frightening. "We need to know who these guys are."

"What about the van you saw at the hit?"

"Nothing there," Frankie answered. "Haven't been able to
locate the R.O. of it. Your thought about a dead owner not saying
anything may be true on this one, but we just don't know."

The time was slipping away. Art knew the bureaucrats in D.C.
would be playing their games, wasting time before acting, but he
was not about to let that happen here. He had heard the tape. It
was real to him. Let them debate its authenticity, he thought. He
had better things to do. "You have your assignments. Let's get
to it."

Within a minute the teams were gone from Art and Frankie's
area. Two would be going directly to Parker Center, headquarters
of the LAPD, to begin running computer checks on stolen vehicles that might match the one they were after. The other six
would be hitting the phones, contacting every car-rental company
in the county and some outside of it.

Art and his partner had another avenue to follow.

"Did Bill give it to you?"

Frankie handed it over. "Quite a list. Sullivan is the consum-
mate bar-hopper."

The list was twenty names long, denoting every watering hole or lounge Sullivan was known to frequent by his co-workers. "We won't make it any shorter by sitting here." Art took the keys from the desk. "I'll drive."

"Good," Frankie said. "Not my favorite thing, you know."

"Driving?"

"No. Looking for some drunk at a bar." Frankie put her coat on. "Did enough of that shit with my ex."

"Well, you don't have to take this one home with you."

Thank God for small miracles, Aguirre thought.

"What does he want?" Merriweather asked, noting that it was ten minutes past the time he had planned to leave for his late flight down to Florida to meet with the CFS representatives.

Greg Drummond sat across the room from his boss, the long fingers of clouds backlit by the moon visible through the DCI's seventh-floor office window. "He said it was urgent. He can make calls like this."

The DCI grunted. He had little time for men like DiContino, and afforded even less to those lower on the political totem pole. His office, Assistant to the President for National Security Affairs, was a Cold War relic that could be done away with in Merriweather's estimation.

"Pete's back tomorrow?" The DCI inquired. Deputy Director of Central Intelligence Pete Miner, the Agency's number-two man, was in Seoul to brief the new South Korean president on the elusive, but very real, nuclear-weapons program in the North. Miner was the occupant of an equally unnecessary position in the DCI's mind. An agency properly run could do with fewer layers at the top. Oh, well. He still had plenty of time to turn Langley's 1950s-vintage machinery into a more efficient operation for the turn of the century.

"A week from tomorrow," Drummond corrected. *So he's no use to you, either.* "He's stopping off in Japan after Seoul."

"Of course." The intercom buzzed, but it was not to be answered. "He's here. About time. I asked the desk to give me some warning. Ready for the show?" Merriweather smiled as if he expected the DDI to understand.

Bud DiContino walked in, his hands empty. He closed the door behind with a forceful shove. *Easy, Bud.* "Anthony. Greg. Your Cuban operation just walked through my door."

"What?" the DCI asked, not really caring what the NSA was to say but curious as to what would motivate a desperate display such as this. *You weren't supposed to be a hothead, DiContino.*

Bud took a seat in one of the wing backs next to the DDI. "The Russians may have left Cuba in '62 one missile short."

"What!" Drummond practically yelled, looking to his boss. The man had an almost bewildered stare on his face.

"And where did you come upon this information, James?" Merriweather inquired, instinctively jotting notes on his legal pad, his manner still outwardly cool.

"The FBI in Los Angeles was investigating the murder of one of their agents and of another man—actually more of an elimination—who turned out to be an assistant to Castro's Russian-language interpreter during the missile crisis. His killers were apparently after a tape he was in possession of, but they didn't get it. The agents did."

"And you believe this man's assertion of who he was."

"I checked it out, Anthony. The library pulled the *Officials, Officers, and Contacts* for '62. Listed as the number-two man for Russian translations was Francisco Portero, now a very dead corpse in the Los Angeles County Coroner's Office. He also had diplomatic status with the UN until a year ago. That was when he defected."

The DDI stood and picked up the phone on Merriweather's desk without prompting, calling the Records Section of the Latin America Desk to confirm the information himself. Leak or no leak, this he had to ask.

Merriweather was genuinely unconcerned, for his own reasons, and it showed. He was going to play this out just for the NSA's benefit, and at the end there would be a very clear lesson in it for him: *Don't screw with my ops!*

"So just how did this happen? The Russians miscount or something?"

All right, asshole. "The Cubans took one. Snatched it just before the pullout was supposed to happen." Bud went on to explain the contents of the tape, portions of which he had heard over the phone with an FBI agent in Los Angeles translating.

"Wait right there." Merriweather laughed openly. "Are you trying to tell me you believe the Russians would have *allowed* Castro to steal one of their nukes? Well, James, take me through the looking glass. I'm waiting."

It was time for some reciprocation. "History, right, Anthony?" He knew it was. "How long did Khrushchev last after the crisis? Eh? Less than two years. Tell me, do you think he would have lasted *that* long if he'd had to go to war with an ally? Christ, he just had his face slapped by Kennedy, practically, and you think he had the wherewithal to face something even more embarrassing?"

"Confirmed," Drummond said, hanging the phone up. "Francisco Portero was the backup interpreter. Trained by Sergei Leonov," the DDI added, referring to the headmaster at Moscow's Higher Institute of Languages in the fifties.

Bud looked to the DCI. His expression had changed a bit.

Parry and thrust. "Your point is well taken, but how would Khrushchev have kept this quiet? His inner circle, particularly the military, would not have accepted him just saying 'Oh, by the way, the Cubans have decided they wish to retain one of our nuclear weapons.' " He smirked, seemingly unconvinced.

"The tape indicates that Castro forced Khrushchev into a cover story, something about an explosion just before the pullout was announced. That was how he could explain the loss of the missile crew and the warhead. Just burned up in a fireball." Bud wondered if the Soviet government of the day had questioned the potential of fallout from a good amount of plutonium going up in smoke. Right—the same folks who tested aboveground weapons just fifty miles from populated areas. The care factor was never much to mention on their part.

Fireball? Missile crew? Something clicked in the DDI's head, but he wasn't sure what exactly it was.

"It is a very engaging story, James, but more fable than thesis, I would say." So far there was nothing, Merriweather knew. Nothing to worry about. It was all right to push a little. "But, given the seriousness of the *possibility,* I suppose you are planning to confirm this."

"And just how do you propose we do that?" Bud asked angrily, tired of the DCI's minimalization of the risk.

"We?" Merriweather laughed, an event uncharacteristic enough to be noteworthy. "*You,* James. The Agency is quite busy at the moment. I mean, an entire missile! Not everything went up in smoke in that fireball, I presume. There must be something to corroborate the story."

That's it! Drummond shouted inwardly. "There may be."

Merriweather's head swung sharply toward his deputy. "What are you talking about?"

The DDI looked to both men, choosing the NSA to explain to. "Our man down in Cuba reported coming upon a graveyard with a couple dozen Russian names on the headstones. No birth years, but the date of passing was '62 on those he could read."

The NSA saw Merriweather bite his lip. "You were part of the review conference back in '62, Greg, weren't you?"

"Yeah. Thirtieth anniversary and all. I also did a paper for the study group on the basing scheme chosen by the Soviets back then. Jeez, that was '78, I think." The DDI had come right out of the Air Force and into the Agency, working his way up to chief analyst, Soviet Desk, in a very short time. His position now was the culmination of a hell of a lot of hard work and some risky calls that had panned out.

"Where was the burial site?" Bud asked.

"South of Santa Clara." The DDI paused, verifying the information in his mental register. "Yeah. An old Jesuit monastery was there. The section chief is still running all the stuff down for the reports." Drummond lit up. The NSA's train of thought was now apparent. "Did he know where the missile was taken from?"

"There was mention of 'associated units' departing from La Isabela. North central coast, I think."

"Right." Drummond's mind checked the information just presented with the data he still retained from his research for the basing report. "Sagua la Grande. Just south of La Isabela. Dammit, yes. The Russians had several MRBMs in the area. The one known as MRBM Site One carried out a full mating exercise the day before the pullout. It went on into the evening. The low-level recon couldn't see it anymore after that."

"Mating what?" the DCI demanded more than asked. His cool hold on events was starting to slip.

"Part of a readiness check," Drummond began. "They bring the warhead out of storage and mate it up with the booster. Then they fuel the thing and put it on the pad."

"KGB had the warheads, though," Merriweather countered. "How would you get them out of the way?"

The DDI thought for a moment. "This was the night before the pullout. If I remember correctly, the KGB units started a move to secure the ports late that evening. We always suspected they had some advance warning before the Radio Moscow broadcast the next morning. Anyway, they had to split their force, leaving only a token force with each warhead. Remember, most were in storage, all grouped together. They had fifteen-man details augmented by Cuban forces when they did one of these mating exercises. Cut that in half, and you have seven men, plus twenty or so generally unarmed missile crewmen."

"Cubans helped in the security?" Bud asked. Merriweather met the look the NSA shot his way this time.

"Right."

"They had opportunity, Anthony," Bud said. "I doubt you'll argue that Castro had the motivation."

How could he? The DCI knew his history better than most. The Cuban leader had been furious when the Soviets pulled out their missiles, at one point even demanding that they fire the weapon at the United States if an invasion appeared imminent. Castro's knowledge of the withdrawal before it occurred had been alleged, even substantiated, by former Soviet Politburo members. Why wouldn't Castro have wanted to humiliate Khrushchev, and get his hands on a very big bargaining chip in the process?

"Motive and opportunity, Anthony. And a smoking gun," Bud said.

The DCI could say nothing. His parry had been negated and his thrust had dissipated to nothingness. *Could it really be?* "That's pretty thin smoke you're blowing."

"Thin, my ass!" Bud exploded. "You want to wait till he has an opportunity to use it?"

"If it actually exists," Merriweather shot back. He wasn't going to go so easily. Couldn't go easily. "All you have is a recording alleging to portray the events you described. It's a good story, I'll grant you, but it's more fable than thesis. And the names in the graveyard—they're Russian. So what? How many Russians have served in Cuba? Maybe a plane went down, or a truck turned over. Why don't you try and confirm that they aren't just a platoon of infantrymen killed in a crash?"

He would have to do that, the NSA knew. But the reality of that was not a hindrance; it was an opportunity. How to do it was the problem that was mated to the opportunity. How would he do it? They couldn't just ask the Russians for the information, because that would likely lead to a revelation of what had been discovered. Not good timing, telling the Russians that the Cubans had one of their old nukes when their radars were down. Plus there were enough hard-liners in government that any revelation to the Russian president might find its way through them to Castro. One more stab at the imperialist West. And if this turned out to be a real threat, what would Castro do if he discovered that his enemies to the north were aware of the missile? *Use it or lose it.* No, anticipating that it was credible, their best defense at the moment was secrecy. To get the Russians to open up their records was just not . . . *Of course!*

"A good idea, Anthony. That way we'll have corroboration."

What? "How . . . ?"

Bud explained for just a minute.

"You can't just go off and use my people to play your games! I sure as hell won't authorize it, and that means your only hope is with the—"

"With the Man," Bud completed the sentence with his own twist. "But first he has to be filled in." The NSA stood. "You want to join me, Anthony?"

This ride to the White House, though silent and filled with contemplation of a very serious matter, would be one of the most enjoyable Bud DiContino had ever taken. *Welcome to my turf, Mr. Director.*

Two BTR-60PB armored personnel carriers led the way along the road. It was a paved one, much to the delight of the convoy's commanding officer. His unit had been running supplies since the opening of hostilities, and most of those runs had been on the overused dirt tracks that cut through the more vegetated, and less open, areas of the countryside. The cover he was thankful for, but the speed was a third, at best, of that which he could make on the paved surface.

This time, however, it had been not a decision of choice, but of necessity. The ten fully loaded tank trucks behind his escorting BTRs would have bogged down before passing through Cienfuegos. That was not the stretch of the journey that concerned him, though. It was the road he was on now. And he was running it under a bright moon.

"Lieutenant, the troops at the rear of the convoy report that one of the tankers has broken down."

"Damn!" the lieutenant swore at the situation reported by his driver. "Leave it. Tell them to have the driver try and repair it. We must move on."

"Yes, sir."

Damn! The lieutenant, standing in the BTR's open hatch, looked to the bright white ball that was sinking slowly toward the hills northwest of Cienfuegos and willed it to hurry into its rest for the night. Darkness was a convoy runner's friend. Darkness and speed, he reminded himself, adding luck almost as an afterthought.

"Wait for the escorts to pass," the sergeant told the gunners just in front of him. It was a perfectly laid ambush using just twenty men, though he could have done it with ten. The targets, after all, were like whales upon the beach.

The thirteen vehicles had been spotted an hour before by a two-man scout unit overwatching the refinery facilities at Los Guaos. Then there had been one more, but the disappearance of one vehicle was not to be worried about. What was approaching was plenty to make quite a noise.

"Ready . . ."

The lieutenant saw the flashes just an instant before he felt the hot sting on his right side. He turned that way but never completed the move, a second volley of machine-gun fire from the hillside ending his life and sending him sliding downward into the BTR. An RPG antitank rocket fired from close in on the opposite side of the road farther up finished off the vehicle itself, the HEAT warhead impacting just forward of the fuel tanks. The white-hot jet of explosive gasses was sufficient to ignite the normally stable diesel. The green vehicle disappeared into a ball of orange-yellow before anyone could get out.

The second BTR made it a bit farther, its driver jinking to the right away from the smoke trail he had seen swoop down on his commander's vehicle. But the farthest he got was the soft shoulder of the two-lane highway. Another RPG came straight down at the BTR's front and punched a hole directly into the driver's compartment, incinerating the upper half of his body instantly and causing the vehicle to continue awkwardly over the roadside. It ended its roll at a nose-down attitude, its hatch-covered top exposed to the hillside. APCs, like all armored fighting vehicles, are lightly armored on top, the thickness in proportion to its thicker side armor. The BTR's side armor was pathetic.

Two heavy machine guns sprayed the top of the BTR simultaneously from opposite sides of the road, opening its roof up like a sieve. A fire started quickly, followed by several small explosions as the soldiers' ammo began to cook off in the heat. No one from either lead escort survived, a similar fate befalling the single BTR at the rear.

The convoy was doomed.

It took little time for the hunter squads to turn the long line of tank trucks into a burning snake of twisted metal. Several of the trucks, strangely, did not burn as furiously as the others, their refrigerated contents venting into the atmosphere as a river of fire flowed down the slightly inclined road from the front to the back.

"Done," the sergeant said. "Let's get . . ."

The sound came from behind. It had been masked by the roar of the raging inferno below, and smoke had obscured any view that might have warned them. The sergeant saw it first and wanted to run, but it was no use. They had killed everyone below, but someone had obviously not died quickly enough.

"Bastards!" Major Orelio Guevarra screamed, his weapons officer in the front of the Mi-28 Havoc giving a thumbs-up at the sight before them on the FLIR display. "Destroy them, Chiuai-gel!"

Sergeant Chiuaigel Montes did just that. A salvo of rockets leaped out of the pods on each side of the attack helicopter as it approached the ambush from the west. Before the first salvo impacted, Montes rippled off another. This he continued as the Havoc flew fast over the length of the burning convoy. Fired from three hundred feet, the rockets spread out to a hundred feet on either side of the highway and created a zone of almost certain death the entire length of the destruction below.

After the first pass, the Havoc turned and approached from the east. Its rocket pods empty, Montes switched to the 30mm cannon that hung like a robotic appendage below the insectlike Havoc's nose.

"Two o'clock," Guevarra reported, this time in a more controlled voice, over the helicopter's intercom. "Right. Right."

The lone figure, represented by a ghostlike white image on the FLIR, was running up the hill, dodging between the trees that provided a lush canopy most of the year. Early autumn, however, was a time of growing sparseness. He had no chance.

"Take this!" Montes said loudly, depressing the Fire button on his directional fire stick at the cockpit's side.

A hundred 30mm rounds burped out of the cannon in less than a second, creating a trail of dust and flying vegetation on the hillside below that ended at the running man's back. Twenty of the high-density rounds connected, literally disintegrating the unfortunate rebel above the waist.

They circled the area for five minutes more, firing on anything they suspected of being alive. A few minutes later it became overkill. Nothing was left. The Havoc turned southeast, heading for its base with no weapons of consequence or ammunition remaining. Just the two AA-7 air-to-air missiles hung beneath its wings, no targets of consequence having presented themselves for their use. The major was ever hopeful, though.

The President looked squarely at Bud, letting the possibilities of what he had just been told sink in. His next look was for the DCI. "Anthony, you obviously disagree."

"Vigorously, Mr. President." Merriweather scooted forward in his chair, his chin almost even with the edge of the President's desk. To his left was the NSA. To his right were the secretaries of state and defense. To his front was the man he had to convince. "Sir, this is so farfetched that it really is ridiculous. I am supposed to be on a plane to the Cape right now. My meeting with the CFS representatives is in six hours. Would I really be thinking of this if these crazy assertions were credible?"

Things had gone well so far, the chief executive knew. The DCI hadn't steered him wrong yet. "Bud, you say there's a way to confirm this to a greater degree?"

"Yes, sir. What we have to do is compare those names our officer in Cuba found with the supposedly murdered missile crew. If they match, then we cannot dispute this. We can't afford to."

It made sense, the President thought. But it was a hell of a big pill to swallow. "All right, how?"

"We have several people working on the archives project with the Russian Ministry of Defense in Moscow."

"Right," the President said, "trying to verify the existence of any POWs."

"And to confirm deaths," Bud said, expanding on the President's observation. "Well, sir, one of the archivists is an Agency employee."

"Hold it." The President's expression went immediately to the far side of serious. "We have a *spy* among the group of archivists? Do you know what the Russians will do if they find that out? Bud, you, of all people, should realize that right now. This is supposed to be the age of trust!"

"Not blind trust," Bud objected, his disagreement careful in its tone. "The Russians, as much as we would like to think not, are still running heavy intelligence-gathering activities on us. The modernization program for their BMEWS does not negate that. What we have in their archives is benign by comparison. Benign and, thankfully, in the right place to help us here."

This wasn't what the President had bargained for when SNAPSHOT was envisioned. It was *not* supposed to involve outside parties, particularly the Russians. "So what do we do with this man in Moscow? How does he get what we need?"

"We already know from his reports that the death records of the Red Army are stored, by year, in the same area as records concerning POWs and other foreign nationals in prison camps. They're not considered sensitive. We can notify our agent through the Moscow station chief immediately." Bud glanced at his watch. "It's almost seven-thirty in the morning over there, so we can get word to him before he leaves the embassy for the workday."

"Mr. President, I have to object," the DCI said before the Man could make a final decision. "To use our agent in Moscow risks not only endangering the modernization program if he should be discovered, but also alienating the Russians in a larger sense. It does not matter if his work is minor, if valuable; they will still see it as a breach of trust. You are correct to be leery of that. Plus, the story purportedly told on that tape—which none of us has heard, I mind you—is factually deficient in several respects."

"How so?" the President inquired, hoping that the DCI could lay a good case. He didn't like opposing his NSA on things with as much *potential* for trouble as this, but what was taking place in Cuba was historic. He wanted nothing to interfere with its successful completion if it could be helped.

"First, there is the last line on the tape, at least as it was reported to us. It instructed the interpreter to lock the tape away." The DCI sat back and straight, his expression signaling puzzlement. "How did this supposed assistant get hold of the tape and keep it?"

Bud wanted to smile, but to do so would make it seem as

though he were gloating at anticipating Merriweather's questions. He didn't even have to look at the secretary of state.

"Sir," Coventry began, "I thought much the same thing when I heard of this, so I had our Records Section at State check on Cortez's status. We did the same thing earlier for the Bureau concerning Francisco Portero. It would seem that Cortez was not seen after the last week of October in 1962. No word of a death, or retirement, though the latter would not be likely when we consider he was but forty-one years old."

"It's very convenient, Mr. President," Bud said. "Too convenient. Cortez disappears, and Portero steps in. Maybe Cortez filled him in before he disappeared."

"That proves nothing," Merriweather commented. "Just because State can't locate some old Cuban government worker, we can't say 'Hey, this means this.' It could mean a good number of things."

"Such as?" Bud asked heatedly.

"Not my job to prove the negative of your theories, DiContino."

"All right, enough," the President said. "Anthony, you said there were several reasons to doubt the validity of the story. What else?"

The DCI nodded emphatically. "Yes. More important than the question about the tape is the reality that a missile left in '62 would most definitely be out of repair by this date. Long before, actually."

What? Bud thought. How would he . . . ?

"Drew, is that a credible observation?" the President asked.

The secretary of defense wanted to choose his words carefully. "A weapon such as the SS-4, which is what the Russians had in Cuba at the time, would have required maintenance over the years."

"Which does not rule out that the Cubans were able to do such," Bud pointed out. "We know that Castro had Chinese and North Korean technicians in his country over the years after he got that crackpot idea to build a space-launch facility like the French have in Guyana."

"But that never—"

"Of course it never flew," Bud interjected, cutting off the DCI. He was determined now to not let the President be wooed by Merriweather's comforting analysis. "Castro has had all kinds of nutty schemes. Biotech. Perfect cattle breeding. You name it, he's tried it. He's unpredictable. We never know what he's going to do next. He doesn't do the logical things." Bud turned his attention directly to the President. "We have *never* known what he is capable of. Therefore it behooves us to be prepared even for that which we are not sure he is capable of doing."

A neat operation! That was a crock, the President thought. Down the toilet. "All right, Bud. Confirm this. If it turns out to be credible, then I want options. Fast options, because it scares the hell out of me to even think that this may be true. In the meantime, we keep things in motion down in Cuba. I'm not going to put the brakes on this without confirmation. Is that clear?" He looked to each man, ending with the DCI. "You get down to your meeting. I expect your deputies can handle this archive thing?"

"Of course." *Damn.* "No problem."

"Mr. President, there are two things that need to be done to prepare for the eventuality that we will confirm the information," Bud said, his plan thought out on the drive over. It took him just a minute to explain it.

"I see," the President said. He was somewhat surprised by the second of Bud's proposals. Bringing the man back one more time was almost too much, considering. As President, he felt some responsibility for what had befallen the man a year before, and still he'd never met him. If he was being brought back again, that fact would have to change. "That sounds acceptable. But, Bud, I want to see him before anything happens."

"All right, sir."

"Anything else?"

There wasn't. The President left with his advisers standing. Merriweather departed immediately after him without a word to his equals in the Oval Office.

"Thanks, Drew. You could have nailed it shut for Anthony."

"Hey, you and I may not see eye-to-eye on everything, but he needs some serious help."

Bud gave the secretary of defense a much deserved slap on the shoulder. "Hope you didn't mind my stepping into your territory there."

Meyerson laughed. "Stepping in? Hell, Anthony damn near appropriated my CT force for his own damn escort service. Your use of them would be a whole lot more up their alley."

"If it becomes necessary." Bud's thoughts drifted back to

something the DCI had said a minute before. "Did it seem strange to either of you that Anthony practically started quoting Missile Maintenance One-oh-one?"

Coventry had caught that also. "I didn't know his knowledge ran so deep." The words were not spoken flatteringly.

"Yeah." Bud didn't know what it meant, but something wasn't kosher about it. That could wait, though. "Can we run through this for a moment?"

The three men sat again. Two floors up, the chief executive would hopefully be getting to bed. He was the decision maker and therefore had to be rested and clearheaded. His advisers were the ones who could do without sleep.

"Okay, if this turns out to be true, what are our options?" Bud was acting in familiar territory now.

"The idea you outlined for the Boss is right on," Meyerson said. "Let's say we confirm this and that we find the thing— anticipating it still works." The secretary had been careful not to give the DCI an ironclad response to his "missile-won't-work" theory. "We can't launch a preemptive air strike."

"Why not?" Coventry asked, leaning back on the couch and straightening his tie. It was a habit, the others knew. Looks mattered little at the moment.

"Decoys," Bud answered for the secretary of defense. "The same kind of problem you run into once a modern ICBM goes terminal. Things called penaids. They're basically decoys that you'd be forced to take out or discriminate from the real warheads if SDI ever got off the ground. The same thing applies to ground-based missiles. We might see *something*, but we wouldn't know if it was *the* something we wanted."

"Makes sense," Coventry admitted. "Ground troops, eh?"

"You heard it," Bud confirmed. "Up close and personal. It's the only way to know for sure."

Coventry suddenly thought of the worst-case scenario. "What if we don't find it? He could fire it."

Meyerson's eyebrows went up at the thought. "Not much we can do there."

"What about Patriot?" Coventry asked, thinking back to the anti-ballistic-missile capability the Patriot missile system had demonstrated during the Gulf War.

"No way. First, we don't know where he'd fire it. Second, we don't have enough batteries in CONUS to cover all the possible targets." CONUS was military jargon for Continental United States. "Third, the Patriot has an upper-altitude envelope of eighty thousand feet, and these wouldn't be Scuds popping up. We're talking about a warhead in terminal phase. Too fast and too small. Fourth, how would we explain SAMs parked on the Mall, or on Ellis Island? You get the picture. It would be like advertising that he should shoot it before it's too late."

"Our only hope is to keep this quiet," Bud said. "Airtight."

"No argument from me," Meyerson said, his thoughts shifting to preventative actions. "You know, time may become a concern in this."

"Meaning?" Bud probed.

"Castro may be motivated to use the missile if things get more desperate."

"It's already pretty bad," the NSA observed accurately.

"But more pressure could set him off. I mean, why hasn't he used it yet?" Meyerson shrugged.

It was a good question. "Jim?"

"If you're thinking what I think you're thinking, you can set it aside. You haven't met the rebel leader. I have. When Anthony and I arranged the conference two months ago in Antigua, all he could talk about was the way he was going to destroy Castro. He despises the man. This coup is as much motivated by hate for Castro as it is by desire for a new system of government."

"But even just a slowdown of their advance?" Meyerson suggested. "Just to buy us some more time?"

The secretary of state's head shook knowingly. "Listen, when Castro executed General Ontiveros after the hijacking, he alienated a lot of his military. Ontiveros was respected, and he was loved. And the only reason he was made to suffer was because Castro perceived him as protecting . . ."

The realization hit Bud and Coventry first.

"Vishkov," Bud said.

"Christ!" Meyerson's head fell into his hands.

"He needed someone with the knowledge to maintain a missile," Bud pondered aloud. "Guess he got him. Son of a bitch!"

"Defection, eh?" Coventry mused, knowing they had all been fooled. They and the Russians, it appeared. "Sounds more like an arranged marriage."

It was the simplicity of design that made some secrets so unbelievable, and made them equally possible. "Castro arranges for Vishkov to come visit the island, probably with an offer of money or whatever if he decides to stay. He might have even allowed him to peddle his nuke designs unhindered. When he meets the general's sister, Ontiveros probably encouraged their get-together. He must have seen it as a way to turn the tables on Castro, to get Vishkov in his camp." Bud laughed, but there was little humor in it.

Coventry saw it all unfolding also. "We knew that Ontiveros was a dissenter in the military. I wonder if he knew about the missile? That would make even more sense. If he has Vishkov on his side, he could literally dictate the physicist's use to Castro. Then when the hijacking happened, Castro saw it as a perfect opportunity to get rid of Ontiveros. Vishkov was just an excuse." Coventry remembered his part in the affair and his suggestion to the Cuban leader that he could deal with Vishkov in his own way. *I might as well have signed Ontiveros's death warrant.*

"You said that Ontiveros was executed," Meyerson said. "What about his sister and Vishkov?"

"We don't know about the sister," Bud answered. "But Vishkov was imprisoned. That's the intel the Agency got through their exile contacts."

"Another check in the value column for him," Coventry observed.

They still needed the confirmation from their agent in Moscow, but this was adding almost undeniable credibility to Bud's belief.

"Bud, you better step up our reconnaissance of the island," Meyerson suggested. "Damn the budget on this one." He knew that Coventry wasn't cleared for *Senior Citizen,* so mention of Aurora was out of the question. The NSA would get his drift.

Coventry still had a hard time fathoming it. "Do you realize what this means? We could have a nuclear attack on a U.S. city at any time." His own words scared and frustrated him. "And anything we do to prevent it might just precipitate it."

"I think we realize it, Jim," Meyerson said.

"And we have to prevent it," Bud said hopefully. The phone call he was soon to make would be a step toward that end.

"Lost!" Fidel Castro screamed. "How?"

Raul waited, his silent signal for his brother to calm himself.

"How?"

"An ambush. The rebels destroyed the vehicles providing security, then the tank trucks themselves. A total loss."

The president looked disbelievingly at his brother. "The shipment must get through to Asunción. It must!"

"It will, Fidel. Los Guaos is preparing another shipment."

"This time with ironclad security," Fidel said, making a fist in the air.

Raul wanted to add something positive to the event. "We did kill all the rebels who ambushed the convoy."

"How did they . . . ?" The president's eyes lit up, and a smile appeared upon the gray-bearded face. Yes. They wouldn't know that there was . . . "Excellent."

Raul nodded. The surprise would not stop the rebels, but it would bloody them. Guevarra was a madman. The perfect madman to fly under these circumstances. "Fidel, soon we must speak of a target."

"Yes. Soon."

"Captain Cresada reports that the patrol never returned," Manchon explained. Night had come to the island, and with it some respite from the day's advance. He, Ojeda, and Papa Tony sat quietly beneath a hastily erected tent in a field outside Aguada de Pasajeros.

"None returned?" Ojeda asked for clarification. "Not a single man?"

"Not one."

Antonio held the latest report from Langley on his lap. The colonel was concerned, obviously at the apparent loss of several men, but also at something Antonio couldn't identify.

"None?" Ojeda asked again, a single nod all the response needed. *There could not be. We made certain.* His thoughts drifted back to a decade before, training with the Soviets in the land that became their own Vietnam. *Not one man . . .* Decimation of the Mujahideen ambushes had been commonplace there also, though not common enough to stave off defeat. "I want any patrols who are out of protective range to be issued shoulder-fired SAMs."

"You think . . . ?"

"We will not take the chance."

*   *   *

It was cheating, but who gave a damn? He owned the lake, the fifty acres around it, and all the fish in it stupid enough to bite at his shiny lure in the dark hours approaching midnight. The light shining down from the dock didn't hurt, of course, but Joe Anderson had convinced himself that if he was going to leave this earth anytime soon, he was going to take as many of his favorite quarry as he could with him, regardless of laws banning night fishing. Correction . . . second-favorite quarry.

"Phone, hon'," his wife yelled from the back door of their house, which was nestled in the trees in Minnesota backwater country. She had gotten quite used to his late-night expeditions to thin out the aquatic population.

Joe looked greedily down at a northern pike hovering below the surface. In a few weeks it would be too cold to fish from the dock, and soon it wouldn't matter at all. So what? He smiled at the fish. "You're mine. Just wait."

He laid his Zebco rod down and went to the back door, picking the receiver up off the dinette table just inside.

He looked to his wife. "This time of night?"

She just shrugged.

"Hello."

"Captain Anderson?"

Shit! Joe thought, knowing before another word was said that the fucking northern pike was going to get away.

CHAPTER TEN

Convergence

"Bourbon, Ted." Sullivan pushed the glass closer to the mirrored wall of beautiful bottles, some clear and others filled with the dirty brown liquid he craved.

"Still early, George," the bartender said. "You gonna pace yourself this time?"

This time? Was he insinuating...? It wasn't worth arguing, George knew. Ted was the guy with the liquor. Ted was his friend right now. Almost his best friend. "Nice and slow tonight." *Last one in this joint, you lousy, overprotective ass.*

The sound was more than beautiful, a sweet, refreshing swish as the bourbon reached down from the neck of the bottle and filled the glass only to the point where the optimist/pessimist debate could ensue. Never enough, the naysayer in Sullivan decided, lifting the glass to his lips, taking in the first taste of the liquid that helped him to relax. Helped him to think. There was much to think about, much to plan. A story to get. His story. *To hell with Bill.*

"Yank my story," Sullivan muttered, downing half of what remained in his glass.

"What?"

Sullivan lifted his head, eyeing the bartender. Not only was he a mother, he was a nosy mother. "Nothing. Trouble at work."

Surprise, surprise. "Maybe you should change your line of work."

"I like being a reporter," George disagreed. "I'm good at it."

"I was talking about your moonlighting," the bartender said, looking at the glass that was nearing empty. *Give it up, guy.* Regulars were good for business, but he hated watching the pathetic ones drink their lives into a toilet.

"I'm good at that, too." George looked away, back to his drink.

Too good, the bartender thought to himself, wondering if this regular put the same amount of effort into the job that paid his tab.

"Strike eight," Frankie said, scratching the establishment known as the Tree House off of their list after getting back in the Chevy.

"Nice place," Art commented. "Remind me never to go there unless I'm drunk first. That way it won't look so bad."

"It's not the looks, partner," Frankie said, wiping the tip of her nose. She looked up at the flashing sign as Art pulled away. "A urinal with neon."

They were getting a good taste of what Sullivan required in a place to get shit-faced, namely "not much." Bottles, barstools, and a bathroom, sometimes all in one room, according to Aguirre's discriminating nose. Art's was less affected. His additional years in the Bureau, particularly his time working the OC hits in Chicago, had seen him observing many an autopsy, where the term "smell" took on meanings it was never intended to represent.

"West we go," Art said without enthusiasm. "Where to?"

Frankie checked the list as her partner swung their car left onto Sunset from Rampart. "A place called Freddy's. Fifty-nine-hundred block of Sunset."

Art finished his turn and slid over into the right lane, slowing as the staggered convoy of LAPD cars, their lights and sirens clearing the way, came at him from the opposite direction.

"Cavalry's got work to do tonight," he said, noticing just a second later that a helicopter was close behind the patrol cars, racing east on Sunset a few hundred feet in the air.

"Just another night in L.A.," Frankie observed. She was wrong.

The Los Angeles Police Department's jurisdiction is divided into four Bureaus—West, Valley, South, and Central—which are comprised of a total of eighteen divisions, not including the elite Metro Division. Each division monitors and maintains its own patrol function, with officers responding primarily to 911 calls dispatched from a central communications center. When things in one division heat up, as is common in a city whose criminal element does not follow the statistical laws of even population distribution, units from adjacent divisions can be called in to assist. Certain happenings mandate such cooperation to a higher degree. At the top of those is one radio call—"Officer needs help."

Why such things happen is a question social theorists and criminologists have debated for decades, and to excess in the very recent past, but none could have predicted or explained the motivation for what began in the streets bounding Echo Park, a slab of green littered with bottles and drug paraphernalia located just inside Rampart Division's area of responsibility.

A jet-black '85 Cadillac Seville, its compressed springs and low-aspect tires identifying it as the ride of choice for gang members, glided slowly up the street on the park's north side, just yards from a group of young men hanging out on the hood of a vintage Monte Carlo parked along the curb. The first words from the Cadillac, which would be seen as benign to most people not familiar with the gang culture, challenged the allegiance of the boys on the Monte Carlo, questioning them as to "who they claimed." The answer, which was as much a statement of pride in one's gang as it was a truthful response, was all the occupants of the Cadillac needed.

Two sawed-off double-barrel shotguns poked through the open side window from the backseat, and a single semiautomatic pistol from the front. The weapons trained on the group of twelve young bangers. Understandably they started to scatter at the sight, but not fast enough.

The fire came quickly and violently, striking three members of the La Playa Flats gang in the back as their homies dove to the ground, pulling out their own hardware, mostly .22- and .25-

caliber pistols. They were not as well armed as their rivals, the Madera Honchos, but did not hesitate to shoot back as soon as their guns were in hand.

On the east side of the park, sitting in their patrol car, two officers of the Rampart Division's P.M. watch were finishing their dinners—Styrofoam bowls full of rice and teriyaki beef strips—when the repeated sounds of gunfire reached them. Immediately they radioed in that they were going to investigate "shots fired," not an uncommon occurrence, and hurried to the north side of the park. They turned from Echo Park onto Park and instantly knew that this was more than an ordinary "shots fired."

The driver of the Cadillac, upon seeing the police cruiser turn toward him, reflexively floored it and swung to the left, trying to make a U-turn in an area that would not permit such for the big four-door. His homies in the backseat, alternately trying to hit their rivals with wild blasts from the shotguns and ducking into the false safety behind the doors, didn't see what the driver had, and, as the Caddie screeched to a stop in its abortive swing to get out of there, they fired again without looking, their shots traveling straight down Park and hitting the LAPD car in the windshield and grill.

"Two Adam Twenty-one! Officer needs help! Shots fired!"

It was as if a lightning bolt had reached down from above and struck every LAPD unit in Rampart, Northeast, and Hollywood divisions. The twelve other Rampart units on patrol that evening, upon hearing the 'Two' in the unit I.D. that denoted it as one of theirs, dropped what they were doing and raced toward the park. Six Northeast units, just north of the park in their own division, also sped off with lights and sirens even before central communications put out the call as a Code Three.

But it was from the west, from Hollywood Division, that the greatest outside response came. Eight units, including one of the LAPD's helicopters, that had been involved in a particularly nasty domestic-violence call left the senior patrol officer of the watch, Sergeant Charlie Burns, to finish up the paperwork and witness statements and headed off to aid their brother law officers who had put out the call to the east of their location. It was a relatively quiet night in Hollywood otherwise, so the immediate loss of nearly all the division's patrol force was not likely to cause a problem.

Sergeant Burns thought that as he climbed into his car near

the intersection of Beachwood and Sunset, his ears tuned to the unfolding situation at Echo Park and his thoughts with the officers who were in need of assistance, unaware that he would soon be in a situation not dissimilar.

Sullivan walked out of Freddy's onto Sunset, wondering if he'd be able to find a cab at this time of night. He took a few steps east on the brightly lit boulevard, his gait slow and measured so as not to test the limits of his coordination. Not a damn one in sigh—

"Get in!"

The hands grabbed him from behind, pushing him toward the curb. A second later a dark-colored car screeched to a stop in front of him, and the back door came open. The hands pushed hard, shoving his head downward just as the police did in the movies. *Could it be?*

Sullivan regained his senses as the back door closed to his right. He was facedown on the car seat and brought his head up as the sound of another door closing filled the car. Who was . . . ?

"Don't move!" Jorge emphasized the words with the barrel of the revolver, which he pressed against the reporter's forehead as he reached over the seat back and held him by the lapels. "Don't say nothing, don't do nothing."

Tomás eased out into traffic, not wanting to draw any attention. Sunset was a busy street, one that they had heard lots of sirens from in the past few minutes, so the automatic decision to get off of it was natural. It was also a mistake.

A car approaching is always cause for caution for a police officer, which made Sergeant Burns's instinct to look up understandable. He saw the blue Chevy's driver just as the man saw him, and there was the unmistakable mask of tension upon his face that most bad guys exhibited when confronted by the cops. That piqued the sergeant's awareness, as did the man's blatant attempt to continue looking straight ahead as he neared the patrol car. He was saying something out of the side of his mouth, Burns noted, probably trying to tell his buddy in the passenger seat . . .

Gun.

The sergeant's head jerked fully to the left at the sight of the revolver pointing into the backseat. Beachwood was a residential street, and therefore not a wide one in the cramped confines of

Los Angeles. The driver and his passenger passed ten feet to Burns's left, then accelerated quickly south on Beachwood.

"Dammit!" Tomás swore, his eyes watching in his rearview mirror as the police car began a tight turn away from the curb.

Jorge was pressed back against the seat when Tomás stepped on the gas, and his eyes caught the sight of the car a hundred feet back just as its light bar came to life. He looked down at Sullivan, the gun pressing harder into his forehead. "I'll blow your head off if you move."

"He's on us!" Tomás shouted above the noise of the Lumina downshifting for a quick burst of speed.

"Lose him," Jorge said, knowing it was more hope than directive.

There was no mistaking it now for Burns. The car was rabbiting.

"Six L Fifty, I am in pursuit," he said calmly, though the adrenaline was already beginning to flow into his veins in appreciable quantities. A veteran of many pursuits, he never found them enjoyable, a fact directly in opposition to the Hollywood portrayal of them. *Get your cameras out, boys,* the sergeant thought, wondering just how long this one would last through Tinseltown.

Next to an "Officer needs help" call, a pursuit takes priority. When both happen simultaneously, there is an expected bit of confusion, a situation that is amplified when the proximity of the two is as relatively close as these were.

"All units . . ." The dispatcher paused, juggling her multiple major cases. *"All units stand by. Six L Fifty is in pursuit."*

Burns followed the car ahead of him through two hard right turns that had them going north toward Sunset. "Six L Fifty," he said into the mike, referring to his division (Six), his unit type (L, or Lincoln, a one man car), and his individual unit number (Fifty, an even multiple of ten, which denoted a supervisor), "car is a late-model blue four-door Chevy, now heading north on Gower approaching Sunset. Two male occupants, one possible in the rear. Suspects are armed. License . . ." The newer white reflectorized California plates made reading at a distance easier. ". . . Four-Nora-Edward-X Ray-Two-Eight-Three. Now passing Sunset."

The dispatcher repeated back the information and waited for available units to announce themselves for inclusion in the pursuit. The silence surprised her, until she checked her status log. *"Any Hollywood units in the vicinity of Sunset and Gower, Six L Fifty needs a secondary unit for the pursuit of a late-model blue Chevy."* Still silence. Her blood pressure notched up a bit. *"Air Forty."*

Miles from the pursuit, hovering over the deteriorating situation at Echo Park, the helicopter heard the call. "Air Forty."

"Air Forty, Six L Fifty is in pursuit, north on Gower past Sunset. Can you intercept?"

"Negative, we have continuing shots fired and multiple suspects."

"Air Twenty," the call came into dispatch from another helicopter that had picked up the pursuit call and was heading north from the South Bureau at top speed. "We'll take it. ETA five minutes."

"Roger, Air Twenty. Six L Fifty, your location?"

Burns was glad he had put his seatbelt on. This guy was driving as though he *really* didn't want to get caught. "Gower at Franklin, going . . . going west on Franklin."

The dispatcher checked her status log again. *"Fifteen Adam Seven,"* she said, calling a clear North Hollywood two-man unit. *"Six L Fifty is in pursuit—can you respond as secondary unit? Location is westbound Franklin from Gower."*

"Roger. ETA is six or seven."

There were now two additional units closing on the pursuit as the backup dispatcher entered the license number into the computer. The result of that would bring another welcome member to the chase. Another unwelcome one would, unfortunately, join in at the same time.

The bright white-and-blue Bell Jet Ranger lifted off from Hollywood-Burbank Airport just as the first "Officer needs help" call went out. Like all local television stations, KNTV Channel 3 monitored police broadcasts to find juicy bits of human drama that its viewers could eat up. Also like other local stations, KNTV had discovered that the helicopter was the perfect platform from which to get fast-breaking news events from the street to the viewer. To this end it had taken the very expensive step of purchasing its own helicopter outright, giving the station round-the-

clock access to airborne pictures. In a business where budgets
were tight, and where most stations simply leased the use of helicopters from respected aviation companies, KNTV had again lived
up to its claim that it would do anything for the story and would
pay the price that an aggressive TV news organization had to.

The news director had no sooner come to the monitor room
where reports from Echo Park were coming in when the first call
on the pursuit caught his attention. "Where's the chopper?" he
asked the control room.

"Coming south from Silverlake. LAPD has a bird up there, so
he has to approach from due north."

Damn the stupid regulations, the news director thought. For
safety's sake the LAPD had persuaded the FAA to issue stringent
guidelines regarding aircraft separation at crime scenes, relegat-
ing the news choppers to higher altitudes. Some stations had just
gone to more powerful, much steadier cameras that could get
better pictures from a thousand feet than they could previously
from three hundred. That sort of gear was expensive, however,
and KNTV had spent its money on the chopper, postponing the
inevitable upgrade of its standard camera setup.

"Any LAPD over the pursuit yet?"

"Not yet."

The news director checked the clock. It was just a few minutes to the start of the eleven o'clock news. If he could get their
chopper over the pursuit for a dramatic lead-in, it could take a
bite out of the competition's ratings for the important 11:00 P.M.
broadcast.

"Send the chopper to the pursuit." It was a smart decision,
he knew. High-speed chases got ratings almost as good as airplane
crashes.

"Left . . . south on Highland!" Burns said loudly, the wailing
of the siren transmitted to dispatch as background noise. The pursuit thus far had reached speeds of seventy miles per hour, fast
enough for the streets of Hollywood. As a supervisor, he had the
authority to continue or end a pursuit based upon conditions such
as traffic and danger to civilians. Another factor was what the suspects were wanted for. The sergeant, having seen the way the gun
was being wielded, had formed an opinion that there might be
someone in the back of the car who was an unwilling passenger.

And that had sealed it. Kidnapping, or suspected kidnapping, was a crime that deserved no slack. This chase was on for the duration.

"West on Hollywood!"

Art and Frankie were three blocks from Freddy's when the radio call came.

"*King Eight.*" It was the office's communication center.

Frankie snatched up the mike. "King Eight."

"*LAPD reports they are in pursuit of blue late-model Chevy. License Four-Nora-Edward-X Ray-Two-Eight-Three. It's your warrant suspects. Presently westbound Hollywood Boulevard from Highland. Three occupants in vehicle.*"

"Three?" Frankie said to her partner.

Art stepped on the gas and activated the Chevy's blue and red grill lights and the under-hood siren. "Idiot!"

"King Eight, we're on it." Frankie slipped the mike back into its holder. She also surreptitiously undid the top strap on her holster. *Get there, Art. Get there.*

George Sullivan knew he was going to die. He was certain of it. These were the guys. They had killed Portero. Now they were going to kill him. *Please, God.*

The man hovering over him kept the gun jabbed hard into his face while he watched out the back window. Sullivan could do nothing. His body was wedged between the front and back seats, his upper body twisted painfully rearward. Only his eyes could move, and they could do little to stop what was certain to happen. He'd already searched the area he could see, but there was nothing. If there had been, what could he do? Fight the guys off? Guys with guns! Not likely. All there was within reach was a set of keys in the coin tray between the front seats. Not much.

But it's something, you wimp! George reached gingerly with his left hand and picked up the keys, actually just one large key on an equally large keytab. He gripped it tight in his hand, swearing to himself that if the guy even twitched on the trigger, he was going to jam the key home into his killer's eye. I'm dead, you're blind, he thought, feeling quite brave but having no idea why.

"South La Brea! Where's the air unit?"

"Air Twenty."

"Air Twenty, we're a minute out." The observer in the helicopter saw the flashing lights of the patrol car, and, quite a ways off, the lights of the North Hollywood unit racing to join the chase. "Six L Fifty, we've got you on visual."

The pilot was going too fast. The pursuit was going to pass below them soon, so he started a turn to the left to set up on a following course. In the process he gained a hundred feet of altitude in a planned ascent.

"There!" Frankie yelled, pointing directly to their front through the windshield.

Art saw the pursuit pass from right to left a block from them, heading south on La Brea and passing Sunset. He slowed at the intersection, a red light causing him to interject caution when he wanted to drive like a bat out of hell.

"Clear!" Frankie said, her eyes sweeping traffic from the right. Lights and sirens weren't some impenetrable shield.

Art floored it through the light, turning tight onto La Brea. Two blocks down he could see the pursuit passing Fountain. What he saw next was in the sky.

The KNTV chopper pilot was eyeballing the pursuit from a thousand feet, approaching it from the east. His cameraman was on the right side, and he knew he'd have to clear that side for a good shot. Plus, he'd have to get lower. He started the diving left turn and checked his airspace for any . . . *SHIT!!!!*

Air Twenty's pilot, a veteran of the U.S. Army who had flown combat missions in Grenada, never saw what hit him. The KNTV chopper, traveling at 110 miles per hour, hit the LAPD helicopter from above and behind, disabling the tail rotor. That damage mattered not at all a split second later as Air Twenty's main rotor sliced into the news chopper's fuselage, killing both occupants instantly and turning the Bell Jet Ranger into a tumbling ball of fire that fell toward the earth.

Air Twenty's crew didn't suffer such a merciful death. They both were conscious as their million-dollar aircraft spun out of control and impacted in the center of La Brea, a block behind Six L Fifty, and exploded into a cloud of black and orange.

*   *   *

Burns saw the flash in his rearview, and it drew his attention long enough that he missed what was happening to his front until it was too late.

Tomás knew the light was red but had no choice. He kept on going, accelerating even, and didn't see the compact car come through the intersection from his left. He clipped the back end, sending the smaller car spinning and a car following it crashing into its rear. The Lumina spun also, its rear end impacting a set of parked cars on the east side of La Brea and throwing Jorge to the left onto Tomás.

George felt the hit but didn't know what had happened. Just a bright flash and the crashing of metal. It was his chance, maybe his last one. He pulled the latch on the right rear passenger door and rolled into the street, his survival instinct propelling his legs faster than he'd run in years east on Santa Monica Boulevard. A few seconds later he was nowhere to be seen.

Sergeant Burns saw the crash ahead too late to brake and maneuver around the second car. He hit it almost broadside, pushing it into the light pole at the southwest corner of La Brea and Santa Monica. He could see the suspect car a hundred feet down on La Brea and someone rolling out of the backseat, but couldn't get out of his patrol car to do anything about it. Looking down, he saw the telltale signs of a compound fracture of his right femur, the bright white bone protruding grotesquely through his dark blue uniform pants.

He reached for the microphone just as the blue Chevy started to move again. "Six L Fifty. TC at Santa Monica and La Brea. Officer down." He glanced into his side mirror and started to cry, but not from the pain. "Air Twenty is down. Jesus."

Tomás got the Lumina moving again, his head searching for other cops as Jorge reached back for Su—

"He's gone! Dammit!" He raised his head, feeling a sharp soreness in the back of his neck, and looked out the . . . open door. *Dammit!* He moved as much as he could as the vehicle's motion closed the rear door, his eyes sweeping the area. Nothing. Sullivan was nowhere.

"What *now?*" Tomás yelled, blood spattering from a cut in his mouth as he talked.

"Get us out of here. Fast!"

Art laid down over a hundred feet of skid marks, the Chevy coming to a stop fifty feet from the inferno that had fallen from the sky. A second glowing column of smoke was rising into the dark sky about a block to the east. He threw the car into reverse as soon as it stopped and backed another hundred feet away, blocking traffic coming south on La Brea. The relay that the pursuing LAPD car had crashed came a second later.

"Call it in," Art directed. He stepped from the car, the heat from the blaze half a football field away causing his cheeks to flush. He slammed the door and went to the trunk, pulling flares out and setting a barrier of small, bright fires across the wide boulevard.

Frankie reported to the communications center that which she was certain LAPD already knew of. *More death. Dead cops.* She got out of the car and walked a few yards toward the hot wall of orange that completely blocked La Brea. Her right hand came up and snapped the thumb-break strap shut. *They're on the other side of that. Just through the fire.*

Art saw his partner standing alone fifty feet away, just staring into the flames. She was statuelike, unfazed by the heat or the thought of what had . . . *Of course.*

"Frankie," Art said as he walked up from behind. "Frankie."

A portion of the white-and-blue tail of the helicopter was protruding from the inferno, but it was soon consumed, changing from a once-beautiful craft to a blackened hunk of metal. *Changed.* Frankie watched it, her partner's words eliciting no immediate response.

"You okay?"

Frankie turned around, facing her partner as the pulsating blaze silhouetted her from behind. "Fine."

Art watched her walk past toward the car, knowing a lie when he heard it.

The DDI made some half-funny joke about burning the candle at both ends that Healy found no humor in. The mere possibility of a leak in Drummond's directorate necessitated that he and the DDO do the grunt work on the new situation involving Cuba. CANDLE would have to wait.

"Our illustrious leader on his way down?" the DDO asked.

"In the air," Drummond affirmed.

"Better than here." Healy had even less respect for the DCI than Drummond did. That came more from his gut than from any overt knowledge. He was an Agency lifer with enough experience in the field that his ability to read people had picked up on Merriweather's real makeup long before he was ever confirmed for the position. The man had been a nemesis on the Hill when he chaired the Oversight Committee, and now he was a more potent nemesis within the ranks. His trust of his subordinates was low, Healy had recognized, giving few of those "underlings" reason to reciprocate with acceptance. The DDO, five years older than his Intelligence counterpart, had seen a lot of changes and personalities in his years at Langley, but nothing on par with this. He had even found himself hoping that the President, if he didn't come to his senses, would fall short in the election just two years off. It wasn't a pleasant thing to contemplate, or very professional, but Mike Healy, like many at the Agency, was at the end of his rope.

And now, he hoped, so would be Anthony Merriweather's career.

"Did Moscow acknowledge everything okay?"

"Yep," Healy said. "Hopefully we'll have something today. God, I hope it's today."

So did the DDI. All the coincidental data—the tape, Vishkov's presence, disappearance of key Cubans—was leading directly to the conclusion that none of them truly wanted to accept, much less deal with. But that they would, regardless of their boss's read on the situation.

"Now it's back to desk days," Drummond said, referring to his time as a "desk" in the Intelligence Directorate's Soviet section. "You and me."

Healy took one of the doughnuts from the box that had been picked up on a junk-food run by one of his night-watch people. He knew he didn't need it. Neither did his waist. "So we're assuming that it's real."

"Have to." Drummond ignored the pastries and took a sip from his Diet Coke. "Now, two things to be done. Response is one, but that's not ours to worry about right now." He knew Bud would be doing enough of that. "Our thing is to find it."

"Forget the old haystack comparison," the DDO said, taking a big bite of the soft, sugary maple bar. "We've got forty-four *thousand* square miles to play with."

Too true. Also too self-defeating to ponder for any length of time, Drummond reasoned. They had to go with what they could do. "What about Vishkov?"

"What about him? I agree that it's a good bet he's somewhere near the thing, but where is *he*?" The Agency had been unable to pinpoint the location of the apparently imprisoned physicist, mostly because to do such had not been a high priority until now.

There was a gentle knock at the door, which opened a second later. "Sir."

"Hi, Sam. Late night," Drummond said. "You can skip my office tonight."

"Okay," Garrity acknowledged. "What about Director Merriweather?"

Drummond looked down to the left of his desk to see if the security detail had come through already to take the burn bags. His basket was empty. "Yeah, you can do his."

"Fine." *Great!*

Healy waited for the soundproof door to close completely. "He sure isn't old Harry," he observed, passing judgment on the new man's somewhat aloof demeanor. "Heard anything about him?"

"Enjoying retirement, I hear," the DDI answered, recalling Langley's former janitor of the seventh floor. King of it, some had said. The old guy had come with the building in '63, making *him* the longest continuously employed person on staff. That said something about longevity in a town where jobs were passed out and taken away depending on which way the political winds were blowing. "Just running his boat around."

"That's me in a few," Healy said. He had done just a short stint in the Navy in the sixties, though he would say that was too long. The confinement of sea duty hadn't agreed with him, but the open ocean did. A sixty-foot sloop had caught his eye a year back, and he was well on his way to procuring it for the day when he hung up his cloak and dagger.

"So where is Vishkov?" Drummond asked the air, bringing the conversation back on course.

"The only thing we have on the prison population comes from our exile contacts, and their folks on the island can't be contacted now."

Drummond frowned crookedly at that. "I don't know if that would help anyway. Vishkov can't be with a general prison population, even in one of the gulags." The Communist regime, despite attempts to deny its existence, had operated several political prisons for decades. Only the media seemed to fall for the denials completely, particularly after Fidel himself gave a guided tour of what he said had *once* been a political reeducation facility. The Agency knew better. Soon the world would also, the DDI hoped.

"What about Paredes?" Healy asked and suggested at the same time.

"I don't know. I thought of that, too, but the security . . ."

"If anyone knows, at least anyone we have access to, it would have to be Ojeda and his staff."

The DDI rubbed his chin, a single finger reaching up to massage the stubble above his lip. "I chewed Anthony out about the reality of secure com links. This would push what he did into the minor infraction box on the scorecard." It was part Murphy's Law and part realization that the least opportune time for the worst to happen was likely the time it would. "But it may be our only way."

Healy nodded. "I'll get in touch with him. You going over to the White House?"

"Yep. Leaving in a few."

"See you back here."

The DDO left quickly. Time might be critical, or it might not. The problem really was that they had no idea what sort of schedule they were on to resolve this. It was still a *possibility*, even though they thought it probable, and that was somehow removing a sense of immediacy from the situation. A man standing with a loaded pistol in front of you got much more attention if you knew the gun was loaded. Is this one? the DDI wondered, almost afraid to accept it. Nukes were passé these days, at least to the press and the public. The Cold War was over. Pantex was taking bombs apart now, he knew, referring to the Department of Energy's former weapons-fabrication plant in Texas. *One weapon? Just one?* Was one stray nuke, though potentially devastating, a real threat? *Ask the people in Hiroshima and Nagasaki.*

He wondered if they really were taking this much too lightly. He wondered that, and he suddenly felt very much the way he had at the height of some of the more recent periods of tension between the former Soviet Union and his country. At those times he had decided that, knowing he'd never make it home to his wife and little boy if a first strike was launched from halfway around the world, he'd simply join the Agency's bank of communications antennae on the roof and watch as man-made suns came to life in the heavens. Of course, he would never have time to register the visual images. He would simply not be. It was actually a very agreeable way to go, if one had to, akin to being shot in the back of the head. You never hear it coming, the DDI thought, afraid that the same reality on a grander scale might be but a breath away.

He pondered that all the way to 1600 Pennsylvania Avenue, even though, just after entering the GW Parkway, the musing began to scare him half to death.

FBI Director Gordon Jones slipped his glasses off and tossed them haphazardly on his desk, letting his head fall back against his chair. Twenty hours, eighteen of those on the job, had been his day so far—and his night. Things were supposed to slow down once you reached fifty, he thought. Weren't old people supposed to need less sleep? Now would be the perfect time for that benefit of aging to manifest itself.

It had been a bad couple of days in a generally bad year. The agent killed the previous day—*Or was it two days ago?*—had brought to three the number of his people killed so far that year. He hated himself for thinking of it in terms of "so far." It was sheer lunacy. Good people dying for doing their job. The stress of that reality, combined with what was now partially on his plate, was pushing his endurance to the limit.

But he had to keep going. The tape from L.A. would be there within the hour, and there was a Bureau translator waiting to give it a close scrutiny. From there it would go to Technical Services for further analysis. Both written and verbal transcripts would then be given to the director so that he could deliver the same to the President in the morning.

Morning. That was just hours away. Jones had a spare change of clothes for occasions just like this, though he had only needed them once in his two years at the helm of the Bureau. They were definitely going to get a second use before the sun was fully up.

His head was swimming now. *There's no way.* He had to get some rest. It would look great if the director of the Federal Bureau of Investigation collapsed while briefing the President. Jones's office had no place to lie down; he had removed the couches to make room for some fine chairs given to the Bureau by Scotland Yard as a gesture of appreciation for assistance in a multiple-murder investigation some months before. There was a long, soft couch in the lounge a floor below. Great! The director sleeping in the coffee room!

But first he had to check on the status of the tape.

"Operations." There would only be two agents on duty in the Bureau's operations center at this time of the morning.

"This is the director. Any word on the delivery from L.A.?"

There was a delay while the agent checked his log. "Not yet. There is an OpRep from Miami."

That would have to be the first operations report from the wiretap team. "Any flag on it?"

"No, sir." A flag—nothing more than a UID (Urgent-Immediate Delivery) stamp on the report's cover sheet—would indicate that the OpRep needed the director's quick attention. Such a flag would also tell Jones that the tap team had gotten information directly related to the CIA leak they were hoping to identify. Without such, and considering that the tap was less than a day old, it was probably no more than an initial report of the operation's beginning.

"I'll grab that in the morning," Jones said. "Secure it until then. I'll be in the lounge."

The director hung up and fiddled with the array of buttons on his watch, setting the alarm to go off in three-and-a-half hours. A full night for some old geezer, he thought, amused at the fact that his state of tiredness might somehow be indicative of his hidden youth.

His memory made him special.

At the age of six, he memorized the capital cities of all fifty states, and ten years later earned his summer money performing "mind magic" at the county fair in the rural Oklahoma town he grew up in. For Patrick Tunney it was second nature. People said things; he remembered them. People did things; he remembered what. People committed things to paper; he stored visual images for later recall.

The last aspect of his amazing talent had helped him get into the University of Oklahoma, and later the Central Intelligence Agency.

He had already burned the twenty-eight names into his brain, in both English and Cyrillic characters, though he was certain if he found them, they would be in the latter. After that simple exercise, which he accomplished using an undescribable form of numerical pneumonics he had somehow stumbled upon as a child, he joined his fellow archivists for the short trip from the embassy to the Defense Ministry annex north of the Moscow Ring Road.

It was a beautiful morning, the sun low in the southeastern sky, and the few wisps of clouds high enough to catch the light and turn it into shades of the rainbow only God could have imagined. Truly beautiful, Tunney observed, knowing he would remember this sight forever.

He closed the door behind as always. There was little need for obvious security. Anything of importance in the Director of Central Intelligence's Office was alarmed. To accidentally trip one of the sensors would bring a contingent of *armed* security officers, and would result in a night of explaining and paperwork.

But Sam Garrity knew from the minute he entered the office that this time would be as simple as all the others. It was sitting right there, after all. For the taking. No effort at all. The spy in Garrity smiled at the simplicity of it. The criminal in him proceeded to do it.

He walked to the director's desk, a generally neat workspace that was not his responsibility, and laid his clipboard down. Next he picked up the blank legal pad sitting square in the middle and tore the top three sheets off, which he then clipped under the stack of cleaning requests on his clipboard. With that, it was done, except for that which he would do later.

That and, of course, the spit-and-polish shine he would give the director's office.

CHAPTER ELEVEN

Masters

"Son of a bitch," Antonelli commented.

"Maj, I'm gettin' tired of this nuke shit," Quimpo commented. "I signed on to smoke bad guys, not play H-bomb."

It was true, Sean thought. Delta's mission, aside from having changed in the last ten minutes, had evolved over the previous years to one beyond the mere rescuing of hostages. They had to adapt. They had to excel. The rescue aboard the 747 a year earlier had been familiar in one respect and alien in many others. This thing was beyond even that.

"So what's the plan?" Captain Buxton inquired.

"First we clear away from these boneheads," Sean responded, motioning with his eyes to the trailer accommodations where the Cubans had finally gone to sleep. "Their Air Force's problem again. Then we run some contingencies through."

"Mission?" Buxton probed. He was a leader of men and, therefore, wanted to know what the goals of any action were before thinking on the operational details.

Sean gave a quick rundown of the scenario as envisioned by the desk jockeys. "Simple, boys."

The collective stares were not accepting of the mock analysis. "And nebulous," Goldfarb added.

Sean couldn't argue with that characterization with little to go on at the moment. It was akin to knowing you were going to fire at a target, but no one had yet revealed what the target looked like or where it was. Or even *if* it was. "First the spooks have to do some digging to give us an aimpoint," Graber said. "Can't very well go around grabbing just anybody's nuke."

"After we grab it, can we shove it up old Fidel's you-know-what?" Jones wondered aloud, his strict Baptist upbringing coming back to temper his descriptive wordage.

"Unfortunately . . ." Sean heard the Pave Hawk approaching. "Captain, we're going to need some stuff from Wally World. I anticipate that this will need to be done fast and in the dark."

"Quiet, too," Buxton added. "What *do* we do with it once we have it?"

"First it has to be found, then we have to do our end, Captain," Sean said. "Let's get the preliminaries out of the way first." He didn't say that he'd been asking himself the same thing since the colonel's call.

"Those things scare me," Buxton admitted.

"Scares everybody," the major agreed. "They're supposed to. MAD, remember."

"Good name," Buxton commented. *Bad idea.*

Joe Anderson followed his escort from the west parking lot adjacent to Old Executive. The Secret Service agent had first validated his identification by pure visual recognition, and a second agent did a more thorough check of Joe's driver's license and Social Security number before he was led to the northwest corner of the West Wing. He had been there before. He had been many places. And it appeared he was going to add one new stamp to his mental passport.

"I *was* retired."

Bud DiContino looked up from behind his desk, coming around to greet his guest. The DDI stood from his seat on the couch.

"Guess it didn't agree with you," the NSA said, half attempting a joke. "This is Greg Drummond, Deputy Director, Intelligence, over at Langley."

Joe shook the man's hand. "Met your boss the last time I was here. Sorry about him."

"Good man," the DDI commented. He knew of Anderson's condition also. "Herb spoke highly of you. So does Bud."

Joe took a seat on the couch, the other two men taking chairs that faced him opposite the coffee table.

"We can order something from the dining room," Bud offered.

"No, thanks." Joe didn't relish food at the moment, an amplification of his appetite of late. "I hope this isn't like last time. That kinda shit can kill you," he said with appropriate gallows humor. The look on the NSA's face said more than any words could have. "No way. You have to be kidding!"

"I wish I were," Bud said.

Joe leaned back into the well-used cushions. He had had enough of this from the job that had sent him into retirement, the permanent kind. As former senior member of the Department of Energy's Nuclear Emergency Search Team, his domain had been everything and anything that spit neutrons, he would say. More than running around looking for atomic bombs, the security of nuclear materials in transit had been his primary duty, other than the two times his unique abilities had been put to the test. The first, a happening still classified, had been a success, and Joe had walked away from it with all his white cells intact. The second had been a different story. Scratch one pseudonuke, and scratch one Joe. Well, at least there was some delay in the final effect. Time for him to get in some last-minute fishing and time with the wife.

Joe looked at the men now tasking him to again do something "only he could do," and wondered if that northern pike was a goner for good. Bad word "goner," he thought silently. "Spill it."

"The Cubans may have a nuclear weapon," Bud said.

Joe laughed, but not at the humor of it. "Another 'may have,' eh? Where'd this one come from?"

Bud explained what they knew, which was little more than a series of propositions strung together by chance. Yet it was enough to put an icy look on Joe's face.

"What is your impression?" the DDI wondered. "I know you haven't had time to look at anything closely but . . ."

"First of all, I can't believe you guys are still sitting here. Where the hell is the President?"

"Don't worry," Bud assured him. "There are contingency plans."

"Contingency plans?" Joe scoffed, laughing this time with incredulity. "Yeah, got any good air-raid shelters around here?" His foot tapped the floor solidly. "I suppose it's good concrete, but you want to test it against a one-megaton warhead?"

"If they have it, and if they aim it here," Bud answered with a supposition and a fear. "What we need from you are a couple of things. First, if Castro does have it, what's the likelihood that it is operational?"

"Not very without maintenance," Joe answered without hesitation. "That goes for the warhead and the delivery system."

Bud was a little surprised at part of the response. "I figured the missile itself would require a lot of work to keep it in working order. But the warhead?"

"You obviously haven't seen them up close and personal, have you?" Joe got head shakes from both men. "I thought not. You see, there's this perceived elegance about the actual bomb part of a weapon. Sure, when it's strapped to the top of a booster or slung in the bay of a B-1, it looks real sexy. But if you take it apart, piece by piece, most have over six thousand components. Those are ours, of course. The Russian ones have fewer, mostly because of the safety systems—or I should say lack of on theirs."

"Theirs?" Drummond asked, wondering how . . . *Oh.*

Joe saw the DDI answer his own question with a moment of retrospection. "Right. Those torps the *Glomar Explorer* pulled up with part of that sub back in '74 gave up a lot of their technology. If we're talking a one-megger from an SS-4, you can expect something at least as crude. Probably more so.

"You see, the safety systems are the most delicate part of the warhead after the actual physics package—that's the part that goes boom. Now, we didn't get what I'm going to tell you from the torps, but you probably already know the source anyway. Soviet weapons predating what are *their* third-generation warheads used mechanical accelerometers."

"Those are the safety systems that prevent it from arming until a pre-set velocity is reached, right?" Bud asked.

"Correct. The Soviets used what are called seismic-mass accelerometers. They're basically a series of springs and pistons preloaded with tension that will resist the force of a small multidirectional weight until the mass increases by way of velocity to a point that the pistons are tripped. That arms the warhead. Actually the more correct term is it *de-safes* it. Primitive but effective.

We use piezoelectric versions that measure the fluctuation in electromagnetic waves, and recently a system that measures actual travel in miles per second based upon GPS readings. There are backups on ours, of course, but my guess is that the one down there would have no backup. If the primary failed, it would arm itself past apogee. At least that's the intel we got."

Drummond knew where the intel had come from, as he was sure Bud did also. He wondered if that agent was still just tending his stall in that Kholkoz market in St. Petersburg. It was something he knew he could never check on. Not if he wanted the man to have the chance to live out his life. "But it would be possible to maintain it?"

"Sure," Joe said, somewhat disbelievingly. "If they . . ." His face went ashen. "Vishkov."

"Exactly what we figured," Bud said.

Joe couldn't believe it. The little prick was coming back to haunt him.

"Okay, they have someone to keep the warhead functional," Bud reluctantly admitted. "What about the missile? I thought maybe the Chinese and North Koreans they had—"

"The Cubans wouldn't need them," Joe interrupted, running a few figures through his head. "Vishkov was a team leader for a few years with the SRF. That was the Soviet's form of quality circles and stuff. They were early lookers at the Japanese way, but it never stuck. The teams were supposed to work out all the bugs from all angles in their missiles. I forget what exact project he was on at that time, but it would have given him the knowledge, at least a basic one, of the principles involved in rocketry."

"So he could have seen to the booster, too?" Bud inquired, his eyes looking toward the DDI. His expression spoke volumes about the growing realization that something terrible had been lurking in their backyard for a long time.

"Let's see. He came over in '82." *Defected,* Joe thought. *We got snookered with that one.* "That would have left at least a twenty-two-year-old booster at that point. Hmmm." His eyes went to the dark floor, the mind behind them filtering and placing what he knew about the topic in a logical order. "The corrosive effects of the fuel and oxidizer would have started by then." *Could he really have . . . ?*

Bud's brow furrowed. "Explain."

"Rocket fuel is notoriously corrosive. That's why the Soviets

stuck with nonstorable propellant mixtures for so long." Joe saw
the nonverbal *huh?* on his student's faces. "Nonstorable propellants were like gas in a tank—you pumped it when you needed it.
Storable propellants, which the Soviets favored once perfecting
them, were made possible by semi—and I repeat *semi*—stable
mixtures. These could be left in the missile's tanks for long periods without causing damage. Even though the SS-4 was supposed to use a storable combination of red fuming nitric acid as
oxidizer and kerosene as fuel, it wasn't practical to keep the thing
fueled since it was a transportable missile. All that extra weight of
the liquids was not easy to move around on the back of the TEL.
That's the transporter-erector-launcher. For all intents and purposes it used nonstorable combos. See, we put a lot of pressure on
Thiokol to perfect solid-fuel motors for the MX. The Minuteman
ran on a Thiokol solid also, but they really perfected it with the
MX. The Soviets never got big on solid fuel until the late seventies." Joe thought he was giving too much in this lesson. "Look,
what I'm trying to say is that if there was a mating exercise, cou-
pled with a full fueling, as you believe, then there's a good chance
that the thing wouldn't fly."

The NSA thought on that for a moment, but the DDI spoke
first.

"You mean they may not be able to deliver it? To shoot it at
us?" Drummond knew he was hoping, but . . .

"Do I mean that's a possibility? Sure. But is it a guarantee?
Not on your life." Joe let out a tense laugh. "Wouldn't bet on
mine, you know. Kinda like throwing down your neighbor's dead
cat as a marker in poker." It was more gallows humor, something
Joe had perfected in the recent past.

"Vishkov could have helped them maintain it, or . . . what,
refurbish it?" Bud asked.

Joe laughed again, though this time because of the role he
was being cast in. "Hey, who are the spooks here? Come on.
Think! Why the hell else would he be there? You think Castro, if
he has a good warhead, would waste it?" *But that would take a major
redo.* Joe was doubting his own exhortations.

"You look mighty convinced," the DDI cracked.

Joe felt the strange aura of *déjà vu* sweep over him. *It was on
this same couch, even.* "Maybe I'm not, but I'm smart enough to
realize that you don't gamble on something like this. You also
don't bluff. Why should Castro?"

There was nothing more to discuss. "Okay, Captain."

"Cut the rank crap," Joe insisted. His Air Force days were long gone. Somehow the title had stuck with him through DOE, probably because bureaucrats thought anyone that knew more than them about something, a reality Joe had frequently been called upon to exhibit, had to be someone of rank or stature. "Just Joe, all right?"

"All right." Bud hated what came next. "Joe, I talked to—"

"Yeah. When do I leave?" Being the only person to ever disarm a live nuke carried with it the curse that you were often considered the only one who *could* ever do it.

"A few hours." To make this man do more, when he had already done so much . . . Given the ultimate in service. "Anything you need is yours."

"All I need is for you to get me to it."

"Kind of a repeat performance," the NSA offered, his knowledge of Joe's biggest job at the forefront of his thoughts. That one had been successful, but it had also been different.

Anderson knew he didn't have to answer. Actually he didn't want to. There were other things more important to say. "I'll do this." He looked to both men with a fire in his eyes that could only have been conjured by a mighty wrath. "But I want you to know I hate it. I spent the best years of my life trying to make sure no one got their hands on those things, and all you guys do is keep them around. You keep making them better. What Castro may have down there is ancient, but it can still kill a million people." That was always a picture his mind trembled at. "A million people. Stop perfecting them, stop making them better, and start getting rid of them."

"No arguments from me," Drummond said.

Joe stood. "My wife is gonna be pissed."

What could Bud say to that? Nothing. The man had maybe a year left, and his government was asking him to come back and give more.

"Maybe I should leave now," Joe said. "I'm sure whoever I'm going to link up with will want to get used to my sunny personality."

"No need," Bud responded. "They're well versed in the ways of Mr. Anderson."

Them. "Well, if that don't beat all. Thought I'd never see those guys again. Rather wouldn't have, actually, but if it has to be someone, there's none better."

202   Ryne Douglas Pearson

"A compliment? Don't worry, it'll stay in this room. I wouldn't want to tarnish your persona," Bud joked. "And you can't leave yet, anyway. The President wants to see you first."

The bureaucratic end of the stick had always been his least-favorite part of the job. Now it was his least-favorite part of retirement. "I'm not the best at political etiquette, you know."

"He's no Boy Scout, either."

"All right," Joe agreed. "I assume you've made arrangements for me to get what I'll need at DOE."

"The secretary will personally be waiting for you at Andrews," Bud confirmed. Andrews Air Force Base was the East Coast staging site for NEST, Joe's old team.

"Fine."

Joe Anderson was gone as fast as he had come.

"He's incredible," the DDI commented. "Like a machine when it's time to go to work."

It was a good way to put it, Bud agreed. "Guess this puts Vishkov in the center, or at least near it. We find him, and we may be able to zero in on the missile. Let's hope we hear something from the rebels."

"What about Vishkov himself?" the DDI wondered. "If we find him, I mean."

Bud's gaze went cold. What he wanted to do to the renegade Russian was not in his power to accomplish, or to order. It was in someone's power, however. "He'll get his justice. I'm sure of that. Remember, we have a very convincing lobbyist with the Man now," the NSA pointed out, his eyes glancing upward. He wasn't referring to the President.

It was very early in the morning, the light of the new day still a dream for those fortunate enough to be sleeping, a luxury not often afforded on a regular basis to warriors engaged in battle. Yet, even in the darkness that was the undeniable friend of the fighting soldier, there was work to be done. Night was the perfect environment for the dispensation of violence. It was also the preferred battleground where the quieter arts of war, the ones disdained by the professional soldiers in uniform, were practiced. It was the common domain of the spy.

Antonio was standing, Ojeda and Manchon sitting on the edge of the truck's rear gate. "You know of him?"

Ojeda folded the paper in half and handed it back to Papa

Tony. "The question should be why does your government now *want* information? They do not tell us this."

Paredes knew he had to stand up to the colonel. Attempted explanations, of which there were none, would not placate him. The truth might, but the CIA officer didn't know what the truth was. The only remaining alternative was insistence.

"They would not request information from you if it was not necessary. Two simple questions, that is all." Paredes noticed Ojeda's gaze soften. "We have given a great deal."

"Yes." Ojeda stood. "We know of him."

Thank God he didn't shoot me. "And where is he?"

Why should the Americans care where a miserable little scientist who had fallen out of favor with the *presidente* was? *Why, indeed?* "Captain Manchon will show you on the map."

The information was transmitted through the facsimile function of Paredes's satellite manpack up twenty-two thousand miles to a Milstar satellite five minutes later. Langley had it seconds after that.

CHAPTER TWELVE

The Turning of Stones

The walk had only been a block and a half in distance, yet they felt as if every eye in the city was on them. But they were now there. To safety.

"Hurry up," Tomás exhorted. His wounds were minor, just a series of scratches on his face and one nasty gash inside his mouth.

Jorge, though, was really hurting. Something was seriously wrong with his back and neck, forcing him to walk as if someone had taken his spine and twisted it like a piece of soft metal, deforming the outer shell until it resembled some grotesque medieval sculpture in motion. "Man, I'm moving as fast as I can."

Tomás turned from the sidewalk to the unwelcomely well-lit walkway that ran in front of the rooms, with Jorge a few steps behind. Theirs was at the inside corner of the motel's *L* where the two sections of the structure met. From there they had a perfect view of the parking lot and the intersection beyond. The plan now called for getting cleaned up and rested before the courier arrived for the tape. And they still had to somehow get Sullivan, though that could wait for a while. Just a while.

Jorge limped up to the door as Tomás was fumbling through his pockets.

"Come on, open it," Jorge said, almost pleaded, his face contorted by pain.

Where is it? "I can't find it. You have it?"

"The key? No. Come on."

"I can't . . . oh, shit!" Tomás softly punched the door as a release. "I left the key in the car. I put it in that tray between the seats. Shit!"

"All right. No big deal." Jorge would have cursed his partner if the pain hadn't been so bad, but all he wanted was to get onto the bed. "It's gone. Nothing will survive the fire, okay? Just go to the night window and tell them we lost it. Okay? Hurry, man."

Tomás still was pissed at himself for doing such a stupid thing. At least they'd torched the car, which they knew would destroy any fingerprints or other evidence of their identity. And also the key, now. He got a replacement from the not-real-happy-to-be-awakened night clerk and went back to his partner.

"Five fucking bucks for a key!" He shoved it in the hole and opened the door, letting Jorge in first. He immediately fell onto the bed.

"This hurts, man. Have we got any booze left?"

Tomás checked the dresser drawer. "A little Chivas."

"Give it."

The remains were gone in a minute, but it would take longer for the effects to be felt.

"Sleep, Jorge. Just take it easy." Tomás went to the bathroom and rinsed his mouth out, checking the gash inside in the mirror. "We'll find Sullivan in the morning." The taste of blood was heavy as he spoke.

"I want him, Tomás. I want him dead. Dead! And I want him to feel it. No bullet-in-the-head crap—ahhh!" Jorge writhed in pain. "God, is there any Tylenol or anything in there?"

"None." Tomás came back from the bathroom. "Sorry."

"Yeah." He twisted and bent his body into as comfortable a position as he could. "Sullivan will be, too."

Art and Frankie pulled up just as the fire department had finished dousing the flames with spray from an inch-and-a-half line. The injured cop had seen Sullivan bail out of the Lumina before it fled from the crash scene, so they anticipated no body would be in the smoking hulk.

"You Jefferson?" the LAPD sergeant asked. He was in a foul mood. It hadn't been a good night for the force.

"Yeah. Anything?" Art stood back while Frankie began examining the steaming remnants of the Lumina.

"Just looks like they pulled it in the alley and set the inside on fire. From there . . ."

It was obvious. The bulk of the once pretty car was now just charred bare metal, save the extreme front and back.

"VIN?" Art inquired. The vehicle identification number was stamped on a small dash placard below the windshield in front of the driver's seat.

"Burned pretty bad. We'll have to pull it off the firewall." A second stamping of the VIN was located on the firewall in the engine compartment in a not readily accessible place. That prevented easy tampering, but it also prevented quick access for the purpose at hand.

"We don't have that much time." Art scratched his head, his fingers finding more scalp than hair. Life was just grand, wasn't it?

"Art."

He walked over to his partner, who was crouched down at the vehicle's rear. It was basically untouched by the intense heat, other than some blistering on the trunk deck. "Look here."

Art bent down, the LAPD sergeant behind him shining his light on the area just to the right of the trunk lock. "Scratches."

"Looks like someone peeled off a sticker," Frankie observed, looking up to her partner. "Like a rental one, maybe."

Art turned to the sergeant. "You got a prybar?"

"Yeah. Why?"

"We're popping this trunk. Rental companies started putting additional copies of the VIN and the owner information on a little plate under the trunk lining last year."

The sergeant nodded. Anything to find the perps who caused the deaths of two good cops and the injury of his close friend. "One minute."

It was less than that. The lock gave way after a few forceful pushes. Art peeled back the soggy carpeting so Frankie could find the placard.

"Got it." She copied it down and went straight to the radio. Their teams checking rental agencies now had a specific target, and those running down stolens could be redirected. She was back from the broadcast in under a minute.

Art had walked to the front of the car, leaving the sergeant to complete his report.

"Step one," Frankie said.

Art was silent, his eyes scrutinizing first the damaged front of the car and then the surrounding area. They were in a mixed residential-industrial area southeast of Beverly Hills, though that proximity did nothing for the neighborhood's aesthetics. The majority of BH was no better, any observer could see upon a short visit. Art had done so on many occasions, each one convincing him that his town house in La Canada was preferable to living in some mansion surrounded by squalor.

The alley jutted off from Rimpau Boulevard, a generous description of the narrow street. Rimpau itself intersected Olympic just a hundred feet from where the alley broke off to connect it with parallel streets. From the spot where he stood, Art tried to imagine where the shooters had gone. Which way?

"Let's take a walk," Art led off to the end of the alley— actually its beginning—at Rimpau. Frankie was right with him.

"They came back this way," Frankie said.

"How do you figure?" Art asked, stopping at the alley's opening, his eyes scanning the neighborhood.

"Backtrack." She took a few steps out into the dark street, looking back at Art. "They pulled in this way, probably came up from Olympic." She pointed down the alley, past the car and in the direction it had been heading. "That way is unfamiliar. My guess is they backtracked out here up to Olympic."

Art's head cocked toward his observant and driven partner. "Let's see what's up there."

The walk-up took just a minute. Olympic Boulevard at one in the morning was as deserted as any other major street would be. There were the expected late travelers cruising the street, but very few visible on foot. It was not a safe area, like much of the city, especially after the sun went down.

"And from here?" Art asked.

Frankie looked to the left, toward the east. The street was almost desolate, and there were no pay phones that jumped out at her. None of the familiar blue handset signs. "Not a cab."

Art thought not. That, aside from being a practical impracticality in this area, would have left a well-defined trail. These guys were too smart, he believed. Too smart to do that. "They didn't walk."

"No." Frankie turned right, looking west, and smiled. "There."

Coming from the west on Olympic, across the street from the two agents, was the graffiti-scarred traveler of the night. Art and

Frankie trotted across the boulevard, holding their shields in the air to flag down the number 28 bus of the Metropolitan Transportation Authority on its last run of the night. The driver pulled his nearly empty coach over on the south side of the street and opened his door.

"Yeah?"

"How often does this line run?" Frankie asked.

The yellow-shirted driver, a small but muscular man whose years behind the wheel had obviously given him the wariness of the streets, narrowed his eyes at the young woman on the first step of his Grumman. Her coat had parted, revealing a gun on her right hip. He wished he could carry one so large, but his was just a little .380 that he kept in a thigh holster despite company and legal prohibitions against doing so. "Every forty minutes after eleven P.M. We went to that schedule two weeks ago." He cast an almost evil eye at the other agent behind the woman. "I've never seen you out here before. LAPD?"

"FBI," Art answered. The man's eyes were powerful, and the wispy gray of his mustache and hair added to that to give his dark black face an air of authority.

"How many other drivers on this line tonight?" Frankie probed. She was intimately familiar with the MTA from her many childhood days spent riding from the family's apartment to the doctor's office and from her part in an undercover operation that had busted several drivers for trafficking in narcotics.

"Two." His eyes narrowed almost to slits.

"Did you pick up two guys in the last three hours?" Frankie pulled out her folded copies of the shooters' composites.

His head shook in response.

"The other two drivers still on the line?"

The driver nodded, wondering just what the FBI wanted with bus riders.

Frankie turned to her partner, her eyes asking, *Well?*

"I want you to contact your dispatchers and have them get a hold of both buses to find out if these guys were on either of them." Art looked to Frankie, but she was already across the street on her way to get the car.

The driver picked up his handset, which was a duplicate of that used on telephones. "Dispatch, this is Forty-Five on the Twenty-Eight, bus number Eighty-six Thirty-nine."

The dispatcher acknowledged the driver's call and listened

to his relay of the agents' request. Two minutes later, just as Frankie pulled the Chevy ahead of the bus, their answer came back.

"Yeah. The one two ahead of me remembers two guys just like that."

Yes! "Where's that bus now?"

It took a minute to get the answer. "Olympic and Alvarado, deadheading back to division."

Art gave a quick thumbs-up to Frankie in the driver's seat. "Tell your dispatcher to hold that bus there. We're on our way."

"Well?" Frankie asked, anticipation in her voice and eyes.

"Olympic and Alvarado. Go. Go. We may finally have a trail."

Frankie floored it back into the traffic lanes. It would take only a few minutes to travel the distance, but she wasn't going to waste any time. Trails could grow cold very quickly, and this was just about all they had at the moment. "What about Sullivan?"

"Let's hope he's passed out on a barstool, nice and safe-like."

"I think we can count on that." Frankie accelerated through a series of greens going east on Olympic. "Hang on."

The bartender looked at the newcomer and pointed to the clock. "Closing soon, buddy."

Sullivan looked up, but the numbers were unintelligible. He'd have to take the bartender's word for it. His second drink was barely touched, which amazed him because he'd been there for more than two hours. For some reason the booze just wasn't calming him. In fact, it was hard to even swallow. There was no relaxation coming from this round of drinking, and that scared him. Really scared him. "Yeah. Okay."

He had come in pretty juiced, and he was not one of the regulars, so the bartender immediately had laid a protective eye on him. Two drinks, he'd decided. That was it. No more. It was *his* liquor license on the line if the guy walked out in front of a truck or something, not even considering if he got behind the wheel. That he had made sure was not a possibility. The guy only had a motel key on him. That was a smart move, though it really wasn't close. Well, the walk would do him good.

Sullivan had that key in one hand and his still-full drink in the other. He stared down at the large plastic tab attached to the key. It had all he needed, all the police would need. Address, room number. He could dial 911 right now, and the guys would be caught. He'd be safe again. No more worrying about his life.

Just the future . . . What was he going to do about that? No job. His house was wrecked. His eyes went down to the glass of liquid. Was it just that? *Liquid?* Was that all it was? Just something to quench his thirst?

Then why can't I . . . ? His fingers tightened on the object that safely held his friend. That was it! It was his friend. It was that. When all others were gone he still had his . . . *booze.*

It was really all he had.

No. His grip on the glass released, and the hand came up to his mouth, covering it for fear that he would vomit. He felt as though he would, and he wanted to drink the— *What is it? Bourbon? JB?* He couldn't remember. But he still wanted it desperately. It was just that he couldn't. Just *couldn't.*

He again looked at the key and just as soon realized what had been presented to him. It was as clear and simple as that. It was a choice. *Prove yourself, George, or drown in the booze.*

The glass was still there, still full, still calling him to drink. To just take it in. To just drink.

He turned away. The key was in his hand, and the grip that had held the glass tightly a moment before now squeezed his only hope. It was his only hope. It was the chance to prove himself. He didn't want to die, not this way. Not now. Not like this.

Give me the strength, Sullivan asked silently, the request directed nowhere in particular. He doubted that God had any time left for him. He was on his own, determined to do what he had to, despite what he and others had thrown before him in the way of obstacles. He had little left of value in his life, just the memory of what he had been. And what he could be. *What I have to be.*

"Hey," Sullivan said, drawing the bartender's attention. "Take this away." He pushed the glass down the bar. "Coffee."

The bartender smiled at the request, but George didn't notice. His attention was focused on the key in his hand. More specifically on the tab. In the morning it would be his starting point. His test. His mission. He was a reporter, a finder of facts, a newshound. It was his job, regardless of the lack of an employer. Some men had to do things for themselves, and sometimes without renumeration for their efforts in mind. This just had to be done.

Regardless of the outcome.

*   *   *

Mrs. Carroll had obviously done a good job describing the suspects to the Bureau computer artist, as the driver waiting at Olympic and Alvarado needed only a quick look at the composites to make an I.D.

"Yeah. Those're the guys." He handed the folded paper back to Frankie.

"Do you remember where they got off?" Her fingers tapped the tip of the pen on her notebook. *Come on. Please.*

"Sure do. Olympic and Vermont. One of the guys walked funny, like his back was hurt." He laughed sympathetically. "I popped an L4–L5 disk myself, so I know the way it looks and feels."

"South side of the street?"

"Yeah. Nearside before Vermont."

"Did you issue a transfer?"

One eye cocked at that suggestion. "This time of night? No way."

"Remember which way they went?" Frankie waited while he thought back.

His head shook apologetically. "Nah, I don't. Sorry."

"It's okay. Thanks."

The driver closed the door as soon as the agents were off his empty bus. He was already thirty minutes late getting back to division, but it hadn't been all a waste. The lady cop was a looker, after all.

"What do you think?" Frankie asked, facing her partner. His eyes were focused to the side of her, his mind in high gear. It was a face she had come to know and respect.

"No car. They take the bus to Olympic and Vermont." Art's eyes finally met Frankie's, his head shaking the barest bit. "Not a great area," Art commented. "One of them sounds like that collision might have messed him up."

"I doubt they were walking too far," Frankie said. "This obviously wasn't the way they planned this to happen, so they probably were just trying to get back to their hole. Especially if one of 'em's injured."

"A lot of motels along Vermont right there, aren't there?"

"You mean rent-a-sheets?" Frankie answered cynically. She had been in the City of Angels long enough to learn that its holy moniker was no guarantee of saintly behavior. "Tons."

"All right, we set up an OP," Art said, the preliminaries of a plan forming in his mind. An observation post was a necessity to watch for the shooters in the area they'd last been seen in. "I want Rob Deans and Hal Lightman on it. Hal's an eagle eye."

"Okay." Frankie was noting the assignments to be called in.

"I want it set so they can monitor foot traffic up and down Vermont from Olympic. Then I want a listing of every motel or hotel in a twelve-block area."

She mentally recoiled at the size of that area to cover. "How are we going to keep an eye on that from one OP?"

"One team at the OP," Art said. "We've got plenty others to use as rovers."

"Yeah, but with that much presence the suspects are sure to know we're out there?"

Art smiled. "Exactly. I want them seen. I want our shooters to know we're out there. I want them scared."

"But if they know there's a net out there for them, they'll stay put," Frankie observed, not seeing the fullness of her partner's plan.

"That's what I want."

"What?"

Art had learned not only the limits of prudence in his line of work, but also the value of it. "We're taking these guys on our terms, when we want them, and how we want them. They have to be in that area, probably in one of those motels."

"But we have to find them, and I thought the operative word was 'fast.' "

"We will," Art assured her, his surety motivated by determination. "We just have to do it right."

"How?"

Art turned and headed back to the car, accepting the fact that cautious behavior didn't always lend itself to easy answers. "I'm working on it." *No screwups this time.*

And that meant for his partner either. "I'll get it set up while you go catch some sleep."

What? "But . . ."

"No buts," Art said sternly. "If you want in on this, then you need sleep. It's been a rough past few days, and I know what can happen to someone when they push it too far. Remember me— super Art? You're not going to end up like me, so consider yourself off duty until seven A.M. Go home, get a few hours shuteye, and kiss Cassie. Once for me, too. Tell your mom I said hi."

There was no arguing with her partner. He was right, and she hated it. She had a little girl who needed to see her once in a while, something she had worked her life around. Until the past couple of days. And she still hadn't told her that Uncle Thom was . . . was . . . "Drop me back at the garage?"

"Sure will. Then you go get some sleep."

That she could do with little problem. It was what came after that that scared her.

Greg Drummond cleared his desk and laid the map of the area surrounding Cienfuegos flat on it. Mike Healy weighted the corners with assorted items just removed from the DDI's work surface. The map was one of the plethora produced by the Defense Mapping Agency, using geological and satellite surveys to create representations of the land, and its features that were the most highly detailed available on earth. This one, of startling detail, was not even one of the newer digitally produced maps that the DMA had started to turn out. Everything was going to computers, even the fine old art of cartography.

In addition to topography, the map had been prepared with the notable facilities denoted as blocks of dark gray. A corresponding notebook or computer database gave precise information on any and all of the man-made landmarks. This particular map had been produced for the Agency's survey of Cuba's industrial capacity, giving it a heavy emphasis on that type of structure. Cuba had developed quite an industrial base in its heyday as a member of COMECON, the economic bloc headed by the former Soviet Union with the goal of fostering development and trade among its signatories and outside countries. Chief among these industries were sugar production, various light industries, and, as a home-grown necessity, oil refining. The refineries at Cienfuegos and Los Guaos were denoted on the map by small, crisp blocks and dots of gray that signified the various buildings, cracking towers, and holding tanks. That was on the east side of the bay. On the western shore were three small manufacturing plants—all closed—and one of Castro's follies, the never-completed nuclear-power plant that COMECON had financed. When the subsidies from the now-dead East bloc dried up, the huge complex had simply been abandoned, just two years shy of completion, despite an offer of funding from the People's Republic of China. It was just one in a string of failed ventures that Castro had attempted over the decades to bring his island nation into the technological twentieth century.

But the symbols on the map also pointed out the daunting task that the two Agency executives had before them. Finding buildings was easy. Finding a missile was not.

"So Vishkov is supposed to be here," the DDO said, pointing at the southwesternmost tip of the Bay of Cienfuegos from his upside-down vantage point. Drummond slid to the side, motioning for him to come around.

"Castillo de Jagua." The DDI recalled the few visuals he'd seen of the eighteenth-century fortress that had once guarded the narrow opening to the bay. "It appears that Castro wanted Vishkov isolated as well as incarcerated. Have you ever seen it?"

Healy shook his head.

"I think the word is *imposing.* Lots of stone. Lots and lots of it. It looks like it belongs somewhere along the Thames."

The thought had occurred to them that Vishkov might be valuable to snatch. He would likely know the precise location of the missile. But any attempt to wrest him from his fortress prison would require a battalion of troops at least, and would blow the secrecy that was vital to finding and securing the weapon. Besides, as Castro had proved through the years, he had little need for those whose usefulness had been exhausted.

"So he's there." Healy leaned over the desk, both fists resting on the map. "Now where's the missile?"

Drummond surveyed the landscape. Hiding places were numerous, but one just didn't pull a thirty-year-old missile out of a warehouse and fire it. It needed a stable launch surface, just as the Russians had built when first bringing them to the island. Fueling equipment would also be required. A missile did little by itself without support. "Take your pick."

"Any longstanding structures?" Healy wondered aloud, checking the DFS (Date First Sighted) notation of the facilities in the area.

"Other than dwellings"—Drummond joined in the search—"none."

"I just thought that if something had been around since the time of the crisis, we could assume it might be a long-term hiding place."

It was a possibility, but not the best one. None of the older structures could be considered secure, and Castro had demonstrated that he was conscious enough about secrecy that he was willing to employ hitmen on U.S. soil. That wasn't proven, Drummond knew, but it was a bet he'd lay money on.

"It couldn't be at the Castillo with Vishkov," the DDI said. "There's very little open area inside the grounds, and the ceilings wouldn't be high enough."

"How high are we looking at?" Healy asked.

"The analysts back then figured a minimum of ten feet for the SS-4 on its TEL. They had to run down all kinds of rumors after the Russians pulled out, that there were still missiles left there hidden in caves and places like that. Problem was, there were no caves with the proper dimensions to hold an SS-4 or the components of it." Drummond saw that Healy was taken aback at that. "No, there weren't folks running around peeking in caves. It just turned out that the Agency had access to pretty complete speleological surveys of the island done before the commies took over. As for the other places, nothing panned out."

"Do you think some of the rumors could have been a product of this missile?" The DDO kept hoping that all this affirmative talk would somehow be negated by the findings in Moscow, but he didn't really believe it would.

"No. Don't ask me why, 'cause it's just a feeling. I think Castro had this planned out pretty well, including the storage of it."

Healy had to agree. "Then where?"

The DDI rubbed his eyes and sat down, pulling his chair forward to the desk. "Let's see. It would need a big area, solid footings. Level, too. Access to roads, yet far enough away that casual observers would notice nothing."

"It's times like this that I wish we'd had more luck getting people into the upper echelons of the PCC," Healy said. The Partido Comunista de Cuba was the singular force in Cuban politics and government, headed, of course, by Fidel Castro as first secretary. The Agency had been unable to penetrate the higher ranks of national politics in Cuba, despite assistance from exile groups and the expenditure of huge sums of money. The DGI, Cuba's equivalent of the KGB and CIA, had been unbelievably effective in keeping the power apparatus of the PCC free from foreign influence, even that of so-called "brother countries" from the defunct East bloc.

"Well, now would be a great time to turn back the clock," Drummond said. "S and T have that time machine finished yet?"

Healy chuckled. "Next week, I hear."

The DDI ran his finger along the outline of the bay, trying to pick out those areas that would fit the bill. "Here."

The DDO bent closer to the map. "Let's see, that's . . ." He paged through the data book that had accompanied the map. "Recio Machine Works. Built in '72 by an East German company. Light and heavy machine tools—mostly high-speed lathes. Armaments, it says. Cannon barrels." It had amazed him and many of the analysts that Cuba had never fully exploited its weapon-building capability. The barrels produced at Recio had been shipped promptly back to the East for assembly into full weapons systems. "Closed in July of '92. Lack of fuel."

"I'd call that one possible." The DDI went on, checking several other sites against the background intelligence. "Jesus, there could be ten or eleven possibles on the west side of the bay. I'm not even thinking about the eastern shore."

"Don't. I doubt they'd have Vishkov traveling all the way over there."

"It's too close to Cienfuegos," Drummond observed, his finger touching the outline of the city of a hundred thousand. "Too many people move around that area." His eyes fell on the old Soviet sub-support facility that was never completed because of U.S. pressure in the late seventies. It was pretty much demolished and rebuilt as housing and various small buildings, none of which would support what they were looking for. Another failed construction project. The DDI wondered if any world leader was as good at starting something and as inept at finishing. . . .

Drummond's attention went back to the western shore, about five miles inland and close to the marshes that spread east from the Zapata Peninsula. It was there, and it was huge. Far enough from any habitations. The people had probably been forced to move. But did it make sense? "Mike, what about the plant?"

"What . . . the nuclear plant?" He carefully studied the lay of the land as best one could from a flat projection. "Sure, it would work, but the rest doesn't add up. The Russians helped build it, and they'd be the last ones Castro would want anywhere near the thing. I'm sure it wouldn't have been there, but there'd have to be signs. Besides, construction didn't shut down until a couple years ago." The DDO stood back up, stretching his back and arms.

"Right. But they could have kept it going." Drummond's head turned left, looking up at his counterpart. "The Chinese, remember?"

Healy's thoughts wandered off to mull that over. "So?"

"So why didn't Castro take them up on it? He had them all over that proposed space-launch complex he dreamed of building out by Holguín. Why not accept their help and finish the plant? We know he could have used the power output. What was it supposed to be—four hundred megawatts off each of the four generators? That would have saved him almost a third of his oil imports! And this is something he knew he'd need. The Soviet Union was a dead dog already when he stopped construction and turned away from the Chinese. Plus, if he'd taken the assistance and proceeded, it would have come under closer IAEA scrutiny." The International Atomic Energy Agency had approved the plans for the plant and would have begun a complete-inspection regime once it was substantially complete.

The DDO turned to the corresponding page for the Juragua Nuclear Generating Plant. "Greg, it's a big sucker."

"I can see that."

Healy read further. "A hundred and twenty separate buildings—the Russians never were good at building things compact, except for crew quarters on their ships and subs." He had thought quarters were cramped during his stint in the Navy, but not after seeing intel on Russian vessels. "Damn, the whole thing is a slab of concrete, it looks like."

"It could launch off the TEL anywhere there."

"Ten thousand acres." Healy looked up from the book. "Over sixteen square miles of buildings, construction, and all kinds of places to hide something like a missile."

The DDI looked to the northernmost part of the map. *Didn't the intel from the past day say the Cubans were retreating to the south?* "Mike, I think we may be onto something here. The government forces are all backing into this relatively small part of real estate with no value other than . . ."

It fit. "I see. What's there to protect? Swamp? And it damn

sure ain't an example of great defensive tactics. Our DOD liaison nearly fell off his chair when he saw the report.''

The thought of thousands of Cuban troops being ordered to defend the area in a desperate setup caused the DDI to shrink away from the map. He eased back in his chair, the DDO turning and resting against the desk, facing his colleague.

''Greg?''

Drummond looked up, his eyes exhibiting a fear his friend had never seen before. ''Mike, if Castro is willing to defend the thing, willing to sacrifice those troops, then it means he's just buying time.'' His voice cracked on the last words, the memories of his youthful experience with Armageddon assaulting his perception of the here and now. ''He really has it, and he's going to use it.''

Healy looked past the DDI to the drawn shades. The sun would be rising soon, and for the first time in his life, he wondered, really wondered, if he might not see it. This was more serious than even the crisis thirty years before that had made it possible. This was really going to happen. One of the goddamn things was in the hands of a desperate man, and he was going to use it. ''What are we going to do?''

The DDI searched the emptiness of his brightly lit office for the magical answer that would make it all better, the same kind of wish he had made when his child walked in front of the ice-cream truck two years before. It hadn't worked then, and it wouldn't work now. Skill had saved his son's life then, and skill this time was all they had.

''Say a prayer and get to work pinpointing it,'' Drummond said, adding that which he believed had really saved his son and hoping that the Man upstairs would help him return the favor by saving a few himself.

Tunney found it amusing that it took the poet Pushkin's use of the thirty-three-character Cyrillic alphabet, known as the ''modified civil alphabet,'' in his writings to bring about an unofficial standard that gave the Russian people a true national language. Before that it had been a contest of usage between the Cyrillic used by the Orthodox Church and that introduced by Peter the Great. State versus the power of God. And a poet had settled it! The Russian language itself was much more difficult for Tunney to master than the mere act of memorizing the stylized Cyrillic alphabet, which he did with ease. He had learned the language with some difficulty after joining the Agency, through courses sponsored by the Department of State. Conversational use of a language was a far cry from committing important phrases to memory, and, though he could easily ask for the bill in one of Moscow's dreadful restaurants—*Dai'te, pazhah'lsta shshot*—he still had trouble understanding the rapid-fire practice of the language that the locals were adept at.

Thankfully this assignment would require no verbiage. Just a comparison of what he saw with what he remembered. His territory.

The stacks of file cartons were surprisingly well organized considering that more than seventy years of military death and prisoner records were stored in such a small space. Actually that made his job easier this day, for all he had to do to put himself in proximity to the area of his interest was to feign disgust with the cramped work area and carry an armful of folders to where he wanted to be.

Once there, it was just a matter of time to locate the Red Army death records for the year of 1962, paying close attention to those departed soldiers whose service jackets showed assignment to artillery units. Two hours into his workday he had found what his superiors had requested. It was time to report.

"Anna."

She turned to see her co-worker gripping his stomach. An *I told you so* look followed. "The bliny and caviar, huh? What did I tell you?"

"I'm sorry," Tunney apologized, assuming the required stooping position to simulate severe cramping. "Can you get me a car back to the embassy? Please?"

The woman stomped off, swearing under her breath that she was not going to let any more of her team members eat in the city until the job was done. Now *she*'d have to pull Patrick's share of the load today. The only justice was that he'd be throwing his guts up back at the embassy.

Tunney followed dutifully, using the skills he'd acquired as a child to fool his mother, but had an almost impossible time holding the laughter in as he thought of asking the chief of station for a note explaining his sudden illness. That would be worth framing!

CHAPTER THIRTEEN

Thunder

Frankie closed the front door easily, only a soft click from the lock signaling that she was home. A single light was on in the living room to her left, and she could see her mother stretched out serenely on the couch, a blue-and-yellow afghan covering her from knee to shoulder. She smiled and took a blanket from the closet and laid it over the woman who had always been there for her and was still, planting a soft kiss on her forehead that caused a slight stir.

She switched off the light and made her way down the hall toward the back bedrooms. Hers was on the right, the door open, and she went to it and tossed her jacket onto the unmade bed. Her penchant for cleanliness and order had been superseded by events. Next she unclipped her holster and laid the weapon in the recessed shelf of her nightstand. There it would be close, not so much because she feared intruders, but she had learned early from the needless deaths in her old stomping grounds that a gun in the wrong hands, of the little variety particularly, was deadly. On the few occasions it was not with her—agents are never really off duty—she kept the weapon in a locked safe high on a shelf in her closet. Little Cassie would someday learn about guns, something Frankie believed was much preferable to her picking one up at a friend's house and not knowing what it was capable of. Knowledge was power, and it was safety.

Little Cassie. Frankie pushed the cracked door open enough to poke her head in. The Winnie the Pooh night-light cast an angelic glow on the singular, constant beauty in Francine Aguirre's existence. She was still a mama's girl, barely four, a quietly intelligent child who never complained when Mommy had to work late but was as possessive as a pit bull when she knew it was "their" special time together. There was never enough of that. Never would be. Looking down on the slender face and the thumb that still found its way to the mouth despite all the talk of being a big girl, Frankie wondered if there ever would be.

She wouldn't disturb her angel's sleep with a kiss, which would surely wake her. It always had. The light-sleeper syndrome, just like her mother. But she didn't really mind those few times when Cassie would awaken. In fact, she had to selfishly admit that it was a purposeful plot on her part sometimes. But not tonight. It was late, actually early, and her daughter was an early riser. Frankie would give her the biggest hug she could in the morning before she went off to preschool. The biggest hug from her, and one from Art, and . . .

Frankie shrank back from the opening, the tears for some reason spilling as though a dam had burst. She backed into her own bedroom and pushed the door almost closed, leaving enough of an opening so she could hear if Cassie started fussing. Her hands came up and covered her face, save the eyes, to muffle the quiet sobs that accompanied the tears.

Why again? she silently asked the darkness. Why was she still hurting so much? Hadn't it all come out the night before? Thom was gone. Gone! She would grieve, she knew, just like she had when her brother died in the car accident a decade before, but why the flood of emotions? It was supposed to ease, wasn't it? Yet it wasn't. It was getting worse. Almost two days later the pain was coming from a deeper place. She remembered the place, but strangely it wasn't where the sorrow had emerged from when her older sibling, her only one, wrapped his new Camaro around the light pole on Mulholland. That was pain. True pain. So was this, but there was something more, a mix of feelings and clouded thoughts that somehow made it worse.

Worse than Johnny's death? How could that be. They were both senseless, stupid things that shouldn't have happened because the victims were both good people. Very good people. Beautiful people. *Why?*

Frankie sat on the bed, falling against the massive stack of pillows that were balled up against the headboard, her face half-buried in one that smelled of the tears from the night before. There was no rhyme or reason to it. None. Johnny had just not been aware enough of his own limitations. He just *had* to try out that damned new black beauty that he'd scrimped and saved to buy. Had to push it up past seventy-five on a curve that was rated for thirty-five. It was just stupidity. His own . . .

At his own hands. A mistake. An accident. Not by design.

Thom's was, she thought, the back of her hand wiping away the wetness under her nose. She sniffled into the pillow and rolled onto her back. It was *Johnny's* time. Was it Thom's? Could it have been? Could it be considered fate when *men* took the existence away from an innocent person?

No! NO!

Was that where the hurt was coming from? Frankie stared at the ceiling for a time that she could not measure, her eyes blinking more rapidly than the flow of tears had caused. The colorless, featureless world narrowed as she continued to search the emptiness above for something. Anything. A form. A spark of light. Something to keep her attention. To keep her from drifting. She wanted to think, to analyze, to investigate, to . . .

Was it really that strong? The hate? That strong? *There's someone to blame for this.* Not just an immortal young guy with a fast car and no sense. This hate was tangible. It had a face. Two faces. Two identities. One victim. One . . .

Avenger?

Frankie let the thought slip way, knowing her subconscious was striving to take over and let sleep come. She wasn't thinking rationally or clearly. Things were affecting her that she could not . . . could not . . .

Frankie Aguirre descended into a light, restless sleep that began, almost upon her eyes closing, to tempt her intellect with sweet dreams of vengeance.

There are four rooms in the executive mansion that the President of the United States traditionally uses for quiet contemplation or private meetings between a few advisers. The Oval Office is first and notable among those. Connected to the Oval Office by a short passway is the second of these rooms, the President's West Wing study. In the main building, near the opening to the East Terrace that leads to the East Wing, is the Library, which contains volumes of the finest of the written word, all by American authors. When the hour permits—tours frequently are coursing through the ground floor on their way to the main attractions one level above—this room can serve as a very private getaway. Finally, on the second floor, with the first family's living quarters, is another study for the chief executive. This room, just off the Truman Balcony, is most often utilized by the President in the wee hours before turning in for the night. Of the four rooms it is the least often used, the most secluded, and the least likely to have attention drawn to it.

Bud DiContino and Joe Anderson skipped the elevator and walked directly from the NSA's office out to the colonnade that was arguably one of the most inviting walks on the eighteen-acre grounds. They passed the Rose Garden on their right, the South Lawn beyond, and the ivory spire of the Washington Monument in the distance, and continued into the ground floor of the main building, turning left after a short jaunt down the vaulted-arch corridor to the stairs.

"You're making me walk?" Joe protested mildly.

"Kitchen staff will be in." Bud checked the time. Breakfast for the President was usually at seven, which was now, though that had been pushed back by the chief of staff. The first lady dined with her husband on most days, though she was away on a trip supporting her cause—adult literacy. Worthwhile and plenty of candidates, Bud thought. "The elevator lets off right near the kitchen and dining room. This way is more discreet."

They continued up, ascending another level after a quick 180 where the stairway opened into Cross Hall on the first floor. Directly opposite the Treaty Room, Bud and Joe ended their climb to the second floor and made a right turn into Center Hall, walking west past the Yellow Oval Room to the President's study on the left. A Secret Service agent gave them a quick look and opened the door.

The President was already there, sitting in a large leather chair, the dark surface of which stood out in a room where light wall coverings and decor complimented the morning just begun. Joe had the strange desire to salute as the Commander in Chief stood to greet them, but offered his hand instead.

"You must be Mr. Anderson."

"Yes, sir." There was a mystique about meeting the President, even for someone with the brash quasi-cynicism of Joe Anderson. "Glad to meet you."

The President motioned to two chairs that faced his. He was jacketless, just a crisp white shirt and a red-striped power tie accompanying the dark gray trousers. "I never had the chance to personally thank you for . . ." *for what, giving your life?* ". . . your service. Especially for the work you did on the hijacking."

My pleasure, Joe almost said automatically before his brain cut off the ludicrous statement. "Just doing my job."

"Mr. President," Bud began, "Ellis suggested moving the meeting up here because he and Jack started getting questions from some of the late birds in the press pool about all the lights on last night."

"That was smart. We don't need to worry about the press right now," the President commented. "Have we received confirmation yet?"

"Not yet, sir," Bud reported. "But we need to be prepared for that eventuality. All indicators are pointing to this being very, very real."

The President tried to mask his expression with confidence, but dealing with incidents such as this twice in his young presidency was wearing on his ability to believe that there was any mode other than "crisis management" in which to operate. That could get to one's manner of dealing with the everyday ins and outs of governing. Not every world leader was filled with such vengeance that he would do something such as that which his country now faced. And not every world leader that might wish to do harm to the United States had the wherewithal to do such. But one apparently had both. And was being backed into a corner. SNAPSHOT no longer had the feel of a great victory to it. Instead, it burned like a sore.

"This is a big one, correct?" the President asked, looking to Anderson.

"One megaton, sir," Joe answered, sensing something behind the President's words. A slight trepidation. Strange, maybe, for the man was known as an excellent debater, able to stoneface his opponents into wondering what was behind the steady eyes. But it was there. Fear. The man was afraid, and that gave Joe cause not for concern but hope. It was a healthy emotion in this situation. "That's the equivalent to the combined explosive force of one million tons of high explosive."

"Uh-huh." The President tried to imagine the power of such a weapon but couldn't. Truly, he did not want to. "I understand from the brief I read this morning that you believe the Russian . . ."

"Anatoly Vishkov," Bud prompted.

"Vishkov. That he could have seen to the maintenance of the missile."

"And the warhead," Joe added.

"Yes. The important part." The President studied the man across from him. "Frail" could not be used to describe his condition, though his physique had taken on a wasting appearance. There was a fire in this man. A drive. Character. A brutal honesty that the President needed at the moment. "The CIA says this isn't a credible threat. You're aware of this?"

"I'm aware that *someone* over there has his head in a hole." *Or up his ass.* The briefing the NSA and DDI had given him said enough about this Merriweather fellow. "And anyone who goes along with that line of thought is kidding himself."

Bud leaned back a bit, feeling the heat of the comment directed at the President. He silently willed Anderson not to push the limits of respect for the Man.

The President, however, took no offense. The warning had been reassuring, in fact. "So it's true what they say about you?"

"They say lots of things about me," Joe responded. "Most of it can't be printed, though. But if you're talking about me sparing the bullshit, then, yeah, that's true. And there's twice the reason now to say it like it is. Having to answer only to myself and you know who kind of clarifies everything. Let's me speak my piece."

"We're not entirely used to plain-speak around here," the President said.

"That's one reason I don't mind retirement."

Once you were part of the D.C. machinery, you realized how much you wanted to be out of it. Or at least how much you wanted to change it. A nice thought, the President had realized long ago. "One of the reasons I wanted to see you was to thank you personally for doing this. The other was to get a straight analysis of what could happen. I can get the rosy picture or the doom and gloom from any one of a dozen specialists. It's like pressing a button. Unfortunately Bud here doesn't know everything about everything, so I have to go out of the circle occasionally. When you're President, you start to realize that a lot of people tell you what they want you to hear, which isn't necessarily the way it is. So, Anderson, I want you to tell me the way it is."

"You may get gloom and doom," Joe warned him.

"At least I won't have gotten it from a cookie-cutter expert from some think tank. Straight. What can this thing do?"

"It can kill a lot of people. What more do you need to know?"

"How accurate is it?"

Joe wanted to stand up and shake the man. Details didn't matter. Couldn't he see that? "Accuracy does not matter when you're talking about a warhead this large and a soft target. That thing does not have to take out a silo, or some command post buried under a thousand tons of concrete. We're talking about a city, and lots of little cities around it, and millions of little people in millions of little buildings. It does not have to land on the South Lawn here to do its damage."

"How far off could it be, Joe?" Bud asked.

All right, if you want the numbers. "D.C. is at the outer-range limit of the SS-4 of the day. Let's assume a major miss. A three-mile miss, which isn't an exaggeration, knowing their targeting systems back then." Joe stood and extended his left hand, pointing to the wall that separated them from the Yellow Oval Room. "That's east. Three miles that way, or thereabouts, is RFK Stadium. Fidel aimed it right here, but ground zero is there. The Redskins are going to need a new home.

"So RFK is dust. I'm guessing a surface or near-surface burst, because that would do the most long-term damage, so there will be a crater over two hundred feet deep gouged out of the earth. All that good stuff will come down later as fallout. But that's later. The real damage comes in the first seconds."

"Heat and blast," the President said, displaying his rudimentary understanding of the process.

"The correct term is thermal pulse and blast," Joe explained. "Blast can actually be subdivided into several distinct phenomena, but for the purpose of explanation, just "blast" will do. Down here, three miles from GZ, the first real effect—other than mass blindness for those looking that way—will come from the thermal pulse. The energy liberated by the detonation, about seventy percent of its total release, heats the air in the immediate vicinity to create the fireball. This fireball emits energy outward in the form of visible, ultraviolet, and infrared radiation, which move at the speed of light away from GZ in all directions. These constitute the thermal pulse that can initially ignite fires miles away. Within three miles, any object with a direct line of sight to the blast will receive a minimum of fifty calories per square centimeter of thermal radiation. That's sufficient to spontaneously ignite just about any material that can burn. Those heavy curtains in the east-facing rooms will spark. The same effect will happen farther out, too, but it degrades with distance. The air will diffuse and absorb more and more energy as it moves farther away from GZ. The actual fireball, which is made of superheated atmosphere, will stop expanding somewhere around the Capitol." Joe paused. "Fire. Not a pleasant way to go."

"The blast wave follows," the President said.

"Basically, yes. A few seconds after the fires ignite, the blast wave will hit here with a force of four-pounds-per-square-inch overpressure. Normal atmospheric pressure is about fourteen psi, so this overpressure will do some nasty things." Joe knew that "nasty" didn't covey the true picture. "Here's a tangible representation of overpressure for you nonengineering types. First, think of it in larger terms. A twenty-foot-long, eight-foot-high wall—just like the side of a small house—has one hundred and sixty square feet. That's over twenty-three-thousand square inches. Multiply that by the amount of overpressure—four psi—and you get more than ninety-two-thousand pounds, forty-five *tons,* of force applied to that wall above what it normally holds. That is a devastating amount of overpressure to most buildings in and around D.C. Every window this side of the Potomac will be shattered and a good number on the other side. Wood-frame houses will collapse like matchstick houses in a strong breeze, though the breeze that follows the blast wave will come in here at over a hundred and forty miles per hour. All these big reinforced stone buildings will act as wind tunnels after their windows and doors, inside and out, give way. Any fire started by the thermal pulse will be fanned into an inferno inside those buildings. All the wood ones farther out, too. It'll be a big one." Joe sat back. "But I don't have time to get into firestorms and conflagrations and all that stuff. Get Glasstone and Dolan from the library if you want a more technical picture. Suffice it to say that little will be left of this city."

A phone rang in the background as Joe finished, and Bud went to answer it.

The President said nothing. The fear that Joe had sensed now showed plainly in the chief executive's eyes. Everyone here could be dead, he thought. Except me. It was a privilege of the office that made him feel small at the moment.

"Sir."

The President looked up to his NSA.

"Langley just received a confirmation from Moscow Station," Bud said. "The names on the headstones are of a Russian missile crew reported killed accidentally in Cuba on October twenty-eighth, 1962."

"My God."

Joe didn't react. He had already resigned himself to the fact that this nightmare was real.

"Bud, what about SNAPSHOT?" the President asked. "I mean, if need be, shut it down. It could push Castro over the edge before we can do anything."

Bud shook his head emphatically. "Drew and Jim and I discussed that possibility, but it could send the wrong signal to Castro." He didn't want to try and explain that the rebel commanders would probably just ignore the directive. "We keep the pressure on."

The President agreed with a nod, then looked to Joe. "You're going to pull another one of these off for us, then."

The attempt at levity was shallow but well intentioned. "Yes, sir."

"Sir," Bud began. "I suggest you keep your schedule normal. We don't want to let on that anything out of the ordinary is going on. That could push Castro into firing the missile."

"Very well. Anderson . . . good luck."

Joe shook the President's hand, then he and Bud headed back the way they had come.

"You have a plane to catch," Bud said as they emerged to the colonnade.

"Yeah. I hate these damn connecting flights." Joe would be flying to Pope Air Force Base in North Carolina to link up with a plane heading farther south.

"Security," Bud explained unnecessarily. "The DCI went down earlier in a pretty blue-and-white from the Eighty-ninth." The 89th Military Airlift Wing was the unit that provided transport for the President and other government officials, the majority of its aircraft sporting the brilliant white-and-blue paint scheme and "United States of America" designation. "We don't want to flood the Cape with too many suits."

Joe looked at the NSA with some distaste for the remark. "I take exception to that, DiContino."

Bud smiled as they walked. "I knew you would."

They continued back into the West Wing. Joe Anderson went to a waiting FBI Suburban for the twenty-minute drive to Andrews. The NSA watched from his office window as the black Chevy carried the acerbic scientist off for . . . *the last* time? *He pushed that morbid thought aside and picked up the phone. It was answered in the Pentagon instantly by a secretary and put right through to another secretary.*

"Meyerson."

"Drew, I need a few things."

The Secretary of Defense recognized the voice, and possibly some urgency in it. "Shoot."

"Get a chopper over here and park it on the South Lawn. Use the off pad."

"The off pad?" The presidential helicopter normally used an area on the South Lawn closer to the mansion than the auxiliary pad.

"Yes. Don't use Marine One. Use Crown Helo. It's smaller." And more appropriate, Bud though to himself. Crown Helo was a heavily modified command-and-control variant of the VH-60, the VIP version of the UH-60 Blackhawk helicopter used by all the military services. Marine One—the designation of the VH-3 when the President was aboard—was a much larger bird that would draw attention if kept ready and waiting on the White House grounds. It—there were actually three identical helicopters—was normally based at Anacostia Naval Air Station when not in use.

Crown Helo? "No problem. I'll have it sent over. And . . ."

"Get Kneecap ready." Kneecap—or NEACAP—was the National Emergency Airborne Command Post, the President's plane to be used as a secure base of operations during extreme national emergency. "Ready" was a relative term for it. It was always in that state, but the NSA's words were meant to ensure that the secretary of defense would make certain that there was nothing that would delay its use.

"My God. Confirmed?"

Bud nodded to himself. "We got the word a few minutes ago."

"I'll have Granger put it out on a readiness check. You want him on board?"

Having the chairman of the Joint Chiefs of Staff on board was not generally planned for, but it would definitely be a plus, especially if the worst happened. "Brief him and do it quietly."

"All right. Is that it?"

"I damn sure hope so."

The night had kept its hold on the island long enough for the convoy from Los Guaos to complete three quarters of its journey in darkness. This time, though, there was little fear of a rebel ambush, at least one that would end as the previous one had. An escort of ten BMP-2 MICVs (Mechanized Infantry Combat Vehicles) were spread out among the twenty tank trucks, a larger number than the first convoy because of the lack of sizable transports. Ninety percent of the refinery's fleet of large tankers were destroyed in the ambush. Overhead, prowling the treetops like an angry avian hunter, the Havoc ensured that no rebels would be allowed any hope of escape if they were foolish enough to show themselves as before.

Major Orelio Guevarra landed his aircraft between two buildings after the last of the convoy vehicles entered the complex. The Havoc's pilot climbed out of the rear seat and ran to a group of officers standing in the long shadows cast by the newly risen sun.

"General Asunción?"

"Yes."

Your eyes are as cold as they say. "Major Guevarra. I am instructed to defend your . . . *command?*" He looked around, wondering what sort of unit could possibly be based here. Possibly one guarding the fuel supplies he had just escorted in. Was the petrol shortage really that severe that it was now necessary to stockpile away from the refinery?

"Yes." Asunción looked at the mechanical sculpture of green-and-black metal sitting in the canyon of pavement that separated the rows of buildings a hundred meters away. "You can operate from here."

"Yes, sir!" The major pointed to two covered trucks that had joined the convoy north of Cienfuegos. "A full ground crew, ammunition, and fuel in one of the trucks. I can fight from anywhere."

Asunción nodded. The abilities of this zealot would only be of consequence to him if there became a need for him to use his beloved helicopter. The general was a footsoldier through and through. These pilots were too full of themselves, he thought.

"General," one of Asunción's assistants called from the row of tank trucks. They had formed up along the tree of pipes where they emerged from below ground.

"Yes, Captain."

The officer looked to the tangle of pipes and valves nearest the lead truck, which had a huge gas-powered pump and a refrigeration unit between the cab and the tank. "This is going to take some time."

"Why?" the general asked, his exasperation with the delays becoming almost unbearable. Answering to the *presidente* was not an enjoyable task.

"The pumping equipment on the lead vehicle is not completely compatible with the inflow valves on the tree. The outflow valve on the pump is a different size than the receptacle on the tree. The larger trucks that were destroyed had the proper equipment, but not these. We have only two trucks equipped with pumps, in fact—one for each type of liquid. We cannot mix the two, of course. The NTO is refrigerated. It must be to maintain it as a liquid. Each truck will have to connect to the respective pump truck to unload its cargo."

"And there is a solution, I anticipate."

The captain nodded emphatically. "We will cut a new inflow valve into the tree using components from one of the trucks."

"Cut into a *fuel* line?"

"General, it is not as dangerous as you must think. I have myself done it before. There will be no combustibles flowing through the line, of course, so—"

"But the vapors?"

"Yes, there will be vapors, but we will purge those through the vent valve on the tree and then pressurize the line with nitrogen. Nitrogen is an inert gas that will prevent combustion as the torch cuts through the wall of the pipe." The captain noticed the continued worry on his superior's face. "It will work, General. As I said, I have done it before."

"And the time?" Time was everything now, as evidenced by the thunder in the distance.

"Several hours. Five, possibly six, before we can begin fueling."

There was no other way, Asunción knew. He could not just wish away the delay. "See to it."

"Uprange five minutes," the pilot warned the RSO. Aurora was three hundred miles from the target and closing on it at a speed of 3,675 mph.

"Systems are synched," the RSO reported. All his sensors would be focused on a relatively small area in central Cuba, though he knew not what the importance of any particular target was. Neither did his pilot. They just took the pictures and let someone else handle the analysis. Those people, of course, would know little of the platform from which the data was collected. Such was the practice of SCI, or sensitive compartmentalized intelligence. It was different from the precept of need-to-know in the fact that the many components of an intelligence-gathering operation were known to many people, but few knew more than one piece, and fewer still knew the whole picture. It was a cumbersome, stifling, sometimes inefficient system, but it worked, provided that the natural curiosities of the involved parties did not get the better of them.

"GPS interface ready." The RSO activated his Global Positioning System interface, a delicate, computer-controlled aiming system from the sensors that used positional readings from satellites to let the image computers know the exact location of both target and platform. It was less for the visible-light sensors than for the SAR, particularly when the mission called for narrow observation, as this one did. The basic premise was that clarity in the representation of the data gathered was dependent upon two things: knowing precisely where the platform and target were at all times during the pass. Knowing the location of just the platform was not enough, as the target was also not in a consistent location, a problem caused by the simple fact that the earth moves, and, therefore, every point on it follows the motion. If the position of a GPS ground station was known in relation to a target that has none, the location of the unknown could be determined. Noting the position of the platform was just a process of taking GPS readings forty times per second. These positional readings were then used to correlate the "picture" created by the SAR and place landmarks and geological features within an overlay of the area of observation. Because of the precision allowed by the GPS interface, the SAR could begin imaging the target while still approaching, giving oblique views that were combined with the overall data package to give extreme three-dimensional detail.

"Uprange three minutes." The pilot checked her performance readings. Everything was fine. This was not the time for a minor glitch to disrupt the mission. "Systems are nominal."

"Shooting now." The RSO activated the SAR with just the touch of a button. Target information had been fed in before takeoff. Three feet below him, and running toward the rear of the aircraft another thirty feet, the powerful radar-imaging system focused on a point 180 miles away. Seventeen-thousand-two-hundred-eighty-inch-square planar radar transceiver/receivers protected within the graphite epoxy housing swiveled toward the target in fractions of a millimeter until the computers decided that the energy was properly focused.

"Receiving data."

The pilot again checked the systems. A bunch of microprocessors told her everything was A-OK, and there was no arguing with that. Flying sure had changed from her days at Colorado Springs and, later, piloting the TR-1, the updated version of the famed U-2. She barely touched the stick—a six-inch form-molded handle on her right console—during flights in her present ride. But looking through the tiny viewport above her head—the windscreen was covered by a retractable shield during the climbout to altitude—she could think of no complaints. Day was breaking 130,000 feet below her, but straight up, a direction she hoped to go one day in the right seat of the Space Shuttle, it was a beautiful indigo with flecks of white still visible. Low and slow was the way some fighter drivers liked it, but not her. High and fast, riding a rocket, was the only way to go. Someday. This would do for now, though.

"That's a wrap," the RSO reported five minutes after the pass began. He immediately began compiling the data for relay to NPIC. He'd have to do no preprocessing on this package.

"Okay." The pilot took one last look upward. "Let's head on home."

Why was he driving like that? The needle was passing fifty, then sixty, then seventy, then eighty.

Johnny, slow down.

He turned and smiled at her, his face as young and smooth as ever. She looked back at him from the passenger seat.

Sis, hang on. This is fun. He glanced into the backseat. *Right, Thom?*

Frankie's head jerked to the left. It was him! Sitting there, just fine! *Tommy! You're all right.*

But he didn't answer. He just smiled, looking like a little boy. *Tommy, why won't you say anything?*

She felt the car go around the corners at a speed that seemed impossible. Her stomach twisted and turned as the speed increased. *Johnny, please.*

Easy, Sis. You're such a crybaby, just like when Mom used to go to work. Stop your worrying.

She looked out the front window again. Telephone poles rushed past and the brown walls of dirt lining the roadway seemed to be one long . . . what? . . . tunnel. No, it couldn't be a tunnel, because she could see the sky.

Hey, who are those guys?

The car stopped instantly, going from a hundred to zero in the blink of an eye. Frankie felt her insides jump, but it wasn't from the motion, or cessation of it. *No!*

Johnny stepped out of the car first, followed by Thom. They walked to the front of the Camaro and waved at the two men approaching them.

Frankie tried to undo the seatbelt, but there was none. Then why couldn't she get out? Why were her legs frozen? *Johnny! Thom! Stay away from them!* She reached into her pocket and pulled out the folded pictures. It was them! The men who had . . . were going to kill . . . She shook her head, trying to drive the confusion away.

Hey, fellas. Johnny motioned for Thom to follow him.

No! "Johnny! Thom! Don't!" Frankie could see the men. They had guns! She reached to her hip for her weapon, but it wouldn't come out of the holster. Looking down, she could see the top strap undone, but it still wouldn't come out. She pulled hard on it, her teeth gritting, as she watched the distance decrease between those scum and two men she cared about. *Please! Please!* One of the men started to lift his gun, pointing it at Thom and Johnny.

"No!" There was a loud sound, a sharp crack, just as her weapon came loose from its holster. Frankie drew it up and pointed it toward the . . . *"FREEZE!"*

A soft whimper broke the grip of the nightmare. "Mom-ommy . . ."

Frankie saw her little angel past the sights of her gun, which was trained on her crying face. "Oh, my God." She moved the gun aside and laid it on the bed before slinking off the mattress to Cassie.

"Mommy. Mommy. Why did . . . ?" The tears were coming in sobs now, from both mother and daughter. A second later the first of three generations of Aguirres rushed into the bedroom.

"Francine, what . . . ?" Amelia Aguirre saw the gun on the bed and the small lamp lying on the floor near the door. Her daughter had always told Cassandra to open the door gently, as it easily hit the dresser when pushed too hard. But why was her gun on the bed? *Oh, no.* "Francine, what happened? You were yelling."

"Oh, Mom. I'm sorry." Frankie looked up to the woman she worshiped as she hugged Cassie as hard as she could without hurting her. "I didn't mean to do it. I was dreaming about Johnny and Thom, and they were . . ." She couldn't explain anymore.

Amelia Aguirre went to her knees and wrapped her arms around her two little girls. "It's okay, *mi hija.* She is all right. She is fine."

"But I could have . . ." Frankie collapsed into the arms of her mother and little girl, they now consoling *her.* There was something not right about it, but also something completely right about it. It was *familia.* It was safety.

"Mommy, are you okay?"

Frankie laughed through her tears at the question. "Yes, sweetie, I'm okay." Her eyes apologized for what she had just done to her daughter, but the responding look told her that none was necessary. "I'm really okay." She looked again at the face, wondering why the expression had changed. "Really. I am."

CHAPTER FOURTEEN

Arrivals

The scene was reminiscent of a team meeting before the big game, but the players here were wearing suits and carrying guns. They also outnumbered their opponents by fifty to one. Yet they were at a distinct disadvantage, a fact well understood by the de facto coach and his players.

"Remember, these guys don't have to play by the rules," Art told the sea of agents arrayed around him. "We do."

The senior agent seemed remarkably controlled in his approach to the situation, much different than some of his fellow agents had come to expect from past experience. The past was the past, they figured, happy to have Art Jefferson running this one with a cool head and measured determination.

"Is LAPD going to step up patrols?" Special Agent Shelley Murdock asked.

"Yeah, Shel. Metro is putting out four uniformed Adam cars to basically do runs around our perimeter-search area." The LAPD's Metropolitan Division was the elite of the department that provided specialized units for use throughout the city. In this instance it would back up the Bureau by increasing the department's presence around the area to be checked. Within the area unmarked but obviously official FBI cars—government cars looked too plain to be anything other than official—would fill the twelve-square-block section around Olympic and Vermont. "If they see anything, they'll call us in. We make the move."

The agents took a last look at their assignments. There were sixty-seven motels or cheap hotels in the area to be covered, though no contact would be made with the individual businesses just yet. That part of the operation was yet to be planned.

"Okay, hit it." Art hopped down from the chair he had used as a riser to address the gathering on the fourth floor. Omar Espinosa was the only one of the agents to remain, and coming through the stream of those heading for the basement garage was the partner Art had sent off to her room some hours before.

"How's everything going?"

Art saw that the chance for sleep had not done much for Frankie. "Everything here is going fine. How about with you?"

She didn't look up from the assignment list on her desk, prompting a worried look between Art and Omar. "Good. I slept a little."

"How much?"

Frankie raised her eyes. "Enough. Now what's the plan?"

So she was still pumped up, Art recognized. Maybe a little too much. He knew he'd still have to keep a close eye on her, for her own good. "Hal and Rob got the OP up and running about four hours ago. So far nothing from them. The teams are heading out to keep our friends' heads down, if they're where we hope."

Frankie sat down. Art did so also, and Omar slid a chair over from an adjoining cubicle.

"Now we have to figure out how to find them," Art said.

Frankie saw the report from the rental agency. It included two photocopied driver's licenses. The pictures on each matched closely the composite sketches of the murderers. *Suspected* murderers, she corrected herself, falling back upon the proper method of classifying suspects. "The DLs check out?"

Art's head shook. "No record of any Juan Quintana or Flavio Alicante with those numbers in Florida's computers."

"Some good counterfeiting," Espinosa observed. The photocopies betrayed no telltale signs of illicit manufacture, something the Florida Department of Motor Vehicles was mighty disturbed to hear of. "Someone has some good resource people behind them."

"More Florida connections," Frankie said. "Still, this doesn't give us much. The names are obviously aliases, maybe onetime identities if this is really something international. Maybe even if they're just hired guns." She looked at the faces closely for a moment. "At least we know our 'puters can put out good sketches."

That was an understatement, Art thought. They were actually photo-representations, mimicking the look of actual pictures. But those would do little good now unless they could come up with a way to use what they had to locate the men pictured.

"We can't just do the rounds with these," Art said, pointing to the color composites. "If we show these to a desk clerk who's been paid to give a warning, then we may cause a mess. I want that avoided at all costs."

"What about calling?" Omar wondered. "What if they used the same names to check in at one of the places? It's possible."

"Yeah, I guess it is, but we'd be taking the same risk of tipping them off." The morning was young, and already the frustration was mounting. "Any ideas, partner?"

None that are legal, Frankie answered for herself. "Unless we get lucky and spot them without them knowing it, then we're going to have to do some kind of approach. That means the desk clerk at every place, or a cleaning person. And it has to be in some way that won't spook them, something that won't set off alarm bells."

"There's the ten-thousand-dollar outline," Art commented. "Now all we need is the ten-cent answer to make it fly." He snatched up the photocopy of the licenses. "Almost as good as our boys could put out." It was a little-known and infrequently used skill that the Bureau's TS Section has mastered: producing counterfeit documents. Sometimes it was necessary to provide an undercover agent with documentation to prove his cover story. With the cooperation of agencies in all fifty states and several foreign jurisdictions, the Bureau had compiled a collection of authentic materials from which the required papers and IDs could be put together. Art studied the fine detail work. "Jacobs would appreciate work like this."

"He'd say he could do better," Omar joked.

"I bet he could," Art concurred, the spark flashing in his brain without warning. His eyes drifted away from the photocopy, the thoughts piling one atop another as they fought for dominance in the plan that was forming in the senior agent's mind.

Omar caught the intensity in Art's demeanor before Frankie. "You got something, Art?"

"I think we might."

Frankie's attention level shot up at the positive tone in her partner's words. "What? How?"

"We're waiting," Omar implored.

"I think with a little help from Jacobs we can pull this off," Art said, without explaining what "this" was.

"Pull what off?" Frankie asked.

Art picked up the phone and dialed down to TS. "We're going to play a little 'lost and found.' "

"What kind of game is that?" Espinosa asked, playing along with Art's crypticism.

"The most satisfying. We're the finders, and our perps are the losers."

"You'll want to buckle up now," the Air-Force lieutenant informed his five passengers. The Gulfstream would be landing on Andrews' east-west runway in a few minutes.

"Give me something, Dick," the *Post* reporter begged. "I go all the way down there with you, hang back in the shadows like a good little reporter, and don't look where I shouldn't. What do I have from that? Nothing."

Congressman Richard Vorhees, chairman of the House Armed Services Committee, laughed at the childlike begging and guilt projection Chick Hill was shooting his way. As the *Post*'s military-affairs correspondent, an assignment with fewer potential stories in the "days of downsizing," he had been invited to accompany the congressman on a short inspection of several special operations facilities. His access had been understandably limited to nonsecure areas of the three bases, which had frustrated him to no end. The congressman had enjoyed every minute of it. The media hated to be told, with no chance for argument, that they couldn't go somewhere or see something. "Childlike" might have been an improper characterization, Vorhees realized; "infantile" was more descriptive.

"Hey, that sergeant offered you a chance to run the confidence course." Vorhees heard the snickers from his staff in the seats behind as the Gulfstream began to descend. "You didn't take him up on *that.* "

Pig. Hill was treading water here, trying to make something of his new beat. The State Department had been a hell of a lot easier to cover than the Pentagon. At least there you could see the comings and goings of ambassadors and the like, things that gave an inkling if something was up. The wrong person in the right place at the wrong time could set the old noggin to thinking. That was the reporters' sense. Somewhere after the sixth on the hierarchy of human senses, he figured. That ability, however, could not easily penetrate a stone wall, the likes of which Vorhees had erected around everything interesting on their short jaunt down South.

Well, so be it. Hill knew that if he couldn't get information he could at least get denials to the right questions. "What about Delta?"

"Delta?" Vorhees asked with feigned ignorance. "What's that?"

A smile. "Weren't you observing a demonstration of their techniques?"

"Whose?" The game was fun to the congressman, a man who had developed a healthy disdain for the press during his tour in uniform. Plus, his professed lack of knowledge was the "literal" truth. The Army had no so-called Delta force. If that name stuck among its members, JSOC, and some uninformed members of the media, oh well. In the Pentagon's nomenclature the unit once referred to as Special Operations Detachment Delta was now known as Special Operations Detachment Trumpet, and that designation would change again in three months. Delta hadn't *officially* been "Delta" for quite some time, giving the politicos like himself a convenient answer when challenged on the existence of the unit. "Don't know where you get your information, Chick."

"Then there is no unit called Delta?"

A careful pause. "To my knowledge we have no unit that carries that designation."

"To your knowledge?"

The congressman nodded.

Well, let's try this. "I heard someone mention that 'some unit' you were observing took off pretty quick from Bragg. Anything to that?"

Vorhees had heard one of his aides let that slip and had chastised the staffer for it. "People on bases move at their own speed. Some slow, some fast. Everyone has someplace to go."

Okay, there's an opening. "Would they be going anywhere in particular? Maybe where the action is?"

Another laugh erupted from the jovial bureaucrat, giving him time to craft a response. "You give me more credit than I'm due, Chick. I'm a pencil pusher, remember?"

"Maybe Cuba?" It was a stretch, but he had to cast his line somewhere.

"Chick, come on. From what I can see that's a *coup d'état* going on down there." Vorhees had no knowledge of any American involvement, but the quick departure of Delta had made the same thought cross his mind. But speculation was not his job at the moment—deflection was. "You're reaching on that one."

Hill could accept that. It would do. *Chairman of the House Armed Services Committee Richard Vorhees, after a tour of facilities housing U.S. Special Operations Forces, denies that any of those forces are involved in the apparent coup under way in Cuba.* Leads often generated as much information as digging for the story. He was certain he and his editors would be getting calls from the Hill concerning their "shoddy, speculative reporting." At least the trip wouldn't be a total waste.

The Gulfstream touched down with the rising sun behind it and turned off the runway toward the secure area of Andrews before backtracking along the taxiway toward the military VIP terminal.

"Jeez, she's a big one, isn't she?" one of the aides commented, looking out one of the aircraft's left-side windows.

Chick turned his attention that way. The observation just heard was adequate, he thought. The white 747 with its long blue stripe running from tail to nose was being pulled from its hangar by a dark green tug. Within seconds of stopping, a truck with stairs mounted on its back pulled to the left—Hill reminded himself of the military jargon: port—side door. As the Gulfstream taxied by, a black limousine pulled up to the stairs and let out . . . *Granger?* He instinctively leaned closer to the window and squinted. It was Granger. That smooth head and blue uniform were unmistakable, his peaked cap in hand as he ran—*ran?*—up the steps into the . . . *That's not Air Force One.* Hill cocked his head and looked as far to the Gulfstream's front as he could through the small glass portal. *It's there.* The President's plane, a modified 747 designated VC-25A, was similar in appearance to the jet they were passing, but its long stripe flared upward near the nose to paint the entire upper front a bright blue. That plane was out on the tarmac in its usual place. The *Post* reporter looked back to the other aircraft, wondering . . .

The Doomsday Plane? It was a flowery, overly dramatic nickname that no Air Force officer would ever utter. The correct name was Kneecap, Hill knew. The National Emergency . . . *Emergency?* . . . Airborne Command Post. Why was it rolling out, and why was the chairman of the Joint Chiefs of Staff *running* up the stairs to it? Granger had been around long enough that everyone in D.C. knew he moved about as fast as he talked. That's why he had chosen the Air Force for his military career path, the joke went, so he could let his fighters do the walking.

Hill kept his attention focused on the hangar where the— what was the damned military designation? E-4B. That was it. He scanned the area around the E-4B. There was nothing else untoward, just a few guards. That was to be expected, he figured. But something still was stuck in his nosy craw. *Granger running?* It wasn't a story; it wasn't even a lead. Yet.

The Gulfstream came to a stop five minutes later, more than two miles away from the aircraft that had sparked Chick Hill's curiosity. The congressman politely accompanied him to the terminal, benignly thanking him for the company and bidding him an appropriately smiling farewell.

"Thanks for nothing, Dick," Hill said after the congressman had gotten into the car waiting for him. *I wonder why that perk hasn't been cut.* The *Post* reporter saw his perk waiting farther away.

"Welcome back," the Jeep's driver said when Hill climbed in, tossing his two-suiter in the back. The kid was low on the totem pole at the paper, hardly more than an intern, actually, and drew the gofer duties often. "Back to the grindstone."

"No. Not just yet." Hill looked down at the cellular phone between the seats of the *Post*-owned vehicle. "I've gotta check something out. You just drive."

"Drive where?"

Hill told him as he plotted out what he'd have to do to get a story out of this, even if there wasn't one. He almost laughed at that doubt. *Anything* could be made into a story.

Jenny MacNamara stared at the thirty-inch display like a child in awe of a new release from Nintendo. But this was no game.

"Where do we start?" Harry Fastwater asked.

"Your ancestral abilities would be much appreciated now," she said, trying to inject some humor into the very serious atmosphere. SCI didn't mean that those restricted by its conditions were without imagination. When one was told to look for an SS-4 missile, especially if that person or persons were blessed with half a brain and a rudimentary schooling in Cold War history, then forming a supposition of what might be unfolding did not enter the category of a difficult undertaking. "Barring that . . ."

Before them was a computer-generated ten-thousand-acre haystack. Somewhere in it was a needle that had the sting of a lance.

"We have to look for the proper access to all those buildings," Jenny said. "Doors big enough to move the thing in and out." She brought the magnification up until the boundaries of the Juragua Nuclear Generating Plant, a complex roughly the shape of a fat inverted T, filled the screen. The top of the T, at the screen's bottom, almost touched the rough beaches west of the inlet to the Bay of Cienfuegos.

"What about the north and south sides of those buildings?" Harry inquired. As the platform passed over the target from west to east, it achieved excellent three-dimensional coverage, with extremely high detail of the structured surfaces in line with the axis of the pass—the east and west walls, or those obliquely aligned with that direction of travel. Those surfaces on the north and south of the buildings received less detail coverage because there hadn't been time to make a corresponding pass on a north-south axis.

"We have some old stills we can use if we don't find anything here." The senior technician entered a command that rotated the view to one that approximated the path of the sensor as it approached the plant, though from a much closer vantage. "Okay, we're going to follow the pass over at ten percent speed. You mark all the access openings that fit the bill from the centerline north, and I'll take the south."

Twenty minutes later the pair had eighty-six "possibles" marked on the working tape of the pass.

"Now we do some geometry."

"How so?" Fastwater asked. His real question was a dumbfounded *huh?*

"Well, even with eighty-plus ten-foot access doors scattered all over, it wouldn't do a damn bit of good to put the thing in there if the structure doesn't have sufficient interior space to hold it."

"Yeah, I get that. We make sure there's more than seventy-eight feet possible clearance beyond the door. But where does geometry come in?"

I should have been a teacher, MacNamara thought, not really minding. "You ever back a car around a corner?"

"Sure."

"Then there's no reason they couldn't have maneuvered the thing in at an angle, kinda like doing a fifty-point turn, or whatever it would take."

The recognition flashed from the junior technician's eyes. "I see. Yeah. So we don't necessarily need a straight shot back from the door."

Jenny nodded. Her junior was a fast learner. "Could be a right angle. Plus, we've got to make sure there's enough room on the outside of the building to get the missile and TEL out. Some of those are pretty closely spaced." She ran a quick computer simulation to come up with the requisite dimensions. "Let's check them."

This process took half as much time as finding the doors.

"Thirty-nine possibles left." Jenny frowned at the display. "Widely scattered, too."

Fastwater noted that a full third of the doors left in their search were in and around a gathering of eight large structures at the southern fringes of the facility, a quarter-mile from the beach. "What are those?"

"Reactor buildings and cooling towers," Jenny answered after a quick check of the database. "Damn!"

"What?"

"There's too many, Harry! We can't send this up saying 'We've got almost forty possible locations. Happy hunting.' There has to be a better way." She took the magnification down in each of the sixteen-square-mile quadrants that she had divided the complex into. A few minutes later the computer spit out a reading of objects that it considered to be nonstructural.

"Big concentration of trucks by the number-four reactor building," Harry pointed out. He scanned some of the visible light images of the same quadrant, but the shadow cast by the tall cooling tower blotted out much of the possible detail. "What kind?"

These readings from the SAR data allowed the computer to guess at the type. "GAZ tankers. Five-thousand-liter jobs." Jenny counted them, and the other vehicles. "Oops, that's one mistake." She zoomed in on a fifty-by-fifty object, a hundred yards from the trucks, that the computer said was a nonstructural—in essence, a vehicle. "That's a prefab building of some kind. A couple vehicles around it. Any heat sources?"

Harry run through the IR images. The pass had taken place in the early morning, before the heat of the day could fully rob objects of their infrared images. "Nothing special, but there is some."

Hmm. "Okay, mark that for reference." She zoomed back in on the tankers. "Any people on the vis?"

The junior technician juggled back to the digitized photos, taking the contrast up to compensate for the shaded area. "Yeah, there's some folks down there. Seem to be pretty busy, all hanging out around that—what is that? a pipe?"

"Pipes," Jenny corrected. "Hmm. Tank trucks. Pipes. Looks like hoses on the ground." She looked to her partner. "You thinking what I am?"

"Fueling." Harry got a sullen nod in response. They weren't stupid enough to overlook what might be going on. "Jesus."

"I think we may be looking in the right area. But where specifically?" Jenny locked her display in on the area surrounding the four big reactor buildings. The missile itself was big, but it was lost somewhere in there. *Hey. Yeah!* "That's a heavy thing we're looking for, right?"

"We aren't following tracks in the mud, Jen."

"No, but a beaten path still shows wear." She took the pass back to a point just before it traveled directly over the plant. "It's slim, I admit, but it's possible."

Harry wasn't hopeful. He watched as she entered a command into the computer, telling the signal-processing subprogram to run the data back in raw numbers directly as received, but adding the proper algorithmic processing loop that would distinguish fine surface detail. The result was a simple forced-choice order for the program, which took the tangible data and processed it through a finite series of "fuzzy-logic" filters to come up with microprocessor-generated guesses. Those suppositions were then compared with their like, and if a pattern could be established, the computer would decide that something was there.

That "something" in this case would be a shallow channel of wear on the concrete surface of the facility where the tires of heavy vehicles might have worn the pavement away, possibly in removing and returning the missile to its hiding place. If a parallel set of grooves running into one of the access doors could be found, then an educated finger could be pointed, allowing for greater scrutiny.

"Flyby time," Jenny said, taking the pass over the plant another time. This one was slower, as the raw-data package was being assembled as the imaginary sensor platform flew over the area. Concentrating on just the small sector encompassing the reactor buildings and their associated structures kept the duration manageable. This was a time-critical task. "Nothing. Huh, that looks like something from that prefab building." A discernible channel ran from the square structure to one of the cooling towers. "Must have been a trench they covered up. Forward." Her eyes bore into the display. "Nothing. Noth— Stop." Her eyes fixed on an anomaly in the signal return, though not from where she had expected. "That's gotta be a data flutter." The bits of digital imagery were sometimes prone to electronic bugs, just as a visible-light image could be affected by a smudge on the camera lens. "No, that's too uniform." The light went off instantly. "Shut the process down and zoom in on this, Harry."

Fastwater ordered the signal processor to disengage from the data package and focused in on the desired area. "Fill the screen?"

"All of it." Jenny watched as the circular structure came up toward her. It was like the other three cooling towers for the reactors. In its intended use the nonradioactive water used to draw thermal energy away from the heat exchangers carrying the reactor coolant would be vented through steam pipes into the two-hundred-foot concrete towers, which were roughly the shape of hourglasses with the extreme top and bottoms sheared off (people had become familiar with the shape while watching coverage of the Three Mile Island disaster in the seventies). The majority of the steam would then condense on the walls, falling back into collecting basins in the interior base of the tower for recirculation.

But there was something different about tower number one.

"Signal strength, pure return," Jenny directed. "Process for strong return and detail."

Harry ran the corresponding data through a simple program that gave high precedence to strong returns from whatever was in tower number one. This gave it a clear, almost photorealistic representation. "Wow."

There it was, dead center in the tower that was now serving as a silo. "Those smart bastards. That thing would never have been seen by the cameras down in there. Not enough light. Check the heat signature."

It took only a minute. "Just ambient."

Jenny surveyed the structure itself. At the base of the tower were several rectangular voids where the radar return had been judged insufficient to process as strong. "There. Look, those are vents. The other towers don't have those. No *cooling* tower should. Cool air is drawn in and goes upward. That keeps the interior temp to just an ambient level."

"An IR shadow," Harry observed correctly.

"Brilliant." Her head shook at the simplistic artistry of it. "And they can also serve as vents for the launch gases." Jenny slumped back in the chair, looking to the quarry that had just been found. The lance aimed at her country. It was a big sucker. Real big. Her eyes narrowed as she sat forward. *Too big.*

Harry caught her puzzled look. "What is it?"

"What's the diameter of the top of the tower?"

He clicked the digitizer on the extreme opposite sides of the circular opening. "Thirty-nine-point-six feet."

"Diameter of the object?"

He wondered why she didn't call it, "the missile." "Ten-point-eight feet. What . . . Wait." He looked at the specs of what they had been looking for. It wasn't what they had found. "Jen, the SS-4 has a diameter of five-point-three feet. This thing's twice that!"

"I know." She saw that the top of the object had a two-step taper from the sharply pointed nose down to about half the radius, then out further to the full radius. "Take a height measurement."

The difference between the returns from the interior floor of the tower and from the nose of the object yielded the measurement. "One-hundred-and-eight-point-two feet. Christ, Jen, that's more than thirty feet longer than the SS-4! What is that thing?"

Jenny did her own measurements on the strangely tapered nose. The top section, an almost perfect cone, was something to be expected. "Thirteen-point-two in length, five-point-three in diameter." She turned to her partner. "That's an SS-4 warhead nose cone."

"And the section below is just a tapered fairing to connect it to the . . . what?"

"Let's find out." Jenny swiveled her chair to the right to face the second of three terminals arrayed around her workspace. "Let's just call up the missile data here and see what we're looking at."

"Comparison search?" Harry asked as he slid closer, looking over his partner's shoulder.

"Manual, Harry. The discriminator on the database has never been my favorite." The desired data file, "Missile Dimensional Characteristics," came up from NPIC's central computer, which was wholly isolated from phone lines leading to the outside world. No possibility of "unclean" data infiltrating the system existed. "Okay, our guidelines here are twofold: liquid-fueled missiles and the proper dimensions. I'm more concerned with the diameter than the height, though we have to be close there also. But that damn fairing is going to throw off any purely identical comparison."

"I can't believe it. They just strapped the warhead to another missile!"

"A bigger one, Harry," Jenny pointed out. She scrolled through the information on known missile systems produced and fielded in the past forty years by any and all nations. "The size of this scratches a lot of the candidates.

"SS-Nineteen," Harry said as information on the Russian-produced missile, known to the SRF as the RS-18, came up.

"About twenty feet too short and a foot too thin," Jenny responded. "Man, this *is* a big thing."

Several more candidates for a match scrolled by. "This is too short for an SS-Eighteen," Jenny observed, referring to the Russian heavy missile known by its NATO designation *Satan*, an altogether appropriate choice of nomenclature. "And the one we have is too fat by about a foot. Damn!"

"That's all of the possible Russian ones," Harry said. "And it's not one of ours."

"The Cubans certainly didn't build it," Jenny said assuredly. She'd seen enough from above to know that Castro's inept government-controlled industrial capacity could be generously given the label of "backward." The capacity had been there at one time, but they'd never exploited it. Another good example of the bearded wonder's lack of foresight.

"But who, then? If it isn't Russian or American, then who? Who builds them that big besides us and them?"

There was one other possibility, but it was a stretch. "The Chinese."

Harry watched intently as Jenny switched to information on the PRC's missiles. "Whoa. Lots of big clunkers."

"They don't build them pretty," Jenny said, scrolling through until two measurements caught her eye. "But they do build them the right size." *That's how* . . .

"CSS-Four," Harry read off the screen. "Exact match on the diameter. Just a foot off on the length. Throw weight of three thousand and eighty pounds. The SS-Four warhead was three thousand pounds. But how?"

"The DF-Five, Harry. The DOD designation is CSS-Four, but the Chinese call it *Dong Feng* Five. That means 'east wind.' The DF-Five is also the basis for the CZ-Three series of space-launching boosters. It's an exact duplicate except for the payload and guidance systems, actually. One carries satellites, the other a very big bomb."

Fastwater, in preparation for his assignment to work with MacNamara on the monitoring of the Cuban military during the rebellion, had versed himself in the goings-on of the past decade as they applied to the capabilities of the Cuban Revolutionary Armed Forces and associated elements. One of those elements was the short-lived Cuban Space Exploration Center project, a farcical attempt by Fidel Castro to construct a launch facility for satellites in the Caribbean to rival that of the French in Guyana. An attempt that received funding and technical support from the People's Republic of China.

"That space fiasco."

Jenny nodded at the screen. "One warhead. One booster. One very big problem."

Harry stared at the visual of the missile squared off in a box to one side of the screen. "It's really big. How far can it fly?"

"Three stages to push it out to seventy-five-hundred miles," Jenny answered. "It can hit anywhere in the United States."

"And a lot of other places," Harry added, as the senior technician picked up the phone and quickly dialed the number she had been told to call immediately if anything was found. It rang on Langley's seventh floor a second later.

"Pull over. Pull over. Here."

The Jeep rolled to an illegal stop next to Pershing Square just across Fifteenth Street from the White House. The morning rush was flowing into D.C., filling the street on the east side of the presidential mansion with legions of cars. Chick Hill looked right past those to the South Lawn.

"This is a ticket here," the wannabe reporter said worriedly, his head looking back, left, and forward for any sign of D.C. cops.

"Stop your whining." Hill opened his door and stepped out onto the sidewalk, taking a few steps forward for a better vantage point looking over the Jeep's hood. The expanse of green between the White House and the ellipse was visible through the bare trees; autumn had taken its hold on the nation's capital.

The driver leaned across the front seat to the open door. "What are you looking for?"

"Anything out of the ordinary."

"Everything looked fine from the front." They had first taken a drive past Lafayette Park to survey the north side of the White House.

"That's the 'show' side, kiddo," Hill explained. "The South Lawn is where things happen."

Hill scanned the area, looking for that one tidbit that would jump out, but from this distance any tidbits faded to clumps of colors blended in with the fall foliage. "Outside pocket of my bag, hand me the binocs."

The driver retrieved the compact Bushnells and passed them out. "Why do you carry binoculars?"

Hill pushed his thick glasses atop his head and began scrutinizing the South Lawn through the 7X binoculars. "Kid, when your eyes get this bad, you learn to adapt. The photogs aren't the only ones who need to see things."

The back of the mansion looked normal, no obvious extra personnel. He swept left, farther south, the ugly gray of Old Executive in the background. The pad used by Marine One was empty. That caused his hopes for some connection to drop. Why pull Kneecap out and have no way to get the President to it? It was looking like some sort of practice run was under way, Granger and all. He continued left. Well, it had been worth a shot. Now he'd have to just go back to Limp Dick's denials about Delta. Oh, we—

What is that doing there? Hill instinctively lowered the glasses away and squinted to see with just his eyes, but the streaking blurs of cars convinced him to give it up. He rolled the focus knob, zeroing in on the aircraft. It wasn't the big one out of Anacostia, he knew. This one was low and sleek, its body a gleaming white with a thin stripe of blue along its side. It had to be from the 89th. He looked for details, of which there were none immediately obvious. There *were* two people on board, in the drivers' seats, and a few outside looking very serious. *Fully crewed?* His hopes began to rise again. *What else?* This had to be a VH-60, one of those airborne VIP taxis that government honchos had at their beck and call. No. He'd been on one of those, up close enough to see that this one was different. All sorts of bulges and small, dorsallike antennae protruded from the fuselage, and there was a—*refueling probe?*—coming out from the nose. Hill's mind searched the mental files he'd made since joining the Pentagon beat. This was that command-post variant of the VH-60, the one supposed to be used by the President during crises when transiting between a ground station and the location of a more fully equipped airborne command post, such as . . . *Kneecap.*

"Hand me the phone," Hill told the driver. "Same pocket as the binocs—black phone book. Look up Congressman Vorhees's office number."

"Didn't you just . . . never mind." He flipped to the *V*s and read off the number.

"Congressman Vorhees's office."

Chick set the binoculars on the hood of the Jeep. "Yes, this is Chick Hill from the *Post* for the congressman. Is he back from Andrews?"

"Yes. I trust you enjoyed your trip with him. One moment."

The moment stretched into four, but Hill had nowhere to be. His companion, however, was still sweating in anticipation of a hefty parking fine.

"Chick, so soon?"

"You know how much I miss you, Dick. Listen, I wonder if you'd care to comment on some peculiar things going on at Andrews and the White House."

A playful chuckle came over the phone. "Sure, why not?"

"Kneecap was rolled out at Andrews when we landed; I believe one of your staffers commented on it. That's what got me to looking. The funny thing was that chairman, Joint Chiefs, was there, *running* up the steps. Then, I drive by the White House, and what's here but that fancy command-post chopper from the Eighty-ninth Crown Helo is what they call it, if I'm not mistaken."

"You're not." The congressman's tone changed perceptibly.

"Anything to this?" Hill listened to the silence.

"The Pentagon runs the show, Chick. You know the routine. They can run readiness exercises whenever they want."

"It's a readiness exercise, then?"

"Must be." What wasn't said, said it all.

"Okay, Dick. Thanks." Hill switched off the phone but kept the handset.

"What was that all about?"

"That was nothing, kid. Watch this." He switched the phone on and pressed last-number redial.

"Congressman Vorhees's office."

"Hi. Chick Hill again."

"Well, hello. The congressman is on the phone right now."

"Oh. He's still on with the White House," Hill said innocently, trying to remove any hint of a question from his words.

"Still? He just got on."

Hill smiled into the phone. "Oh. No problem. I'll call back later."

The driver stopped his worrying long enough to admire the devious digging just witnessed. "Tricky, but what does that get you?"

"It gets me a lead," Hill said after climbing back into the Jeep. *"The sudden, unplanned deployment of emergency airborne command posts at the White House and Andrews Air Force Base prompted Congressman Richard Vorhees, Chairman of the House Armed Services Committee, to contact unnamed White House officials for an explanation of the actions."*

"How can you spin that from the call?" the driver asked incredulously.

"All true, kid." It occurred to Chick that he didn't even know the kid's name. "Just deductive reasoning."

It sure wasn't what the driver had learned at Columbia. "I don't know. What comes after that is weak."

"Kid, lesson number last: The lead is everything." Chick watched the White House disappear behind the balding trees.

"What comes next is fluff. Anyone can fill in the body. Only a pro can give you a winning lead."

"Fluff?" the driver asked with more disbelief than before. "What about facts?"

Hill snickered at the traffic ahead. "The best facts are guesses that turn out to be on target."

Major Sean Graber took the SATCOM radio's handset from the Pave Hawk's crew chief. "Graber."

"Major," Colonel Cadler drawled. "The spooks found you a target." He went on to explain the location.

"What's the aimpoint?" Sean asked. As in practice, you did not just fire wildly at a target—you chose a specific point on it. "The missile is one thing, sir, but it sounds like the way it's set up now doesn't point to someone just standing there and pushing a button."

"My thought exactly, Major. The eagle eyes found one of those prefab sons o' bitches that smacks of Chinese construction. Real close to those control bunkers we took a look at in Iran last summer."

Sean had been up close and personal for that one. Almost too close. "And once we secure it?" He never thought in terms of "if" when it came to a mission's outcome.

"There's a DOE tech guy comin' down with the gear y'all ordered from Wally World." Cadler didn't expand, an unseen smile on his muscular face.

Another one of those. Sean knew Delta didn't have a stellar record in keeping technicians from the Department of Energy safe when in their care. His thoughts momentarily went back to the man condemned to death during the last and only mating of their talents. He wondered how Anderson was doing.

"We'll try and give this one back in one piece," Sean said with some levity.

"Deal. Any assets you think y'all might need?"

"Let me talk to Lieutenant Duc." Lieutenant Cho Duc was the Pave Hawk's pilot. "We'll run through an insertion to see. Are there photos on the way down?"

"The com center o'er on Crocodile Road should have 'em 'bout now."

"Okay. We'll get to it."

"Fingers crossed, Major."

"Fingers crossed, sir."

The satellite photos were retrieved from the Cape's com center and delivered to Sean and Lieutenant Duc, who were sitting in the open port-side door of the Pave Hawk. Duc, a twenty-eight-year-old child of the Nam experience whose earliest memory was of the American Hueys buzzing his family's village north of Saigon, was a member of the Army's 160th Special Operations Aviation Regiment, commonly referred to as the Nightstalkers for their inhuman ability to fly low and fast in total darkness. They were less well known as Delta's taxi service.

"Long flight," Duc commented, looking at the map. He was a small, thin man, whose neck was strangely overdeveloped from the constant wearing of NVGs during the Nightstalkers' "normal mission profile" flights.

Sean watched him trace a line around the east end of the island before turning west, past Guantánamo Naval Base, to their target west of Cienfuegos. "Not overland?"

"Not with a war going on," Duc answered, his voice inflected with the choppy influence of his native tongue. "We got two AWACS up, one in the Gulf and the other this side of the keys. They say there's still a bunch of SAM radars up and running. Plus, one lucky shot can ruin your whole day."

"Then we go around past Guantánamo and come in from the water. We'll have to tank, right?"

Duc nodded. "Ten men, four crew, a little gear. Probably a six-hour flight to avoid getting shot at until we want that." He smiled deviously. "We'll tank once east of the island and once right before we go in."

"We should get a Combat Talon alerted," Sean said. "The MC-130H Combat Talon was a Special Operations version of the C-130 Hercules. Its capabilities included communication, navigation, refueling, and in-flight extraction of troopers using the Fulton STAR recovery system, an E-ticket ride if there ever was one.

"You didn't know? The Talons are all grounded," Duc said.

"What? Why?"

"One of them took a beaucoup beating yesterday when one of the nose prongs came off in flight. Knocked out two engines and took a chunk of wing with it." The nose prongs, normally folded back against the fuselage, were extended to form a forward-facing *V* when a pickup using the Fulton system was in progress. The prongs would catch a line hoisted skyward by a helium balloon and hold it until it could be fed into a winch system. On the other end of the line a trooper or troopers would be yanked from their earthly bonds and pulled into the aircraft. "They want to make sure it's not metal fatigue."

"But we don't really need a Talon. We can go with a Shadow." Duc referred to the HC-130 Combat Shadow, the Talon's cousin optimized for in-flight refueling of multiple helicopters.

"Okay." Sean knew that the lieutenant could be trusted implicitly when it came to getting them into and out of potentially hot LZs. And this might get hot, he thought, looking to the two-pintle-mounted 7.62mm miniguns. "Think those will be enough?"

"I don't want to have to find out. How about we get some backup? Something that can ruin the Cubans' day if we need to."

Sean nodded agreement. "Anything else?"

Duc thought for a moment. I wouldn't mind having one of those AWACS dedicated to watching our ass."

"I'll tell the colonel." That meant the colonel would get it for them. Bill Cadler had clout, and a hell of a loud voice.

"Look at those," the lieutenant said, pointing at the images of the plant. "Power masts all over the place. We gotta watch those." His eyes traced a path around the logical path for any lines between the tall metal structures. "We gotta come in right."

"We should be able to get one or two run-throughs down," Sean said, hoping they would have enough time. There wasn't much time for preparation on this one. "I'll let you know when we're ready."

"Gotcha." Duc took one copy of the map and satellite photos to the front of the Pave Hawk to begin planning the precise flight plan.

Sean stood and took a few steps from the helicopter before looking back. This would be the first real test of this version of the Pave Hawk. It was a formidable-looking bird. The stubby wings that held the 230-gallon outrigger fuel tanks forward and above the side doors could also add to the twin miniguns' firepower by holding air-to-air or air-to-ground missiles. There were also systems to prevent the Pave Hawk from being hit. Chaff-and-flare dispensers, tied to missile-launch detectors, could pump out the radar and infrared countermeasures from just behind the cabin, and the entire helicopter was covered in a black-and-green infrared-suppressing paint scheme. To help get it to any target, there was a FLIR system and a Terrain Avoidance/Terrain Following radar that allowed Lieutenant Duc to fly so close to the earth that new threats of collision had to be planned for. That was taken care of by the sharp, forward-facing blade protruding upward from the Pave Hawk's fuselage a yard forward of the main rotor shaft. This was protection from wire strikes, the very real possibility of clipping a power or communication line as the helicopter skimmed low to the ground. Any contact above the nose and below the four-blade rotor would direct the offending wire into the sharp blade, slicing it in two and—hopefully—saving the Pave Hawk. The system had proved itself during training flights, leaving certain local utility companies in the South and West scratching their heads as to how their lines came to be cut.

All the systems inherent to the Pave Hawk were meant to make it one of the safest and most stealthy taxis for the special operations forces—Delta, in this case. It was a matter of mating the best with the best.

The major's attention shifted to the east-west runway just north of where he stood. From over the Atlantic a dark green C-130 descended and touched down gracefully. There were no markings visible on its exterior, which told Graber that it was the Herky Bird from the 23rd Air Force that was bringing down the gear he'd requested from Bragg, plus the technical expert from DOE. Sean watched the aircraft taxi to a blue Air Force Humvee, which waited for a single passenger to deplane and climb in. A second vehicle, which would get the equipment brought down, pulled up to the stern ramp as the Humvee drove away. In a minute it stopped just short of the Delta major.

"Can't you grunts do anything without me?" Joe Anderson asked loudly as he stepped from the vehicle. There was the slightest smile on his smallish face.

Sean recognized the faint expression as the highest compliment from the man who had just added the final element to a team that was now, without a doubt, the best for the job that lay ahead.

The American Airlines flight from Dallas–Fort Worth landed on Los Angeles International Airport's runway Two-Four right just as Angelenos were halfway through the morning weekday rush hour. It was the milder form of the red-eye, just a three-hour jump from the sprawling Texas airport to LAX. Most of the eighty passengers were businesspeople who had risen before the dawn to catch their flight. Two of those passengers, as much businessmen in their own eyes as any of the others on board, had connected from an earlier flight from Miami. From one panhandle to another.

The two men, dressed in sweatshirts and jeans that gave them the appearance of youthful student travelers, took their carry-on bags and followed the crowd out to the baggage-claim area in Terminal 4 on the south side of LAX's two-level loop. There were few people at the rotating oval baggage conveyers; businesspeople had learned to travel light, for fear of losing a needed bag. The two young men, however, knew that carry-ons had one disadvantage for the business traveler in their line of work—the X ray.

The single blue Samsonite, which had been checked at the desk in Miami, slid down the ramp and was snatched up before it could start its transit around the stainless-steel racetrack. The men went next to the Budget Rent-a-Car counter and took possession of a subcompact car that was assembled by Chevrolet from parts imported from Japan. Five minutes later they were on the 405 freeway heading north, with traffic, toward the 10. That would take them into downtown L.A.

Then the work would begin.

CHAPTER FIFTEEN

Return to Sender

Becoming a spy was frighteningly easy.

Samuel Paul Garrity had done so because, like others who chose treason as an avocation, he wanted to get back at a government, at a system that he believed had prevented him from living the American Dream. That concept was no more than a pipe dream fed to the eager masses who wanted something better, he knew, and had for a long time. There was no dream out there. Just a bait, an illusion to satisfy the desires of those who wanted more. But they could never reach it. Like Garrity, they were treading water, unable to get ahead enough to keep from falling behind. It was a cycle of desire, appeasement, and denial that he had decided to step out of. No longer was he in the loop. In fact, he was so far out that he didn't even retain empathy for those still in it. Sam Garrity had found his brass ring, and to hell with those who were stupid enough not to go for their own.

As an employee of the Central Intelligence Agency, Garrity had at one time been a loyal citizen who found some pride in serving his country, even in the oft-considered menial work he did. The job had once been a source of fanciful dreams and musings as to what the Agency really did behind the red doors that marked the secure areas he could never hope to enter. But the natural curiosity had led him to seek out, on his own, the knowledge of what the wondrous things might be. There were

259

dozens of companies in the area surrounding the nation's capital that carried the "latest" in electronic and surveillance equipment that those in private security and investigative fields used in their daily work. These showrooms were also open to the general public, as a buck was a buck, and there were thousands of bright, shiny toys to cause the amateur sleuth to drool uncontrollably.

Sam Garrity found himself in awe of the gear that was out there in the open, for the taking—with the liberation of a large amount of money from his savings. As he ogled at the plethora of "spy" toys, he came upon a device that he could combine with his passion of the moment—a high-end personal computer that had already eaten up a good chunk of that savings. It looked much like a small photocopy machine or, to an educated eye, an expensive scanner that converted documents or pictures placed under its cover to bits of digitized data to be stored on a computer connected to it. It was exactly that, and much more, and he had, after a particularly effective sales pitch from the store's manager, taken it home with no idea what he would one day do with it.

This day, though, after a long night cleaning the mess left by the obscenely well paid executives who ruled Langley like the appointed monarchs he saw them as, Garrity knew exactly what to do. As usual he took a short nap when he arrived at his two-bedroom home, then, later, went into his "playroom." In it were his babies, the computer and the machine hooked to it that had helped change his life to one where *he* was in control.

He repeated the same procedure each morning after work, though there was not always a yield from his efforts. First he switched on the IBM and started the program, called *Deep Reader,* that ran the scanning device. Next, he took the sheets removed from the DCI's legal pad and scanned them one at a time into the computer memory that the program had set aside for the task. Several sensitive lasers swept over the blank pages and "read" the indentations left by the pressure of writing instruments on the sheets above. The process was familiar to law-enforcement agencies, who often used it to uncover the most mundane scribbles to tie criminal activities, or the plans of such, to certain individuals by way of handwriting analysis. Garrity knew who had written that which *Deep Reader* was scrutinizing and separating into distinct word patterns from the different pages. That man had made his path of treason all the easier with his incessant scribbling, something Sam had noticed during several of his late-night cleaning sessions while the director worked at his desk, despotically pointing out areas that needed more attention with the sweeper or the polish rag. At first he had taken the sheets on a lark, just to see if his new toy would work. Then, when references to individuals and groups he was familiar with started showing up, he made the leap from sleuth to spy, offering his services to the first one on the list. Surprising to him, they had accepted and were paying generously into a Canadian bank account that would ensure a very comfortable retirement beyond what he could ever have hoped for otherwise.

"What's on the director's tiny little mind today?" he asked the screen, watching the digitized hourglass drain as the five-minute-per-page process wound to its end. It was more complicated than just scanning the page for indentations, a trick that had once been accomplished by a method known as electrostatic detection. That was archaic compared to this. *Deep Reader* not only "saw" what was on the page, more important, it sorted through the numerous words and scribbles from potentially tens of pages above to piece together the logical word strings and other writings of that day. Because there could still be "leftovers" from the previous day, the program "looked back" at what had been culled twenty-four hours earlier and disregarded it. So much data had been stored since Garrity first began his homespun business that he had to install a tape backup to dump the excess to; his hard drive just wasn't big enough.

A bright blue FINISHED flashed in the graphically raised icon box. Garrity clicked on that with a sweep of the mouse and saw that *Deep Reader* had discerned seven separate pages of notes the director had made. He scrolled through them slowly, looking first for any notations that pertained directly to his paymaster. Those that didn't were delivered as well. What happened after that was not his concern.

The fourth page yielded what he wanted. He had trained himself to decipher the director's exaggeratedly left-leaning—no pun intended—penmanship. The letters were always spaced close together, some overlapping, especially the cases where there were two of the same next to each other. This one looked as though he was jotting down something someone else was saying, as the thoughts were far too coherent to be his alone.

"Shit!" Garrity said loudly, too much so, as evidenced by the "What's wrong, dear?" from his wife in the kitchen. He dispatched with her question and went back to the notes. "They know," he said more quietly. "But how . . . ?" He found the answer on the next page. "Oh, my God." *That guy wasn't just blowing smoke after all.* He instinctively looked around the room, afraid for the first time since beginning his treachery that there was a real danger of being discovered. He knew that the DDI, that Drummond asshole, was looking for a leak in the wrong place, but what the Agency knew now could lead to his employers, which could lead to him.

He had to warn them that the Agency knew. He quickly saved the data and switched the computer off, then went to the front room. "Where's the paper?"

"The *Post*'s on the couch," his wife answered from the other room.

"No, the *USA Today*." His eyes frantically searched the living room.

"Probably on the porch." The back door closed, and the motor of their new Taurus started up as his wife headed off to work.

Garrity was out there and back with the desired paper as his wife pulled out of the driveway. He flipped hurriedly to the sports section and looked for the . . . *The Cards did it again, defying all . . . A.* That was it. *A* was 1. The keying system was simple enough. Find the seventh word in the first story on the sports page concerning the dominant sport in season. There was none more dominant than baseball. The first letter of that word would then yield a number. *A* was 1; *B*, 2. And so on, stopping at 4 and starting with 1 again when *E* was reached, and again four letters later. The corresponding number was then added to the telephone number of a phone booth Garrity had preselected, and that number was then to be entered on the touch-tone phone after dialing his contact's pager. It would then be reverse-deciphered, giving his contact a place to reach him in one hour. That was the drill—one hour from the time he entered the number.

For added security he never called the pager from his home phone; that he would do from a pay phone chosen at random as he drove. He grabbed the keys to their old Audi—he and his wife, because they worked nonconcurrent schedules, always took the nicer Taurus to their respective jobs—and went out to the double-wide driveway. The cracked vinyl of the Audi's front seat squeaked under his weight when he climbed in. He pumped the gas several times in the ritual they had mastered over the years to get the finicky car started after a long time dormant. From the gas gauge it looked as if neither he nor his wife had driven it in days. He turned the key, keeping his foot on the accelerator. The starter spun, the engine coughed, then a series of rapid clicks came from the front, and the coughing ceased. He twisted the key again, getting the same clicking, but no motor sounds at all.

"Damn!" It was the starter! He'd replaced it just three months ago with that reconditioned one his wife had warned him about. "*Just buy a new one.*" She'd been right again.

He got out and raised the hood in the expected and useless way. There was nothing under there he could fix. The damned thing needed a new starter . . . again!

Why now? He couldn't walk to a pay phone and just hang around for an hour, not in the neighborhood surrounding his quiet residential enclave. The phones there were frequented by drug dealers, and often by the police busting them. That he couldn't chance. There was only one way, and it was a breach of the security measures he'd agreed to. But there was no other way. He walked into the house and dialed the number of his contact from memory, adding the *1* to each of the digits in his home phone number as he entered them with ten touches on the keypad.

"DiContino," Bud said into the phone, checking the time on his Casio. Drummond would be there any minute.

"Bud, it's Ellis. Listen, I don't know what's going on, but I just ran interference for the President with the chairman of House Armed Services. He called and wanted to know why Kneecap was rolled out at Andrews with General Granger on board, and also about the chopper out back."

Vorhees was such a control freak, Bud had come to know firsthand. His domain was his, and in a way the NSA could understand that from recent experience, but he took his legislative duties to the line where oversight blurred with command. *Never made it past colonel, did you, Richard?* Maybe this was his way to get what had been denied him by that mine. "Ellis, you did right. Just spout the party line if he keeps bellyaching. The Pentagon is quietly calling it a readiness exercise."

"That's what I figured, and I told him so," the President's

chief of staff explained. "But Vorhees isn't the big problem. Jack just got a call from the *Post* asking for confirmation that the congressman had contacted the White House asking about 'emergency relocation procedures' for the President." Jack Duffy was the White House director of communications, the newly in-vogue position that had replaced the press secretary as the President's point man with the media.

"Damn. Is it spreading?"

"The senior White House correspondent from ABC is digging. If they get any sort of confirmation on this, we can expect something on the tube."

"Jack didn't give the *Post* anything even close to one, right?"

The COS snickered. "He's going to 'get back to them.'"

"I suggest he takes his time," Bud said. "The day's half-gone already."

"Tomorrow, then?"

"Things should be under control by then." *I hope.*

Gonzales heard the words "under control" louder than the rest of the weak assurance. "Bud, is there anything I *need* to know? Anything the Secret Service detail should be aware of?"

Bud knew he'd have to expand the loop, because the COS had a right, and a responsibility, to know the story now that things were accelerating toward some sort of resolution . . . or confrontation. "The DDI is due here anytime. Where are you?"

"My office."

The COS's office was just down the hall from the NSA's. "Why didn't you just walk over for this?"

Another snicker. "Your deputy is as much a pit bull as I am when it comes to protecting his boss."

"Nick takes his job seriously. Why don't you come over and sit in with Greg and me. We'll fill you in."

"Bless me with your gatekeeper?"

It was Bud's turn to laugh. "Done."

"Now is the time, Fidel." Raul had never seen his brother like this. He no longer resembled the charismatic, vigorous leader that he was just hours before. There was a look about him that was peaceful, of all things. A sort of resignation, but without the sorrow he had expected to see. Was the revenge they were going to unleash really that redeeming for him? Raul could think of no other reason for his brother's demeanor.

"Yes."

Raul unfolded the paper he had jotted his notes on. "There are several target options, Fidel. Of course, there is the obvious one of Washington, but I believe others should be considered."

The president's eyes looked upward as he leaned back. "The guilty parties must pay. Those responsible for destroying the Revolution must feel its wrath."

"They will. There is no doubt." Raul took a chair and pulled it next to his brother, sitting and leaning close to him. "But there are options other than the American capital." He put on the glasses he hated so much and looked to his notes. "A very good target would be New York. The destruction of that city would disrupt the financial dealings of the *yanquis* for years. Their vaunted stock exchange would be leveled. The headquarters of many of their largest corporations are located there. It would be a crushing blow."

Raul went to the next on his list of three. "There is also Los Angeles, on America's West Coast. While not as financially important to the capitalists as New York, it is a heavily used transportation center vital to communications and distribution of manufactured goods. It is also the dominant port of trade with the East. And its population is highly vulnerable. Also, with the warhead being fused for a surface burst, the radioactive fallout will be carried by the prevailing winds eastward over the heartland of the country. There could potentially be millions more deaths over several decades from that effect alone."

Fidel took in a slow, deep breath and continued to give his brother the time to plead his case. There was no reason not to. That which had to be done would come to pass.

"Finally, Miami. We have many enemies there, and some of the insurgents are likely from that population. It is also an important center for commerce in the southern United States." Raul could see that his brother seemed disinterested in his propositions, especially the final one.

"Fidel, you must choose a target. General Asunción needs to program the guidance system."

"Yes." A smile came to his face. "They must be punished."

"The target, Fidel."

"I have chosen it."

Raul suspected correctly that his presentation had been for naught. The president's mind had been made up for some time, he realized, knowing that the seat of power of a mighty nation was going to be targeted.

His musing was only half-right.

Gonzales said nothing after hearing the NSA's explanation of the situation to him. His family had fled Cuba when Castro seized power more than three decades before, and he had thought when the rebellion began how much his late father would have loved to set foot in the land of his birth just once more. And now that bastard in Havana was planning to kill potentially millions because he didn't accept the handwriting on the wall.

"I'm glad I filled you in before Greg got here," the NSA admitted. The DDI had been delayed waiting for imagery of the area where the missile had been found. There was also a possible complication, he had told Bud, but did not want to discuss it on the phone. Even a secure one. Drummond didn't wave red flags for no reason, leaving Bud wondering what could possibly complicate the situation any more than it already was.

"Holy cow," Gonzales commented mildly, though his eyes hinted at the language he truly wanted to use.

"You can see why we've got to keep this airtight. Jack doesn't get this, okay? That way he's not lying when he is sweetly noncommittal."

Gonzales nodded. "Do you know what this is?"

"What? A repeat of '62?" Bud had seen the eerie parallel early on. "Let's hope we're better at keeping it under wraps than they were."

A few heavy footsteps through the connecting office of the deputy NSA signaled the DDI's arrival.

"Sorry it took so . . . Ellis." Drummond laid the security case on the coffee table.

"He's in, Greg," Bud said, going on with his own complication. "We may have a press problem."

The DDI sat down on the couch and began removing the pictures he'd brought over from the case. "We may have a bigger one than that. Look."

Bud sat next to the DDI on the two-person couch, with Gonzales standing to the side.

"Good shots," Bud commented. He could tell they were from Aurora's SAR, but Gonzales wasn't cleared for that knowledge. To him they would just be amazing overhead imagery.

"NPIC processed them F-A-S-T. This is straight from the analysts who did the workup." He handed a synopsis of their findings to the NSA.

"What! A CSS-Four?"

"Or a CZ-Three space-launch booster," Drummond said. "Though that's a matter of semantics. They're identical in all respects except for what goes on top." He pointed to the best image that showed the weapon's huge diameter. "Fidel is proving to be adept at these secret 'arrangements.' First Vishkov, and then this."

"The Chinese supplied him with this!" Bud's neck reddened by the second. "That space-facility thing was just a sham, then?"

"It's looking that way. If it ever came out that this booster was there, he could try and explain it away as just part of the process to build the facility. A mockup or whatever. And to be truthful, without knowing that he had something to put on top, it would have looked like just part of his loony schemes."

Gonzales saw that it was much bigger than the missile described by Bud a few minutes earlier. "How did we miss this?"

It was the question the Agency—"we" invariably was translatable to "you"—forever found itself answering when things didn't go as those in higher places expected they should. "The Chinese were in Cuba working on the space facility in the first months of '91, which were pretty busy for us, you know. If it came in, it was probably then. And remember, this was *one* missile which we knew nothing about. The Navy lost a whole freighterful going from North Korea to Iran not long back, and they *knew* what they were looking for. The Agency is not the all-knowing, all-seeing power that a lot of folks think it is."

"I'm not blaming, Greg," Gonzales explained. "It's just hard to fathom that Castro would go to such lengths."

That struck Bud. *Why would he?* He read over the report again, picking out the details on the CSS-4's performance, particularly the estimated-range data. "This thing has a seven-thousand-five-hundred-mile range."

That was an academic statement to the DDI. "Yes. So?"

"Ellis has a point," Bud said. "Why *would* Castro go to the lengths he has to give himself a delivery system that is overkill? There were other missile boosters out there that he could get a hold of that would be easier to hide and to base. The Chinese sold some CSS-Ones to Saudi Arabia awhile back. That would have had plenty of range to reach any target in the lower forty-eight, and it's quite a bit smaller. Or those SS-Fours the Russians were 'destroying' after INF.'' The Intermediate Nuclear Forces treaty between the United States and the former USSR required the destruction of all surface missile systems with range envelopes of three hundred to three thousand miles. "We know that some of those made their way to Iran. Why not Cuba? Wouldn't that have made for an easy match? Old warhead to newer booster of the same type.''

Drummond's mental process put on the brakes. "Wait, what are we assuming? That the original booster never worked, or that it stopped being functional at some point?''

"Or that Castro decided it wasn't what he wanted anymore,'' Bud suggested ominously, more so in his own mind. The scenario was beginning to take shape.

"I don't follow you,'' Drummond said.

Bud walked to the globe that sat in the far corner of his office. It was no more than a showpiece—something he thought looked nice. He spun it almost half a world past the United States. "Oh, my God.''

The exclamation was spoken softly, as if a prayer.

"What is it, Bud?'' Ellis asked.

The NSA still faced away from the men. "Greg, you're versed in Castro's ways from the missile crisis.''

"Yeah.''

"Who did he blame for it all collapsing?'' A hand rested softly on the globe's surface.

"The Russians. Why?''

Bud's hand lifted a bit, leaving just one finger to trace on the uneven surface west from the Urals. "The speech he gave at the fifth party congress last year—do you remember the text?''

"Sure,'' the DDI said. He had read the translation of the five-hour speech in full in preparation for a roundtable discussion hosted by GW University. "He went on for hours haranguing all the 'enemies of the Revolution.' ''

"Were we among those?''

"Right near the top.'' Drummond's mind seized on one of his words.

"Near? Who was at the top, Greg? Who did Castro say had committed the greatest crimes against the Revolution?'' Bud's finger straightened and pointed down upon a single city.

"Oh, no," the DDI said, looking at the still-unaware chief of staff. "It can't be."

Bud turned back. "The extra range isn't overkill; it's necessary."

"For what?" Ellis nearly demanded.

"To reach his target," Drummond said in a shaky voice.

"What target?" The COS saw both men go a shade lighter before the answer came.

"Fidel. The target?"

They had done worse than attack the Revolution, Fidel Castro thought—they had forsaken it. That transgression must be avenged. It must.

"Moscow."

Chapter Sixteen

Plans and Action

Art looked at the small card just handed him. One look was all it took. "Dan, this is beautiful."

"Thank the computers and Luke Kessler," Dan Jacobs said. "He got the information we needed from the Florida DMV *muy pronto.*"

Frankie took the card. Without a *real* Florida driver's license to compare it to, this one could pass for legit. It might have to, she knew. "It'd be just our luck that one of the desk clerks is from Florida."

"More likely Calcutta," one of the dozen agents gathered around Art and Frankie's area commented. It drew a few agreeing laughs.

"All right," Art said, motioning for the agents to move closer. "We are going to do this right, so listen carefully. Omar and I will each be directing the two search teams. Frankie and Shelley will be doing the actual casting of our bait."

"Using their feminine ways," the same agent as before cracked.

"I'll 'feminine way' your family jewels," Shelley Murdock shot back, getting a better response than her verbal nemesis.

"Enough locker-room crap," Art said, getting them back on track. "Frankie and Shelley will each have one of these." He held up the counterfeit Florida license produced by the lab. It was a real representation of one of the licenses of their shooters shown on the photocopy from the rental agency. Dan Jacobs had taken the color composite photo put together from Mrs. Carroll's description, cleaned it up using their suspect's picture from the copy, then shrunk the image on the computer and added it to a close approximation of a Florida driver's license. It was an FBI-produced forgery to rival the forgeries the shooters had been using. It was also the bait. "Six of us on each team besides them. Their job is to go to the desk clerk at each of the motels on our list and play like they're delivering a lost wallet to the guy on the license. They'll say they work at some store and that Mr. Flavio Alicante—aka whoever—called and asked if a lost wallet was found. They were supposed to hand-deliver it to him at such and such motel but didn't give a room number. If the clerk recognizes the name and face and gives a room number, then we've got 'em. If not, we move on."

"How do we know they used the same names to check in under?" an agent asked.

"We don't, but either way we should be okay. These desk clerks deal with enough 'John Smiths' and 'Joe Blows' that a false name on the register won't spook them. It's the picture that will get us our shooters . . . not the name."

Deputy SAC Lou Hidalgo had listened from the back of the group. He was not there to pass judgment on Art's plan of action, though Jerry Donovan had cautioned him to do just that. What he had heard didn't bother him in the least. It was a smart operation. But he did have some questions. "Art, what's the separation on the two teams going to be?"

"Two short blocks," he answered. Los Angeles, like many cities, was a patchwork of rectangular blocks with short and long sides. "If we get a hit, the other team can be there in a minute."

"And the rovers?" Hidalgo went on.

"Sixty agents out there now. When we find them, we lock the area up tight and get any innocents away from the scene. LAPD will set up a perimeter, and we make our move . . . even if that's just waiting."

Hidalgo nodded approval. Art Jefferson, despite Donovan's worries, didn't need watching anymore. At one time, maybe, but no longer. His choice of Omar Espinosa, a tough, straight-shooting agent, as a second in this case only added to that belief. "Do it."

Frankie took the wallet and slid the license into the plastic cover that would prevent too close an examination when showed to the desk clerks. Shelley Murdock did the same. The choice of the two female agents to do the point work was a practical one. Women were less threatening. It was societal, and Art was willing to use whatever tricks he could muster to catch the killers of Thom Danbrook. A suspicious desk clerk could ruin it all.

"Okay, partner, showtime," Frankie said.

Art checked the communications rig on her. It would allow her to speak to the three Bureau cars tasked with watching her backside, but not to hear them. An earpiece would be too obvious. Almost as obvious as her anticipation of this. "Right. You just keep talking. Let us know what's going on."

"Easy enough." Frankie tucked her holster farther back than it usually rode, hiding it under the loose jacket.

"We'll keep you in sight," Art said. It was more of a promise. It was also a need, he worried.

"Okay," Frankie responded quickly. "Let's get to—"

Art grabbed her arm and pulled her into their cubicle. The other agents had filtered toward the elevator, leaving them alone.

"What?"

"Frankie, this is for real."

She looked up at her partner with an expression of puzzlement and anger. "What the hell do you think I think it is?"

"It certainly isn't a fucking dream," Art yelled in a hushed voice, one eye on the group of agents just boarding the elevator. The look of recognition in Frankie's face washed away the other emotions. "Yeah, that's right. Your mother called me."

"What did she say?"

"She said she's worried about you. Just like I am." He let go of her arm. "What is going on up there, Frankie? Huh? This is not some personal vendetta you can let your mind dream about, because I am not willing to let that cross over into your behavior. No chance."

She swallowed hard, her eyes locked on those of the man she respected more than any other. On the man she hated almost as much as herself at the moment. "It won't."

"I can take you off of this, Frankie."

"Then why haven't you?" It was a simple question, and a more difficult challenge.

"Because I have faith in you, partner." He glared down at

her. "And in your professionalism. Don't give me any reason to doubt that."

"I won't," Frankie said, meaning it at the moment. It was the future that she wasn't sure of.

"Then let's get going."

Frankie watched Art turn and walk toward the elevator, leaving her alone. Very alone. "Yeah, let's."

No booze. No broads. Just a too-soft mattress and the first hangover in years that he hadn't doused with bourbon.

Sober mornings were pretty shitty, George Sullivan thought upon waking to his first in a long time. But it was the first, he realized. Maybe, like the booze that had kept him from experiencing them, they got better with age.

He rolled to a sitting position on the motel bed, the soaked sheets twisted around his body. Instinctively he looked to the nightstand for the bottle, but there was none. He had brought none. That reality made him snicker to himself. Was this Step One of the Twelve? he jokingly mused.

There was something on the nightstand, though. George took it in his hand, his half-medicated thoughts from the night before returning. Go there? he wondered, looking at the address on the keytab. They might be . . .

The fear made him want to drink. Want it really bad. The want was the demon to conquer, not the booze. To conquer it, he would have to get past the fear. Have to face it. To prove that he could. It was his job. It was his life.

It was his last chance.

George stood from the bed on wobbly legs. His head immediately began to spin. Neither malady, though, would deter him. He clutched the key tightly and looked around the room for his clothes. There was no time for a shower. This story couldn't wait.

Garrity picked the phone up on the first ring. "Hello."

"Yes."

The lightly accented voice was unmistakable. "We've got trouble."

The contact noticed the absence of traffic noises in the background. This sounded like . . . "Where are you?"

Garrity gulped. "Home."

"*What!* Are you out of your fucking mind! What the fuck are you thinking!"

"Listen, I had no choice. My car is dead, and I have something that can't wait."

A loud breath blew through the phone line. "Goddammit!" There was a pause. "What is so fucking important that you can't follow procedures?"

"There *is* a missile still there. There really is."

There was more silence. He wasn't supposed to know that. "What do you . . . Do you mean they think there is one?"

"No. This isn't like before. This time they have some sort of proof."

Oh, shit! "Are you sure? Positively?"

"I got it off the director's desk last night. Some guy in the White House, his name's DiContino, told the director that they have some sort of evidence."

"What evidence?"

Garrity looked at the printout of Merriweather's notes. "It doesn't say. His scribbles don't always make sense."

"Fuck."

"I figured with what's going on that you'd want to know this fast." Garrity listened for some kind of validation, but there was none. This man, these people, were his rainbow that led to the pot of gold. He had to do them right. But . . . "Is this true? I mean, that guy a while back wasn't just making it up?"

"That's none of your fucking business."

"Yeah. Okay. But, am I in any danger? I mean, could this lead to me?"

"Not if you keep your fucking mouth shut."

"Yeah. Okay."

"Don't ever do this again. Never. Do you understand? You follow procedures from now on."

"Okay."

Garrity hung up as the line clicked off. A hand came up to his face. It was wet with perspiration, and it was trembling. His contact didn't sound very sure of the situation, or of his semiguarantee that this wouldn't lead to him. To him. *My God.* That was a thought, a possibility, that Sam Garrity could not comprehend. Discovery. Prison. *Prison.*

He looked down at the phone and then to the sheets of

printout in his hand. This was no fucking game anymore. It wasn't fun. *A missile? A nuclear missile?* This was way beyond what he had envisioned.

"What have I done?"

"Got it!" Sanz said jubilantly. "The son of a bitch used his home phone."

"Where?" Testra pressed.

"Area code two-oh-two. Washington Metro." Sanz picked up the phone without prompting.

"Run it down," Testra directed his partner. "Christ! Talk about self-incrimination! 'Off the director's desk' and 'some guy in the White House.' Man, this guy is stone-cold gone."

The phone to the Miami office was still ringing. Sanz knew they needed a trace fast. "We gotta get a warrant before that guy gets too spooked."

"He sounded pretty far gone already." Testra thought back to the conversation. "What do you suppose that stuff about a missile was?"

"We'll know soon enough," Sanz said, as his call was picked up on the other end. "Yeah, this is Freddy. I need a name-number search pronto."

Anthony Merriweather drank slowly from the Styrofoam cup. He forced himself not to cringe each time it touched his lips. "President Alvarez, I believe your priorities are quite well-thought-out. Your main distractions, as you say, will most definitely be the loyalists who remain after the defeat."

"Several dozen processing camps will do nicely," José-Ramon Alvarez stated. "Your Marines from Guantánamo can have them constructed very quickly."

"Yes. Yes, you are right." Merriweather put his half-full cup down on the nondescript end table. They hadn't been able to provide accommodations with any higher state of acceptability for a future world leader. But, as with many things, it would do. Very soon it would not have to.

"It is very nice of you to wait with us, Señor Merriweather," Alvarez said hollowly. His guest would not see that. He could not. That such a brainless academic-turned-politician could be chosen to run the CIA was almost beyond belief. But Alvarez could not look a gift horse in the mouth. Least of all this dimwitted old stallion.

Merriweather dipped his head a bit. "It is my pleasure to see you off, Mr. President."

Your pleasure, indeed. Soon the fool would rue the day he ever came to be associated with them, Alvarez knew. But by then it would be too late to extract himself from the careful web they had spun. The idiot was theirs, literally under their thumb, and he didn't even know it yet. That pleasure of disclosure would come in due time.

"Mr. President," Gonzalo Parra said softly as he leaned toward Alvarez from behind. "There is a call you should take."

Alvarez looked up over his shoulder. "Can you not handle it?"

"You should take it, sir." Parra's tone was firm and convincing. It also triggered an alarm in Alvarez.

"Very well. Señor Merriweather, your pardon please."

"Yes."

Alvarez lifted his girth from the chair and followed his closest aide into the adjoining room. "What is it?"

Parra ignored the annoyed tone and handed his leader the cellular phone. "It is Avaro. There is trouble."

José-Ramon put the small black phone to his ear. "Avaro."

"Yes," the contact replied in Spanish. It was the agreed-upon language of their conversations.

He recognized the distress in the voice. "What is the problem?"

"The missile. They know about the missile!"

Alvarez jerked his head toward Parra. He could see that his aide already knew. "Who knows?"

"The CIA. The White House. Our agent got the information from the director's notes last night. They have some sort of proof that the missile is there."

"But how? The fool is here with me, right now, and he is calm. He would not be here if it were so."

"I don't know why, but our agent was certain."

"This cannot be. Could they have found the tape?"

"They must have. How else would they know?"

Dammit! "If it is so, then why is the director here?" He looked to Parra as he spoke. "Why?"

"A trap?" Avaro suggested.

"Or he still does not believe it," Parra suggested. "As before."

Alvarez nodded slowly at his aide's thought. That was it. The fool was still blind to it, even with his government telling him otherwise! "It is not a trap. They have no way to know that we know of the missile. There is no connection to us."

"Except for Tomás and Jorge. They know too much."

"But you took care of them, Avaro, yes?"

"Yes."

"Then we have nothing to worry of," Alvarez said confidently.

"But the missile," Avaro said. "It will not be ours."

Alvarez chuckled. "It most certainly will. All they have is a tape. It does not tell them where to find the missile. *We* do not even know, Avaro, but once we are in power, we will locate it. The Americans will only be able to scratch their heads and wonder. It will be our country, Avaro, and our missile."

"Yes. I suppose it will be."

"Do not suppose," Alvarez said. "Believe."

"I will."

"Besides, it cannot be true," Alvarez said jokingly. "Our friend the director says there is no missile, so there must not be. Not for a while, at least. If there was, it would make him look bad. We would not want him to lose his job. He does such a great service. A very valuable service."

Avaro allowed a very infrequent laugh. "Yes, he does, Father."

Alvarez switched off the phone and folded it shut. "That damned interpreter!"

Parra took the cell phone from his leader and laid it on the table. "Your words to Avaro were true. It is too late for anything to stop us."

"He is my son, Gonzalo. I must ease his fears. But to have the Americans looking . . ."

"As you said, they will not find it. When the country is ours, they cannot just snoop around without our permission. Of course they will want to, but want and will are two very different things." Parra knew his words were having the desired effect. Even men of power needed reassurance in times of great events. "We will have a country. We will have the weapon with which to guarantee our sovereignty. We will have the director right where we want him. And from all those things we will amass great wealth."

Alvarez hoped it would be so. Hoped it would be as they planned. "Soothe me, Gonzalo."

Parra smiled with just his eyes. "In six months we will have the economy of our country moving in the right direction. In twelve months enough commerce will have returned that the moneys flowing in and out of our banks will be sufficient that the tracing of funds will be impossible . . . without the government's assistance, of course."

"You will make a fine minister of finance, Gonzalo."

"*Sí*, Mr. President. And I will see to our laundry business as if it were my child." It was, actually. Parra had first suggested the lucrative use of the island's financial institutions. There would be plenty of customers on the international market. Dirty money was a commodity of almost limitless supply among the world's less savory power players. Someone had to "clean" it, and that someone was rightly due a very large commission for services rendered. "In eighteen months we will be generating more than one hundred million dollars a month. In three years that will more than triple. In five years . . ."

"Your words are like the touch of a fine, fine masseuse, Gonzalo."

Parra nodded. His session was not finished. "By then we will no longer need the services of our friend in there. The money generated by our 'sales' division will be meaningless by then, and so will his protection. That we will be able to purchase. No one, I guarantee you, no one, will be able to refuse the sums we can offer. What we want will be ours."

"He doesn't even know he is working for us yet, and already we have signed his pink slip," Alvarez joked. He thought of the amount earned from the director's busy pen. It was peanuts compared to what lay ahead. Peanuts. "I love money, Gonzalo. I truly do."

"Money is power, Mr. President."

Alvarez nodded. There was much power to be had . . . in many forms.

"Bob, you know it's good," Chick Hill said as his editor ran through the story a second time.

"Good, sure, but is it true?"

"Old Limp Dick does not call the White House for nothing," Hill reminded his boss. "Party line or not, they don't like him, and he don't like them."

Bob Christopher, national editor for the *Post*, had no argument with that. Congressman Richard Vorhees had surprised many by not always falling in line with the President and his secretary of defense. Some said he was promoting his own agenda. The ones who didn't say it simply agreed with those who did. "All right, morning edition."

"Morning!" Chick's hands went to his hips in a futile display of disagreement. Christopher's look told him that. "All right."

"Get it to copyediting."

Hill took the hard copy and walked it down one floor to the copyeditor for the national pages. "Morning edition."

The middle-aged man looked up. "Why didn't you just transfer it?" All the *Post*'s word processors were connected to a Local Area Network that allowed copy to be transferred to other machines. It was standard to "send" a story to copyediting by pressing a button, not by hand-delivery.

" 'Cause I needed the walk," Chick answered sarcastically, reaching for his cigarettes as he walked away.

"Asshole," the copyeditor said openly. Dealing with these prima donna "journalists" was his least favorite part of his job. At one time he had gotten some satisfaction in using them and the information they dug up to increase his net worth, but that part of his "night job" had slacked off in the recent past. His employers no longer craved the written word as they once had as if it were gold. Now he was much more often used simply as a message boy, the link somewhere in the middle of a chain whose other end he knew nothing about. And he'd continued to be blissfully ignorant as long as the end he did know of continued to pay him handsomely.

Back to the day job. Reading and rewriting, fixing the mistakes that these "highly educated journalists" made with comical regularity. Chimps at the National Zoo could do better.

Hold on. He read over the first part of the story again. Then the rest. "Well, isn't this interesting." He knew from experience that he would not be the only person to see it as such.

He picked up the phone and dialed the number from memory that he had so many times before. Doing so was not even that unusual. Part of his job included checking facts, and one of the stories in his basket was about the new economic-treaty provisions that the republics of the former Soviet Union had just agreed to. Where else would he get the confirmations he needed?

The call was answered at 1125 Sixteenth Street NW and forwarded to the third secretary for consular affairs. Five minutes later, after a trip to the photocopy machine, the copyeditor left on his regular lunch break. A car departed the Russian embassy at the same time.

CHAPTER SEVENTEEN

Design and Circumstance

The Pave Hawk appeared from behind the unmaintained gantry at Launch Complex 12 and raced across the green earth of the Cape at fifty knots toward the target. From a mile away, visible clearly in the unfamiliar daylight, the helicopter appeared to be skimming the ground, its altitude governed by the two groups of dark forms hanging below the fuselage, one higher than the other. As it drew closer to the target—an abandoned range-safety bunker that had once been a haven for crash crews during launches—the dark objects became distinguishable as men. Actually they were much more.

Twelve hundred feet from the bunker, the Pave Hawk slowed, its nose flaring slightly as it dropped twenty feet toward the ground. Four Delta troopers, suspended on STABO rigs below and behind their five comrades, hit the ground running, their weapons in hand. A single pull on their release handles freed them from the fixed shoulder harnesses. They began moving quickly to their right toward a group of drums arrayed in a large circle.

Lieutenant Duc, after depositing his first package right on the money, released the aft STABO rigging and nosed down toward the primary target a quarter-mile dead ahead. He dropped twenty feet more in altitude, leaving a clearance of just that same distance between the boots of the troopers hanging from the

forward rig and the ground. Crossing Central Control Road, he
accelerated to sixty knots, pushing the dangling troopers toward
the rear in a steady sway. The five men remained facing forward,
a product of the STABO rig's designed stability, their stubby
MP5SD4 submachine guns trained on the low gray structure that
was coming at them fast. Very fast.

"On target," Duc said, alerting the men twenty feet below to
"prepare for landing."

Major Sean Graber heard the warning in his earpiece, but
there was no need to key the mike on his right chest and respond.
He, like the four others arrayed to his sides on the rig, bent his
knees slightly and kept his legs close together without letting
them touch. Their boots caught the ground as Duc flared the
Pave Hawk, the bunker practically in their face. They all released
and went for the two entrances, one each on the north and south
sides. Sean, Lewis, and Goldfarb took the south; Antonelli and
Quimpo the north.

Graber heard the STABO rig hit the ground a few yards away
as the Pave Hawk cleared to the south, away from where the
power masts and the lines strung between them would be. His
moves, like all the troopers', were quick and crisp. They went to
each side of the door in crouches. One trooper reached for the
top of the hinge side and stuck one end of a gray strip there. The
other end hung straight down against the door as a plumb line
would, a small wire trailing to the hand of the trooper who had
placed it there.

Step one, Insertion, had just been completed.

"Go!" Sean said into the mike.

The triangular shaped det cord exploded as the troopers
closed their eyes to avoid the bright flash, though that was more
a concern in darkness. A hollow core of aluminum inside the
explosive strip, shaped like a V pointing toward the door, focused
the force of the blast against the old steel door. It ruptured along
a straight line running from top to bottom and tilted inward,
swinging toward the latch side, before falling to the concrete floor
with a *clang.* On the north side, the same process was repeated
within a second of that on the south.

Step two, Entry, was done.

The proper entry of a room or building where hostiles might
be is choreographed long before any attempt is ever considered.

When done simultaneously from several points—the preferred method in order that those being assaulted should be surprised from multiple directions—the planning takes on an even higher importance. Shooting a friendly is a distinct possibility in these situations, and this is why each trooper is given an area of responsibility to watch. His slice of the pie. His own personal killing zone.

Lewis was first through the south door, Graber behind him and Goldfarb bringing up the rear. The trio turned to their left, covering the west end of the open, single-room bunker. Lewis claimed the southwest corner and everything between it and him as his. Goldfarb did the same for the northwest corner. Sean took the middle and was the de facto backup should any surprises present themselves. To his back Antonelli and Quimpo had divided the east side of the room into just two sections.

Step three, Assault, was finished.

"All right, outside," Sean ordered. The run-through, their second, had gone better, and faster, than the first. There would only be time for one more. The biggest hindrance was that the practice runs had all been "dry"—no firing. The makeshift facilities at the Cape were just unsuitable for that. Too much of a chance for ricochet existed, and any chance of that right now was unacceptable. The only other negative was the light conditions. Daylight practice, when the real thing would be going down at night, did not translate fully into complete situational awareness. They were unable to use the NVGs—attached uselessly to their titanium helmets so as to give the "feel" of the real thing—or the LAMs attached beneath the suppressors on the business end of their MP5SD4s.

Ideal, it wasn't, Major Sean Graber knew, but then he and his men weren't paid to work under the best conditions—they earned their money by making any situation the most favorable for them and the converse for any bad guys. That, he was confident they could do.

Sean waited for Buxton to trot over from the "cooling tower" with his team. "How's your timing, Bux?"

"Fifty seconds from touchdown," the captain reported.

"Good." Sean checked the timer on his watch. "We were in and done in twenty seconds from touchdown. That means under two minutes for the show." The "show" was the most interesting part of any mission, namely the time when getting killed went from possibility to probability. "I want to shave five more seconds off our transition on the last run-through."

"Cho flew that one perfectly," Antonelli commented as the Pave Hawk circled in and landed a hundred feet away. From its cabin Joe Anderson climbed out and approached while the crewmen retrieved the jettisoned STABO rigs for the final practice.

"Fifteen minutes, troops," Sean said, giving his men a short break before they again took to the sky. "Bux, you're with me."

Graber and Buxton walked to meet Joe halfway to the helicopter. "Nice ride, Mr. Anderson?"

"Your flyboy should be running the rides at Disney World, Major," Joe observed. He didn't know that would be taken as a compliment. "And that is where you want me because it's *safer*?"

"You got it," Sean affirmed. "I don't want you on the ground until we have the area secured."

"Yeah, the nine of you, your whirlybird, and that firebreathing Hecky bird." Joe's eyes rolled. "Good luck."

Buxton looked to his commander. "He may have a point, Maj. Once we take out who we have to take out, things could still get interesting. There were a lot of troops in the area according to that last bunch of overheads we saw."

"Yeah." Sean's mouth contorted in reluctant agreement. No matter how fast Delta was, there was liable to be a large, unfriendly force nearby, if not on top of them. The Israelis had to deal with the same problem at Entebbe, with Ugandan soldiers running around in the dark. They had done the smart thing and eliminated the bulk of them before they had a chance to officially become "the enemy." Sean and his men would have no such firepower behind them. The AC-130 Spectre gunship, a modified C-130 with 25 and 40mm cannons, a 105mm howitzer, and the advanced targeting systems to accurately fire them at night and in bad weather, was worth a lot of men on the ground, but there was no substitute for those, Sean knew, despite all the ballyhoo about the supremacy of airpower. Delta would need some help, but from where?

"Why don't you just rustle up some airborne guys to come in after you?" Joe asked.

"Because doing that makes it all the more likely that Fidel will know something is up before we get a chance to do our job,"

Buxton explained. "Moving anything bigger than what we're already moving could blow the whole operation."

Joe looked at the distance from the Pave Hawk to the circle of drums that represented where *his* target would be. "I'm gonna have to go across four hundred yards of open ground to do *my* job, and all there'd have to be is one lucky Cuban out there to take me out? To take any of you out?"

All it had taken was one lucky Ugandan to kill the commander of the Israeli operation at Entebbe, the mission's only military casualty. Terrorists were supposed to be the real enemy there, but finding a nemesis was rarely a difficult endeavor if one looked hard enough. There would be opposing forces to spare down in Cuba. Delta had to get in, secure the missile, let Anderson do his thing, then get out of there, all while the loyalist Cubans had the opportunity to take potshots at them. If only the loyalists would suddenly defect to the other . . .

That was it. Sean smiled at Buxton. "I think we have our security force."

"Who?" Captain Buxton asked, unsurprised that the Maj had again sparked on something. It was his way.

"Our enemy," Sean answered. "The trick is convincing them to do it."

That, he knew, would be the job of another.

"Holding court" was not the exclusive domain of the president of the Russian Federation.

Interior Minister Georgiy Bogdanov walked directly from his Zil limousine across the darkened Kremlin grounds to the office of the president and handed him the report without hesitation. "State Security received this less than twenty minutes ago," he said accusatorially. "Tell me to keep trusting the Americans!"

Konovalenko read over the report, actually a news story to be printed the following morning in the paper of the American capital. That Bogdanov had received a copy of the translation in advance of him or Foreign Minister Yakovlev was not surprising. This had gone straight to State Security, as it was not from their CIA contact, and it was no secret that Bogdanov had allies in the upper echelons of the intelligence service. KGB holdovers entirely. Did nothing ever change?

But it was disquieting. The look on the president's face belied that as he handed the sheets to Yakovlev.

"The Americans have started relocation procedures for their President," Bogdanov said quite unnecessarily. It was all in black-and-white. "*And* a *raket* submarine is missing? All while our warning radars are shut down!"

"Georgiy Ivanovich." Yakovlev laid the report on the president's desk. "This is an unverified report."

"Yes, from an agent *you* have chosen to handle the most delicate of tasks!" Bogdanov's neatly combed brown hair fell forward as he shouted. A sweep of his hand pushed it back in place. "You cannot argue trust anymore, my good president. Do you not think the Americans would know these actions would concern us at a time like this? Why, then, have they not informed us in advance? Why?"

The question was proper, Gennadiy Timofeyivich Konovalenko admitted. So were the fears that motivated it. He looked up to Yakovlev. "Has there been any word from Marshal Kurchatov on the American submarine?"

"Just that an air search has begun in the Caribbean," the foreign minister reported.

"A search!" Bogdanov said sarcastically. "How very convenient this all is."

"We will figure this out," Yakovlev assured him.

"No."

"No, what?" the president inquired.

"This cannot be tolerated," Bogdanov said with a force that only a man unafraid of defying his leader could. "You cannot simply sit here and think of an explanation."

"What do you suggest, then, Comrade Interior Minister?" Konovalenko demanded. His puffy cheeks flushed a red that even his hardest drinking could not match.

"See if the good American President can explain this."

Konovalenko sat back in his chair, rocking as he pondered what had to be done. He was treading very dangerous ground, part of which he had created by lack of foresight. His strongest ally in the military establishment, the defense minister, no less, was half a world away in the camp of his nation's ... *enemy?* Bogdanov's faction in the government enjoyed the support of several high-ranking officers, men who might be unafraid to challenge the Motherland's leadership with Kurchatov so far removed.

He had to counter anything that would give Bogdanov and his hard-line cronies an excuse to move on his leadership. He had to prevent that. Disaster could only follow. Before they could take a mile, he would give an inch.

"Igor Yureivich, get the translator." The president slid the multiline phone to the center of his desk and scooted close to it. "I hope this satisfies you, Comrade Interior Minister."

Satisfying me is the least of your worries, Bogdanov thought. "Let us hope so."

"You are kidding?" the President inquired hopefully, but with the knowledge that one did not joke about such things.

"I'm afraid not, sir," Bud said. Sitting next to him, across from the President, was Greg Drummond.

"And you, Mr. Drummond, you concur?"

The DDI was not a regular attendant at briefings in the Oval Office—Anthony Merriweather had reserved that task for himself—and the years that he had on the man sitting across the desk from him could not diminish that somewhat unnerving fact that the most powerful leader in the world was asking him for his opinion on a matter of extreme importance. He actually felt queasy at the moment. "I do, Mr. President." The Man kept his eyes focused on the DDI. He wanted more. "The target makes sense considering Castro's expressed hatred of the Russian leadership. They abandoned Cuba, in his eyes. The longer-range Chinese missile also points to Moscow as the target."

The President removed his glasses and rubbed his eyes for several seconds before laying the bifocals on his desk. "Let me see if I have this right. We have a missing missile sub, the Russians have no early-warning radar functioning, and there is a thirty-year-old *Soviet* nuclear warhead targeted on Moscow. Well, gentlemen, if this is true, we have just been visited by Mr. Murphy himself."

"Sir, we need to talk to the Russians," Bud said.

"And you think they'll believe this?"

"We can't afford to assume that they won't," Bud responded. "Showing trust doesn't always mean that the picture is rosy, but if something happens and we didn't tell them, then they will most certainly see the worst. And we won't be able to convince them otherwise."

The President looked away from both men, his eyes falling upon the picture of his wife. Unlike his many predecessors, he did not reserve the credenza behind his desk for the obligatory family photos. Several were on his desk, where *he* could see them. They might have looked better for the cameras arrayed behind him, but then he'd never considered life, or this job, to be a photo op. Pictures held more meaning than that, and the very recent one he was gazing upon was more important than most. The first lady's growing stomach added a beauty to her that he'd never dreamed possible. The media was joyous for their own reasons; for the first time in decades the White House would echo with the patter of little feet. To the President, it was the little feet that mattered, not the anticipated media circus that would accompany the birth of his first child.

His stare shifted off the picture and to the room as he thought. All of this could come to an end. All of it. And for no reason other than a madman's singular, vengeful act. "He has no idea what could happen, does he?"

"Probably not, sir," Bud answered. "We are living through the collision of design with circumstance. With that combination we can only imagine the result."

"God. Bud, can't we do anything quicker to take that missile out? Bomb it or something?"

"Mr. President, a surgical strike might have a ninety-nine-percent chance of destroying the weapon. Delta would have a ninety-nine-point-*one* percent chance. Point one is not much of an improvement, but the extra certainty is worth the time and effort. If a bomb misses, all it would take is the press of a button to fire the weapon. We would not have time to react. Troops on the ground can adapt to the situation more quickly than any other force we can employ. If the command bunker they hit is the wrong one, they can shift to another target in seconds. Moving more aircraft in after a failed strike, even if the weapon hadn't been fired, would be worthless; the surprise would have been lost. This is the best way."

"I know. It's just the chance that something could happen before Delta goes in that worries me. I just keep wondering why Castro hasn't done anything yet?"

"We were, too, Mr. President, but we think we figured it out." The DDI knew this was his territory. "We figured that Moscow was almost certainly Castro's chosen target from a number of things. One of these was a recent speech he made where he laid blame squarely on the Russians for 'forsaking the Revolution.'

Rhetoric, if ever there was, but he also said something else very telling. He said, 'One day the Russian people will awake from a night's slumber expecting to see the sun, but they will find only the darkness they themselves have created.' "

The President looked to Bud. "My God."

"A wake-up call for the citizens of Moscow. If we're correct, that would mean a launch in about ten-and-a-half hours," Bud said. "Thirty-minute flight time. Arrival just in time for sunrise."

"Why didn't he do that this morning?"

"Fueling, Mr. President," the DDI explained. "Imagery from a reconnaissance pass showed tank trucks at the site earlier. They might not have had time enough to fuel the missile for a launch today. There's no doubt they'll be ready for one tomorrow."

"So he's sitting there waiting, a nuclear missile ready to fly, with his finger on the button. All because he wants to fulfill some grandiose prophecy." The President's head shook slowly. "How could *any* man be that cold and calculating? Does he realize how many innocent people will die?"

"Of course he does, but you can't apply a thinking person's logic to a madman," Bud said. "And that is what he is. It is what he has always been."

Cuba was going to be free. That was how this all started, the President thought. Now what would happen? He couldn't answer that to his own satisfaction and could not afford to spend time pondering it right now. The liberation of Cuba was now on the back burner. The survival of the Russian capital, and possibly of much more, was in the forefront. "How do we do this, Bud?"

"Carefully," the NSA began. "You have to speak to President Konovalenko personally and be very honest. If you have to, tell him about the rebellion, but assure him that the Cuban military approached us. He needs to know that we're not keeping anything from him. Anything."

"All right." The President reached for the phone to call the head Russian translator—one was always on standby in the White House—but it rang just as his fingers touched the handset. "Yes."

"Mr. President, we have an urgent direct voice call from the Russian president. His translator is on the line."

"Speak of the Devil."

"Really?" Bud said.

"Urgent, they say. He already has his translator on the line."

It would take several minutes to get the White House Russian speaker in place, and "Urgent" had a special meaning to it in superpower communications.

"Take it now," Bud said. "Konovalenko's translator can handle both ends, and our guy van verify the tape after the call. Just remember to be straight with him."

"But why is *he* calling?" the President wondered aloud. There was only one way to find out. "Put it through."

"Mr. President, thank you for taking my call," the translator said, repeating the Russian heard in the background.

"It is my pleasure, President Konovalenko. Your translator will have to handle both ends of the conversation, as I did not want to delay speaking with you. There is . . ."

"Thank you for preventing any delay. This is of the utmost urgency. The utmost."

The President's brow furrowed at the double use of "utmost." "What is the problem?"

Problem? Bud thought, too late to realize that something was terribly wrong.

"Why, Mr. President, are your wartime airborne-command posts on alert with your highest military officer aboard?"

Bud didn't hear the words on the other end. All he saw was the President go absolutely pale.

"Command posts?" the President said, reacting with a denial-like question for lack of any other response. It was also the worst thing that could have been said at the moment.

"Whoa!" the signals-watch officer at NORAD exclaimed. His position was in the main control room of the facility, among a hundred other watch officers who continuously monitored their displays for any events that could be considered hostile toward the United States. "I have *never* seen this before."

"What is it, Captain?" the duty officer inquired, looking over the officer's shoulder.

"The Moscow ABM system just fired up, Colonel. Man! Those radars are putting out some major signals." A SIGINT—or Signals Intelligence—package piggybacked onboard one of the Defense Support Program early-warning satellites had just registered the spewing of radar energy from the Pill Box phased-array radar, located north of Moscow at Pushkino, that supported the sixty-four ABM-1 Galosh long-range antiballistic missiles ringing the

Russian capital in eight sites of eight missiles each. "Whoa! There go the others." The Flat Twin radars supporting the thirty-six shorter-range ABM-3 Gazelle missiles had now come to life. "We didn't hear of any Russian ABM exercise, did we?"

"Not to my knowledge," the duty officer said. *They'd better not be fucking with us. Not at a time like this.* The thirty-year colonel looked toward the door up the twin stairs. Behind them might be the answer, but he couldn't just go ask. As a duty officer, he was privy to the special happenings at NORAD for the next couple of weeks, and he also knew that *this* was not supposed to happen. No, he couldn't ask the Russians sitting in watch of his country's strategic forces just what the hell was going on. But someone could. "Get CINCNORAD down here, pronto.'"

Colonel Ojeda's stare sliced into the eyes of the CIA man opposite him. It was a test. A man's eyes, he had learned early in life, told all. If he was fearful, they shifted. If he was truthful, they would not shrink from the challenge of another's gaze. If he was lying, the eyes would be like hollow orbs. Papa Tony's met his with an equal test.

"The stories were true, it would appear," Ojeda commented, his eyes still on the American. "Eh, Captain?"

Captain Manchon nodded as he, too, surveyed the face. "It would appear, sir."

"What stories?" Antonio asked. The visual contest ended with his question. The midday sun blazed down around the shade tree that they stood under, and a pervasive wetness had invaded every crevice of the CIA officer's body. He undid three more buttons on his sweat-darkened uniform before his wondering was answered.

"Of the missile," Manchon began. "For many years there have been rumors of such a weapon. They began after the Russians left. At first we disregarded them as nothing. Soon they began to die away, except among many officers. Officers of rank and privilege."

"General Ontiveros himself often mused on the effect such a weapon would have on the Revolution, in private, of course," Ojeda revealed. "I asked him once if the stories were true." The colonel paused and remembered the moment. "He looked away and said nothing. The general was an honorable man."

Paredes knew he could not judge the man Ojeda respected above his many other superiors. Much had been said of General Eduardo Echevarría Ontiveros by the briefers from Langley, none of it very flattering. He was a staunch Communist, in opposition to the president because of his disastrous policies that had destroyed the nation's economies. Whether he could have done better with his own brand of the same ideology was highly unlikely. But he had imparted something to the men he commanded, something beyond even loyalty. It was a wisdom of sorts, one that challenged his subordinates to challenge the ideas given them as gospel in search of a better way. Ojeda had done so, and had come to the conclusion that the ways championed by the general were not the ways of the future. In one spark of realization he had become Ontiveros's most loyal critic, an act of quasi-treachery that might have earned him a date with the firing squad under men of less character. From the general it had won him the highest respect an officer could give a man under his command. How could he judge right and wrong in such an unconventional mating of ideals? Antonio wondered. If Ontiveros had done nothing else, he had made Colonel Hector Ojeda the man that he was.

"The retreat toward the plant makes sense, now," Manchon said.

"As does the presence of the Russian your government inquired about," Ojeda added. "Now they ask for another thing."

"Yes, we do," Paredes affirmed, his choice of words very careful.

"The map." It was handed to Ojeda by Manchon. The colonel studied it for a moment, his eyes surveying the options of advance for his new mission. "Captain, you will move the brigade as planned toward Guilermo Moncada. The loyalists will be forced to advance toward you. If not, it would allow you access to the coastal roads. They will come to a fight. As you do this, I will take three companies to Juragua. We will skirt the swamps and be in position to do as our American friends wish."

"The swamps, Colonel," Manchon said, biting his lip. "Even if you do not enter them, you will have no roads, no vehicles to carry heavy weapons."

"We will carry what we need." Ojeda looked to Antonio. "Will we not, Papa Tony?"

I had to say "we," "Yes, we will."

"Get the men ready, Captain," Ojeda ordered. "We have a long walk ahead."

"From the lab, sir," the director's secretary said as she handed over the report. "Plus a UID from Miami. *And* your mail."

"Thank you, Sally," Jones said politely, not wanting another scolding from the person who kept his office—and the Bureau, sometimes—in order. He paged through the workup the Audio/Visual Section had done on the tape. "Ninety-two percent probability that it is Castro speaking," he read aloud. Any doubts that he or anyone might have still harbored had just gone out the window.

All the Bureau could do now was try and find the guys who had killed the keeper of the tape—and of one of his agents. That search was about to swing into high gear according to the latest briefing from the Deputy A-SAC of the L.A. office. Jones's role was limited to waiting. He had become proficient at that over the years but had never come to enjoy it.

Miami. Jones turned his attention to that. It looked as though the tap team might have come up with something. He opened the envelope that had been sealed down in the crypto room and read the summary first. A.D.C. number. A name. Samuel Garrity. Referred to . . . *What*? *"The director's desk"*! He flipped through the transcription of the conversation, reading it only once. Greg Drummond was gonna love this. So would a jury in the near future, Jones thought, if this Garrity guy didn't cop a plea bargain. The director wondered who the guy was to have access to the head of the CIA. He'd know soon enough, after a quick call to the DDI. Arrest warrants would be issued soon after that.

Jones dialed the DDI's office and waited, paging through his mail as Drummond's secretary checked to see when he was due back. He came upon the other report from Miami, the one he should have read after his wonderful night of sleep in the lounge. He scanned the summary, which always preceded any verbatim transcription of a recorded conversation, and stopped cold on the mention of a single name: Portero. Jones read further, then on to the transcription. *My God.* These were the murderers of his agent, and they were being . . . *controlled?* . . . by the same person who . . .

"What the hell is going on here?" Jones asked the air.

"Director Jones, Mr. Drummond should be back from the White House in five minutes."

"Thank you." Jones punched up a clear line. "Get me L.A."

He looked down at the transcription again. *An address, even.* "Stupid sons of bitches." Whatever was going on, however it was connected to the CIA leak, at least he knew exactly where the killers of Special Agent Thom Danbrook were, and he cursed himself for not reading the report when it came in. It would have saved L.A. a lot of legwork, among other things.

"Damn the fool!" General Alexander Shergin swore. The loudness echoed through the antiquated secure telephone system that connected the underground headquarters of *Voyska PVO* to Moscow.

"His intelligence prostitute no longer seems so credible," the interior minister said from his fourth-floor office near the Moscow Ring Road. Sixty kilometers away, the commander of the nation's air-defense forces grunted angrily.

"A fucking R-12 left in Cuba," Shergin scoffed, using the old Soviet designation of the missile known to NATO as the SS-4. "And a new *Chinese* booster. Hah! And Castro has it pointed at us! What other fairy tales did the American tell?"

"None of consequence. Of course, he promised to provide *evidence* that his fantasy is true." Bogdanov stubbed his cigarette out and swung his chair to face the window. Flecks of white pierced the darkness as he looked to the city center, toward the lighted ornate spires of the Kremlin. "He and Yakovlev are sitting there now trying to convince themselves that the Americans' story is somehow possible."

"With the evidence, no doubt." Shergin laughed. "The Central Intelligence Agency is adept at uncovering 'evidence.' "

"Yes," Bogadanov agreed. He took another cigarette from the case on his desk and lit it, using the lighter his father had given him. "He had "liberated" it from a dead German at Stalingrad half a century before. "But this will not end in their favor. The time to move has come."

There was a surprising pause from the general. "When?"

"Before the sun rises. Before the Americans have a chance to play out this little scenario they have concocted in order to lay blame on Castro." Bogdanov blew the smoke from his lungs loudly. "Before that *missing* submarine has a chance to loose its missiles. Yes, Aleksandr Dimitreivich, before that can happen, we will be in power, and the Americans will learn that even though the Motherland is blind, that does not mean even for a second that she is without strength, or without the resolve to use it."

"And Marshal Kurchatov? He could be a problem, even from where he is."

Bogdanov laughed. "A man with no voice is as dangerous as a child. Cut him off."

Chapter Eighteen

Best-Laid Plans . . .

Art watched from his Bureau Chevy parked half a block from motel number three, an inviting sort of place that had no name, just a price listed in faded neon. In his early days with the Bureau, when stakeouts and tails were procedures still to be learned, he had wondered why bad guys, especially the ones who could afford not to, would choose places like these to hide out in. The answer came not in the accommodations, but in the management, who ran their businesses with a see-no-evil, hear-no-evil attitude. Literally anything could go on behind the numbered doors, and as long as the bills were paid—in cash, up front—there was no need to question the activities.

"She's going in," Andy Harriman reported from the passenger seat next to Art. He lifted the binoculars to his eyes for just a second and checked the front of the motel. "No visual. It's a bad angle."

Art took the mike from its clip on the dash. "King Eight to King Six and King Four."

"Go, Eight."

"Go."

"Frankie's in."

Two acknowledgments of the information came immediately. Art and Andy's unit, King Eight, had the best vantage point. They were parked on Vermont south of Eleventh, and were focusing their attention farther south on the "$22.50" motel, which occupied the southwest corner of Vermont and Twelfth. Agents Dan Burlingame and Drew Smith in King Six were a half-block south of the motel, parked in a strip mall on the opposite side of the street. King Four, with agents Tina Mercer and Tim Russo, was parked on Twelfth, nosed east toward Vermont and had a very limited view of the scene. All three units, however, could be to Frankie in just seconds.

Art cupped his left hand over the small earpiece connected to the receiver. His right hand dropped down out of habit and ran across his jacket. The move did not go unnoticed to a smiling Harriman.

"Mr. Smith okay?"

"Right where he should be, Andy," Art said unabashedly. The ready signal from Frankie sounded in his ear. "One more time."

"Hi!"

The desk clerk looked to the lady across the counter with little care for her bubbly personality. "Room for two?" Were there ever any rooms for one?

"No. No. Nothing like that," Frankie responded with mild embarrassment. "I'm returning a wallet." She reached into her oversized purse and retrieved the item. "Mr. Flavio Alicante called our store and said he thought he'd left it there." She flipped open the "license" and avoided holding her breath. "But he didn't give me a room number. He just gave this address."

The clerk eyed the picture, then the lady, then the wallet again. It was bulging with something in its recesses. Money? *Hmmm.* "You want me to give it to him."

Yes! "No, it's got, you know, kinda a lot of money in it, and he made me promise to deliver it in person." She smiled apologetically.

"Yeah. Okay." He glanced down at the keyboard beneath the counter. "He and his buddy are in one-oh-six. Out the door and to the left."

Frankie's smile dissolved instantly. She dropped her bag and pulled out her shield and weapon, which was pointed upward. "FBI. Do not move, do not say anything."

The young man's eyes tripled in size as his hands slowly came up. "Yeah, whatever you say, lady."

* * *

"Yes!" Art slapped the steering wheel, but a radio call from headquarters interrupted his celebration. He reached for the mike, looking right, and took no notice of the yellow taxi passing to his left and heading south on Vermont. He also missed the lone passenger in back.

"There it is," the man said to his partner in the driver's seat.

"Got it," the driver acknowledged, sliding the small compact into the northbound left-turn pocket for Twelfth Street. He stopped before reaching the intersection, however, and waited for a break in the midmorning traffic coming south on Vermont. The last car in the traffic wave was a yellow taxi, which turned into the driveway immediately to his left. He cranked the wheel and followed it in. "Time to go to work."

The man in the passenger seat undid the restraining strap on his shoulder holster. "You got it."

"Art, we've got the address of where the shooters are staying." It was Lou Hidalgo calling from the office.

"What? We just found them, Lou." Art looked right to Andy, who returned the perplexed look. "How did you find out?"

"I can't explain everything. It'd take too long. But listen, this thing runs deeper than we thought. Much deeper."

Lou had full knowledge of the whole story, unlike the rest of the agents working on this. What the hell did "deeper" mean in this situation? What *could* run deeper? "Wait, Lou. We found them. All we do now is set up the plan to take them."

"There may not be time, Art. A wiretap team in Miami recorded a conversation between those guys and their boss, or their contact. We don't know exactly. But whoever it was, was sending someone out to get a tape from them."

"A tape? *We* have the tape," Art said.

"I know, but that's not the point," Lou explained with frustration. "The whole conversation, even the way they made contact, was set up to keep locations secret. The contact was *not* supposed to know where they were, but he asked directly for it, *with* full knowledge that they didn't have *the* tape. Just *a* tape."

"But why would the person running these guys break security procedures to . . ." Art froze with the realization.

"They wouldn't. The shooters could have express-mailed the

damn thing back to Miami faster than it would take to send someone out here to get it," Lou said. "And with less risk. Who-ever's coming is not here to play messenger."

"Goddammit!" Art keyed the mike. "Okay, I'll get LAPD to seal off everything fast so our visitor can't get close."

"Or visitors, Art," Lou added.

"Wonderful." He laid the mike on the seat and pulled his earpiece out. "You listen for Frankie's signal to close in."

"Trouble?"

Art picked up the cellular. "I don't know, but I want blue suits out here fast."

"Is there anyone else in the office?" Frankie asked as she walked behind the counter, one hand grasping the clerk's collar into a bunch.

"No, just me."

She glanced into the small room off the office. A bed and nightstand were visible, as was an open door to a bathroom. "Any-one in there? In the bathroom, maybe?"

"No. I swear."

The young guy was too scared to lie, she knew. They had them.

"King Eight," Frankie said, tilting her head slightly down-ward toward the mike behind her lapel as she looked across the parking lot and down the street toward her partner's car. Another vehicle passed in front of the office window, catching her atten-tion before she could finish the message. When she saw who was in the backseat, the word she uttered was not the one those listening were expecting.

Drew Smith lowered the binoculars, a questioning grimace on his face.

"You see something?" Dan Burlingame asked, his third doughnut of the morning half-gone.

"I'd swear the guy riding in that cab was the reporter."

"You mean Sullivan?"

"Yeah," Smith answered. "And a car going north turned into the motel right behind. Two guys in it. Nice clean compact."

"Are you sure about the reporter?"

"Not positive, but it's still a lot of traffic for that place this time of day."

Dan Burlingame nodded, swallowed, and reached for the radio.

"Sullivan?" Andy repeated with surprise.

Art looked right as he waited for the Metro Division lieutenant to come to the phone. "What?"

"She says Sullivan just pulled in in a cab. Into the lot."

"Shit!" Art dropped the cellular and reached for the mike, but King Six's call cut him off.

"King Eight, this is King Six. We may have some movement. One cab and one blue compact just entered the lot."

Art looked back to the motel, following the cab Frankie had mentioned as it came to a stop in the lot. Behind it, pulling into a space, was another car with . . .

"Damn!" Art dropped the car into gear—you never waited with the engine off while covering another agent—and keyed the mike. "King Four and Six, move in! *Now!* Watch occupants of blue compact! Possibly armed!"

Art turned the wheel hard into traffic lanes and stepped on the accelerator but had to brake almost as soon as a wave of cars shot by, the lead vehicles honking at the intruder into the lane. Over a block away King Six was moving to pull out of the strip-mall lot, Drew Smith weaving the car through pedestrians and other vehicles. Only King Four, sitting on Twelfth Street, was able to move immediately toward the motel, but neither agent had been in a position to see what the others had. They were going off only the barest instructions.

In just more than a blink of an eye, with careful planning being tossed aside because of circumstances' intervention, almost everything that could have gone wrong had.

George Sullivan handed the driver a twenty and looked toward the two-story motel, then to the key in his hand. Behind him there were car doors closing, but he was focused on what he had to do. On where he had to go. Straight ahead. The same number as on the key tab. Room 106.

Were the guys who wanted to kill him in there? He'd tried to convince himself that they wouldn't be. They would have taken off by now, right? Hanging around would be stupid. All the indicators told him that he'd be able to open the door, find the room empty, and rummage around to see if there was anything he could use to make a story. All the logical things told him that.

And then there was the annoying voice from a higher plane of realization that kept saying "Yeah, right!" And it said it louder.

But he couldn't listen to it. There was no other way to prove himself. Giving up the bottle, if he could keep it up, was a personal victory. He needed a public one to make his life worth living. He *had* to have this story, had to find out who the killers of Portero and the FBI agent were. And the path to that end lay a few feet away.

The barest opening in traffic appeared. Art didn't hesitate. He floored it and squealed the tires into the right lane. In the distance he saw the red and blue grill lights of King Six coming in the opposite direction. To his right and ahead, agents Russo and Mercer had stopped their car on the street, the motel building preventing its being seen from the lot. They were advancing along the north wall toward the lot.

That left only . . .

"No!" Art screamed. *What are you doing?*

Frankie Aguirre made the decision in a split second, based upon factors that she could not control but had to confront. There were two known murderers less than fifty feet from her, and a man *they* wanted to kill was heading for their room. She had no two-way communications with the teams watching her backside and had no way of knowing when they would get there. Quickly, for sure, but quick might not be fast enough. Frankie knew that things were gong to start happening in seconds.

She was there. She was alone. She had to do it.

"Stay down," she told the clerk as she pushed him to the floor and walked through the glass door to the lot. Sullivan was at the door of 106, something in his hand. The door started to open before she could shout a warning to him. It was going to be two against one, she realized, catching her mistake in ratio a split second later.

Tomás heard the key turning in the lock, grabbed his Browning, and jumped into the latch side of the doorway. As it began to swing inward, he flipped it with one hand and stepped into the opening, his gun pointing at . . .

"Sullivan?" Tomás said it with a surprise that caused his bedridden partner—who had expected just an overzealous cleaning woman—to sit bolt upright despite the pain.

George Sullivan was equally shocked. His jaw dropped, then his eyes left their lock on the face and saw the gun. "You ... You ..."

Tomás reached for Sullivan with one hand and pulled him toward the doorway. As he did, he saw past the stupid reporter—little more than a walking dead man, now—and to the parking lot. Walking toward him were two men. One was lifting something in his left hand, and the other was reaching under his coat.

"*Freeze!*" Frankie yelled, startling the two men who had appeared with guns. Their heads jerked to the left, then the nearest one began to turn the same way, his hand emerging from the hidden side of his body with a ...

Her Smith & Wesson was already pointed at them, and she squeezed off two quick shots at the nearest one. He immediately fell backward, toward his companion, who was also now spinning her way. The second one was a lefty, which meant that his gun would take just a hair longer to rotate enough to fire. But that hair was too long. Frankie fired twice more, one of her shots registering in the head of number two, which briefly was crowned by a grotesque halo of pink and red mist that was lit by the morning sun. It disappeared as he crumpled to the ground, his partner collapsing atop him in a heap.

Tomás froze briefly as he watched the shootout erupt in front of him. Why were the cops shooting each other? The two guys coming at him with guns had to be cops just following Sullivan, but who had shot them? And how did Sullivan find them? There were too many questions, too many things racing through his mind, and too many distractions for him to notice that the dead-eye shooter, some chick, was almost on top of him.

Art heard and saw the exchange from a hundred feet away. He slammed on the brakes through the intersection of Twelfth and Vermont, cranking the wheel right and skidding up over the curb to a stop. Andy already had the mike in his hand.

"King Eight! Shots fired! Agent needs help!"

*   *   *

"Drop it!" Frankie said with as much authority as she could muster but obviously not enough to overcome the determination to die in the perp pulling Sullivan into room 106.

Tomás jerked the reporter past him, tossing him to the floor, and leveled his Browning at the chick with the gun. His sights were almost on her, his mind wishing the sweet young thing a nice trip into the hereafter, when a strange, cold blackness spilled in front of his eyes, like a waterfall of darkness cascading over his body.

Frankie's two shots were right on the money, placed where they had to be—the head. The perp's torso had been blocked as Sullivan was thrown inward. Both 10mm rounds entered through the cheeks, one below each eye. They exited straight back, taking large chunks of brain stem and skull with them. The wet red spray was visible on the dirty white door as number three fell.

One was left. One of Thom's killers. Frankie continued her fast walk to the doorway, turning in and crouching with her weapon, sweeping the room from right to left. Outside, in her peripheral vision, she saw a head peek around the corner of the building on Twelfth. Behind she could hear footsteps, running footsteps, and car tires grabbing hold of asphalt with the terrible sound of a panic skid.

All those things were inconsequential, though. Her senses were narrowing their focus to the scene before her. The scent of gunpowder and whiskey was pulled through her nostrils with every rapid breath. Hands grabbing for something, a glass tumbling to a carpeted floor, and the pleas of the condemned assaulted her auditory filters. The gun felt hot and very light in her hand, as though she were holding a feather. And her eyes . . . Her eyes saw everything in the room at once and then focused with an instinctive, highly selective tunnel vision on what mattered most.

"Drop it!" she said, stepping toward the man on the bed. His gun was pointed at Sullivan, who was half lying, half sitting in the corner nearest the bathroom.

"I'll kill him!" Jorge screamed, his words broken as though tortured by pain. Tears streamed down his face, and the pistol trembled slightly in his hand. But he kept it pointed directly at the whimpering reporter. His finger pressed on the trigger a hair. *"AND I WILL BLOW YOUR FUCKING BRAINS ALL OVER*

THE ROOM!'' Frankie said, stepping still closer. And closer. And closer, until the smoking barrel of her weapon touched Jorge's temple. He winced as the hot steel burned the tender skin on the right side of his face.

Art swung into the room as Russo and Mercer approached from Twelfth. "Behind you, Frankie," he said. A quick look to the ground at his right confirmed that the guy in the doorway was very dead. He knew that to his rear Burlingame and Smith were covering the other two recipients of Frankie's shots, though he didn't know their condition.

He also didn't know the condition of his partner. Slowly he slide-stepped toward her and the perp, coming up easily on her right.

"I said drop it," Frankie repeated, her grip steady, the Smith & Wesson barely moving. *"Now."*

Jorge squeezed the trigger a slight bit more. "I mean it. I'll kill him." Another gun appeared to his front, and his eyes shifted to see straight into the barrel.

"She means it, too," Art said, his own finger applying pressure to the trigger. "So do I."

Death suddenly seemed certain for Jorge. Death. The end. Over. Defiance and bravado lost their appeal with that revelation. He did not want to die. Not for the sake of finishing a lousy job. No way. He backed off pressure on the trigger. "Okay. Okay. I give."

"Finger off the trigger, and lay it on your lap," Art directed. The perp followed the instructions without hesitation. "Cover me, partner."

"Got him," Frankie said robotically as Art reached in and picked up the Browning.

"You all right?" Art asked Sullivan, who sat wide-eyed, his chest heaving, in the corner.

"I ... I ... I ..." It was all George could get out as his breaths came in deep, heavy waves. He was alive. Alive! "I'm alive."

"Yeah," Art reacted. "Good for you." *Fucking idiot.* There would be time for that later. "We got him."

Frankie pressed the barrel harder against the perp's head, until he began to lean away and down to the pillows. *You killed Thom. YOU KILLED THOM!!!*

"Partner." Art swiveled his aim slowly left until it was centered on the man's head. He didn't want to move it anymore. "Frankie." *Don't make me do it. Not again.* "Frankie."

She heard her partner's words. They were almost pleas, but pleas for what? For her *not* to do something? Just like this scum hadn't done anything to Thom. Like . . . Like . . .

"Bring your right hand slowly to your back," Frankie said, waiting for the suspect to comply before having him bring the other back. "Cuff him, Art."

"Gladly." Art holstered his weapon and brought out his handcuffs. A sigh of relief escaped his lips, for many reasons. Their suspect was now in custody.

Frankie backed away and holstered her own weapon. She felt as though she hadn't breathed in hours, in days even, and took in a deep, cleansing taste of air. Looking down, she saw Sullivan, now in a semifetal sitting position, his chin tucked between his knees. He looked like shit, and she hoped he felt like it, too.

"Next time, hotshot, someone might not be there to save your ass," Frankie said directly to him. His eyes came up, then looked away. Frankie walked through the door without commenting further, passing Dan Burlingame on his way in.

"You keep your face down," Art said to the suspect. "You so much as move, and I'll shot you just for the fun of it."

Burlingame came up from behind. He eyed both Sullivan and the perp before speaking. "The two outside are dead, Art. Three total."

The sound of approaching sirens began. Art knew there'd be a symphony of them in the next minute. "Jesus, Dan."

"Hell of a job of shooting," Burlingame commented. "Four on one, and she cleaned up."

"Yeah," Art agreed without glee. Killing was killing, even when justified. It was never the best way. Sometimes it was the only way. This time it didn't have to be. "Watch him," Art said to Burlingame. He was standing over Sullivan a second later. "You sorry sack of shit."

George looked up, his eyes red but dry. There were no more tears left in him. Hardly any emotion. Just a sobering realization that his life was poised on the edge of the drain and ready to slide in.

"You nearly got my partner killed 'cause she had to save your ass," Art bellowed. "And why? Why the fuck did you come looking?"

"I . . . I needed the story." Sullivan swallowed hard. "I need something."

Art spit out a disgusted breath. "Yeah, you need something, all right. You need a fucking lesson in life. Look around, huh. You see what you caused? What you caused because you 'needed a story'? Bullshit! You're a fucking little crybaby who only has his booze to keep him company!"

"No more booze," George said simply.

Art wondered if the claim was true. Probably not, despite the fact that the guy seemed stone-cold sober. "Wonderful first step, hotshot. Now try and fix all this."

Sullivan looked to his left, leaning forward to see past the plain wooden dresser. The body of the man who had dragged him in the room lay against the doorframe. Beyond that, in the parking lot, were what looked like two more bodies. And farther still, leaning against the hood of an awkwardly parked car, was the woman who had saved his life.

"Tina," Art said, calling the other agent in. He took what he hoped would be a final look at Sullivan, and he didn't know what to feel about him right now. It couldn't be pity; that would be too generous. Hate? For what, for being an idiot? Anger in part. But what else he should think of George Sullivan eluded him. Only distaste was prevalent in his mind at the moment. "Get him out of here."

Art turned away as Mercer lifted and led Sullivan from the room. He took a few steps toward the bed and rolled the suspect over. The movement caused a grimace of pain. "Listen carefully, whoever you are, you are under arrest. You have the right to remain silent. . . ." Art finished the Mirandizing of their suspect, then lifted him with a one hand grip of the man's shirt to a sitting position against the headboard. There was another wince. "Now we're gonna have to talk."

Chapter Nineteen

Connections

General Walker finished relating what he had just been told a few minutes before. The story was met initially by silence from Marshal Kurchatov and Colonel Belyayev.

"You have just answered your own question, General Walker," Kurchatov said. "I, too, would activate the Moscow ABM system if such a thing had been told to me."

"Yes, but this appears to be an action taken not because of prudence, but because of mistrust," Walker explained. "Your president's tone was very provocative, I am told, and I say that not to challenge his motivation, but just as a point of concern."

"Well, President Konovalenko, unfortunately, has more than just himself to answer to. And those who demand such satisfaction in times like this are not the most accommodating people." Kurchatov smiled with the knowledge of one who had juggled both the political and military hats in his career, a process he knew was unfamiliar to CINCNORAD. "And distrust is their ally, not their enemy."

"Your words are calming, Marshal. Possibly they can be for President Konovalenko as well."

Gennadiy Timofeyivich would be feeling the pressure, Kurchatov knew, and he was well aware who from. *Yakovlev and Shergin.* The interior minister he could do nothing about, but Shergin was his subordinate and was at the end of the direct line

311

temporarily connecting NORAD with the *Voyska PVO*. Neutering the commander of the Motherland's air-defense forces, at least temporarily, would split him from that weasel of an ally of his. Yakovlev would then stand alone, without an inroad to the military. Gennadiy Timofeyivich could then eat him for breakfast.

"I will speak to my people, and then I will speak to the president," Kurchatov said, thinking on what his words would be for the latter. "One of our missiles in Cuba, eh?"

"At least in part," Walker expanded.

"Yes. The part that matters, apparently. It is not so hard to believe. I was but a young captain during that time. Things were very confused, and information was hoarded as if it were gold." In these days as if bread, the marshal thought. "As I gained rank and experience, I learned that there are many *impossible* things that are actually realities cloaked in secrecy." Kurchatov smiled knowingly. "Someday, possibly, I can tell you of such things."

Walker returned the expression. "And I to you."

"So such a thing as you tell it is not beyond my belief, but . . ." The pause was punctuated by concern. "Those who are not here, those who cannot see and feel that you are in no way trying to deceive us, well, to them such a happening could be seen as less than fact. Even as a threat."

"That's my concern," Walker said straightforwardly.

Kurchatov nodded concurrence. "And mine. Let us try to calm any fears that may be developing. Colonel Belyayev."

Kurchatov and Belyayev followed General Walker from their quarters to the force-monitoring console. A new duty officer was in the left seat and stood respectfully as the Russian defense minister took the seat to his right.

"This one?" Kurchatov asked, pointing to the handset lying in the unmarked cradle. A nod affirmed his question, and he picked it up. The predialed sequence, routed through three secure voice communications switching centers, searched for a connection at *Voyska PVO*. After a first failure—which took less than a second—the switching computers tried again. Another failure.

"No connect," a microchip reported in a disembodied male voice.

Kurchatov pulled the receiver away, looking at it in a reaction that was as natural as it was unproductive. Colonel Belyayev took the phone from him, pressed the cradle switch down, and waited for the connection again.

"No connect."

"Something is wrong," Belyayev said. His words were tinged with the barest amount of a question, and his eyes silently waited for CINCNORAD to answer.

The same result came from General Walker's attempt. He picked up another phone and called NORAD's communication center—its own switchboard. "I want an analysis on the direct line between the force-monitoring console and Russian Air Defense Headquarters . . . fast."

Belyayev and Kurchatov alternately watched CINCNORAD and the displays, the tension obvious and growing. Everything so far had been as the Americans had said. Everything. Even the Cuban revelation, though unexpected, was not the thing to cause confident hearts to stir. But this. A malfunction at this time? In combination with all else? If this became known to the president's enemies in Moscow . . . The defense minister isolated by a communications *failure?* That discovery could be very dangerous. Marshal Kurchatov hoped, simply, that the sarcasm in his thought would turn out to be baseless.

The phone buzzed, and Walker snatched it up. "Yes." He listened for less than thirty seconds. "You're certain?"

"General Walker?" Kurchatov said after CINCNORAD had hung up.

"The direct circuit has been disconnected. Cut at the source."

The defense minister's eyebrows arched to the center of his forehead. *It cannot be* . . . "Why would you do this? Why would you isolate us?"

Walker's head shook. "Not *us,* Marshal. *You.* The link was severed at your end. In Moscow."

The thick black lines of hair over Kurchatov's eyes shot upward, ending the expression of anger. The emotion now was plain fear. "Dear God."

Greg Drummond stood personally by the secure fax and took the pages as soon as they came out. He made a duplicate copy and was in his office a minute later. Mike Healy was waiting for him.

"Here," the DDI said, handing the copy to his Operations counterpart.

"Sam Garrity?" Healy said skeptically before reading the word-for-word wiretap transcripts just sent from the Bureau.

Drummond had given him only what he had learned from Gordon Jones's quick call, namely that they had a suspect in the leak, and, the big twist, that the leak's contact was also directing two men wanted in the killing of Francisco Portero—the keeper of the tape.

Drummond ignored the question and read through the conversation, picking out important details first. " '*Off the director's desk*'? '*Scribbles*'? What the hell is he saying? There's no way to get anything written off this floor. Security would have caught it in their sweep. Anything Anthony left on his desk would have gone in the burn bag."

"Well, he got something," the DDO said. " 'Cause he knows about the missile. And so does his contact—whoever that is."

"Gordy's guys down in Miami are setting to take him real soon," Drummond said with pleasure. Only nailing the man who'd caused his directorate to become suspect would bring greater joy.

Healy scanned farther down the transcript, his mind seizing on two passages. "Greg, look halfway down. You see that?"

" '*This isn't like before,*' " Drummond read.

"And then: '. . . *that guy a while back wasn't just making it up?*' " Healy looked up. "You don't think . . ."

Deputy Director, Intelligence, Greg Drummond, not a man prone to violent urges, knew exactly what he'd like done to the man filling his thoughts at the moment. "He had to know, Mike. The asshole had to."

The DDO glanced back down. "You're right. If this is accurate, then it's the only way Garrity would have known." His eyes looked right, to the wall that separated them from the DCI's office.

"But how?" Drummond wondered aloud.

Healy thought for a moment, which was all the time he needed to make the decision. "I don't know, but we sure as hell are going to find out. First step is to find out more on the man who brought the knowledge into the country."

"Portero?"

"Exactly. We're gonna check with our INS liaison in Florida and see just what he did when he came over."

"Anthony won't like us talking to *his* people," Drummond countered, though the conviction behind his words was less than halfhearted. ·

"Fuck what he thinks. From where I see it, he is on assignment," Healy said. "Deputy director is out of the country. That makes me acting director."

The DDO had a few years service on the DDI, but Drummond didn't mind the hierarchy one damn bit. Not for this. "Let's do it, boss."

"I'll check with Florida," Healy said. "And I assume you want to handle Garrity."

"You assume correctly," Drummond confirmed, nodding emphatically. "I'm going with the FBI team that's going to pick him up. There are a few things I want to ask good old Sam."

"Do it right, Greg. We need connections here to tie this all together."

"We'll get them," the DDI said. *And him,* he added hopefully, referring to the man whose empty chair sat but a room away.

Three floors below the office of the deputy director, Intelligence, in a roughly square room with no windows and lighting that never dimmed, the first connections Mike Healy had desired were being made without him even knowing it. And those connections came in the form of ones and zeros.

DIOMEDES, the Science & Technology Directorate's computer link to the world's financial institutions, had been sorting through trillions of bits of binary code (ones and zeros), searching for links between accounts controlled by Coseros and those belonging to known criminal types, namely drug cartels or their fronts. The process was much like following a multigenerational family tree that branched out in all directions. Once a link to a certain account in bank X located in country Y was found, then an attempt was made to identify the owner of those funds. With the strict financial-security laws of some countries, this was not always a direct task. Other links had to be determined that might point to the ownership, and more links to verify those. It was a tedious, time-consuming exercise in electronic investigation, pseudoillegal, and quite suited to the twin Cray computers dedicated to Project DIOMEDES.

"Got a cross-link," a technician announced, the data freezing on her screen. Her supervisor came over to see.

"Where?"

"Here," she said, pointing to the display. "Coseros transferred seven hundred grand into this account in the Bern Central

Bank. It's another CFS account." They were finding more and more offshore accounts belonging to the Cuban Freedom Society, though there was nothing patently illegal about that. Nothing that could be proved, that is. Yet. "Then look who transferred into the same account. Victor Feodr."

"Feodr?" the supervisor said aloud. The name rang a bell, but not loudly. He had heard it before in his time with DIOMEDES, some years back, but exactly when he couldn't . . . *Him?* "The Bulgarian?"

"The same one who the KGB used as a money funnel," the technician reported.

"Who's paying his bills now?"

She pointed lower on the screen. "An account controlled by the Russian Foreign Ministry. Usually used for diplomatic travel expenses."

The supervisor scratched his head. "Any back transfers from those funds to Coseros?"

"Nope, but look at these." She scrolled the information slowly. Account after account flowed upward from the bottom of the screen, all of them listed as "depositors" to the CFS account in Bern. "These accounts are all controlled by different agencies in over forty governments. Look. This one is controlled by a front for Israeli Intelligence."

"Mossad?"

"Never get them to admit that. This one by the PRC. This one by an Iraqi with liaison duties to the UN. The list goes on, and on."

"I still don't get this. Nothing back-transferred to Coseros?"

The technician willed her supervisor to see the real discovery, but he didn't put the obvious together. "We have been looking at the wrong bad guy. Coseros isn't in the shit up to his elbows. The CFS is. He hasn't been funding them. The whole fucking world has. For what reason I don't know, but these are not just donations. Not from these folks."

The supervisor looked down at the young lady who'd just proved that the best damn computers were worth diddly-squat without a human brain to look at what was spit out and cull the diamond from the coal. "Damn good work. I know some people who are going to be very happy with what you've found."

There would also be some who would not.

* * *

"Sir, one can't just pick up a phone and dial Russian Air Defense Headquarters," Bud explained. "Whoever cut Marshal Kurchatov off knew that."

"But why, Bud?"

"We can't be certain." The NSA was standing. He had too much energy built up to sit. "But it cannot be good."

"You would think they'd want someone watching our missiles at a time like this," the President said. "I guess this means I wasn't too convincing."

"You were at a disadvantage."

"And just how did Konovalenko know about Kneecap, and about Granger on board?"

Bud knew the question was not directed at him. It was simply asked in wonder. But he felt compelled to offer some sort of explanation, or a supposition of such. "Mr. President, when things happen as fast as they have been on this, things get said. Things are overheard. The press digs things up, just like the *Post* and ABC have been today. Leaks happen, and all it would take is some 'agricultural officer' from the Russian embassy to be in the right place at an opportune time."

"So I get waylaid by the Russians, and everything I tell them then sounds like an after-the-fact rebuttal to their concerns." The President turned his chair left and right as he thought. "This is beginning to scare me, Bud. I thought when we figured that Castro's target would be Moscow, we could breathe a little, but now I'm not so sure. If the Russians don't believe us about this . . ."

"Sir, President Konovalenko would not do anything rash," Bud said with confidence. "He is not a reactionary. But he is cautious. He did not walk into the modernization program without questions, and he did not proceed without answers that he found satisfactory. He is not who we have to be concerned about."

The President scowled as he thought of the men his NSA was referring to. "Those people never see the writing on the wall, do they? They just keep looking to the past for some kind of salvation from the hardships of undoing the damage done over three-fourths of a century. I'll tell you, Bud. I have more respect for Konovalenko each and every damn day he keeps pushing ahead, despite the polls and the threats from the hard-liners."

"He may need you to cheerlead very soon, sir."

The President wasn't sure that would be the right thing to

do. Or the timely thing. "No, Bud. We did that for him once before, but he didn't have his defense minister over here incommunicado then. This is more serious, meaning we have to step further in if he needs and wants it." He caught sight of the tan desk phone. "Maybe we can do something to reverse the situation."

Bud saw the beginnings of a satisfied smile as the President picked up the phone.

"And this may be the way to do it," the President said, twisting the receiver in his hand. "Bud, get the translator in here."

Sean found Joe giving his equipment a final check in the privacy of an empty office off the hangar the Pave Hawk had been rolled into. For the work that lay ahead, and for any work involving the kind of shit that Anderson dealt with, for that matter, the major had expected to see the type of highly sophisticated, hideously expensive equipment that the physicist had used during the previous pairing of their talents. What he saw was quite the opposite.

"You ready for another run with us, Anderson?" Sean asked. It was an idle question, breaking the inherent seriousness of the moment. And a moment was about all they had for such luxuries. Delta and their special passenger would be departing very shortly.

Joe rolled his two pieces of electronic equipment into padded cloths and placed them carefully in the rigid black case, filling half its volume. The tools that would take the remainder of the space lay in a neat row before him. "I'd rather be fishin'."

"Yeah, we all would," Sean said honestly. His eyes studied the odd mix of hardware lying in front of the kneeling Anderson. "Pretty low tech."

Joe looked up. "I don't need lasers to do what I've gotta do."

"I guess not, but a hammer? A handpick?"

"You forgot the pry bar," Joe said. "Look, any physicist worth his salt could sit you down and go into the most excruciating detail on how to design and build a nuclear bomb. There is nothing magical about it. It's just hard to do. But ask one of those same braniacs what to do if the thing goes haywire and has to be defused, and you know what their reaction would be? They'd try and overengineer what needs to be done. Every damn gadget they had access to would somehow find its way into the process. But RSP ain't that difficult."

"RSP?" Sean inquired.

"That's right. You mainly play with guns and little things that go boom. Render Safe Procedures. It's EOD—that's explosive ordnance detail—acrospeak. And RSP for the thing we're going after does not need any fancy gadgets. I've got an ammeter to show me where the current is flowing, a high-speed saw to cut through anything getting in my way, and these babies."

Sean snickered. "You look like you're better set up for demolition than defusing."

"What's the difference?"

"Huh?"

Joe paused, thinking of what he was about to do very quickly. "I'm going to tell you something that I would definitely go to prison for, but then that would be a waste of space. I've already got a death sentence."

Sean lowered himself to the floor.

"Nineteen Eighty-four, Francis E. Warren Air Force Base, Hotel Flight, Missile number ten."

"This is the one you told me about on the plane last year," Sean said.

"I didn't tell you anything," Joe corrected him. "You came to your own conclusions from some innocent remarks on my part. This is the real thing, from the old mare's mouth."

" 'Need to know,' Anderson," Sean said with a joking wariness. "The walls might have ears."

"Then hear this, walls," Joe said loudly, his tone coming down to continue. "We damn near had a Minuteman Three warhead go off. The LCC got a nonresponsive 'launch enable' report, then, before they could check the circuits, they received a 'launch execute' light. Now these blue suits were really starting to sweat. The commander of the Ninetieth Strategic Missile Wing called in one of his emergency response teams and sent them, in their APC, to the silo and had them park the damn thing on the lid. If a launch actually occurred, the APC would have fallen in when the blast door slid away and disabled the missile . . . or so they hoped.

"But there was no launch. The press reported it as a 'computer malfunction.' Believable enough, but not the truth."

"What was?"

"The truth was that the arming package on one of the three warheads zapped out for some reason. Bad inspection and maintenance procedures, we figured out later. About a minute after the APC was parked on top of the silo, the LCC got a 'missile away' report. Talk about shitting your pants. Well, there was no missile away, but the computers wouldn't believe that. You see, our ICBMs have a downlink-only telemetry package on them that transmits back to the LCC, and through them to the associated headquarters, a diagnostic on the warheads for two minutes after launch. By that time the thing should be armed. If it isn't, then the boys who target the things have to scratch one set of MIRVs from their roster. Not that I ever thought it would matter. I mean, in a nuclear war, a few misses really don't mean much except to the bean counters who keep track of the megatons."

"Sustainable war," Sean said.

"Exactly. They want to know if they have to retarget something if the thing doesn't arm. Anyway, the computers kept saying that the thing was armed. Well, guess what? It was."

"No shit, Anderson. You're serious?"

Joe laughed, thinking back to it. "Those were my words when CINCSAC filled me in on the 'problem.' So, I had to go into the silo through an access tunnel and, well, use a little reverse engineering." Joe spread his hands across the line of hand tools.

"You mean you just took it apart?"

"Took it apart?" Joe parroted, surprised at the question but knowing that he shouldn't be. The major dealt with precision in his operating methods and was assuming that Joe did the same. "Hell, no. I tore the fucker apart. Cut the wires, broke the explosive lenses into little chunks. Man, I did a job on that thing. And CINCSAC wanted to know why I 'messed up' one of his three-hundred-and-thirty-five-KT bombs. Can you believe that? I told him to shove it. He thought he'd have my ass in a sling for destroying his warhead and talking to him like that, but I got a presidential citation—classified, of course—for it, and he got the boot for letting the maintenance schedule on his birds get so slipshod that this could happen."

Sean laughed quietly, his head shaking and his arms wrapped around his knees where he sat. If anyone could talk to a CINC like that, there was no better candidate for it than Anderson. Only a civilian had a chance of surviving such an egregious breach of etiquette and decorum. Military men, particularly career officers like the major, hated the upper-echelon bullshit that frequently interfered in the execution of what was necessary, but few were willing to trade their uniforms for a few choice words with a bozo wearing brass.

"I would have loved to see that," Sean said, the last bit of laughter trailing off. "So you figure this one will be armed."

"It doesn't matter one way or the other," Joe answered. He began rolling the tools into the black cloth they lay on. "I've got to get to the pit in any case."

"The pit?"

"The plutonium," Joe explained, setting the remainder of his gear in the hard case and snapping the lid shut. "Old Soviet warheads were what we called 'sealed-pit' designs. That means there's no access to the sphere of plutonium that's the first-stage core of the thing. The explosive lenses that focus the implosion on it to compress it to supercriticality are sealed, meaning I have to cut or break through them to get the thing out."

"Out?" Sean said warily.

"Yeah. What did you think, we'd just bring the whole warhead back with us? That thing weighs at least a ton and a half, and from what you've told me, I won't have time to do a surgical removal of the whole thing. This is going to be a crude extraction with no anesthesia, Major."

The reality of what to do with the thing once it had been neutralized hadn't hit Sean completely until right then. "And it's coming back with us."

"You got it. Just think of it as a big nickel-plated basketball that weighs about as much as ten bowling balls," Joe said. "The rest of the stuff we leave. It's of little use without the first stage."

"I guess I should have taken one of those physics lessons you mentioned," Sean said.

Joe decided a quick one was in order. "Stage one is the plutonium bomb, in simple terms. Running from stage one is a rod of uranium surrounded by lithium deuteride and an outer skin of more uranium. Neutrons released when stage one goes supercritical ignite the uranium rod and skin, causing a massive flood of neutrons into the lithium-deuteride assembly. *Voilà!* Fusion. A thermonuclear explosion. That's the basic course, so don't go out and try to build your own without more instruction."

"No problem there," Sean said. "So you leave the second stage?"

"Right. One reason is that it's too dangerous to get in to remove the uranium. You see, lithium deuteride is pyrophoric, which means it ignites spontaneously in contact with oxygen. Plutonium is also, but the pit is encased in another material, usually nickel, which isolates it from any pyrophoric reaction. To get to the uranium initiator rod, I'd have to go *through* the lithium deuteride, and unless you can get me and it into a vacuum chamber, then it ain't gonna happen. We don't need that stuff burning."

Visions of Chernobyl came to Sean. "No, I guess we can do without the fallout."

Joe chuckled at the dual meaning of the major's observation. "A comedian and a killer. Man, you're talented."

"Maj, time to boogie," Lieutenant Duc said as he walked through the slightly parted hangar doors.

"Need a hand with that?" Sean asked.

Joe gladly put the handle of the forty-pound case into the major's outstretched hand. "You young 'uns is so polite."

"Gotta be nice to our elders," Sean said with a smile.

Joe returned the expression and walked to the Pave Hawk with Delta's XO. Ten minutes later, after loading and securing their gear, the nine Delta troopers and their civilian specialist joined the four crewmen aboard the MH-60K. With no reason for delay the black-and-green bird, which bore no external markings, lifted into the warm afternoon air and headed out over the rippling blue surface of the Atlantic Ocean. Ten miles out the Pave Hawk turned southeast. The first leg of its journey would take it north of the Bahamas before it turned due south to meet up with its tanker east of Cuba.

Once again, the real thing had begun.

"We are ready, General," the Cuban lieutenant reported smartly, his hand jerking up and down in an overdone salute.

"How long now?" Asunción asked. Looking at the grotesque tangle of newly welded pipes, he would not have been surprised to hear a year as an estimate.

"Six hours," the lieutenant answered. "Possibly slightly more, but I do not think so."

The crack of several explosions reverberated from between the buildings. These did not come from across the bay, however. They were emanating from the north.

"Go ahead. And quickly. I want no more delays."

The lieutenant waited for the general to walk away before

summoning the crew of the pump-equipped tank truck. "You will see to the pumping of all the NTO. Is that clear?"

"Yes, Lieutenant," the crewmen responded willingly, though why they had to be responsible for *every* driver's load was beyond them.

"Come on," the second crewman said as soon as their commander was out of earshot. "The sooner we start, the sooner we'll be done."

"You're too much of an optimist." He pulled the fueling hose over to the newly installed inflow valve and twisted to the locked position. After he did so, his eyes followed the length of pipe that left the tree and dived underground a few yards away. "Are we pumping that way?"

"No. That way. There must be a tank near those towers." It was a big game of shuffling fuel supplies to safer storage areas until the *yanqui*-inspired coup was crushed. The damned Americans! Thinking they could control anyone who did not fall in line with their imperialist ways!

"Well, how far does this line go the other way? There's no cutoff valve on this side," the first crewman complained.

The second crewman walked off the distance to the underground tank, noting where the outlet valve was before returning to his partner. "I estimate forty-five meters."

"You mean we're going to backfill forty-five meters of empty pipe? And what do we do with the remainder? Huh? This tree is above flow level, and it is going to act like a trap." The crewman's knowledge of chemicals might not be to the level that those who made the devilish substances was, but he knew that you *never* left a line full of cryogenically cooled nitrogen tetroxide. That liquid had to go into a similarly refrigerated tank. "Is there enough room to drain the leftover back into that other tank?"

"No, the lieutenant said it's full, remember," the second crewman said. "That's why we're not pumping to it."

"Well, how are we supposed to do this?" He surveyed the tree. The work was adequate, but no one had thought to install a backflow valve to prevent what he was trying to figure a way around. Forty-five meters of empty line! *Empty?* "Aha!"

"What?"

"Is there a fill pump on the outlet of the full tank?"

"Yes," the second crewman answered without knowing what his partner was thinking.

"There! We have it. Just prime the line with some of what is in that tank. It's the same chemical. Then, when we fill the empty, we drain the line back into the full tank."

"I may be the optimist, but you are the genius."

The crewman nodded acceptingly. "Of course I am. Now start that pump and prime this line so we can get out of here." Another explosion thundered through the complex from a distance. Someone must want something around here, he thought, with no knowledge that his "genius" had just altered the value of that desired by an appreciable degree.

Gennadiy Timofeyivich Konovalenko set the handset easily and slowly into its cradle. It was a forced calm, one with rage behind its tranquil facade, as the foreign minister could readily see.

"The line from Air Defense to Marshal Kurchatov has been severed," the president said, relaying that which his American counterpart had just informed him of. The rest of the conversation took just seconds to relate.

Yakovlev shared his leader's stonelike expression and let out a breath, one equal in both relief and dread. "So, it is happening."

"Georgiy Ivanovich and his cohorts could not let such an opportunity pass," the president observed. "We knew this would happen eventually."

The interior minister looked to the clock behind the president. A gift from the American ambassador, it blended perfectly with the Spartan decor that the president preferred. Once owned by the great American Benjamin Franklin, the timepiece, an intricate set of springs and gears inside a polished maple case, now held a place of honor in the office of the president of the Russian Federation. It was a reminder of what was possible when a people were sailing the uncharted waters of history, as the Russian people now were. And of the perils. The making of America had not been without its challenges. Neither would be the making of the new Russia. Anticipation of those challenges was the first step in overcoming them. The rest required only determination . . . and some luck.

"It will not be long, then, until there is some movement," Yakovlev said, mentally noting the time. "Either a missile at dawn or rifles before."

The president picked up the phone. Enough time had passed for the Americans to complete the switching that was required, and which they had offered. "The Americans will handle the missile, Georgiy Ivanovich." He pressed a single button, making the connection immediately. "And we have a few rifles ourselves. . . . Yes, Mr. President. We are ready."

Art left room 106 and walked into the parking lot. Already there were three dozen agents, and half as many officers of the LAPD, milling about the area. The streets were shut down for two blocks in all directions, and the nearest crowd of ghouls was a full football field away up Vermont.

And then there were the bodies. They lay where they had fallen, no attempt yet made to cover them. Those formalities would come after the Bureau photographers arrived to memorialize the crime scene on hundreds of rolls of film. Art walked past the pair of bodies, the foretold "visitors" from wherever, probably Florida, and to where his partner stood a dozen feet away. The two agents who had stayed with her politely drifted away.

"How are you?"

Frankie looked up from her focus point on the cracked black asphalt, but not at her partner. Not at anyone. "I could have killed him, Art."

"I know." Something in him wanted to reach out and put a hand on her shoulder, or even to pull her close and hug her, telling her that it was okay, that he understood. But he didn't understand. And he couldn't do the other. It wasn't what she needed at the moment.

"But I didn't," she said. It was almost an admission, as though there was something unnatural in *not* blowing the guy's brains out. "Why? I could have done it. I've even dreamed of it, of having the scum in my sights and he doesn't have a gun and I shoot him over, and over, and over. I was craving the chance, but I . . ."

"You what?" Art asked obligingly. The thought needed to be completed, but by her.

"I realized it was real. It wasn't some fantasy that I could play over and over until I got it right, because it never got right." Frankie finally looked at him. "Doing it wouldn't have been any more right than dreaming it."

Art smiled a bit and nodded. "I told you I had faith in you."

It was Frankie's turn to smile, her first true one in days. "So, what does he have to say?"

Art glanced back at the room. "He suddenly became mute. You know the type."

"Won't rat on his *familia*, huh?" Frankie asked, her gaze traveling down to the bodies of the first two to die.

"His loyalty may be a bit in excess, considering," Art commented, the idea coming simultaneously. "Hmm. Maybe we should fill him in on just how loyal his employer was to him and his buddy."

"I think he has a right to know," Frankie agreed with a bigger smile.

They were back in 106 a few seconds later. Omar Espinosa cleared the room for Art, leaving just the two agents and their suspect.

"Still don't want to tell us your name, 'Flavio'?" Art inquired, knowing the chance was unlikely to be seized by the perp.

Jorge rolled a bit and cocked his head to look up. The spade and the broad were there, standing over him. The door leading out was open, and lying in it was . . . Tomás. "Go fuck yourself, nigger."

Art just laughed it off softly. He'd been called "nigger" by more dangerous and influential people than this pile of human waste. "Tough. That's a good thing to be. Tough and loyal. Never rat on your buddies. That's a good code." He stepped back and sat on the second bed, staring into the eyes of the man he wanted to break like a matchstick. Beating him mentally, though, would be more satisfying. "It's a bitch when your buddies don't think the same way."

Jorge looked again to Tomás, then to the lady pig. She was the one who had shot him. She had to be the one. So what was this nigger talking about? "Don't play head games with me, boy. It won't work."

Art gave a single, slow nod, then bolted from his sitting position and grabbed the perp by one arm, jerking him off the bed to a standing position. There was a muffled cry of pain, but Art ignored it and dragged him to the door, inches from his partner's body, and directed his face with a strong hand on the chin to look out the door.

"There is your fucking loyalty, asshole! Look!"

Jorge looked down once more to Tomás, moving only his

eyes, then out to the parking lot at the two bodies lying together as one. There were . . . guns? . . . on the blacktop near the corpses. Two guns, shiny stainless-steel revolvers. Revolvers. The tool of . . . his trade, and of theirs.

"Quite a well-armed pickup service," Art said, the perp's head swiveling to look at him. "Oh, yeah. We know that you were expecting someone to pick up a tape. Only I don't think they were coming just for that. Do you?"

The motherfuckers! He had done everything to bring the job off perfectly, just like he had for them before, and they were going to repay him with this?

"You owe *us* your life, *boy*, 'cause these fellas were coming to smoke you." Art pulled him back to the bed and lowered him against the headboard. "My partner here saved your ass."

"But she killed Tomás," Jorge said, his voice wavering as it had when the guns were pointed at him.

Art mentally noted the name. "And he was going to kill her. She was faster. The point is that you are alive *not* because of any of your so-called friends. Your buddy over there would have been dead anyway. And so would you."

Frankie watched in silence as her partner wore the guy down. His manner was reverting to that which it had been when death was staring at him from the barrel of a gun. He wasn't able to handle the fear of his own mortality. He was a coward, as most bad guys were when confronted with something they could not seize the initiative on. When killing Portero and Thom, this guy and his partner had been in control. Now the surviving member of the duo was completely without that human need, and he was coming apart.

"What's your name?" Art asked directly, his clear, steady eyes staring into the tear-filled ones of his prisoner.

"Jorge."

"Jorge what?" Behind, Frankie had removed her notepad.

"Jorge Alarcon, and it's . . . it's behind the dresser."

"It?" Art asked, Frankie was already looking for whatever "it" was.

"This, partner," Frankie said, holding up the cassette. A simple General Electric radio/tape player sat on the dresser. She opened the tape deck and dropped the cassette in.

"It's Portero and some guy," Jorge said with a sniffle. "That's not what we came for."

Well, you had the right to remain silent. Art didn't care if the guy hanged himself with his words. "We have that one."

Jorge's face showed complete surprise at the revelation. "But how?"

Frankie smiled as the tape rewound. "Wrong pocket, buddy."

Jorge's head dropped until his chin rested against his chest. They had blown it. Now he had also. He was broken. Having always seen himself as smarter than the cops who were his de facto enemies, he had learned that the reality was quite the opposite. Whatever lay ahead, he considered his life to be over here and now.

A loud click signaled the end of the rewind. Frankie pressed the Play button and adjusted the volume.

The first sound after the opening static was the ringing of a phone as it would be heard through the receiver. Art knew the sound. "Phone mike."

Frankie nodded. The sound was a telltale indicator that someone was using a simple microphone, attached by suction cup to the listening end of the receiver, to record a call.

The ringing ceased, and a voice answered with the customary "Hello," though thickly accented.

"That's Portero," Jorge said. He had no reason not to tell them.

"His voice is clear," Frankie observed. "He's the one recording this." Her eyes narrowed as she listened to the other voice, obviously at the opposite end of the line. "But who is that?"

The voice was familiar, but Art couldn't place it. He had heard it. His mind traced backward for familiar links. It was in a group of people. That was it. A speech. His ears strained to match the sound with a visual image tucked away somewhere among the trillions of neurons. *A speech. Where? When? Who?*

The progressing conversation began to steer Art's mental search on a narrower path. Certain words and the way they were spoken caused brief images to flash in his mind, but he could not seize on any one. *Who are you?*

"Mr. Portero . . ."

"No, *please*, señor. *Francisco. We are speaking as friends. Francisco.*"

"Yes. As I was saying, Mr. Portero . . ."

That was it! What was being said was important, but who was

saying it, and to whom, was what mattered most. "The son of a bitch."

"Who?" Frankie asked. "That's nothing new. Portero was just telling some guy what he knew. And whoever it was didn't sound like he believed him."

"Or didn't want to believe him," Art countered. "You don't know who that was, do you?"

"No." Frankie pressed Stop and ejected the tape. "Who?"

Art looked over his shoulder at their prisoner. "I'll have to tell you later. Give me the tape. I've got to get this to someone."

"Art?"

"You give your statements. I'll fill you in later."

Her partner was on his way out the door, instructing Omar Espinosa to take charge until Lou got there. Frankie watched him jump into King Six—his own car, King Eight, had a flat from skidding to a stop over the curb—and pull out of the lot with haste. She saw the blue and red rear deck lights come on before he turned and disappeared from view and heard the Chevy's underhood siren come to life just after that.

"Frankie," Omar said. "We should start on your statements."

"Yeah," she answered, the wail of the siren fading with each second. Her partner was pushing it fast, real fast, which only made her wonder more just what was so important about who he had recognized on the tape. But wonder was all she could do for the moment. There were three bodies scattered across the $22.50 Motel, all brought down by her hand. And she would have to justify each and every shot. Killing within the law, unlike the handiwork done by the whimpering perp they had just busted, was not so easily set aside, professionally or personally. Special Agent Francine Aguirre would answer the questions, write the narrative, dot every i and cross every t, and then, at some time in the foreseeable future, she would go home to her little girl and try to explain why Mommy had to kill three people. If only that were as instantly easy as the six pulls on the trigger. "Let's get this done."

CHAPTER TWENTY

Conference Call

There were five Bureau vehicles and six Miami PD cars in the convoy, which exited the Airport Expressway going south on Twelfth Avenue and slowed to a crawl just as it turned west on Twenty-third Street. Two of the marked police units had already dropped off, blocking Twenty-fourth and Twenty-fifth streets, and at this point the remaining Miami PD units moved quickly to the other four intersections that would effectively isolate Thirteenth Avenue between Twenty-fourth and Twenty-fifth. Number 2744, an older single-family house, was located almost in the middle of that block, on the east side of the street. That address also graced the warrant held in the lead Bureau Suburban.

The first Bureau car to approach the house was an older bronze Volvo, chosen for the task because it looked so un-law-enforcementlike. The two agents looked casually toward the house as they passed. Nothing looked out of the ordinary in the last-minute reconnaissance. "It's clear," the driver reported over the handheld radio.

With that the service of the search and arrest warrants began. The Volvo swung left at the end of the block and sealed off Thirteenth from that side, a block closer in than the marked unit. The five other vehicles, including four Chevy Suburbans carrying the FBI equivalent of a SWAT team, accelerated to the house and came to quick stops, two in the empty driveway, one on the lawn, and one in the street. The follow-up car blocked the end of the street opposite the Volvo just as the *whop-whop* of a helicopter came from the east.

"Go!" the team leader shouted over his hands-free radio. Twenty helmeted agents, clad in indigo jumpsuits and body armor, streamed from the vehicles and moved to their appointed areas of responsibility. As half of the team surrounded and secured the exterior of the house, staying low and covering every opening, the entry team moved as a single entity toward the front door. Two agents in the lead held a black steel battering ram, which they brought back as they neared their target. Upon reaching it, they swung forward, aiming for the lock side, and punched the wood-paneled door in with hardly any effort.

"Federal agents! Search warrant! Get down! Search warrant!" The scream was continuous as the first three agents entered behind the partial cover of a view-ported shield. They moved through the house, toward the back, followed by their seven colleagues, who secured each room, hallway, or closet as the penetration progressed.

"Freeze!" the leader of the point group yelled at the sight behind the door just kicked. His reaction was instinctive, yet what he saw caused him just the slightest pause. They didn't often come upon *this* in a warrant service, and they certainly hadn't expected it here. "Keep your hands in the open."

Avaro had heard them come through the front door but had no time to react. The gun under his right leg could do nothing now. His hands, clad in fingerless black gloves, came up slowly so there would be no doubt as to his intentions.

Two of the agents from the follow-up team put their guns on the suspect from the doorway as the rest of the house was checked and secured. The team leader then stepped gingerly into the room, his MP-5 trained on the man. Proper procedure dictated that the suspect be instructed to "go prone," but that was obviously not an option in this case.

"Do you have any weapons?"

Avaro's eyes fell on the yellow "FBI" stencil on the agent's chest. *The idiot had to call from his house! Fucking fool!* "Under my leg."

The agents' fingers placed the barest amount of pressure on the triggers of their submachine guns at the admission. One stupid move was all it would take.

But that move would not happen. The team leader side-stepped to the man and reached under his right leg. The bone in the atrophied limb was easily felt through the thin cotton pants. He eased the 9mm pistol from between the leg and the cushioned seat of the wheelchair and laid it on a table to the side. "Anything else?"

The barrel was a few inches from his face, and he looked through the sights in reverse to see the blue eyes of the FBI agent staring down the right way at him. *The stupid, fucking fool!* "No."

"Baker King, this is Baker Leader, we have house secured and unknown male in custody."

"On our way." Agents Christopher Testra and Frederico Sanz got to the back room just as the house's only occupant was being cuffed and Mirandized. That he was in a wheelchair surprised them, but only momentarily. What the rest of the room held was infinitely more interesting.

"Nice setup," Testra commented. The compliment had a purpose beyond the commentary.

"Thanks," Avaro replied.

Thanks . . . The voice sounded identical. Testra got a nod from his partner. "You're welcome."

"So your guys page you, leave a number of a phone booth, you call them there, and . . ."—Sanz gestured to the sophisticated communications setup on the table—"What, you use this to keep in touch with your boss?"

Testra visually examined the multiline cellular system spread across the table. Two phones, indoor antennae, a coax cable going out the window—to a roof antenna, no doubt. And . . . *Hmm. You are a serious player.* "An encryption package?"

"Well," Sanz said in a very teacherlike fashion. "We are a very smart fella. Now why don't you be even smarter and tell us your name and who you work for."

Avaro stared stoically at his inquisitors. He would say nothing, and there was no way they could make him talk.

"Mum's the word, eh?" Testra picked up one of the cellular phones and dialed a number from memory. "You were right to think we couldn't tap your cell calls, at least not without a whole lot more trouble." He bent forward and smiled at the defiant face. "But that don't matter now. . . . Hello, this is Special Agent Christopher Testra, Miami FBI. Blue Rainbow Sunset." The confirmation of the code phrase came from the phone-company supervisor without pause. "I have a federal wiretap warrant, and I need the name of the registered user of this number and a list of all calls made from it for yesterday and today. I'll wait."

Their prisoner's expression changed as the seconds of waiting dragged to minutes. "I ain't done nothing, man."

"We'll see about that," Sanz said. "My guess is that your fingerprints are all over this stuff. I didn't see any ramps from your doors, so my guess is you're pretty much a homebody." A quick flash of anger resulted from the comment. "Which ties you to this place quite nicely. And we have you on tape talking to a very bad boy about some very naughty things. No, I figure you've done plenty."

Testra scribbled a few things on his notepad before thanking the supervisor and hanging up. "Well"—he looked down at the name—"Avaro Alvarez. Pleased to meet you."

Alvarez? Avaro *Alvarez?* "Did they have the call list?"

"Ten minutes, Freddy." Testra caught the speculative tone of his partner, then the name clicked. He had worked too long on the Coseros case to forget the name of Alvarez. "Do you think his daddy knows what he's doing?"

Sanz smiled. "We should know in about ten minutes."

Some arrests required force. Others required guile.

"Hey, we got a gas leak."

The booming voice from the porch startled Sam Garrity. His nose tested the air as he walked through the living room to the front door. There was no obvious rotten-egg smell, which had come to be associated with natural gas, though that was produced by an additive to the odorless gas. But smell or not, it was nothing to fool with. There had been problems in the neighborhood before with leaks in the underground lines. He didn't need the added distraction on this day especially, but what was there to do?

"Where's it this time?" Garrity asked the worker after opening the door. He was a stocky black guy, dressed in the blue jumpsuit that gas-company workers wore when the work got dirty—*Great! Digging again*—and carrying a probe that looked like a vintage metal detector less the sensor plate at the bottom.

"Not sure, but we got pressure-drop warning," the worker explained. "We're checking all the streets and all the houses. It should take just a couple minutes. But if the sniffer detects anything, I'll have to shut your meter off for a while."

A "So what?" look flashed on Garrity's face. "Who needs gas when you've got a microwave?"

The worker smiled, but not at the joke. "Sure, but cold showers ain't no fun."

"Yeah. Come on in." Garrity stepped aside and let the worker pass through before pushing the door closed. . . .

But it stopped against something, which his eyes identified as the foot of the worker just before he felt the touch of cold steel behind his left ear.

"FBI. If you move, you will be dead." The agent tilted his head toward the microphone concealed under the jumpsuit. "Whiskey One. I've got him."

In seconds there were two more agents in the front room. The trio put Garrity on his face, searched him, and cuffed him before lifting and setting him in a straight-back chair one agent had dragged in from the adjoining dining room. More agents, cops, and who-knew-who-else were arriving, and soon the street in front of Samuel Garrity's modest Hyattsville home was impassable. One agent showed the stunned man the search and arrest warrants, reading the pertinent portions of both along with the requisite Miranda warning, then stepped out of the way as another man entered the living room.

"Hello, Sam," Deputy Director, Intelligence, Greg Drummond said. "I hear you've been moonlighting."

Garrity's face, painted with surprise, followed the DDI as he strolled around the room like a disappointed parent who'd just caught his teenager in a lie. A very big lie.

"I'm just curious, Sam. Why?"

There was no answer, just an averting of the eyes.

"I see," Drummond said knowingly. It was money. He had dealt with treason in many forms, and one thing that always stuck out when those motivated by ideology were caught was their willingness to slam the system they'd struck out at with their actions. Those motivated by greed had no such conviction that could "explain" their acts, even if they thought otherwise.

"Mr. Drummond, you should see this," the supervising agent said, leaning through the doorway of a room down the hall that bisected the house. "We have some interesting stuff in here."

Drummond saw Garrity's eyes widen a bit as he looked to the agent speaking. "One minute. Well, Sam, how do we do this?"

"What do you mean, sir?" He added the "sir" out of habit,

and subconsciously in the hope that it might bring some mercy.

"I mean that you can tell us everything—*everything*—and then we can see if anything can be worked out."

The offer was thin, but then what else did he have? Everything they needed to hang him was in the room they were now pawing through. Garrity was far from a genius, but it took much less to realize that things were going to happen with or without his cooperation. He decided to get on the boat before it sailed without him. "All right. I'll tell you whatever you want."

"Good." The DDI turned to his Agency bodyguard. "Pick a room and get the stenographer in here. We have a story to hear."

Mike Healy paused after the Agency's Florida liaison to the INS finished recounting what he knew. Getting him to do even that had taken some strong words from the DDO. CIA officers were not prone to disobeying direct orders from a superior, in this case the DCI himself, but then disobeying a deputy director had about as much appeal to it. It was the choice of who was on the other end of the secure phone.

"You are absolutely certain of this?" Healy asked after processing the believably unbelievable.

"Positive, sir," the officer affirmed. "I did just like director ordered. When Portero came in for an interview, he gave me this big long story about a missile and said he had proof of some kind. I thought he was a bit loony at first, but his past checked out. Plus he knew things that only someone in a government position would know. So, I got all the pertinent information and passed his story to Director Merriweather, just as ordered."

"Pertinent information?"

"Right. Name, address, phone."

"Anything after that?"

"About a month later the director called me personally and told me to forget what Portero had told me. So I did."

Healy was thinking ahead of himself, trying to add this new piece to the overall picture. "No notes, correct? No hard copy of any kind?"

"It never happened, sir," the officer said. "Just like the director told me . . . I forgot. Until now, that is."

"Forget it again," the DDO directed. "This time on my order. Anthony, what have you done?" he asked after hanging up. Whatever it was, he couldn't use the officer he had just talked to to prove it. The Agency relationship with the INS was quasi-legal at best but very necessary, which meant he could jeopardize neither the officer nor the ongoing operation. And that, in turn, left no way to use the information to hang his esteemed boss high and dry.

"There has to be a way," Healy told himself, wishing that determination were enough to make his desire a reality.

Nick Beney caught his boss coming through the door. "That was fast."

"You said hurry. What's up?" Bud asked, setting his bottled water on the deputy NSA's desk.

"More now than when I called you." Calling anyone *out* of a meeting with the President took guts, precisely the reason Bud had chosen Beney as his deputy. "Greg Drummond is on a mobile and Director Jones is at Hoover, and Mike Healy just got in the queue. He's at Langley. All urgent, to use their words."

"Wonderful," Bud said. Urgent had to mean something about Cuba, and a trio of calls from the integral players in the situation could hardly signal anything positive. Life wasn't that fair. "Let's not make anyone wait. Conference it, and I'll pick up in my office."

Bud walked behind his desk and twisted the window shades closed to cut the glare from the afternoon sun. He finished the water with a quick gulp and lifted the handset. "Hello, everybody." He was answered by three return greetings. "First of all, nobody is on speaker, right?" None were. The speakerphone was too much of a security risk, allowing those within earshot to hear things that were never intended for their ears. "And this is a four-corner conversation here, so let's keep the interruptions to a minimum. Gordy, do you want to start?"

"Sure." The FBI director could be heard flipping pages on his end of the line. "Our Miami field office served search and arrest warrants on the occupant of a house who a wiretap indicated was receiving information from a CIA employee. Greg was in on the warrant service up in D.C."

"This was the leak you were worried about?" Bud asked.

"Yeah," Drummond answered. "What did you get, Gordy?"

"The person receiving the information was Avaro Alvarez, son of José-Ramon Alvarez."

"The head of the CFS?" Bud asked.

"Exactly." Jones confirmed. A barely audible *"Jesus"* came from the DDI's end of the line. "Avaro Alvarez was also directing the actions of two men in Los Angeles who killed Francisco Portero and one of my agents."

"Son of a bitch," Drummond said clearly this time. He knew just about everything after talking to Garrity, but not that. "You're sure? Directing them?"

"The tape does not lie," Jones said. "And we should know more soon. I just got word a few minutes ago that one of the gunmen was captured alive by the L.A. office. But let me tell you the rest. Avaro also had a sophisticated communication scheme involving pagers and phone booths worked out. He used this with the men out West and with the CIA leak. His name's Samuel Garrity. Anyway, Garrity broke security and used his home phone. That's how we nailed them. But he also had an encrypted cellular-phone system set up to keep in contact with his bosses."

"Encrypted. Like a voice scrambler?"

"No, Bud. Beyond that. It was one end of a multi-user package. Any phone with the same coded package can decrypt the transmission and convert the signal to simple audio. Without the package all someone would hear is white noise. It's a pretty fancy system for a user like Alvarez."

"So the other end has to have the same equipment," Bud said.

"Right. Actually the properly coded microchip," Jones explained. "And guess who was at the other end? Avaro's cell-phone records indicated calls exclusively to one number. That number is of a cellular phone registered to a company called Onotronics."

"Wait," Drummond interrupted. "Onotronics out of Fort Lauderdale?"

"I knew you'd recognize it," Jones said. "A major manufacturer of secure communications systems. They even did work on WASHFAX and SECVOCOM. And the company is owned and operated by Gonzalo Parra."

"Number two in CFS," Drummond expanded.

"And the calls in the previous two days have all terminated at a cell node near Shelton College, on the Cape."

"Dammit," Bud said softly. *Why them?* There were plenty of legitimate Cuban-American groups longing for their nation to be free again. Bright, patriotic, honest people. And too quiet in this case. The CFS had made the most noise making a name for itself, and had garnered much of the attention that should have been directed elsewhere. It was little wonder the rebels chose to contact such a "high profile" group, and less surprising that Anthony Merriweather had anointed them as the chosen ones. His chosen ones.

"It's all very incriminating," Jones said. "But not direct enough to prove CFS involvement beyond Avaro Alvarez. From this there's no way to prove beyond a reasonable doubt that Parra or any other CFS official was at the receiving end of those calls. We have him cold on espionage and conspiracy to commit murder, but we can't legally extrapolate that to his father or anyone else without more evidence."

"I think I can give some of that," Drummond said. There was a determined edge to his voice that came from the revelation that murder was side by side with treason in the CFS's repertoire. "Garrity came clean. Completely. The leak I thought I had in my directorate was actually in the next office."

"What?" Bud said, the suggestion hard for even him to comprehend. "You mean Anthony?"

"Yes, but he didn't even know he was giving just about everything discussed in his office to Garrity, and by way of him to the CFS."

"How?" Bud asked.

"Anthony's incessant scribbling and note-taking."

"But that all went into the burn bag," Healy said. "I thought we discounted that."

"The notes, yes. But Garrity didn't need those." The DDI explained the janitor's exploitation of the device to decipher indented writing.

"*We* use *Deep Reader*!" Jones said, making the same mental note as the DDI to see that more stringent security measures be implemented regarding note tablets.

"But how did this Garrity link up with the CFS?"

"Chance and availability, Bud. When Garrity decided to use his toy for some moneymaking, he just went to the top of the list. The CFS was the big topic of the moment for Anthony, and they were reachable. Not like some of the other parties in his notes. Garrity couldn't very well just go up to the Chinese embassy, or wherever, and say, 'Look what I can do for you.' But he could easily slip away to Florida, like on a vacation, to make his pitch to Alvarez and his bunch."

"The money," Healy said.

"Yep," Drummond said. His counterpart had made the connection. "Garrity was passing pilfered intel to the CFS, and they were selling it to any and all takers. A financial trace that S and T was running identified a long list of contributors to a CFS account in Bern. The Chinese, the Israelis, Russians—all through intermediaries. It goes on and on."

"The Russians," Bud said with a slight chuckle. "I guess it wasn't just my convincing that got them to come on board."

"You laid the groundwork, but catching Anthony's thoughts on the modernization program might have been the convincer," Drummond said.

"So there is no druggie connection between the CFS and Coseros," Healy observed.

"Maybe in the future, but all Coseros has done so far is pay for information."

"No wonder he could avoid indictment," Jones commented.

"Right. Every time I went in to brief Anthony on a new surveillance of Coseros, the same information made its way to him through the CFS."

"Wait a second," Bud said. "A CIA leak was supplying Anthony's notes to the CFS through Avaro Alvarez. They were then selling this information to Coseros and others to fill their coffers. Plus, the son of the CFS head was also directing the actions of two men who killed the man who had the tape of the Castro/Khrushchev conversation. My question is why the CFS would have any interest in Portero?"

"Because they knew about the missile," Healy revealed.

"How?" Bud and Drummond asked simultaneously.

"I can't tell you exactly how," the DDO said, the word "can't" obviously translatable to "won't." "But Anthony received word soon after Portero came over that he had a story about the missile, and some sort of proof. A month later the person who informed Anthony about this was told to develop amnesia about the entire affair."

"And you cured that, correct?"

Healy didn't respond right away. "Something like that."

"Bud, we suspected from some of the wiretap transcripts that Anthony might have known, but we didn't know how," Drummond said. "Now we do."

"So the CFS learned about Portero from Garrity."

"And they must have contacted him," the DDI finished the NSA's thought.

"And believed him," Bud added further. "And now we're about to put a group of corrupt scum in charge of an entire country."

"With a nuclear weapon," Healy said.

"Not once we're through with it." The NSA's words were like a wall of determination, impossible to breach. "That was obviously what they thought, but they can forget it."

"Gordy, with what we have right now, who can we nail?" the DDI asked.

"Just who you have. That's it."

"But we can't let those guys take power in Cuba! The rebellion is going to succeed, probably within twenty-four hours, from what the reports tell us."

"Greg, it isn't as easy as that," Bud said. "These men have been given the tacit approval of the United States government to assume power in *their* country. By your boss, by the Congress, by the President. If we try and prevent that without an absolute certainty of being able to prove their involvement in this, we will all be out of a job."

"A fucking *job*, Bud?" Drummond practically yelled. "We're talking about the leadership of a country!"

"Not the same one, Greg. I'm talking about our own. Possibly others," Bud said. A strong American government sometimes meant a stronger government somewhere else—like Moscow. "If we arbitrarily stop Alvarez from assuming power and can't justify it, the whole thing will point first at your boss, then at you and everyone at Langley, then at Jim Coventry for helping broker the arrangements, then at me for not knowing, then, my friend, the finger will point right at the President for approving the fiasco in the first place."

"So, what, we just let things happen as planned?" Drummond said with mild sarcasm.

"No," Bud countered. "But we have to do it right. We have to be able to nail something criminal on them. If we can do that, we can stop this thing and deflect a good deal of the criticism that will follow in any case right on your boss, where it belongs."

"The President will still feel the heat," Healy said.

"He can handle it if he's shown that he took immediate steps once *evidence* of illegal activities was discovered. Otherwise," Bud went on, "nothing he does will matter. The press will crucify him. And so will everyone else, right or wrong."

"We have to get Anthony out, too," Healy said.

"Has he done anything other than make a bad decision?" Jones inquired.

"Legally, no," Drummond answered. "He hasn't violated any security rules either."

"Greg!"

"Mike, what do we have?"

"So the CFS goes and Anthony stays?" Healy could be heard falling back in his chair.

"Now wait. Anthony is secondary right now." Bud knew his observation, though right, would not find favor with the DDO. "We have to—"

A few rapid knocks at the NSA's door preceded its opening. "Bud, there's—"

"Nick," Bud said, one hand covering the phone and his eyes asking what the interruption was for.

"Sorry, but there's a call from an Agent Jefferson," the deputy NSA said. "He said he couldn't get through to the director. Then he got a hold of Ellis, and Ellis said you'd want this right away. Jefferson said to tell you he has another tape."

"Another tape of what?"

Beney shrugged. "Your flashing line. Do you want it?"

Bud drew in a short breath. All the unknowns were coming together, and instead of making the situation clearer, they were complicating it. Now this, whatever "this" was. "I'll take it." Bud removed his hand from the mouthpiece. "The three of you hold on for a minute." He put them on hold and pressed the flashing line. "This is DiContino."

"Sir, Director Jones's secretary would not put me through because he's on a call," Art explained.

"With me. What's this about another tape?"

"Of Francisco Portero discussing the missile."

"With who?"

"I'm not a hundred percent certain, but I know I've heard the voice before, at a speech."

"Who, Jefferson?"

"I think it's the director of Central Intelligence, Anthony Merriweather."

A momentary void of silence greeted the FBI agent's disclosure. "Discussing the missile?"

"Yes. It sounds like Portero recorded a phone conversation with Merriweather."

Bud thought quickly. This might be what was needed to do what mere suspicion could not. "Any warning beeps?"

"None," Art answered. In order for phone conversations to be legally recorded without a wiretap warrant, both parties had to be knowledgeable of and agree to its being done. In addition, a distinct *beep* had to sound every fifteen seconds as a reminder that the conversation was being recorded.

It was just a shot. Merriweather would never have allowed himself to be recorded talking to Portero. And a surreptitious recording without a warrant was blatantly inadmissible as evidence. But as evidence of what? Even this wasn't illegal. Borderline improper and damned stupid without a doubt, but that wasn't enough. Bud wanted Merriweather gone as much as Mike Healy. His remaining in the picture while the CFS was being accused—and telling all, no doubt, to bring down anyone else with them—would point to the President harboring the man responsible for their recruitment. He had to go, but how? Recordings or not, there wasn't enough on him to force him out. Or on the CFS, Bud reminded himself. With all the technology and all the manpower they had at their disposal, time was the one obstacle he could not see them being able to surmount. Merriweather and the CFS had to be dealt with before the time came for the changing of the guard in Cuba, or not at all.

"I appreciate you letting me know, Jefferson, but you know as well as I that you're describing an illegal recording."

"I know, but . . . he's the *director* of the CIA. Are you saying that he can just talk about a potential national-security issue over an open phone line, and no one is gonna care?"

"I don't care if he's God, Jefferson. We can't use it, even if it is him and he's discussing something he shouldn't." Bud knew that even this wasn't beyond the bounds of legal, though it would certainly take Anthony down if it could be admitted as evidence in a case against one of the others. "If he had been warned he was being recorded, then that . . ." A thought occurred instantly, and Bud seized it before going on. ". . . that would have been different." *Very different.*

"So this means nothing?" Art asked with irritation.

But didn't notice the tone. The thought he had had a second before had become an idea, which was playing over and over in his mind. After a few seconds the idea became a plan, with both a beginning and an end. And with participants.

"Maybe not," Bud said. He checked the time. It would have to happen fast, preferably before Delta's operation was over. And it would have to be quiet. Beyond even hushed. Entirely because half of what he was envisioning was more unethical than anything Anthony had done. But Bud was willing to step over that line for this. In fact, he looked forward to it. For this the circle could not expand, meaning he would have to use people already in the loop to tighten it around the necks of two different men. "Jefferson, your partner knows about this, correct?"

"Yes, sir."

"Hang on." Bud gave the same direction to the other three still waiting and dialed the NMCC. "This is NSA DiContino. Give me the secretary."

"Bud."

"Drew, I need a fast plane for two in the Los Angeles area, pronto."

"What? Bud, we're kind of busy here," Meyerson said. "Delta is on their way, the Russians have their ABM system on alert, and you've got us crossing wires like some telephone-switching crew."

"Dammit, Drew!" Bud drew back and cooled down. "Look, I don't have time to explain. Not now. Please. Something fast that can get across the country."

"Just a minute." The minute was only thirty seconds, thanks to the ability of the National Military Command Center to almost instantly locate a piece of hardware anywhere on the globe. "All right. I've got a VC-Twenty-one at El Toro Marine Corps Air Station. It's CINCPAC's plane. He's on a visit, and he's not gonna be happy with you taking it."

"Thank you, Drew. I'll call you back in a minute with a flight plan for it." He brought Jefferson back up. "Okay, you and your partner get out to El Toro, and fast. I don't care how."

"Sir, my partner was just involved in a—"

"I don't give a damn what he was involved in, just—"

"She, sir," Art said loudly. "Her name is Frankie Aguirre, and she just shot three bad guys dead. Okay?"

Bud knew he had to come down from the high his mind had put him in. "I'm sorry, Jefferson. But this is very, very important, and we can't let anyone else in on it. You and your partner are already in, and what needs to be done is a nonevent."

"I don't follow."

Bud explained it briefly. "Do you have a problem doing this?"

Art remembered what he had done to protect Bill Sturgess from a legal system that could not comprehend his anguish. Now he would have to lie again, actually just not tell, about a similar act, though this time a quite opposite goal was the motivation. "I can do it."

"And your partner?"

"No problem."

"Good. You'll get more instructions in the air." Bud went back to his conference call. "Sorry, but it was well worth the interruption."

"What was it?" Jones asked.

"A couple of your agents in L.A. got a tape from Portero's killers that has Anthony listening to Portero tell the story of the missile. Problem is, it's an illegal recording."

"Christ!" Healy swore. "Why are we tiptoeing around this? Legal, illegal. I know we have to follow basic principals, but Anthony is the highest intelligence officer in the land, and he's fucked things up royally. God knows what his backdoor shit is going to cost us in the long run, and I mean lives, not dollars!"

"Mike . . ."

"Greg, he's right," Bud said. "Gordy, the agents who handled the wiretap—can we use them for something?"

"For what?"

Bud told him without attempting any justification of his plan. "I'm leaving out what follows."

The director of the FBI wasn't a rocket scientist, but then he didn't have to be to take the NSA's thought process to a conclusion. "You know that's a crime."

"I haven't said anything," Bud pointed out correctly. "The part your agents will play is completely legal. What comes next—"

"I'll handle," Greg Drummond said, jumping in. It was also clear to him, and it would be a pleasure.

"I suggest you do not know the rest, Gordy."

Jones was a lifelong Bureau man, sworn to uphold the law. He had a particular dislike of those in government who used their positions to skirt the rules of society that John and Jane Q. Public were bound to follow. And he was a pragmatist above all else. He also could not forget that he had once run interference for a colleague who'd taken too much of a liking to the tables in Atlantic City while involved in an undercover operation. Looking the other way was infinitely easier than bearing false witness, but no less challenging for the soul. "I'll inform the agents down South personally," the director said, hanging up immediately.

"I can do this, Greg," Bud offered.

"Right. With that missile still there and the Russians on the edge."

He was right. Bud's place was in D.C., with the man who would be making decisions, not running off to involve himself in something that he should be physically removed from. "You'll have to face him down, Greg."

"Bud, I've been in this town a long time. Longer than you, even. If there is one person out of all the shitheads that I am not afraid to tangle with, it's Anthony Merriweather. I think I'll even enjoy it."

Bud wondered if any man could enjoy destroying another at the moment of its happening. He was also suddenly glad that it wasn't going to be him doing it.

"If this all works, then we have a new problem," the DDO pointed out. "Who is going to take the reins in Cuba?"

"I'll talk to Jim," Bud said. "He brokered the original agreement. Maybe he has some idea on this. And you, Mike, you need to get in touch with your man in Cuba."

"I guess they will want to know there's been a change." Healy considered something for a second. "It might be good if Jim and I do the talking together."

"Good idea." Bud took another look at the time. "You better get a move on, Greg. We need you in position to coordinate."

"On my way."

Both CIA men hung up together. Bud kept the phone in his hand and rang the office of the chief of staff. "Ellis, listen. I need to see the Boss again."

"You just left him."

"Get him back to the Oval Office," Bud mildly demanded.

Gonzales realized he shouldn't argue, considering the way

the "request" was delivered. "It's done. Is this about Jefferson's call?"

"What call?" Bud asked, his tone hinting at the answer he expected.

"Oh."

CHAPTER TWENTY-ONE

Forces

"The advance scouts are turning south toward Juragua," the radioman reported as he walked, the heavy radio and its whip antennae bouncing with each quick step.

Colonel Ojeda, a third of the way back in the twin columns that totaled three hundred men, considered the situation and his mission briefly before responding. "Order them to cross the highway to the east and prepare an ambush. In one hour they are to spring the trap and set up a defense to draw the loyalists to them."

A *defense?* Antonio thought, the unfamiliar rifle suddenly feeling very present in his hands. *With twenty-five men?*

"They know, Papa Tony," Ojeda answered, the look on the CIA officer's face asking the question he had heard many times. Those for whom command was an unknown often expressed horror at the thought of their fellow men used in a sacrificial maneuver. Leaders of warriors, however, lived with the horror of having to do so.

Antonio switched the rifle from hand to hand and cinched the straps that held his satellite manpack snug against his back. He looked away from the colonel, focusing on the rutted dirt track ahead and trying to think of something other than the scouts. Twenty-five men four miles ahead, all about to give their lives. A hundred more immediately in front of him and twice that number behind. He found himself wondering how many would survive what was to come, and whether he would be among the living. Or would he join his father as yet another casualty in the struggle to free his homeland?

A staccato burst of fire from the front ended Antonio's questioning. Ojeda reached out and pushed him down to the right. He fell on his side, consciously protecting the satellite radio from impact damage. Looking up, he could see the lead element of the column running left into the cane fields and right for the edge of the marsh. A half-dozen men had fallen by Antonio's count before any fire was returned. Ojeda's men were disciplined and knew the value of ammunition when far from their supply lines.

"Papa, get up and follow me," Ojeda said. He led off into the marsh, the setting sun at their rear coloring the edges of the sharp grass rising from the water with a fiery brightness. Two squads of men, twenty in all, were ten yards in front of the colonel and his five-man headquarters detail.

"Jeez!" Antonio said, cringing as several bullets ripped through the thick grass above his head. The water was waist-high, already lapping at the weatherproof radio on his back. Short bursts of return fire from the two squads sounded to his front. Then more in return, and more from another direction, and all the while Antonio was moving, following the colonel, instinctively crouching into the soggy marsh as much as he could and having no idea in hell what he was supposed to do.

Ojeda's hand came up just in front of Antonio. He followed the colonel's lead, stopping and sinking deeper into the water until just his nose and eyes were exposed. The taste of thick, dirty water seeped through his lips, filling his mouth. He continued breathing through his nose, smelling the staleness of the marsh and the decay that was an ever-present part of its ecosystem. They stayed still, almost fully submerged, for several minutes, Antonio's heart beating faster with every passing second.

CLICK.

The sound came from Antonio's right. He turned his head easily to look, then back at the colonel, who was staring intently toward the direction in which his men had moved. Then back to the right.

CLICK.

Antonio ran his fingers along the body of the submerged Kalashnikov until he found the safety. Remembering the colonel's brief instructions he moved it up one notch, to single shot, and started to bring the weapon to his eye level. He turned the rest of his body slowly right, disturbing as little of the coarse vegetation as possible as he did, causing just a few crackles as the sharp-edged blades of grass rubbed against each other, and stopping when he was facing the direction of the sound. The distinctive top of the Kalashnikov broached the surface of the water. Antonio's eyes looked past the sights into the gently moving forest of light green blades. His eyes moved, searching, his body still except for the soft up-and-down caress his finger was giving the trigger. He watched, expecting to see someone not unlike him staring back from behind another AK-74. But there was none. No movement, no sound.

"Papa Tony."

Antonio's body jumped at the colonel's voice. He let go of the trigger and stood, lifting his weapon out of the water as he did. "I heard something."

Ojeda scanned the direction of the CIA officer's interest and discounted the claim very quickly. "We killed three of them," he said, looking back to Antonio. "More escaped."

"Three? I saw at least six of our men go down."

"We were fortunate. A well-executed ambush could have killed ten times that number." Ojeda saw the surprise in Antonio's eyes. "This is war, Papa Tony. Welcome to it."

The colonel turned and headed back out of the marsh. Antonio looked once more over his shoulder, still expecting to see someone with the means and the desire to kill him lurking among the vegetation but finding only that which scared him more: the unknown. He turned and followed Ojeda, his right hand squeezing the Kalashnikov's rear grip more tightly than he'd thought possible.

The first unit of the 106th Guards Air Assault Division to leave its base northeast of Moscow was the reconnaissance company. In wartime, after having been inserted in the enemy's rear by airdrop according to the still-followed Soviet doctrine of battle, the two hundred officers and men of recon would be tasked to seek out and identify the enemy units in their area. This morning, however, the objective was not elusive, and they expected no resistance to their advance.

Just after the witching hour, in the bitter chill of the ever-

longer Russian nights of autumn, a single Russian Army staff car
rumbled through the main gate and turned south onto the M8
highway. Twenty BMD-3 Infantry Combat Vehicles of the recon
company followed their commander's vehicle but would not even
attempt to keep up. Unlike in battle, his job was to announce
their presence before they would strike. Next came ten BMP-2s,
the larger and slower cousins of the lead element, and these were
followed by 160 trucks that would stagger their departure in
groups of five every few minutes. By the time the last of the
division had passed through the brown-painted gates, adorned
with the blazing white parachute emblem of Russian airborne
forces, the lead elements would be a quarter of the way to Moscow, and their commander would be well on his way to deliver the
requisite message to the president.

Force, after all, was most effective when employed as a threat.

"We're going where?" Frederico Sanz asked.

"The Cape," Chris Testra answered, still trying to figure out
the call from the director.

"To do what?"

"Didn't say. He said we'd be briefed once we got there by
someone named Drummond."

"Drummond?" Sanz let the name roll around in his head for
a minute. "Drummond. You don't mean . . . ?"

"I don't know," Testra said. "So don't think it yourself. If the
director didn't tell us, maybe we ain't supposed to know."

Sanz closed the hard case that held their recording gear and
started for the van.

"Don't lock it up, Freddy," Testra directed his partner.

"Why?"

" 'Cause we're supposed to bring some stuff with us."

Sanz looked down at the silver suitcase. "This? I hope someone has a warrant."

"Don't need one," Testra said. "Remember where we're
going?"

Lieutenant Duc brought the Pave Hawk down to eight hundred feet after an easy two-hundred-mile cruise out to sea at three
thousand. A hundred miles east of Great Abaco Island, a crescent-
shaped finger of land at the northern end of the Bahamas chain,
he nosed the helicopter to starboard, making his course just east

of due south. They would be meeting up with the Combat Shadow in two more hours off the eastern tip of Cuba. Until then, the plan called for staying away from the more inhabited land masses and skirting shipping whenever possible.

"Yo, Cho. Look."

Duc heeded his copilot's direction and shifted his attention briefly left, looking over the Pave Hawk's instrument panel to the white capped sea below. He scanned the scene for a few seconds, then pressed the intercom switch on his yoke. "Major, take a look to port. Coming up off about a hundred yards."

Sean undid his safety belt and crouch-walked past his team members to the port-side gunner's door, the coiled wire of his headset dragging and sagging behind. "What is it?"

Duc took another brief look. "Looks like a debris field to me. Got some orange floaters down there, a few pieces of something, but I don't know what from."

Sean took a pair of binoculars and stared past the minigun to the sea. "A whole bunch of stuff, Cho. No oil slick, though. Anything about a plane going in?"

"Not that I've heard. Nothing about a ship either."

Well, something had either sunk, crashed, or blown clean up, and there were no people in any of the dozen or so life vests bobbing in the swells. No bodies, either, as far as Sean could see. But that didn't mean none were down there. "Cho, better report this over SATCOM. Just to be safe."

"Gotcha."

Sean swept the area once more with the glasses. Still no sign of life. Hopefully a closer look would find someone. If the Pave Hawk hadn't been fitted with the most sophisticated communications suite possible, that closer look might never come. To report it in that case, they would have had to broadcast on the standard radio, giving off an omnidirectional message of "Here I am." SATCOM, which bounced its directional signal off a satellite, was far less likely to reveal their position, and then only if someone was looking for them. The latter was not in the cards.

Sean went back to his place on the rear-facing bench seat and put the thoughts of the people who might be below away for the moment. His mind had to focus on what was just four hours away, and on keeping the men surrounding him alive.

*   *   *

"We will have to deal with the Hundred and Sixth," Colonel Belyayev said in Russian. The American air-defense commander, standing just behind, did not need to hear.

"Of course we will," Kurchatov said without surprise. The husband of Natalie Shergin, sister of the *Voyska PVO* commander, would not wish to disappoint his brother-in-law. He owed his job to the man, after all.

"They are the closest to Moscow," Belyayev pointed out grimly. "No one is between them and the city."

"How long?"

"Three more hours," Belyayev answered after a quick calculation.

Before the sun would rise. The thought of Moscow waking to another test of leadership made his stomach want to turn. There had to be a way to stop this. "Why couldn't his damned division be based in Irkutsk?"

"That would matter little. They could simply do as trained and float from the sky."

"Yes," Kurchatov responded. There was not much one could do to keep paratroopers from their objective. Not much at all. Not much indeed, he thought, a smile of discovery coming to his lips. "Yes."

Belyayev heard the difference between the marshal's twin uses of the word. One was spoken with resignation, the other with hope. "Marshal?"

Kurchatov smiled fully at his aide, then looked up to a bemused CINCNORAD. "How do you say, General Walker? We shall fight fire with fire."

CINCNORAD hadn't the slightest idea what the Defense Minister meant by the remark, but it obviously had pleased both him and the colonel. That, he could tell plainly as the marshal picked up the phone and was connected immediately, via an amazingly rerouted series of switches, with the Russian Army's main communications center just outside Moscow.

At another communications center, five thousand miles from its dissimilar cousin in the Russian capital, the captain in charge of the Miami Coast Guard Station was wrestling with his own dilemma of force.

"Navy says no, sir," the bosun's mate reported as he hung up the phone.

"For Christ's sake, what do they expect us to do our job with?" The captain noticed his grease-pencil-marked status board. They couldn't even give him the simplest of computers to keep track of his meager forces. And then they took those! "Looking for God knows what!"

"That's the Navy, sir."

The captain snarled at the reminder from his subordinate. They might have the bigger boats—those ugly gray things—but that did *not* give them the right to appropriate his entire SAR force. Except when his boss, a full admiral, said to do so. "What the fuck are they looking for that's so important that they need all our ships and our birds? Can't they do a search on their own?"

The bosun's mate glanced at the heavily marked status board. The captain wasn't exaggerating. Everything *was* gone. Cutters, choppers, and the 2 C-130s. All heading north to the Atlantic off Virginia, and leaving them nothing with which to check out the report relayed to them via the Joint Special Operations Command at Fort Bragg. One of their special-ops planes returning from a training mission had flown over a possible crash site northeast of the Bahamas but was unable to remain on station because of their fuel status. So it was up to the Coast Guard to take a closer look. But with what?

"Damn," the captain swore, allowing himself a final spurt of disgust before turning to the business of finding a solution to the problem. "All right, what commercial ships are out there?"

The bosun's mate looked at his log, which carried notations from radio traffic and from the last pass of a Coast Guard plane five hours earlier. "A Japanese bulk carrier, a hundred and fifty miles north."

"At fifteen knots—if the bastard would waste the extra fuel—it'd be tomorrow before they get there," the captain observed, discounting option one. "Next."

Next was nothing. That was the closest commercial ship. Well, the closest truly commercial. "Just a Russian trawler loitering about sixty miles east."

"Waiting for bluefin, no doubt."

"Right," the bosun's mate agreed sarcastically. "They just call 'em in with those antennas."

The Russians obviously hadn't lost interest in the launches from the Cape, one of which, a fully military one, was set for the following week. "Well, he's out there, and as a *commercial* vessel, he has a responsibility to respond to a ship or aircraft in trouble."

"It'll piss him off," the bosun's mate observed.

"Reason number two to do it." Reason number one was the seaman's code. "Get word to him."

"Aye, sir."

Art pulled through the intersection of Twelfth and Vermont and stopped at the motel with more control than he had the last time he'd approached the place. The car used at that time was just being pulled, flat tire, bent rim, and all, onto the back of a tow truck. He walked right past it to his partner.

"How are you?"

Frankie had seen him coming and had noticed *that* kind of walk he was using. It was his "We gotta do something" stride. "I'm fine."

"We're just about done, Art," Omar said. The narrative portion of the report was several pages thick already.

"Well, it'll have to wait. Frankie and I gotta do something."

Frankie smiled slightly. Getting to know how Art Jefferson operated hadn't taken long. He wasn't a complicated person, really. That was sort of nice in a man and made working with him as a partner an enjoyable, bullshit-free experience.

Omar reacted with surprise. "Art, this *is* required procedure when this happens."

"I know, but required can wait in this case."

"What's going on?" Lou Hidalgo asked as he walked up. The rise in Omar's tone had alerted him.

"Lou, Frankie and I have to do something. I can't tell you what, but it's"—Art hushed his voice a bit—"on orders from the White House. And the director knows about it."

The White House? Hidalgo saw Art's steadiness. It didn't surprise him anymore, but it did merit notice. "When did you become so fucking important?"

Art snickered. "This old pavement pounder? Get outta here, Lou."

The group of four agents looked up and to the north as an Aérospatiale helicopter of the LAPD approached, preceded as always by the rapid chopping pulse of its rotors. It descended and landed a half-block north on Vermont, which had already been closed for its arrival by the police.

"Our ride," Art said.

The Aérospatiale's rotor continued to turn at speed after setting down. Its crew had been told that this trip had to be made fast, and sitting there didn't take any time off the journey. "Let's go," the pilot said over the external loudspeaker.

Lou reached out and gripped Art's shoulder. "Whatever you're doing, be careful."

"Piece of cake, Lou," Art assured him above the noise. "Come on."

The pair trotted off to the helicopter, instinctively ducking lower as they passed under the main rotor. They climbed in the passenger compartment and were handed headsets by the police-department observer, which they slid on, pulling the boom mikes close to their mouths.

"What's this all about, partner?"

"We're heading south."

South could mean a lot of places. "Mexico?"

"No," Art answered. "My old stomping grounds. The Deep South."

The whine of the turbines rose quickly and massively above their heads, the helicopter responding to the increase in power with a gentle jump from the ground. Seconds later it was climbing above the buildings, gaining more altitude as it banked slightly left. "El Toro in about twenty minutes," the pilot announced.

"Why El Toro?" Frankie inquired.

"We have to be there fast, and the military has the things that move," Art answered, looking out the left side of the helicopter to the midday city below. The blight that was prevalent at street level almost disappeared when looking from above. L.A. from a thousand feet actually looked nice.

"Art," Frankie said, nudging him. "What are we going to do?"

"To nail the guy who could have prevented all this."

Prevented. "All of this?"

Art looked at his partner. "Yeah." He said no more, but he could tell she was reading *"And Thom might be alive"* from his statement.

The familiar feeling of the previous days passed through her again, lingering briefly as a heaviness in her chest, then faded away when it found there would be no eager host as before.

Vengeance had come, and it had gone. What remained was a job to finish.

"Let's go get him," Frankie said, caring not at all who the man was.

Lieutenant Duc brought the cyclic back a hair and lowered his collective, slowing the Pave Hawk while maintaining its altitude. The maneuver backed the helicopter out of contact with the flexible drogue boom through which they had just topped off their tanks from the HC-130 Combat Shadow. The tanker accelerated and turned forty-five degrees to the right, heading almost directly into the setting sun low on the southern horizon. The Pave Hawk made the big bird's course its own, following like a good little chick. The next and final tanking wasn't far off, and after that they'd be on their own. Almost.

"Raptor is on station," Duc's copilot reported after switching from the SATCOM back to intercom. Raptor was the AC-130U Spectre that would be in the area to provide a little muscle if it became necessary. "On station" meant off the southern coast of Cuba, dead ahead of them, loitering at a discreet distance.

"What about the AWACS?" Duc asked.

"Sandman is there, too, fifty miles west of Raptor. We've got good coverage."

All that remained was word that the rebel ground force tasked to provide assistance was in position. "Raptor and Sandman are in position, Major."

"Good," Sean answered back. Only Anderson looked up when he spoke, and Sean gave him a reassuring thumbs-up, which sent the civilian back into his trance. The major saw his shoulder muscles bulge upward as Joe tightened and released them repeatedly, but they were smaller than when he had last watched the man perform the same limbering exercises. The disease was taking its toll.

The other members of the team were universally silent, spending the last hours before the show began in their own private contemplations. Then, of course, there was Antonelli. He had left the Walkman at Bragg, this time, but had remembered his new favorite toy, a handheld arcade simulator from some upstart company that made the games from the big names look archaic. Next to Sean, Buxton was staring at the floor, past his open paperback, thinking about whatever. Makowski, strangely, had his small Bible closed but held it tightly in both hands. Prayer, Sean thought, ready to accept any help Delta could get. The rest were very quiet, very still, all their eyes closed, though none was asleep. That was impossible this close to going in.

"One more time."

Sean looked left. It was Buxton, leaning in close to speak over the noise. "And they pay us to have fun."

The captain smiled. His former squad leader, now XO of the entire unit, was a damn good guy, and a hell of a soldier. "How long you gonna do this, Maj?"

Sean didn't expect the question, and it was somewhat strange considering what he'd been thinking of in recent months. "I don't know. Can't very well settle down and have a normal family life if you're flying off all over the world to smoke bad guys."

Buxton's eyes flared open. "Settle down. You mean . . . ?"

Sean couldn't help the smile that came to his face. It happened whenever he thought of her. "Mary's been an angel, Bux. She's waited a long time."

"Man!" The captain was surprised but not shocked. He'd never considered that the major would be out of uniform; he was the kind of guy you figured had the khakis tattooed on.

"My tour's up in a year and a half," Sean said. "I figure I've done my time. Going out on a high note is the way I've always wanted it." Being XO of Delta was higher than he'd ever thought possible.

Buxton smiled again and nodded. It was a blessing of Sean's decision from a comrade, and that mattered more than anything.

"One for the road, Maj."

"Hopefully the last."

Major Guevarra and the commander of the Cuban Army unit securing the Juragua Nuclear Generating Facility hurried to the small building that was known as the command bunker, though neither knew why such a small structure out in the open would be termed such. General Asunción was waiting for them outside one of the two doors.

"Colonel, the enemy has cut the highway north of here."

"What?" the Cuban commander asked with disbelief, his

eyes narrowing to slits. "We already have a force to the north. A large force and they are engaging the rebels."

"To *their* north, yes, but the bastards have slipped into their rear," Asunción said.

"How many?" Guevarra asked.

"No reports, but however many there are, they are fighting like wild men." Asunción turned back to the commander of the ground troops. "Colonel, take your force and secure the highway between us and the rebels. Send a unit to attack and destroy them once you have."

"But the plant, General."

"Leave a small unit here. We will have Major Guevarra remain to react if any more rebels have slipped through."

"Yes, sir."

"Major," Asunción began as the colonel moved off. "I want you ready to defend this facility at a second's notice, is that understood?"

"Yes, General Asunción!" Guevarra saluted smartly, then trotted back to his helicopter and its ground crew. "Prepare to fly, quickly!"

"We have a target?" Sergeant Montes asked hopefully.

"Possibly. If it shows itself, then we must be ready."

The crew chief approached the major. "The weapons load, sir. What do you wish?"

Guevarra analyzed what he might be asked to do. Rebel forces slipping behind the lines. They would have light weapons and would be able to scatter themselves quickly. He would need weapons that could attack a large area with lethal results. "A full load of thirty-millimeter ammunition for the cannon." He paused. "And eight rocket pods, all with flechette rounds." Flechettes, small, needlelike spears, were packed tightly ahead of a burster charge in the warhead of each unguided rocket, essentially creating a massive shotgun shell that would fire after launch. The effect, as had been proved in battles from Vietnam to Afghanistan, was utterly devastating on troops in the open. Precisely where Guevarra hoped to find his targets.

"But, Major, you need protection from aircraft," the crew chief implored. "Let me load two air-to-air missiles."

"What aircraft?" Guevarra demanded angrily. "Our targets will be running, on the ground, not up with us. We rule the sky, my friend. Now load the weapons which I have told you. They will be of use."

"Yes, sir."

Guevarra watched his crew chief hurry back to begin the job, which would take but a half hour. He then looked up to the darkening sky and listened. The sound of nothing was just what he wanted to hear.

CHAPTER TWENTY-TWO

Cavalry

The president of the Russian Federation has two offices. One is located in the Russian Federation Building, ironically called the White House because of its alabaster finish, which overlooks the Moscow River where Kalinin Prospect crosses that body of water. The second office, which had been the official seat of power since the demise of the Soviet Union, is the same working space used by the leaders of the former USSR. Situated near the northern corner of the roughly triangular Council of Ministers Building, the office affords a view of Red Square that is only mildly obstructed by the monolithic Lenin Mausoleum off to the right. Directly across the square is the GUM Department Store, which, even with the depressed and stagnant economy of Mother Russia, usually has throngs of Muscovites pouring in and out of its doors.

But the square was empty as President Gennadiy Timofeyevich Konovalenko stared out upon it. No shoppers meandered away from GUM. No tourists admired the neoclassical architecture surrounding them. Moscow was asleep, its residents, except for the hardiest drunkards prowling the frigid Metro stations, at peace. *At peace.* The president hoped they would wake to such a reality.

The motion of an approaching Zil limousine caught his attention. It sped past St. Nicholas's Tower and disappeared through an unseen gate in the massive stone wall that surrounded the seventy-acre Kremlin grounds. The president turned back from the window, nodding to his foreign minister. "I believe we are about to receive visitors."

Yakovlev nodded back and sat down, shifting his chair slightly to better face the door. The president went behind his desk and sat also, rolling his sleeves back into the neat cuffs that had loosened during the hours of waiting.

"Let us hope that this is just a delay for dramatics," Yakovlev said. They could have done without such very easily.

The president brought his hands up to his chin. His eyes were locked on the twin wooden doors leading to his secretary's adjoining office, which itself led into a wide hallway. Not a sound could be heard. The silence lasted for several minutes before the synchronized tapping of heels upon the wooden floor began. Two distinct sets. As expected, the good interior minister had brought company.

The doors opened without a knock. "Gennadiy Timofeyevich! Your lunacy has gone on too long!"

Konovalenko barely moved as his interior minister bellowed the proclamation. At his side was a man not unfamiliar, in full uniform, a pistol at his side. At least it isn't in his hand, the president thought. "Georgiy Ivanovich. You brought a guest."

"I bring General Pavel Suslov," Bogdanov said. "And the six thousand men of his division."

The president's eyes mockingly scanned the room and the hallway through the open doors. "I see only two men, and I am not certain they can be classified so highly in the social order."

Bogdanov steamed. Even though the pig knew he was finished, he continued to throw insults! "They are very near, Gennadiy Timofeyevich," Bogdanov said, continuing his international nonuse of the man's title. "And they will see to your removal, and to the removal of all those who have supported your abuse of the Motherland."

The faintest sound reached the president's ear. He had been waiting eagerly for it. *A few more minutes.*

"Georgiy Ivanovich, you will be shot for this," Yakovlev stated.

"Only if I do so myself, Igor Yureivich." The interior minister spoke his words with almost exaggerated smugness.

"So you are here to remove me from office." Konovalenko

stood slowly and walked around the desk to face his nemesis. He gave General Suslov a cursory, a disdainful glance but saved the weight of his attention for Bogdanov. "And you believe there will be no resistance?"

Bogdanov smiled, but he might not have had he seen Suslov's eyes narrow as a familiar sound began to reach his ears. "General Suslov's division is the only force of consequence near the city. The Kremlin guard would not even cause them pause."

Konovalenko saw, from the corner of his eye, Suslov's head turn toward the window. The sound, a far-off droning, was rising. "But others will, Comrade Interior Minister."

"What others?" Bogdanov asked with little expectation of an answer that would cause him alarm . . . until he heard the sound.

The president stepped back and walked to the window, his head tilting upward toward the sky. The droning was almost overhead now. "Comrades, I think you may wish to see this."

Bogdanov went to the window, his mind racing as it began to fear what might be happening. A step behind, Suslov had already realized his fate. Yakovlev caught the look of resignation as the general passed him. He held out his hand, palm up, and took the officer's pistol as it was handed over.

"Beautiful, wouldn't you agree, Georgiy Ivanovich?"

Bogdanov didn't even hear the question. His attention was fully absorbed by the sight before him. From out of the darkness dozens of dark green canopies descended into the white lights of Red Square. The nylon mushrooms collapsed as the men dangling beneath them landed and cut themselves free of the chutes. The first troops to land moved directly to the north and south ends of the square, and the second wave of paratroopers, arriving less than a minute later, went straight for the Kremlin gates.

"I don't understand," Bogdanov said honestly.

"The Ninety-first Guards Air Assault Division," Foreign Minister Yakovlev informed him from behind. "The heavy equipment they could load on such short notice is landing at Shermatevo Two as we speak."

Shermatevo Two, an airport north of Moscow normally restricted for government use, was but twenty-two kilometers away. Thirty minutes at the most. The 106th was still an hour outside the city.

"You see, there will be a fight," Konovalenko said. "And

General Shergin will be receiving a visit from the Ninety-first Guards, as well.'' Those aircraft had already deposited their troops, if all was going as planned.

"But how?"

"You underestimate the power of Marshal Kurchatov, Comrade Interior Minister.'' That title the president used only for the sake of convenience. It would soon be stripped from Georgiy Ivanovich Bogdanov. "Did you think he would remain silent once you cut him off?'' Konovalenko laughed, still looking to the square as dozens upon dozens of loyal troops floated from the sky. "He is more a man than that. More a man than you can ever hope to be.''

"Comrade President,'' Suslov began very formally. "I request permission to contact my division and have them cease their advance.''

"What? No!'' Bogdanov spun around.

The foreign minister finally stood. "Your friend the general is wise, Georgiy Ivanovich. Russians fighting Russians in the streets of Moscow will produce no winners.''

"Tell them to return to base, General Suslov,'' the president ordered without turning.

Bogdanov swung angrily around to face the president. "And the Americans! They assisted you with this, didn't they?''

"In a manner of speaking, yes.''

Bogdanov's eyes became slits as his head shook. "You are a bigger fool than I thought. You have let the Americans destroy you, Gennadiy Timofeyevich. Possibly us all.''

Konovalenko was aware of the time. "We will know that one way or the other in a short while.'' In the distance he could see more paratroopers descending toward Lubyanka Square. All around the city they would be arriving, he knew. "And you will wait here, with myself and Igor Yureivich, and greet the morning.'' He turned and faced Bogdanov as the drone of aircraft continued. "What happens then . . . We will see, but I have placed my trust in the Americans. Enemies of ours once, yes. But now their threat to the Motherland pales when compared to the likes of you.'' He looked to the general. "Suslov, present yourself to the guard to be put under arrest. Your grasp of the situation will be considered in your trial.'' Back to the interior minister. "You. Have a seat.''

*   *   *

Ojeda split his force into three groups as they approached Juragua, the last trace of daylight just a reddish-orange sliver on the horizon. One group of seventy moved east through the abandoned warehouses a mile from the objective. From there they would set up a hasty defense if any loyalists should approach from the north once the operation began. The second group, consisting of fifty men and the only heavy weapons—two mortars—the rebels had carried with them, approached along the beach, and positioned themselves to provide support for the main group. That force, 180 men under Colonel Ojeda's personal command, arrayed themselves in the jungle a mile west of the objective. They were split into sixty-man groups as planned, each with their own specific task. Once all were in position, there was but one act remaining before the show would begin.

"Pilgrim, this is Toolbox," Antonio said into the SATCOM radio's telephonelike handset. Ojeda was ten feet from him, scanning the approach to the plant through the NVGs.

"Toolbox, we copy," Mike Healy responded from Langley, a single satellite "bounce" from the jungles of southern Cuba.

"Pilgrim, we are in position. Awaiting signal information."

"Copy, Toolbox. Your signal will come from Raptor. He will be airborne CP and can provide assistance from above." Healy knew that Paredes would be aware of just what Raptor was. "Gambler will be your visitors. Due in on a no-wait warning from Raptor. Sandman will be eye in the sky. All your communications should go through Raptor once the operation commences."

"Pilgrim, I copy." Antonio noted the information mentally and expected to switch to the alternate net that would put him in contact with Raptor.

"Toolbox, we have a change in plans to inform you of."

"Go ahead, Pilgrim."

"Your original guests will no longer be able to make the party due to circumstances beyond our control."

Unable? "Pilgrim, that is . . . that can be a problem." Ojeda was expecting to turn power over to a civilian government headed by the CFS exiles. What the hell would he do now that they weren't coming? And *why* weren't they coming? "This was all arranged to avoid a power struggle."

"Toolbox," a different voice came on. It was Secretary of State James Coventry. "We are trying to arrange for alternate leadership, but it might take time."

"Time," Antonio said a bit too loud. He turned his body away as eyes locked on him. "If there is a power vacuum after this is over, we could end up with a fight for leadership that could leave Cuba with something as bad as it just got rid of. There are still opportunists in the military, even among the rebels. Not all of them are as honest as Ojeda."

There was no reply immediately. The silence made Antonio realize what he'd just suggested without intending to do so. His head turned back to the colonel. *Could he do it?* "Pilgrim, I have an idea."

"We thought so, Toolbox."

The unmarked white van pulled up to the gate and was met by a stern-looking Air Force guard. The Cape was an Air Force installation, albeit one with more public access than most, but the two weeks before an entirely military shuttle mission always saw increased security.

"Your purpose, gentlemen?"

Chris Testra produced his FBI shield, as did Freddy Sanz. The guard examined them and their faces with a shine of his flashlight. He had been told to expect them and further told not to question them about what they were there to do.

"Very good. I have you on my list. You can follow the signs to Flight Control Road. Turn left there."

"Thanks," Testra said, reaching to drop the van into gear.

"Hold it, Chris." Sanz pointed through the windshield to the fence, more specifically to a sign on the fence. "You know, it might be kinda fun."

Testra turned to the guard. "Hey. Mind if we borrow that for a while?"

No questions, the guard remembered. That also implied no arguments. "Be my guest."

The Agency Learjet landed at the Cape just after a vaguely similar aircraft bearing the markings of the United States Navy. Both taxied to a seldom-used tarmac south of the single runway and stopped a hundred feet apart. A white van with two men standing in front of it was waiting in the same area. In less than a minute the passengers of both jets and the men at the van were standing together.

"I'm Greg Drummond, Deputy Director, Intelligence, of the Central Intelligence Agency."

Sanz nudged his partner.

"Yes, the CIA," Drummond confirmed, noticing the gesture. "You must be agents Testra and Sanz."

The two Miami agents shook the DDI's hand and those of the other two people.

"Art Jefferson, L.A. office. This is Frankie Aguirre."

"Hi," Frankie said, nodding to the Miami representatives of the Bureau.

"Well, we have some bad guys to nail," Drummond said. "We need the same thing from both of them. You two"—the DDI pointed at Testra and Sanz—"will take the real bad boys into custody once we have the evidence we need. Jefferson and Aguirre here will get what I need from the second target. But *I* will handle him. None of you are to be involved with that. Clear?"

They all nodded.

"Jefferson, you have the tape?"

"Right here," Art said. "And something to play it on."

"Good." He looked to the Miami agents. "And I trust you have the equipment we need?"

"Right here," Sanz said, touching the hard case on the ground with his foot.

Greg Drummond smiled, feeling an anticipation he hadn't felt for a very long time. "Good. This is what we're going to do."

The Pave Hawk backed out of its final tanking twenty-five miles off the coast and turned north, heading for the beach southeast of Cienfuegos.

"Major, Raptor on the radio."

"Switch me over," Sean said. He left his black titanium helmet on his lap, next to the MP5SD4, and pushed the boom mike against his lips. "Raptor, this is Gambler. Go ahead."

"Gambler, we have a thumbs-up from Toolbox." It was Colonel Cadler, twenty miles west in the AC-130U. The drawl was unmistakable, even after traveling more than forty thousand miles through space. He would be acting as the central coordinator of air and land actions for the operation about to begin.

"Roger, Raptor. We'll be feet dry in fifteen."

"Sandman shows a clear air plot. You and me are the only things flying."

"Roger that, Raptor. Glad to hear it."

"Fingers crossed, Gambler."

"Fingers crossed, sir." Sean heard the radio switch back to intercom. "Cho, she's all yours. I'm going on my body mike."

"Yes, sir, Major. Fingers crossed."

"You, too." Sean removed the headset and inserted his radio earpiece before pulling his helmet on. The attached NVGs, flipped upward to allow for unobstructed vision, made his head want to tilt forward. "Mikey. Chuck. Check the STABO rigs again."

Antonelli and Makowski had the no-snag duffels containing the STABO rigs setting between their legs. A steel oval ring, which would attach to the twin connection points under the Pave Hawk, stuck through the cinched opening of each bag. The two troopers tested the spring-loaded safety bar on each oval, letting it snap back after depression several times. A thumbs-up told the major everything was a go.

Joe Anderson, sitting in the middle of the forward-facing bench seat, watched the preparations with mild interest. The nine troopers were readying themselves, checking weapons, cinching straps, testing equipment. They had those thing to do. He had just his thoughts to occupy him. Thoughts of another job. Thoughts of his home, his wife. Thoughts of his life. What he had done, what he would miss. He could have let sadness and bitterness envelop him, had it not been for the reality that his sacrifice had saved a lot of lives. He wasn't a hero for doing it, just as these men didn't think themselves deserving of accolades, but he, and they, could all take satisfaction in doing a job and doing it well. It might seem simplistic, even insincere, to those who could not understand the motivation to do something, even if dangerous, because it needed to be done, but it was what counted. Success meant the good guys won. To Joe, and to those he proudly joined on this mission, winning was a very private victory.

"You ready, Mr. Anderson?" Sean yelled across the two feet that separated them.

Joe lifted his equipment case and nodded. "Always, Major."

The noise picked up as the door gunners, one on each side of the Pave Hawk just behind the cockpit, slid their respective windows open and swiveled the pintle-mounted miniguns into the open. The weapons locked into position, and the gunners tested the built-in stops that prevented the guns from rotating too high, lest they inadvertently put a stream of 7.62mm shells into the 230-gallon fuel tanks that hung from the high mounted wings on each side. A low whine emanated from each mount. They were now powered up, ready to fire if need be, just the pressure of their gunner's finger required.

"Test your LAMs," Sean ordered. He lowered his NVGs and activated the LAM mounted underneath his MP5SD4's integral suppressor with a touch to the grip-mounted pressure switch. A beam of infrared light sprayed from the unit, a focused red laser dot in its center. Sean moved it around in the darkened cabin, placing death spots on three of his comrades before he was satisfied that all was working properly. He flipped the NVGs up again and checked his watch. "Five minutes to first stop! Lock and load!"

The nine troopers pulled the loading levers back on their weapons and slid them easily forward, chambering the first round.

"Safety on until we're swinging, then set on controlled burst!" Sean checked the left side of his weapon, making sure the selector switch was to its top position: safe. He looked left to Buxton. "Move fast, Bux."

"Like lightning."

"And keep your head down," he added, not knowing quite why.

"Then I won't be able to see all the fun."

Sean nodded and motioned for the team to switch on their radios. "Test check." He got eight nods in response. In sequence the other troopers transmitted over the short-range system. "Cho, you got us?"

"Five by five, Major. Two minutes to tippee-toes."

Sean held up two fingers for Anderson, who did not wear a radio.

Joe saw the victory sign and gave a thumbs-up to the confident gesture. It was nice being among the best of the good guys.

The Communications Vessel *Vertikal,* a former whaler that had taken its share of leviathans from the deep during its former life, plowed through the mild Atlantic swells at seventeen knots, churning a bright white wake that luminesced in the low moonlight. There was barely any spray over the high bow, even running at her top speed, and the captain of the ship stood confidently just outside the wheelhouse, the thought of wearing a slicker blasphemous on such a warm night.

"Debris in the water, dead ahead," the lookout reported.

"Where?" the captain asked skeptically. They weren't supposed to be near the reported site for another hour. Flotsam could not have drifted this direction, nor this distance since the American Coast Guard contacted them.

"There, Captain."

He scanned the swells, and there it was. The unmistakable blob of orange floating and bobbing on the water. And more. The captain counted ten separate pieces of debris. But of what? And how did it get here? An aircraft going down would not have spread its remnants over twenty nautical miles. Nor would a ship going down. There would be a greater concentration of debris in either case. It was as if it had been spread across the ocean from high above. *Or far below.*

But it could not be that. *Or could it?*

"Launch the boats. Bring back everything you find. Fast!"

First Lieutenant Duc made his altitude fifty feet as the Pave Hawk skimmed the choppy waters toward the deserted beach near Playa Rancho Luna on the eastern shore of the Bay of Cienfuegos.

"Nothing ahead," Second Lieutenant Sanders reported. His eyes were focused on the LLTV and the FLIR sensors, both of which stole the darkness from the expanse of white sand that was to be their first stop. The copilot flipped his NVGs, which were specially designed for use by flyers, down and scanned their flight path. Duc had them on a straight run in. Reconnaissance had showed no troops in this immediate area, and any civilian stupid or lucky enough to catch a glimpse of them would have little time to sound a warning. The objective was just minutes from here.

"Here we go, Maj."

Sean did a quick look around the cabin, his eyes falling upon Anderson last. "See you in a few!"

Joe barely heard the shout. "Don't mess up my missile!"

The major smiled and gave the signal to open the doors. The chill of an eighty-knot breeze instantly filled the cabin of the Pave Hawk.

"Feet dry," Duc announced.

Antonelli and Makowski gripped their duffels tighter as the sound of the rotors changed. It became a deep, throaty pulse before the Pave Hawk's nose flared, slowing the helicopter and reducing altitude.

"Go!" Sean yelled into his mike as they settled at five feet above the sand.

The troopers piled out through both doors, Antonelli and Makowski turning as they hit and going beneath the floating helicopter. They attached the hooks to the fore and aft STABO connectors respectively and pulled the duffels out from below, Antonelli going to the left with the short rig, and Makowski to the right with the aft rig, which was longer by ten feet.

"Good hooks, troops. Double check." Sean lined up in a prearranged row with the rest of the entry team: Antonelli, Goldfarb, Lewis, and Quimpo. They attached the paired connectors, one to each shoulder, and made themselves a semirigid unit with carefully placed handholds on each others' web gear. One hand was dedicated to that. The other held their weapons. "Bux?"

"Ready."

"Safeties off." Nine selector switches moved down one notch to the controlled burst setting. "Let's make 'em pay. Ready, Cho. *GO!*"

Lieutenant Duc needed no time to ease into the maneuver, which he had practiced countless times and used for real in several tight spots before. He brought his collective up with the helicopter in a hover, lifting Sean's group first, then, a second later, Buxton's group clear of the ground. When the latter was thirty feet above the sand, he added more power and nosed the Pave Hawk down, gaining speed and maintaining his altitude. The two groups of Delta troopers, nearly invisible in their coal-black working suits, swayed backward, away from the direction of travel, their HKs held forward in preparation and anticipation.

"Raptor, this is Gambler," Duc said over the net. "Two minutes out."

Twenty miles southwest and three thousand feet above his men, Colonel Bill Cadler sat in the soundproof battle-management center just behind and below the flight deck of the AC-130U. The middle finger of his right hand slid over the index finger as he counted off the seconds. The required wait dissipated quickly. "Take us in," he instructed the pilot over the intercom, switching back to the radio net immediately. "Toolbox, this is Raptor. Move on my mark."

"The fueling is complete," the beaming officer announced.

General Juan Asunción let out the breath he had been holding for days and leaned on the command center's console, staring down at the few switches and buttons he would manipulate in but a few hours. Then the vengeance would be wrought. A fitting target the *presidente* had selected, Asunción believed.

"Remove the trucks from . . ." His head swiveled toward the overhead vent shaft, through which the sound was entering the small structure. "What is Guevarra doing up?" he asked the air. Then the *kind* of sound caught his attention. Guevarra's craft did not sound like . . .

"General?" the young officer said, seeing the elder man's face go pale.

"Damn them!"

The Pave Hawk crossed the perimeter of the plant at ninety knots, Duc maintaining his altitude with only minor adjustments in course to avoid buildings. Ahead, through the NVGs, he saw the cooling towers to the right, and straight to the front the target. "Gambler to Raptor, on target."

Cadler keyed the mike. "Raptor to Toolbox. Execute."

Chapter Twenty-three

Donnybrook

The eight guards patrolling the perimeter fence on the west turned toward the sound coming from the east. They never heard what came next.

The Kalashnikovs in the tree line burped briefly, felling the eight loyalists with no resistance. Ojeda's group, divided into three 60-man sections, needed no further signal. They raced toward the fence in staggered columns, their numbers spread out along a quarter-mile front. At the head of each section were soldiers carrying what appeared to be small backpacks. Fifty feet from the fence all but these men went to ground. A second later they, too, dived for cover as the breaching charges arched through the air in unison.

The roar of the Pave Hawk's turbines reverberated off the endless concrete slab as Duc flared the helicopter perfectly, setting Captain Buxton and sergeants Makowski, Jones, and Vincent precisely two hundred yards south of cooling tower number one. They released themselves from the STABO rig just before their feet met pavement and made a quick turn to the right, running as fast as possible toward their objective.

Duc freed the empty rig and nosed forward, dropping a few feet in the process, the main objective coming at him quickly.

Fifteen feet below, Major Sean Graber slid his thumb upward

on the MP5SD4's grip, activating the LAM. Next his finger moved onto the trigger, and his left hand eased its grip on Lewis's web gear, ready to reach for the release handle on his harness.

The feeling was one of surprise, then wonder, then realization, then anger. Major Orelio Guevarra looked toward the sound and saw the shadow of the helicopter pass between him and the star-flecked southern sky.

"Chiuagel!" Guevarra screamed as he bolted for the Havoc.

Sergeant Montes ran after his commander, joining him at the MI-28's front. "Where did it come from?"

"Dammit, who cares." The major pulled his helmet on with haste and clambered into the aft seat of the helicopter, plugging his communications umbilical into the intercom/radio jack as Montes dropped into the front seat.

"We have no missiles," the sergeant said. He opened the power circuits to all his weapons as Guevarra fired up the twin Isotov turbines above and behind them.

The major looked left and right. *A damned ground attack, eh?* "No, but we can still fight." He recalled the wide, flat profile of the craft streaking across the sky. A transport, he knew, though it could not be the type he had initially thought. But still a transport. More correctly it was prey. And he was the predator.

"Systems on line. Checklist?"

"To hell with the checklist," Guevarra said, pulling the collective up in a steady motion, the Isotovs responding with a surge of power. "Switch to cannon," he ordered as the Havoc leaped into the darkness.

"Bolt those doors," Asunción directed the officer with him. He went to the firing controls as his orders were carried out. He had performed the motions repeatedly in his mind, and an equal number of times in preparation of the day when he would do so for real. That day, that moment, was now at hand.

He flipped the two rows of safety covers up, exposing the switches that had to be thrown to give control of the power and pumping functions to the missile. With his right thumb he threw each switch from manual to auto. Asunción cleared another safety cover to the right and pressed the single black button beneath it, locking the preprogrammed target codes into the missile's guidance system.

Then he lifted the final plastic cover. The others were black. This one was red. Beneath it was a circular button of the same color.

"Raptor, this is Sandman."

"Sandman, go ahead," Colonel Cadler said, acknowledging the call from the E3C Sentry thirty miles to his rear.

"We're showing a second air target northeast of Gambler. Distance is about a half-mile. Just coming up from zero AGL. Heading is southwest. No IFF, Raptor. This one's a Bandit."

Goddammit! Cadler swore silently, switching to intercom. "Captain, step on it. Gambler has company."

"On target."

The Delta troopers swung forward in the motion of a pendulum as Duc flared the Pave Hawk and dropped toward the ground. They pulled their release handles almost in unison and sprinted toward the squat gray structure fifty feet away. Lewis, Graber, and Goldfarb broke left to the south-facing door; Antonelli and Quimpo right to the north. In fluid motions Goldfarb and Quimpo pulled the pre-cut strips of det cord from pouches on their webbing and reached up, attaching the adhesive end to the top of each door on the latch side. They stepped quickly to the side, the thumb-switch detonators in their hands.

No nod was needed. Sean already had his hand on the chest mike.

Buxton's group reached the base of cooling tower number one unopposed. They split into two pairs and took up overwatch positions a hundred feet apart, ready to deal with any threat, except for the one that was taking shape inside the walls of the tower at their backs.

"Go!"

The det cord exploded with a bright flash that the troopers did not see. The energy created by the blast was focused inward along a vertical line and severed both doors inward of their latches. The steel slabs twisted inward as the sound of the explosion cracked inside the concrete walls. Without hesitation the entry team moved through the portals.

Practice, in this case, had made for a perfect entry. Lewis, the first through, was met by the sight of a single figure near the west wall. The LAM painted the man's form with IR light, giving the Delta trooper a clear picture of his target. Armed or not, the man was a target. And the pulsating dot of red on his chest was the bull's-eye.

Sean came through the opening, stepping on the steel door, just as Lewis fired a single burst. He caught the scene in his peripheral vision. The target suddenly moved backward as if a massive fist had punched it in the chest, then collapsed like a felled tree. The movement of Antonelli and Quimpo to his right registered in Sean's vision, and Goldfarb's hand touched his back as he entered and passed to the center. The sensory input at that moment was tremendous. The sights of the first shots; the staccato popping as though a child were making a machine-gun sound; the feel of his team members; every tiny motion.

Motion.

Sean caught it first as the LAM swept the far end of the room, beyond where Lewis had fired. That target had blocked the sergeant's view of the scene beyond, and Goldfarb was not yet in position to see what his commander was seeing.

Asunción had ducked as a reflex when the crack of an explosion invaded the command bunker. But duty quickly overcame his natural reactions, and he began to rise, the launch button right there, just inches from the finger that he was stabbing toward it.

Man. His back was to Sean. Hands moving. The laser dot danced across the target's back to a point between the blades before Sean squeezed the trigger. A three-round burst of 9mm rounds spit from the front of the MP5SD4 with hardly a flash. There was a sound to accompany the meeting of lead with flesh, but it was not from the weapon. Not from Sean's, that is.

General Juan Asunción's final act was hardly a difficult one, but it set in motion a complex series of actions that were to culminate in a disastrous event, though not that which he had envisioned when his finger came down upon the launch button.

The first manifestation was probably the least involved. A minute electrical current traveled five hundred yards through a wire, buried with many others in a conduit running from the command bunker to Tower One. A backup radio signal would have been transmitted if there had been a problem with the power, but there was not. The pulse of energy reached a sequencer box just behind the missile's guidance package. Here it "tripped," in sequence, a series of electrical switches. The first initiated a wholly separate signal that ordered the explosive bolts securing the missile to its launch pedestal to fire. All twenty did, breaking the bonds that held the weapon in place. The second switch started four separate pumps near the base of the booster's first stage. Two of these were primary and two secondary, and all four began drawing the two liquids from their separate tanks in the first stage but were stopped from delivering the propellant combination to the combustion chamber. The final switch in the sequencer removed the intended blockage, activating a series of piston-driven drop valves that allowed the hypergolic mixture of undimensional dimethylhydrazine and nitrogen tetroxide to flow under tremendous pressure into the bulbous first-stage combustion chamber.

It was there that the mating of the two products, which should have reacted with a predictable violence, began to do something very unexpected, though quite preventable.

The combination of UDMH and NTO, a standard fuel/oxidant mixture used in Russian and Chinese liquid-fueled rockets for decades, was ideal for the purpose because it required no ignition source. The two liquids reacted on contact with each other, in essence exploding in the confines of the combustion chamber, which contained and directed the energy of the reaction through the gimbled thrust nozzle at the missile's base. As expected, the reaction occurred, spewing a massive jet of flame downward as the powerful engine began to push the Chinese-built missile upward toward the opening of Tower One. Everything was working perfectly. The guidance system was already reading the thrust level and minute attitude shifts, and began factoring the "actual" with the "planned" to correct any deviations that could alter its six-thousand-mile flight course to Moscow. Pumps were whirring robotically without care for the limited life they would have. All was as Anatoly Vishkov had seen to. All, that is, but one thing that he could not control, but that he had warned of. The sharply pointed nose cone was within a yard of clearing the confines of the tower when the unseen error of the fueling crew manifested itself completely within a fraction of a second.

UDMH and NTO, like all combinations of fuel and oxidant, require a precise mixture quotient to react at a level that is proper for their use in a set space—the combustion chamber, in this case. The concentration and amount are critical, and here they had been altered by the use of the contaminated NTO as a primer during fueling from the tank trucks. The nitrate infiltration that Vishkov had feared did happen when the rainwater filtered through the nitrogen-rich soil into the supercooled NTO. The water, in contact with the frigid gas in liquid form, instantly froze, creating a layer of highly crystalline ice atop the oxidizing agent. What nitrates had been held in solution with the rainwater then settled from the ice sheet and contaminated the NTO solution with salts of nitric acid, which again dissolved and upset the delicate balance needed for a successful and controllable hypergolic reaction. In effect the NTO had been diluted by the addition of stable nitrates to the solution, which meant that a higher than normal ratio of UDMH to pure NTO was reacting in the combustion chamber. What occurred when that ratio drifted past the 3 percent variance in favor of the UDMH was similar, though quite a bit smaller, than the effect the opposite end of the missile was designed to unleash.

In less than the blink of an eye the loss of equilibrium in the reaction caused the energy level to rise dramatically and instantaneously. The additional UDMH overtook the reaction, increasing the controlled explosion to a point where the design limit of the combustion chamber was surpassed. The chamber literally fractured into hundreds of sections as the force of the explosion pushed outward in all directions. Traveling upward, it destroyed the pumps, feed lines, and finally the lower tank of NTO. The upper tank of UDMH ruptured a fraction of a second later. Before the liquids could join, they were acted upon by the fireball rising upward and were themselves added to the mix, feeding the uncontrollable inferno. At that point the effect became that of a very large bomb, whose force searched for avenues of escape from the already failing cooling tower that contained it. One route was through the exhaust vents at the base, but the larger opening at the top saw most of the energy pass through it, rising from bottom to top, generating a force that propelled all things in its path skyward.

One of these was the warhead.

Lieutenant Duc had the Pave Hawk in a tight left turn when the night became day for a few seconds.

Joe strained against his belt to look out the open left-side door as the helicopter reached a due-west heading. "Dammit!"

The fireball was rolling into the sky, a mass of orange and black and yellow that curled outward and in upon itself. Joe followed the inferno to its source, looking for the structure from which it had come. But it was not there. Just a spreading sheet of flame and smoke lay where Tower One had been. *And where those men were supposed to be.*

Seven feet ahead, Lieutenant Duc was realizing the same loss when the net came alive.

"Raptor to Gambler, you have company. Sandman reports a bandit at your—"

The report abruptly ended as a burst of 30mm cannon fire ripped through the Pave Hawk from somewhere to port. It stitched across the cockpit, left to right, and continued back into the cabin, drawing a line of the inch-diameter rounds through the gun stations on both doors. Duc's copilot received four hits, all traveling through his midsection before continuing out and through the helicopter's windscreen, leaving gaping holes in front of the pilot. Other rounds impacted the metal structure between the cabin and cockpit, penetrating and ricocheting, one passing just an inch from Duc's chin as it severed the line from his headset to the radio and intercom. Behind him both door gunners were dead, like his left seater, but Anderson had received only a superficial wound from a metal fragment blasted free by a 30mm round.

The lieutenant had a myriad of things assaulting his decision-making processes at the moment, the most important of which was that somewhere very close—too close—was something trying to kill him. Putting distance between his bird and whoever was out there was the first order of business.

"Hang on!" He screamed and would have been surprised to know that Anderson, himself wondering what the hell was going on, had heard the warning plainly above the cacophony of noise that seemed to be rising appreciably.

*   *   *

"A hit!" Guevarra yelled joyously. "Good shooting, Chiuagel!"

"He's running," Montes said, watching as their target banked hard to the right, staying close to the earth as a fine stream of smoke began to trail from one of his engines.

Guevarra got his best look yet at the craft as it silhouetted itself against the light of the blast reflected off the buildings. It was a Blackhawk, and the way it was being flown could mean only one thing. "He is an American, Chiuagel! Kill him! *KILL HIM!*"

Montes swung the cannon fully right as Guevarra followed his wounded prey. Falcon and pigeon, the sergeant thought, as he pressed the fire button a second time.

"High!" Guevarra screamed as the stream of fire passed over the banking helicopter. "I will get closer, then destroy him!"

The light of the nearby explosion reached the command bunker just before the awful roar. Sean and his team secured the one-room structure, making sure their targets were very dead, before stepping through the north door into the glow of the fireball rising from where Tower One had been.

"Bux," Sean said softly, then reached up and keyed his mike. "Bux!"

There was no response.

"Maj," Antonelli said, pointing up and to the east.

Sean forced himself to look away from the inferno. "My God."

"Where did that come from?" Goldfarb practically demanded.

Sean watched helplessly as the Pave Hawk, a ribbon of smoke marking its path, sped away, a second helicopter right behind, its turret-mounted Gatling gun spitting fire and lead.

"Maj, what do we do?"

There was nothing they could do about the Pave Hawk, or for anyone on board. Including Anderson. Cho would have to run for cover, which meant that what remained of Graber's team was on its own. "We do what we came here to do. Until we know otherwise, we have to assume the warhead is in there somewhere."

"In that?" Goldfarb said skeptically.

"Until we know otherwise," Sean repeated with authority.

"But what about . . . ?"

Quimpo's words were cut off by Sean. "Listen! We have a mission to complete! You think I don't feel like shit right now? Well, I do, but I lived through this before, and we sure as hell ain't gonna run away like we did then!" The nightmare of Desert One seemed all too real at the moment. The fire. The drone of aircraft. The feeling of failure. There Delta had hightailed it out of harm's way before it could do its job. Men had died there. Sean looked to the fire, knowing that very good men, very good friends, had fallen here also. But there was no ducking this one. For the moment, at least, they were on their own, and there was still a job to do. "Two and three. Mikey, you guys work around to the east side, by those far buildings. Stay clear of the fire. We don't know if there's anything left in there that could blow." Like a nuke? he wondered. "We'll take this side. Stay in contact until our reinforcements get here."

A series of small explosions echoed from the distance. Sean hoped it wasn't the rebels getting bogged down in a fight. He desperately wanted some more firepower on the ground right now.

BOOM.

The distant explosions became a singular one very close as a rocket-propelled grenade fell short after being fired from the corridors between the reactor buildings three hundred yards to the northwest.

"Damn!" Antonelli cursed. "I'm hit!"

Sean and Lewis dropped low and sprayed multiple bursts in the direction of fire. The shots were met immediately by a volley of full automatic fire from the reactor buildings.

"Inside. Hurry." Sean tapped two more bursts off, but the effective range of the suppressed MP5s was severely limited. They were close-in weapons, not battle rifles. He would have traded a year's pay for a few M-16s right then.

Quimpo and Goldfarb dragged the big lieutenant back into the bunker. Quimpo went to cover the south door, while Goldfarb, the team's medic, went to work on his comrade's nasty leg wound. Sean and Lewis backed in and took cover as round after round peppered the beautifully thick concrete walls.

"At least the Chinese can build decent prefab," Lewis joked.

"It won't mean shit once they get around us," Sean pointed out. They needed help fast. He switched his radio from the local channel, which allowed the Delta troops to talk freely without distracting communications from the net, to tactical. This linked him with the only assistance he could count on for the moment. "Raptor, this is ground. We need some help here."

"Okay, ground, whaddya got?" Cadler's welcome voice inquired.

"Unknown strength to the northwest of our pos in the bunker. Autos and RPGs. We have multiple casualties. Can you assist?"

There was no hesitation in the reply. "A-ffirmative, ground."

"Launch! Launch!" The NORAD threat officer said loudly. Thousands of heat-sensitive receptors on a DSP satellite, looking down upon the Western Hemisphere from twenty-two thousand miles over Gibraltar, had registered a surge of energy from a single point, and the signal-processing computer had judged the event significant enough to warrant a FLASH warning to NORAD.

General Walker hurried down from the command center's upper deck. "Where?"

"Central Cuba, thermal-launch signature." The officer processed the information further, the expression on his face signaling that something was not right. "Very concentrated. Similar to a silo hot launch, but then it spread way out. Going from a thermal of three-thousand-point-eight on a narrow aspect to one thousand even on a wide one."

Walker's heart was beating faster, enough so that he thought he could hear more than feel it. "Better location."

A few seconds passed. "Cienfuegos, west of the city."

"Damn." CINCNORAD walked three consoles down to the position he would occupy during the real thing. Whether this was or not, he did not yet know, but he also could not wait to do what needed to be done. He picked up the tan-colored phone that sat away from the other communication devices before him. It was picked up immediately in the NMCC.

"This is CINCNORAD. I am reporting a NUCFLASH event, central Cuba. Possible launch. This is not a drill."

Yakovlev pulled the phone away from his ear, a puzzled look on his face. "*Voyska PVO,* sir. Urgent."

President Konovalenko saw Bogdanov rise slightly in his chair. "Put it on speaker."

A raspy click sounded from the white box on his desk. "You

fool! You send men here to arrest me, and now the Americans have done it!''

Konovalenko recognized the voice as Shergin's. "Have done what?''

"Launched a missile at us, you idiot! *YOU FOOL!*''

Bogdanov's head sank at the revelation. "You . . . You . . .''

"From where?" Konovalenko demanded, keeping his composure. "Exactly.''

"How do you expect an exact report? The Caribbean, idiot. Is that precise enough for you?''

"No. Is it from Cuba?''

"You are blind! There is a submarine out there that has just fired a missile at us! A Trident missile!''

"Could it have come from Cuba?" Konovalenko pressed the question.

"I cannot believe this!" Shergin practically screamed through the phone. "How much proof do you require?''

"More than you are offering." The president released the line. "Igor Yureivich, suggestions?''

"We get out of here!" Bogdanov answered for the foreign minister. "Before the damned thing kills us all!''

Konovalenko ignored the outburst. "Quickly.''

Yakovlev refused to believe they had been wrong. They had come so far, building a trust with their onetime enemy. That trust had to continue. "Call the Americans immediately.''

The Communications Vessel *Vertikal* was running a circular course around the growing debris field, her foredeck covered with growing piles of material as her pilot boats continued to bring it aboard. Some of the more interesting items were already in the wardroom.

"Can you read it?" the captain asked. He knew enough conversational English to excel at his job, but the written word had never been his to master. His signals officer was doing those honors.

"A logbook. A captain's log." The officer carefully separated the waterlogged papers and laid them on the steel tabletop. He examined the cracked plastic holder that contained them. "A seaman's folio. I have seen this in Spain before. During our port call last winter. It is normally waterproof and is made of a buoyant material. This is why it floated.''

Ryne Douglas Pearson

"But from where?" the captain wondered. "Or what?"

"*Pennsylvania*," the signals officer said.

"Hardly," the captain replied, assuming his subordinate had made a joke.

"No, sir. The *USS Pennsylvania*," he said, pointing to the stencil on the folio's mangled cover.

Pennsylvania? The captain snatched the object from his signals officer and examined it himself. It said as he was told, but how could it be? There were no other ships in the area even searching, and surely. . . . Of course. There was a search under way farther north. Radio intercepts had indicated that. And they would have no way of knowing where to look, if this was true. A *raket* submarine. He looked again at the name.

"Go through these papers immediately. Find out all you can and say nothing to anyone but me. Is that clear?" The captain headed for the door.

"Of course, but where are you going?"

"To the radio," the captain answered. "This is worthy of an immediate report." And of a promotion, he thought.

"No radar track, no exhaust plume." The threat officer looked up to CINCNORAD and the two Russians standing behind. "Whatever it was, it stayed on the ground."

Colonel Belyayev leaned close and studied the data carefully. The survival of Motherland's capital might be at stake. He could trust, as Marshal Kurchatov had shown him, but he must also verify.

"Colonel?"

Belyayev returned to upright. "I see nothing. Residual heat signature."

CINCNORAD noticed that the exchange was in English. He thought it might have been otherwise at a time like this. The relationship truly was different. Not only between their countries but between the people. It was different, and refreshing. "Marshal?"

Kurchatov nodded. "I am satisfied. Let us contact President Konovalenko."

"Toolbox, mark your pos and keep your head down."

Antonio looked up, seeing nothing but hearing the faint sound of engines as the AC-130U approached.

"Colonel! Stop the advance!"

Ojeda snapped his head toward the American. "What are you talking about, Papa? We are almost to the objective. These loyalists are paper-thin in numbers."

Antonio knew he had little time to explain. "Maybe so, but farther on the American unit is pinned down, and someone is going to be laying some heavy fire on the area in less than a minute."

Ojeda followed Antonio's gaze upward. He heard the sound also. "Back! Fall back!" He reached for a termite grenade from an aide and pulled the pin. "Where?"

"Here. We'll be safe on this side, then."

Ojeda tossed the incendiary device around the building's corner and trotted back the way they had come. A pronounced *pop* came a few seconds later.

"Gunners, we have a friendly marker west northwest. One klick from the target. Check fire west of marker."

The gunners aboard the AC130U noted the fire-control officer's directions and prepared to make some noise. The forward weapons station consisted of a single 25mm Gatling gun, located just aft of the cockpit. Closer to the rear, just forward of the aircraft's loading ramp, were a 40mm cannon and a 105mm howitzer. All the weapons fired to port, requiring the pilot to put the aircraft into a controlled orbit around the target.

"Ten seconds," fire control announced.

Cadler keyed his mike. "Ground, take cover."

All three stations would be used in this attack. The gunners already had the target located on their low-light targeting systems. With five seconds to go, the pilot gave the AC130U an additional five-degree bank, allowing the weapons to have free play on the target during the tight orbit.

"Commence firing."

Fifty of the loyalist forces had just begun dashing across the open area toward the bunker when the ground around them turned to dust and sparks. It was the last thing any of them saw. Thousands of 25mm rounds showered the vicinity of the target with a show of dancing colors as the lead and steel shells impacted the concrete. The stream of fire, accompanied by the terrible sound of a buzz saw, followed a gentle curve to the reactor buildings. As the rounds stitched across the buildings' roofs, the 40mm cannon opened up, concentrating on the minicanyons between the structures. The 105mm howitzer boomed next, firing straight into the mass of troops scurrying away from the devastation. The 25mm gun also shifted to them a few seconds later. After one half-orbit there was no movement visible, and no fire coming from the reactor buildings.

Ojeda ordered his men to advance as soon as the airborne battery had checked fire. The loyalists that had impeded their advance just minutes before were now fleeing north through the dozens of buildings. Calling for his radioman, he instructed half of the northern group to move south and contain the retreating loyalists, lest they escape. No one, he swore, would get away.

"Helicopters!" the rebel gunner yelled, his body turning as he tracked both aircraft with the SA-14 Gremlin SAM resting on his shoulder.

"No!" Ojeda shouted, running to the soldier and yanking the weapon away. He put it on his own shoulder and tracked the targets with the optical sight, waiting for the high-pitched screech that would signal that the infrared seeker in the missile's nose had acquired a target. Muzzle flashes from the second helicopter dazzled his vision, then series of sparks fell from the lead craft. *What is this?* he asked himself as the craft both banked right, one following the other. *Following . . . or hunting?*

The lock-on tone screeched from the small annunciator on the Gremlin's firing unit. Ojeda listened, following the path of the helicopters as they turned sharply east. He had a lock, but he could not fire.

"Colonel?" the gunner said as Ojeda lowered the weapon and switched off the firing unit.

"One of those has to be the Americans," the colonel explained. "The other . . ."

"But you could have fired."

Ojeda handed the weapon back. "If there is one thing I have taught you, it is that you do not fire blindly just for the sake of doing something." It was a lesson in war, and one in life. He reached to the ground and picked up his Kalashnikov. "Papa Tony."

Antonio had watched the entire episode, and it had allayed any fears he might have had about his suggestion to Langley.

Ojeda was a warrior, for certain, but he was a thinking warrior. He was also a giant of a man. "Yes."

"Let us go meet your friends."

The Pave Hawk took its fourth hit in the starboard outrigger tank, which broke free of its wing mount and burst into flames as it fell away.

"Hey!" Joe screamed for what seemed like the thousandth time as his body was thrown left, then right, as the pilot maneuvered violently to evade whatever was trying to kill them.

But his call went unheard. Lieutenant Duc was in the midst of something that came totally from instinct: survival. Helo jocks, even those in the 160th, were not given much training in aerial combat. That was usually saved for the fighter drivers in the other services. Yet that was precisely what he was having to do.

A fifth volley of fire struck as Duc turned hard left, heeling the Pave Hawk over on its side. These hits set off amber warning lights on the control panel and also robbed him of 20 percent of his power. His bird couldn't take much more.

He continued the hard left until he was heading west again, almost a mile north of the huge fire still burning furiously. His pursuer would be behind and above him, Duc knew, and he kept the helicopter jinking left and right as he searched for somewhere to go, for some way to escape. He was just about to pull a hard turn to the right when the obstacles he was going to avoid suddenly presented him with a hope. Their only hope.

"Hang on tight!" Duc screamed as loud as he could, then put the Pave Hawk on a straight course, cutting his altitude as he guided the dying bird by dead reckoning, knowing he had to do this just right to keep salvation from becoming suicide.

"The bastard is ours, Chiuagel!" Guevarra yelled. His eyes were locked on the easy target ahead and below. The American was not even trying to evade anymore. Possibly he thought there might be an offer to surrender. Ha! That would not be. Guevarra increased power and closed on his prey. "Open him like a tin can, Chiuagel."

"With pleas— *Major!*"

Duc knew he had to hit it just right, if doing such a thing purposely could ever be termed "right," and that he did. The lowest power line, which stretched a hundred yards from mast to mast, hit the Pave Hawk's windscreen with a loud slap, breaking the already punctured lexan into a dozen irregular panels that blew into the cockpit. The wire, though, slid upward along the metal window brace and was fed into the wire-strike blade, which sliced the inch-and-a-half-thick cable in two. A jolt shook the helicopter as its forward momentum was abruptly slowed by the hit, then it nosed down and continued on, Duc adding as much power as the helicopter could muster.

The pursuing Havoc had no such good fortune. There was no protection for wire strikes installed on the Russian-built attack helicopter and it would have made no difference if there had been. Major Guevarra flew his helicopter into the second power line above that which his prey had cut. The cable hit the bubble canopy that encased the pilot, then bounced upward, catching on the main rotor shaft, causing the helicopter to pitch its nose upward. The rotor hub failed a split second later, unable to tolerate the abuse. Spinning uncontrollably, the main rotor, now separated from the shaft, sliced into the forward portion of the Havoc as it went almost vertical from the impact. Then it fell back, toward the ground, a shower of sparks falling with it. It rotated and hit the pavement on its port side. The rockets that had been intended to do damage to the rebel forces instead detonated and destroyed their host in a fountain of fire.

Lieutenant Duc brought the Pave Hawk around for a final turn and looked immediately for a place to set down, as the increasing number of amber lights were quite clearly telling him to do. He also saw, as the turn was completed, the remnants of his attacker for the first time. The sucker had been tenacious but had wanted the kill too much. That was a fatal flaw, Duc knew, wondering why the other guy had not been blessed with similar knowledge.

The ground beyond the burning wreckage was clear and flat. Duc gingerly took the Pave Hawk below the lowest power line and set down on two flat tires a hundred yards beyond the inferno. He shut down his engines and undid his harness, climbing through the cabin to check on his crew. But he had no crew left. Only Anderson was alive, sitting ramrod-straight against the aft bench seat, his equipment case clenched tightly between both legs.

"You okay?"

Joe swallowed and nodded. "Who the hell was that?"

Duc removed the headset and cord from one of the door gunners, ignoring the carnage that had once been a friend. There would be time for those feelings later. "Cubans, I guess."

"Did we get him?"

"He got himself," Duc answered. "Hang tight here." He handed the other gunner's headset to Anderson and instructed him to put it on before climbing back into the cockpit. He plugged the working set in and prayed that the radio was still among the living. "Raptor, this is Gambler. Do you copy?"

"Gambler, hell yes!" Cadler bellowed. "What's your situation?"

"We're down, but so is the bandit. We have multiple KIA on board, but our civie is A-okay."

"Copy, Gambler." The colonel's tone was no longer that of a relieved commander. "Toolbox is moving your way, and we show no enemy forces near your pos. We will keep you under watch."

"Copy, Raptor."

"Gambler, what's burnin' near you?"

Duc looked over his shoulder, through the cabin and out the port-side door. "That's the bandit, Raptor. A hundred yards behind." The smoke from the blaze was drifting east, blown by a light wind.

"No, Gambler. To your front."

Duc and Joe both looked through the open front of the helicopter. The barest glow was visible beyond a lot of machinery. "Don't know, Raptor. Looks like a little one, whatever it is."

"Not on the FLIR, Gambler," Cadler said. "It's radiating better than your bandit."

Duc's head shook. Behind him, Joe Anderson's eyes went wide. "Can't be, Raptor. No way."

"Yes, it can," Joe Anderson said, just before pulling off his headset and jumping from the helicopter, his gear bag in hand.

CHAPTER TWENTY-FOUR

Render Safe

"Marshal Kurchatov believes there is nothing to worry about," Konovalenko said after hanging up the phone. "And the Americans report that the event our satellite detected was the missile booster exploding. They still do not know why."

Bogdanov's head nodded disgustedly. "And you believe them. Of course. That fat fool Kurchatov is under their spell. The Americans can show him whatever they want him to see, and they can then obviously convince you of anything."

The president walked to the front of his desk and took General Suslov's pistol from his foreign minister. "Do you see this, Georgiy Ivanovich? Do you? Well, let me make this clear to you. If you are right, and our ABM radars detect warheads descending on Moscow—which they should be able to do in the next few minutes, I understand, if there are any to detect—then I will put this gun in my mouth and pull the trigger. Right in front of you as I kneel and beg forgiveness from the Motherland! Is that enough for you?"

Bogdanov disregarded the president's theatrics and looked at the clock, watching as the seconds ticked away. A minute was gone, then ninety seconds, then, as the hand moved around to end its sweep, the phone rang.

"Yes." Konovalenko listened intently for a full minute. "You have no doubts? . . . Good. Thank you."

"What did *Voyska PVO* have to say?" Yakovlev asked cautiously.

"It was not *Voyska PVO,*" Konovalenko replied, looking at Bogdanov. "It was State Security. Your comrades, Georgiy Ivanovich."

The barest glimmer of salvation dangled before the interior minister. State Security, though not party to what he and the military elements had attempted, were without a doubt of the same mind. Possibly now they were exercising the influence they still held to rescue him from the president's treasonous activities. That hope survived only until his nemesis spoke.

"An intelligence-gathering vessel operating off the east coast of America has recovered debris from the *USS Pennsylvania.* That is a *raket* submarine, Georgiy Ivanovich. The one that was missing."

Bogdanov felt the last of his strength drain away. He could accept that he might have been wrong about some aspects of the previous days' events, but not about the trustworthiness of the Americans. Yet the leaders of the Motherland were too blind to see that. The wonder as to why left him without hope. His world had simply come to an end.

"I will face my firing squad, Gennadiy Timofeyevich. That will be my punishment for attacking your authority." Bogdanov stood, ready to present himself to the guards outside the door. "But your punishment will be much worse. The Motherland has little mercy for those who forsake her."

Konovalenko smiled and nodded. "I agree. It would seem, then, that a firing squad will be but the beginning of your punishment."

"Ground, this is Raptor. Toolbox is approaching from the west. He's acquired some transport."

Six Jeeps pulled up to the bunker a few minutes later. Sean and Lewis kept their weapons trained on the convoy until it stopped.

"Major Graber." The voice was decidedly American.

Sean stepped into the open, his weapon coming down until the suppressor pointed at the ground. The NVGs were flipped up on his helmet. "Here. Toolbox?"

Antonio climbed out of the back of the lead Jeep, followed by the front-seat passenger, a tall man with huge white eyes set in hollow black valleys.

"Antonio Parades. This is Colonel Hector Ojeda."

Sean gave the Cuban a quick salute and shook the CIA officer's hand. "How many men do you have?"

Ojeda looked down upon the American officer, who had directed the question to Papa Tony. "I have three hundred men."

Sean realized his breach of etiquette. This was a Cuban matter, after all. Not another Bay of Pigs. "Very good, Colonel."

"You have nine men?" Antonio inquired.

"Five left," Sean answered tersely. "One of those is wounded."

Half of his force gone? Antonio noticed where the fire was for the first time. He had seen the flash and the fireball from a distance, but not where it had come from. "It blew up?"

"Yeah." Sean's earpiece crackled. "Go ahead, Raptor." He listened for a few seconds, his expression changing from melancholic to very serious. "Copy."

Antonio's radio was in the Jeep. "What is it?"

"We've got to get somewhere fast," Sean said. "A mile and a half that way." He pointed northeast, beyond the burning remnants of Tower One.

Ojeda turned and ordered three of the Jeeps brought up. "We can go in these. Do we need more men?"

"No, Raptor says the area is clear." Sean called into the bunker. Goldfarb and Quimpo helped Antonelli into the second Jeep, and Lewis climbed into the third vehicle with Ojeda's radioman and another soldier. Sean, Antonio, and Ojeda got into the lead Jeep, which moved off at speed for the new objective.

Joe stopped fifty feet short of the warhead, which lay in the open on the far side of the equipment park. Duc ran up behind him.

"What is it?"

"It's burning."

Duc instinctively stepped backward. "The *warhead*?"

Joe stepped a few yards closer, leaving the pilot behind. The steel casing was fractured, he saw, and a good chunk of concrete had been dented where the warhead had impacted, then bounced to where it lay. Just like that Titan warhead back in the States, except that one had landed in a lot softer ground, leaving the casing intact. This one was split right open, and the innards were burning, and burning hot. There were only two fuel sources in the thing that would generate that kind of heat.

"Stay back there." Joe dropped to his knees and opened the case, removing only the pry bar and hammer.

"Wait. Isn't that shit radioactive?"

"Yep, and it's gonna get a lot hotter if I don't stop it." Joe ignored the few safety items in the case. Goggles. A flash hood. They were useless for this.

"But you . . ."

Joe turned his head. "Listen. There's a city of a hundred thousand people across the bay, and none of those people asked for any of this. I can't educate you in physics here and now, but what's burning now isn't the worst that's going to happen. If the plutonium burns, you'll see a lot more smoke, and that will mean fallout over the city."

Duc saw that the little smoke coming from the thing was drifting skyward and east in the breeze, a bright whitish glow lighting it from where it emanated. From behind, the sound of racing engines drew his attention, three American-made Jeeps emerging from the darkness and stopping just short of his position. Graber was the first out.

"Anderson!" Sean yelled, running toward him. Duc grabbed him before he could pass.

"He says to stay back, Major." Duc turned as the glow intensified.

"You heard him, Major!" Joe shouted back. "Keep your ass away from this!"

Lewis ran up. "Maj, he can't stand that."

Sean said nothing but nodded just enough for Lewis to notice.

Joe had no time to think about the consequences. It was a one-way ticket. He circled around the mangled warhead, approaching it from the crumpled nose. Staying upwind, he inched closer, rising to his tiptoes every few steps until he reached a point, ten feet from the thing, that he could peer inside the opened case.

Dammit. It was good and bad news concurrently. The cylinder of lithium deuteride encasing the uranium initiator rod for the warhead's second stage was burning. Pyrophoric like the sphere of plutonium a few feet forward, the compound combusted spontaneously when the inner case broke open on impact, allowing air to enter the sealed chamber. Joe estimated by sight that a fifth of the lithium deuteride had already burned. As more ignited, the fire was growing, and soon it would be hot enough to burn the explosive lenses surrounding the plutonium. Then the nickel plating that sealed the PU 238 would be breached. After that . . .

"Get me dirt!" Joe yelled back to the group watching him. "A lot of it! And hurry!"

All but Graber went off to collect whatever dirt they could find among the endless stretches of concrete. Joe would need that to try to snuff out the fire. But before he could do that, he had to make sure that the plutonium would not ignite, and there was only one way to accomplish that.

"Anderson! No!"

Joe ignored the screams from the Delta major and went straight for the warhead. Specifically to the forwardmost section. The heat from the burning second stage was intense, but he twisted his body so his face was shielded and started tearing away the shards of metal and bracing structures that blocked access to the circular first stage. He was close enough that the smoke wafted around his body, passing over his face and filling his nostrils with an acrid smell that also became a taste. He tried to spit it from his mouth but gave up the futile attempts and concentrated on what had to be done. On what he had to do.

Antonelli hobbled on his own from the Jeep to stand by his commander. "Jesus, Maj, that stuff is going to kill him."

Sean propped his lieutenant up with a helping arm and watched with him. "I know." *So does he.*

The metal bands gave way as Joe leveraged them with the short pry bar. Their ends snapped, and the buckled center sections that wrapped around the lens assembly broke much too easily. This wasn't all from the impact, no matter how violent. This was lousy material.

"Ivan builds them worth shit!" Joe told his audience.

"Can't we do anything?" Antonelli asked helplessly. His leg wound, just above the knee, was wrapped tightly under an olive-drab battle dressing.

"No," Sean answered. "We can't."

Lewis returned first from the scavenging expedition, his helmet filled to overflowing with a rich brown soil.

"Set it here until he needs it," Sean directed. The others did the same and joined the line to watch.

The final obstruction broke away, and Joe went right for the lenses. He brought the pry bar up, holding it over his head like a vampire slayer about to plunge a stake into his quarry, and brought the sharp end down, burying the tool in the hard blocks of explosive. Once it was in, he worked it around in a stirring motion. As chunks of the stable explosive came free, he tossed them aside. He repeated the same plunge-and-clear process over and over, the fire to his right intensifying, until the shiny silver surface of the pit was visible. Then he worked with his hands and the claw end of the tool, digging away the destroyed lenses to give access to the plutonium. When half the material was cleared, he nudged the pit with his hands. It moved, jostling back and forth.

A flash erupted from the secondary, showering Anderson with intense white sparks. He ducked and brushed those he could see or feel off, but several stuck to his jumpsuit on the back, setting small patches to smolder. Still, he ignored it. With both hands pressed tightly around the pit, he leaned into the case as far as he could, trying to get enough of a grip to lift the sphere of plutonium out. His body was weakened by the disease that was destroying his blood cells, an almost laughable malady considering what he was subjecting himself to, but he pushed his hands down, farther, deeper between the lenses and the pit, reaching . . . for . . . enough . . . of . . . a . . . hold . . . so . . . he . . . could . . .

He fell backward, out of the growing haze of smoke that enveloped his body before rising into a deep black column that leaned toward the Bay of Cienfuegos. The heavy basketball-size pit came out with him. Joe held it tightly to his stomach like a medicine ball and rolled to the side, small fingers of smoke still coming from several spots on his clothing. He looked up to see Graber make a move toward him.

"No!" Joe yelled forcefully, the command ending in a hacking cough that sounded painful and unnatural. "I'll bring it closer."

Sean laid his weapon on the ground and forced the others back. All but one followed his order.

"Colonel."

Ojeda again looked down to the shorter man. "He is doing this for my people when he does not have to. I *will* help."

Joe got to his knees, pulled the pit up from the ground into his gut, and struggled to his feet, his face grimacing in pain. Each step was labored as he traversed the fifty feet to the two men waiting with outstretched arms. "Take it!"

Sean and Ojeda followed the raspy command and cradled the heavy pit between them, its mass enough to test the steadiness of their knees.

Joe collapsed to a crouch before looking up. "It's not hot enough to hurt you," he explained, his voice almost gone. A trickle of bloody saliva ran from the corner of his mouth, clearing a channel on his soot-covered face. "You guard that son of a bitch with your life, Graber. It could kill a lot more than just me in the wrong hands, or in the right hands."

"We need to get you out of here," Sean said.

"No. You need to get yourself out of here, in case this breeze changes." Joe pushed himself up to his feet. "I have to put that thing out. Gotta take its oxygen away."

"Anderson," Sean said, his eyes locking on the civilian's. The blue centers were still clear and full of fire, but he knew that the well was almost dry.

"Just get your ass out of here and let me finish this."

Joe took three of the dirt-filled helmets and walked back to the warhead, unafraid of the fire, or the smoke, or the invisible particles that had already sentenced him to a much quicker death. He dumped the damp earth into the fissure in the casing around the lithium deuteride. One helmet at a time. Then he walked back for a brimming bucket that one of the men had retrieved. The contents of that spilled into the opening, robbing the pyrophoric reaction of some of its strength. The white-hot glow simmered slowly down as he added more and more dirt, losing intensity until the flames barely licked from the casing. A final bucket of loam stopped the fire completely. Joe pounded on the fill, compacting it to remove all channels for air to reach the compound. He was satisfied after a minute's work and stepped back from the warhead, looking upon its ugliness for what he knew would be the last time. Then he turned and walked halfway to where Graber still stood.

"I told you to get out of here."

Sean stared at the man, his eyes feeling warm and moist. He had lost men today. Too many men. And here was a man who did not have to die but chose to do so that others would not. "We can get you to a doctor."

"You can get a decon team in here to seal this thing up right," Joe countered. The cough that followed this statement was heavy with blood, which he spit on the ground. "I'm hot. There's residue all over me, and in me."

Jesus Christ, Sean thought. What was he supposed to do?

"Get out of here!" Joe shouted in a weaker voice. "Now!"

Sean moved away, watching as Anderson lowered himself to sit on the ground. It wouldn't be long. The blood was from his lungs, which were undoubtedly hemorrhaging. He was going to drown in his own blood.

"Major, we have the thing in the back of the Jeep," Antonio told Sean, though the Delta officer did not look at him. "And Raptor is calling another helicopter to get you and it out of here. Colonel Ojeda says the plant is secure."

"Good."

"What about him?" Antonio asked, just as Anderson fell backward on the pavement, his hands dropped to his side.

"He's going home."

Testra knocked hard three times on the door. It opened inward, a burly man looking much like him blocking the entrance. "FBI. Move your ass."

Sanz followed his partner in, his hands pushed into his coat pockets. Testra looked around the room for the objects of their interest but saw only lackeys. The door at the far end of the room was his next stop.

"FBI," he said as he walked through the door, surprising the two men sitting on the couch. He recognized both. A folded cellular phone in the pocket of Gonzalo Parra caught his eye. Sanz came in behind, shutting the door as his eyes scanned the room, then went for a desk on the near wall and leaned comfortably against it, his hands braced on its edge.

"What is all this?" Parra demanded, but a wave from José-Ramon Alvarez told him to cease his questioning.

"This, gentlemen, is to inform you that your son"—Testra looked to Alvarez—"is under arrest for espionage and conspiracy to commit murder. There'll be more, I guarantee you. You see, when you kill one of our own, we get just a little angry."

"Avaro?" Alvarez said with concern.

"The cripple?" Sanz said, moving away from the desk. "Yeah. We nailed him. Plus we have some interesting tapes, you know, talking about missiles and stuff. Real interesting."

Parra stood. "Whatever a man's son has done, that man cannot be held responsible for. Avaro is an adult." He knew that the young Alvarez would not implicate them, and he was certain that they were fully insulated from any legal connection to the activities. He just had to keep José-Ramon from saying something foolish in the hope of aiding his son.

"Maybe, but we'll sure be checking on it," Sanz promised, opening the door.

"Oh," Testra added. "By the way, your flight to Cuba has been canceled. Those nonrefundable tickets are a bitch, aren't they?"

The door closed behind the federal agents, leaving the leaders of the Cuban Freedom Society alone.

"Gonzalo, we have to get Avaro out of there!" Alvarez stared at his aide. "He can't be in jail. He can't."

"Listen to me, José-Ramon. He knew the risks when he chose to work with us. Your son is no child."

"But he was following instructions," Alvarez implored. "My instructions!"

"Dammit, José-Ramon! Do you want to join him in prison?"

"But they have the tape. You heard what they said. And the FBI agent—"

"*Goddammit!* Listen to me! If you don't get your head on straight, you're going to end up saying something you regret! So what if one of their agents is dead? Is that for us to be concerned about? No, unless you say something that implicates us."

"But I gave the order for Portero to be killed. Avaro just passed on my instructions. He didn't intend for that agent to be killed."

"And did you? No." Parra's blood pressure was ticking upward now as his leader inched closer to losing his grip on what was important. "We did what we had to do. We made bold moves. That is the way of the strong, José-Ramon. Portero was a pawn. He was useless to us, but he was also a danger."

Alvarez stared at the wall and shook his head. The thought of his Avaro behind bars, with the lowlifes and faggots. It just could not be!

"We still have a great fortune, José-Ramon. Remember that. The director has provided for us well."

"And Avaro will be blamed for that, also. That, too, was my doing, and him following *my* instructions."

Parra threw his hands up in frustration. "Will you not even try to underst—" Sounds from the adjoining room cut his words off. The two FBI agents entered the room a second later.

Sanz went to the desk and reached under its edge, removing the miniature transmitter he had affixed there. "Thanks, fellas."

Testra smiled and pulled out a pair of handcuffs. "Looks like we have that evidence now."

Parra's eyes flared. He was a businessman, well versed in the laws of the land. "You cannot just record conversations without the authority to do so! Without a warrant! And you have none, do you?"

"You know, Freddy," Testra said, looking to his partner, "I don't think we do."

"No," Sanz agreed, reaching behind and under his coat. He laid the sign on the coffee table before Alvarez. "But we do have this."

Alvarez read the placard silently. *This is a United States Government Military Facility. Right to pass is subject to approval. All activities on this facility may be monitored by electronic and nonelectronic means without prior notice. Please behave accordingly.*

"You should have behaved accordingly," Special Agent Chris Testra observed. "Now stand up and put your hands on the wall. You are both under arrest."

Two hundred yards away, in a separate trailer that had been set up for the use of the guards watching over the CFS, Director of Central Intelligence Anthony Merriweather sat unaware of the events that were transpiring across the Florida Straits, or across the vacant tarmac. A knock on the door signaled the beginning of the end of his ignorance.

"Anthony."

Merriweather's eyes grew behind the distortion of the thick glasses. "Gregory, what are you doing here?"

Back to Gregory, is it? Drummond stepped in. Art Jefferson and Frankie Aguirre were right behind him.

"Who are these people?"

The DDI introduced his companions. "They brought something you might want to hear."

Art set the cassette player on the television and pressed Play. The conversation began, prompting the DCI to test each of his would-be accusers with a look. None looked away from his weak attempt at intimidation. In just a few minutes the familiar exchange was over.

"And this is for what, Gregory?" Merriweather sat back confidently.

"Can you excuse us," Drummond said to the FBI agents, who left with glances of distaste for the DCI.

"Your company should learn manners," Merriweather commented.

Drummond reached under his gray jacket and scratched his chest through the new shirt he had chosen just for this occasion. "Why, Anthony? Why did you do it? You knew that Portero had something, and you ignored it."

Merriweather laughed quietly and with pity for his Boy Scout deputy. "Gregory, Gregory. You have so much to learn, and the tragedy of it is that you never will."

"Anthony, there *was* a missile down there. Portero wasn't lying." Drummond searched for some kind of recognition in the DCI's face. Some kind of regret. "Anthony, good men died cleaning up what you could have prevented."

"Prevented? I didn't even know there was a missile." For the first time Drummond saw his boss smile, though it was not motivated by joy. It was a smile of arrogance. "And that tape is inadmissible as evidence. I'm sure you're aware of that."

"I just wanted to know why. You led us to the brink of something that could have spiraled out of control. The President listened to you, Anthony. He took your advice and made bad decisions about SNAPSHOT."

"Gregory, a President gets advice because he has to. All Presidents need it." The DCI chuckled. "This one needs it more than others."

Bingo. "He wouldn't appreciate your attitude."

"It would probably have to be explained to him."

"You certainly aren't the poster boy for loyalty," Drummond commented.

"Loyalty has so many meanings, Gregory. I am loyal to what

needs to be done. Cuba needed to be done, and I knew how to do it," Merriweather said smugly. "The President could not have conceived SNAPSHOT, or anything of lesser complexity, without me there to hold his hand."

"I see," Drummond said, nodding as a smile came to his lips. *Click.*

"What was that?"

The DDI reached inside his jacket and removed the recorder, unplugging the hidden lapel microphone. "Your head on a platter, *Tony.*"

Merriweather pushed himself forward on the couch, his teeth bared like an animal who'd just been caught. "You son of a bitch."

"Foul language. That will get you nowhere. And before you complain about illegal recordings, remember where you are." Drummond rewound the tape, ejected it, and dropped it in his shirt pocket.

"What do you want?"

"It's not what I want. It's what you will do, which is submit your resignation to the President for, let's say, personal reasons. Tomorrow would be a good time."

"Or else?"

"Or else this tape will find its way into the court case that's being prepared against your CFS friends." Drummond saw the coming question. "Yes, the cuffs are on them right now. Espionage. Conspiracy to commit murder. You hooked up with some really bad boys, Tony." The DDI thought he would relish this, but it wasn't all that enjoyable.

"I still haven't done anything illegal," Merriweather protested.

"No, but the things you said about the President won't do anything for your reputation. You won't be able to find a job teaching shop in high school."

"So if I resign, that tape gets lost."

The DDI tipped his head a bit, a few teeth showing. "Looks like you don't need it explained to you."

Merriweather drew in and let out a huge breath. "This is blackmail."

"You really are smart."

"Why are you doing this?"

"Because the country doesn't need another scandal just because you led the President into a corner," Drummond explained. "The President doesn't need it, either."

The DCI's head shook. "All right. We do it your way. Lose
the tape, you naive little boy."

"I prefer the term 'loyal,' if you don't mind," Drummond
said, before leaving his former boss alone to ponder the meaning
of the word, as well as his future.

Epilogue

Passages

It was a sight the citizens of Havana could scarcely remember. Not since Batista had a leader of their nation appeared on the balcony overlooking the plaza without a military uniform on. For their new leader, too, it was an unfamiliar experience. Yet it was a statement, possibly the strongest, that the interim president of the nation of Cuba could make. People, he was saying by shedding his uniform, would rule the country. Not the military. Not idealogues. People.

"It was a fine speech," Antonio Paredes said as President Hector Ojeda returned from the balcony.

"I do not give speeches, Papa Tony," Ojeda objected. "I simply speak."

It was a lesson Antonio wished he could transfer to every politician across the straits. But then this man was not a politician. He was a patriot. There was a vast difference, Antonio had learned.

"Fine words, then, *Señor Presidente*."

Ojeda did the strangest thing in reaction to the CIA officer's revised observation: He smiled. "Becoming accustomed to the title will take some time. Rank is an easier concept to grasp."

"I doubt you will have any problems adjusting."

Ojeda accepted the comment hopefully. "And you, Papa

Tony, I owe you . . . the country owes you many thanks for what you have done.''

"Many people made this day possible," Antonio added humbly.

"Many lives given," Ojeda continued. "Cubans. Americans."

Every great victory had its cost. Often that was measured in human terms. This momentous achievement was no different.

"What will you do first, *Señor Presidente?*" Antonio asked, moving the conversation to the future.

"It is not a difficult thing to decide," Ojeda said. "I have learned from the chaos and the glory as new countries were born from their old selves. I will simply let the people have a voice. They will have the opportunity to send me on my way."

Antonio chuckled. "You've learned well from our example, I would say. But, remember, any American could sit for hours and complain about what is wrong with the country."

"And at night they go to sleep knowing that the next day they can rise to continue their complaining," Ojeda said, turning the American penchant for naysaying into a beacon of stability.

"I've never quite seen it that way."

"I did not expect you would," President Hector Ojeda said with a very knowing grin. "You were looking from the inside."

Antonio Parades knew what the *presidente* meant. Perspective truly was everything.

He was breaking his own rule. Sort of.

"You'll like it," Art promised.

Frankie eyed him with doubt, the chili-covered monstrosity cradled in both hands. "I want you to know you're the only person I would do this for, and only then because you have a gun."

"You agreed, Aguirre," Art reminded his partner, motioning for her to take a bite.

"The game was rigged." She sneered as the thing approached her lips.

"Fair and square, partner. Four of a kind beats a full house."

"Four twos," Frankie pointed out. She had to lose the hand to *that?* And now she was Art Jefferson's Pink's surrogate for the next six months, until his next allowed venture into cholesterol land. If he had a craving, she had to vicariously fill it. "There's something about this in that Geneva thing."

"Eat."

Frankie closed her eyes and opened wide, taking the first gooey bite. She chewed the bacon-chili cheese dog tentatively at first, then her eyes opened as she began to experience the taste that was unique to Pink's. "Hey," she said through the first bite, "this is pretty good."

Art beamed knowingly. "You just wouldn't listen, would you? See what you've been missing?"

"Yeah. I guess so." Frankie took another bite, savoring this one more than the first. It was getting better! "This was the best bet I ever lost."

"Yeah, I . . . Hey! You're not supposed to be enjoying this. I mean . . . I'm supposed to be . . . Not you . . ." Art leaned against the counter, a frustrated, hungry man. "Oh, forget it."

Frankie winked at her partner and bit again into the deliciously messy conglomeration.

"Seltzer, Mr. Jefferson?" the clerk inquired.

Art looked over to the kid. "No. Another bacon-chili cheese dog for the lady. And hurry. Can't you see I'm hungry?"

Major Sean Graber sat staring at the maroon carpet, the words of the chaplain echoing throughout the John F. Kennedy Special Warfare Center Chapel. His eyes came up only when he knew that the padre was reaching the point in the memorial service that required him to do so. It was a show of respect for comrades fallen. For his men.

"Captain Christopher Herald Buxton. Sergeant Charles Steven Makowski. Sergeant Gerald Morris Jones. Sergeant Alfred George Vincent." The chaplain paused, closing the book that held the names of Delta's departed troopers. "The Great Jumpmaster watches over our comrades now. Let us not grieve over their loss, but, rather, let us use them as an example as we cross the next barrier, meet our next foe, defend freedom, and destroy tyranny. Let us not grieve, but let us not forget. Amen."

"Hoo-ah," the assembled troopers responded.

Sean stood with Colonel Cadler and walked to the back of the chapel, meeting each family member as they departed. It was a private service, intended only for the families and the men of Delta. Despite what the chaplain had said, it was a time to grieve. But it was also, as he professed, a time to remember. In a way, that was more painful than the grieving.

The last family member drifted toward the cars lining Fort Bragg's Ardennes Road. Sean walked away from the chapel, stopping near a stand of pines that flanked the hallowed building. Cadler joined him there a minute later.

"Major."

Sean looked around, smiling at the colonel, thinking before saying what he wanted to say. "We lost too many on this one, sir."

Cadler looked at the damp, needle-covered ground, his lips pouting. "One is too many, Major. Ten is too many. But missions don't come with a set loss ratio. Y'all know that as good as I."

It was a correct statement, but that still didn't change what Sean was feeling. Four of his own men were gone. Three from the 160th. And Anderson. Being a Delta trooper was his life. It was all he had wanted to do from the minute the unit was formed. But now he found himself fearing what came with Delta's hazardous mission profile. Death was no longer just a possibility. It was all too real. He could accept it for himself, but for men working for him? For soldiers who followed his lead? He no longer knew if this was for him, and that doubt itself, he believed, made him ineffective as a Delta trooper.

"You haven't mentioned my request, sir."

"I was hopin' you'd change your mind 'fore I had to act on it," Cadler explained. "But it seems to me that y'all are pretty sure about this."

Sean nodded. "Very sure, sir."

Cadler nodded with regret and acceptance. "We're gonna miss your ugly ass around here."

"I'll drag it back once in a while so you can kick it into shape," Sean joked.

"Can't touch no civilians, Major."

Civilian. That had a scary ring to it. Sean had known little other than the Army life. What lay outside the comforting walls of Bragg was alien to him. Uncharted territory. New adventures.

"You did good, Major," Cadler said, offering his hand.

Sean took it, fighting the urge to salute. Habits would be hard to break. "Thank you, Colonel."

"Now go find that little lady of yours and make some babies."

"Is that an order, sir?" Sean asked with a smile.

"The last from me to you, Major."

"Will do, sir," Sean said, giving his commander a crisp salute before turning and walking away down Ardennes.

"God speed, Sean."

The plot was set among a circular clearing ringed by Douglas firs, except for the section that afforded an unobstructed view of the pristine lake below. As if in deference to the man being laid to rest, the water churned with fish broaching the surface and splashing back into the deep blue lake. It could not have been planned more eloquently.

Only twenty people were gathered at the gravesite, located in the Minnesota backwaters not far from the dock where Joe Anderson had cast his last line. Most were family, but there were two outsiders, one of whom had asked to say something at the service.

"There is not much that need be said about such a man," the President observed, concluding his words without the aid of cards or prompters. "It is sufficient, and utterly appropriate, to say that he did what had to be done when the call was made. And that he answered that call not for the sake of glory, or for any less honorable reasons. He answered it because he heard it, and because to turn a blind eye or a deaf ear was not his way."

The President went to Joe Anderson's widow, spending a long moment with her. Then it was time to go, to leave the family to remember without the intrusion of outsiders. Bud followed the President along the wooded path, two Secret Service agents ahead and two behind. They emerged from the trees to the waiting limousine, but the chief executive did not immediately get in. Instead, he stood still and smelled the sweet, damp air.

"He picked a good resting place, Bud."

"Yes, he did, Mr. President." Bud tasted the freshness himself, pulling in the scents of the forest. "If only the rest of the world was this peaceful."

"If only." The President still could dream, even if such musings were inevitably overcome by reality. "You know, Bud, even with the losses we suffered from this, it could have been so much worse. I hate to even imagine what could have happened."

"The important thing is that it didn't, sir," Bud reminded him. "In the end you have to count your losses and pray that you've learned something from the ordeal that will help you avoid similar situations in the future."

"The future." The President studied the trees for a moment before looking back to his NSA. "What frightens me is that this all came at us from the past. I remember a professor of mine back at UCLA saying 'History is not the study of what has happened before; it is the study of that which we *know* has happened before.' " He thought to himself briefly. "What else is out there that we don't know of, Bud?"

The NSA considered the question in the quiet of the forest, looking skyward as the answer came to him. "You're asking the wrong adviser, Mr. President."